WINTER PALE

WORKS IN GREEK

The light in darkness (To fos sto skotadi)
Novel, Kedros, 2011

Scavenger (Rakosyllektis)
Short stories collection, Lykofos, 2021

Secret room reloaded
Stage play, Théâtre du Soleil, Plaka Athens, 2009

SHORT SCREENPLAYS

Athens – Berlin
2nd Odysseus award, London Greek Film Festival (LGFF), 2021

The clay shoes (Ta pilina papoutsia)
Nominated, London Greek Film Festival (LGFF), 2012

A mellow dusk: Visual translation of Emily Dickinson's "Because I could not stop for death"
Odysseus award winner, London Greek Film Festival (LGFF), 2008

We
Fiction short film, Director: Panagiotis Kalantzis
Thess International Film Festival, 2007

WINTER PALE

A WW2 drama

MARINA KOULOURI

Independent author

WINTER PALE

For information contact:
Marina Koulouri
info@marinakoulouri.com
https://www.marinakoulouri.com

Cover design by Ilias Karampinis
iliaskarampinis@gmail.com

Edited by David Flack
peet.df@gmail.com

ISBN (Print): 978-618-86242-0-7
ISBN (E-book): 978-618-86242-1-4

First Edition: 2022
10 9 8 7 6 5 4 3 2 1

Contents

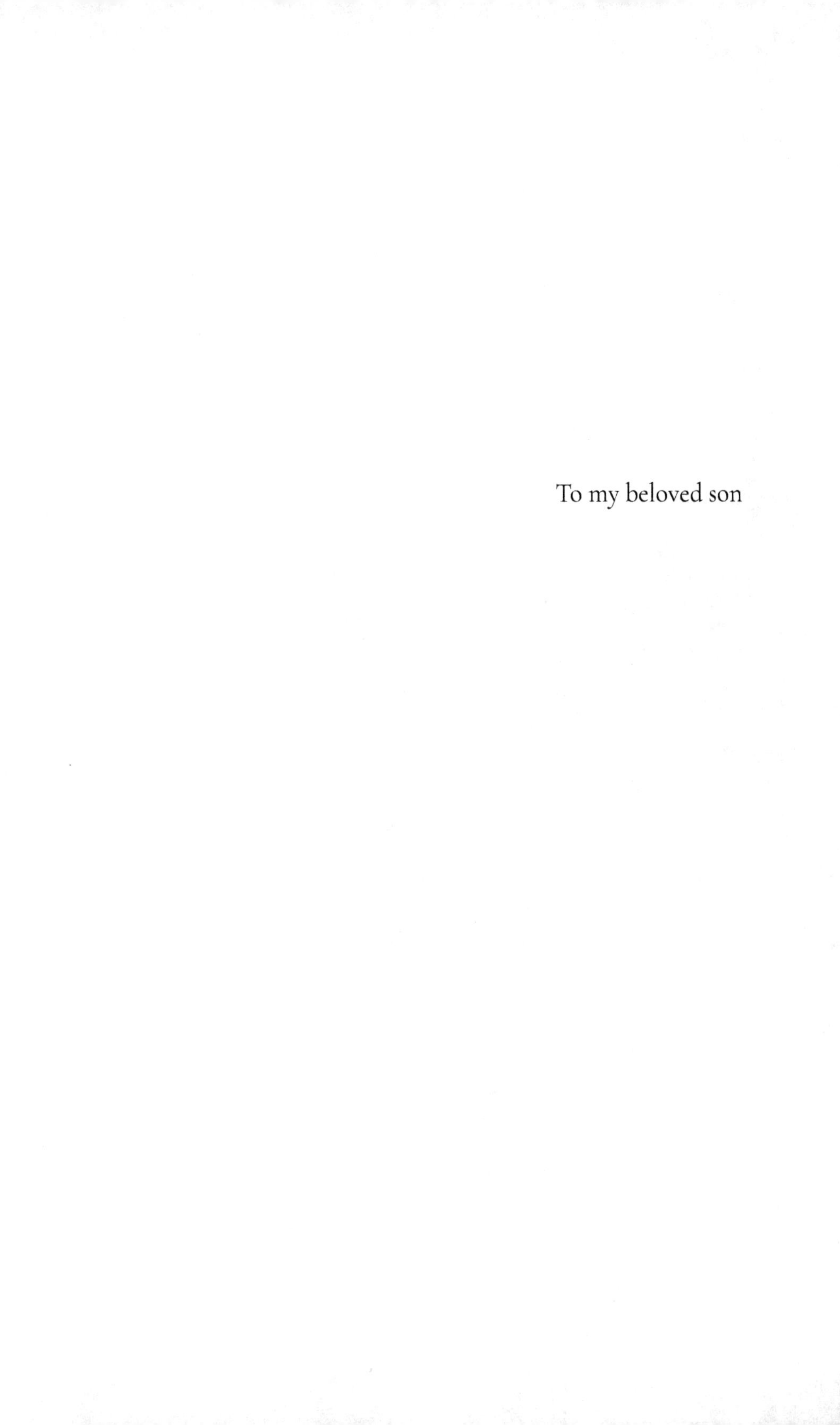

To my beloved son

Prelude

It's snowing. I'm looking at the falling snowflakes. Look, if you can. But you can't. You can't anymore. I'm looking instead of you. Snow is falling; a thick white blanket has already covered everything out there. The first snow of winter, the first snow of this new life: it always snowed inside of me as it snowed all around, but this is a different kind of snow. Or there's a different eye looking at it.

I remember you. Every single day. Every minute. I could never forget you, even though, now and then, I wish to. The memory of you hurts, but it reminds me I'm alive. I cannot forget you. Oblivion is death, like memory. If I remember you, you must have died. But if I remember you, you come back to life.

The snow is heavy, frantic snowflakes descend from the sky. People make all sorts of frantic attempts to thaw their inner snow, and they make all sorts of mistakes. A ray of sun and the snow changes, it turns to water, it becomes steam. Then it's gone. When you loved me, everything was certain.

The snow is swirling in small spirals at the slightest breath of wind. I used to think of life as a circle: same losses, same pain, over and over. Why could it not be a finite straight line, where one could move forward, leaving everything behind? But life is not a straight line. And life does not make circles. Life is like those spirals of snow outside the window. It looks as if it continually repeats itself, but each time you're at a different level. My life was a circle until you came and made it a spiral.

I'll go to sleep now; the snow will keep on falling while I'm asleep. It may still be snowing even when I wake up. The universe continues to exist regardless of us. And we are born on an icy night, just like snowflakes, a frenzied dive from the cradle of creation and onto earth: this earth with its earthly passions, which bring people closer or completely tear them apart.

Suppose we let it snow inside of us as it snows all around, let the sun in to change it. Let it carry us back to the cloud of our birth to meet there once again before we turn to snowflakes and, if we are lucky, fall anew together, some other night, on another earth.

I

A sprig of heather

Ever since she was little, people always called her a pretty girl; long hair, golden like a field of wheat, soft skin as white as snow, two earthen dollops for eyes. And she used to laugh a lot, a smile making her face always look more beautiful. She was innocent and carefree, blessed with loving parents whom she adored. Perhaps it was love dressing everything in pure light and beauty. Or perhaps it was because she lived life as a fairytale:

In a faraway kingdom, there lived a rich merchant and his daughter, a beautiful little girl with long straw-coloured hair and almond-shaped eyes, brown like a doe's.

"Like me, Daddy?"

"Yes, my princess! Just like you!"

But this little girl had lost her mother, and the merchant had married another woman, who had her own two daughters. When the little girl's father died, too, her wicked stepmother and step-sisters made her suffer all that no poor orphan should. And because she had no place to sleep but in front of the fireplace, every morning waking up covered with cinder, they would mock her and call her by the name...

"You're not going to die, Daddy, are you?"

How does one explain life's inevitabilities to a child! He would speak of vast green meadows, where the sun shines forever, and everyone is surrounded with happiness and love. But when the time came, she could only wonder why heaven had to be so far away, why she could not go with him, see him, and love him like before. It was the tenth summer of her life. And since then, no summer had been the same again; nor any other season.

Once Mother and she moved to France, hoping for a new beginning, their last link with that incomparable past was forever broken. Living in a foreign country, stranger among strangers, poorer than the poor, with no one to ask for help or even talk about their misery. Foreigners, interlopers, outcasts. Like fleas infesting a newborn puppy, they sucked the blood of society and culture. 'France belongs to the French!' they would shout. 'Catharsis!' and 'Throw out the hordes of foreigner invaders!' They had moved there for a better life. Sadly, they had jumped out of the frying-pan into the fire.

Some neighbours had once said to Mother, 'Pray that God won't give you everything you can endure!' Instead, Mother insisted on saying 'Thank God'. Thank God that they were alive and still going strong, that they did not have to look for a place to sleep under the bridges of the *Seine*, counting holes in their ragged clothes and searching for leftovers in the rubbish. Thank God that they were not locked up in any of those concentration camps for the unwelcomed, where they would surely die, if Stepfather's knaveries had not for once been for their good, ensuring their French citizenship. And thank God for his surname 'Dupont', which was put down in the official documents instead of their own, giving them the freedom to go about without fear, but, no, she could not say it, because she never felt like a 'Dupont' and that name meant nothing to her or Mother. They would always be the girls of John Pale the shoemaker. Sometimes, she felt the twins were just as well the offspring of John Pale the shoemaker, even though they had Christian's blood running in their veins. There was something remarkable about Stepfather. He was a kind of long-lived and durable parasite that poverty and disease could not touch, and war could not either.

As the war was coming, everyone said that it would not happen at all; later, that the French were ready for war. Even when the government had evacuated every public building and had burnt the state's archives in front of the stunned citizens' eyes, abandoning the capital altogether, no one believed the Nazi boot would walk the streets of Paris. They would not believe it, but they left anyway. Temporarily, to the south, for safety. By whatever means they could find, by trucks, on animals' backs, on foot. With the few things they could carry on their backs, in makeshift trailers, in their babies' prams. Everybody wanted to leave. Families from their homes. Workers from their jobs. Even patients from hospitals got up to leave. And it was heard that some, too sick to follow, asked for a lethal injection.

Once the Germans entered Paris, the city sank into silence. One could almost hear the sadness slapping behind shocked eyes, while lips, marked by fear and awe, admired, in the triumphant parade, the conquerors' regularity, their uniforms, how robust they looked. And she was happy, for a moment she was happy that those who had been staring at them like pests would now be forced to realise others were in charge. Then, she woke up to the reality of what this defeat for the French would mean to them and she was terrified. And it terrified her just as much every time she heard those steel army loudspeakers sound, '*Achtung! Achtung!* [1] The city has been occupied!'

The city had been occupied, and the conquerors were in command. Gray uniforms and loud steps, whistles and gunshots warned the offenders. Road signs previously written in French changed into the German language and new German ones were placed in central posts all over the city. Every afternoon, a legion of armoured Germans, both foot soldiers and horse riders, appeared on the *Champs-Élysées*; and as they vigorously chanted their unintelligible marching songs, on the roadside, ordinary people, no less surprised than the first time, still stared at the strange parade in amazement. Many who owned houses, nice houses, not like theirs, had to leave, because the conquerors were to stay there. The power supply was limited and people had to dig out candles and oil lamps. And when the first winter came, one could see improvised chimneys of improvised heaters, burning, with no exception, from coal and dried wood to old books and furniture. All necessities were immediately rationed–fuel, food, clothing, soap, everything. Legal trade completely collapsed, while the black market flourished. And indeed, how the citizens loved to haggle in the black market! The housewife next door; every single wage worker; one's bench seatmate; the pupil at school. It would not have surprised her if the parish priest tried to hammer out a deal behind the candle stand or inside the confessional.

Eventually, Parisians would refuse to be disheartened by the harsh and alert eye of the occupation army, and they would return to their homes and to their jobs after a while; and they would resume their habitual visits to the entertainments, theatres and cinemas and fancy dinner shows, right before the curfew, but they would. They ran for the last *métro* all dressed up in their bow ties and polished brogues, with fake fur coats hanging heavily over their liquid stockings, because nylon was in shortage and ankle socks did not look good with evening gowns. Paris would always remain Paris and Parisians would make certain they made justice to the reputation.

For two and a half years, everybody had been trying to convince everybody else that everything was as it used to be; that peaceful and cooperative citizens had nothing to be afraid of, as was so often announced by the loudspeakers. Contrary to those other ones who had every reason to fear: the Resistance! Everyone learnt about these stouthearted men and women. They had started a dangerous struggle, inspired by the dream of freedom, the dream of taking back what they once had or perhaps the dream of gaining what they did not have but wanted. Well, naturally she admired them too. How could she not? And yet she was convinced that whoever survived this war, at arms or not, should equally be considered a hero; in her mind, there was no struggle more titanic than the struggle to survive.

The arrival of the Germans had forced Mother to miss every opportunity for a regular job. Had it not been for the twins, to make a little money out of beggary or steal some potatoes, a handful of dried beans or a loaf of bread, no doubt they would have starved to death. Poor babies, they had been seriously roughed up by Stepfather those first days, when, being totally unpracticed to swindling and begging, they came back empty-handed. But necessity always made people incredibly inventive and the twins soon became geniuses of deception and they also found companions, children from other neighbourhoods, entire gangs scouring the city, sneaking around like rats and snaffling whatever they could hide inside their clothes. And then they made a run for it. They laughed and bet on who would run faster. They played with fire, but it was not fire they were afraid of–they were only afraid of their father.

Their father, who had considered it unimportant when, a little later, they fell ill, and blamed Mother for overreacting, because she had been terrified it might be that fever ravaging the common people, especially in their parts of the city. Until a place in a cabaret was offered to Mother; and then he made a big issue out of it, suddenly asserting the twins needed a doctor and they needed medicines, but who could pay for all that, unless...

One night, well past midnight, a strange wind blew against the window next to which she was sleeping. It was broken in one corner, her frozen legs annoyed her sleep, it was easy for her to wake up. She got up and saw Mother having just returned from work. She stood unnaturally and slumped down on a chair. With a rough move, she threw a bunch of wrinkled, sweaty banknotes onto the table.

"Mum?"

The sound of her voice shocked the woman, and she hurried to hide her face: "Don't look at me! Don't touch me!"

Mother curled up in a corner and cried out of shame. And she was even more ashamed, because, for the sake of her and the twins, Mother had sold her entire self out. Only Christian was pleased enough, and so were the twins, who recovered from their illness and started feeling perky again. It was not until later that they would wonder why Mother had stopped hugging them or looking them in the eyes.

She had but one wish: to go back home, to feel the sun shining warmly upon her face and lie on the grass with Mother's kitchen delights once again tickling her nose. There were mornings when she still woke up with the bells of bikes tinkling in her ears, hearing the horn of the only car running up and down their neighbourhood, the voices of the neighbours' children, the chatter of housewives... On Sundays after church, Father and she would sit down and tell stories of princesses and knights.

And he would read to her–poetry from a scrapbook he diligently kept and supplemented with his favourite pieces. Hardly did she understand what the poems meant to say. But Father insisted that was the beauty of poetry: you did not have to understand; you just had to feel it.

"A sprig of heather shudders in my hand
Autumn is dead you should remember
We'll never see each other again upon this land
Bitter fragrance of the season sprig of heather
And remember that I wait for you forever." [2]

In the afternoons, even under the drizzling rain, they would take long walks to see Big Ben or the Palace, and, sometimes, they would spend hours at Trafalgar square where she loved to shoo away entire flocks of pigeons, otherwise quietly bobbing their heads in search of food. Birds and balloons in the gathering dusk! A festival of raindrops and clouds! It always amazed her to watch the mimes and clowns on Oxford Street, thrilled at their colourful chiming hats and the noise they made at their every move. One night, she had dreamt she had one of those on, and, as she had sneaked in to get some sweeties from the cupboard, she woke up the whole family and the neighbourhood people, who would stand there looking at her in utter disapproval.

Their neighbourhood today would not wake up even if all the city bells rang together. A complete dump, the ultimate shelter for the rejects of life. The cemetery across the street was full of such miserable misfits–dead and alive. Ghost figures, many of whom were victims of last March's bombing, hiding from their fate more than from anyone else. But their fate they could not escape from and they would carry it on them, like the clowns' chiming hats, cling-clang, cling-clang, cling-cling-cling-clang, a rigid, unavoidable master ...

The old clock on the wall struck the time, taking Winter's mind off her thoughts. One, two, three, four... Seven o'clock. She looked down into the street, where two figures entering their building caught her attention.

"Mum! Christian just came in with someone wearing a uniform!"

Mother was getting ready for work. She was brushing her hair, miraculously still maintaining its natural brown colour, putting on makeup, wearing her best dress.

"The twins!" she mumbled, fully alarmed, and approached the window to anxiously take a glance. A few moments later, the apartment door opened to attract both their agonising looks. "Christian..." Mother's anxiety soon turned into surprise: "Jules, is that you?" The man in *Milice* uniform, who accompanied Stepfather, was an acquaintance to Mother. Winter knew him, too: one of Stepfather's buddies–same breed, same group–and she recalled having been offered a blow or two by that man's rough hand. "I didn't know you joined the *Milice*!"

The dramatic exaggeration in Mother's voice brought a smirk onto Winter's lips. Jules's affiliation with the French Gestapo, which the Germans had welcomed to help them terrorize the city, would have given him neither the manners nor the dignity he had never had. At best, it would have expanded his already over-developed ego.

"You should be grateful, Carole! You have benefited from my good offices in ways you are not even aware of!" stated Jules and squinted at Christian, awaiting his confirmation.

"If that's so, then I do thank you, Jules. May God give you back the good you've done for us a hundred times more!" Mother replied in her perfect French, which allowed her the freedom to speak her mind exactly in the way she intended. "And now you must excuse me, Jules! I would love to stay and entertain you, but, as you well know, I have to work!" she added with a fake smile, and Winter simpered once more, very much enjoying the implication.

"Which brings us to the cause of my visit, dear Carole!" Jules responded, making certain to look down upon the two women. "We are currently reviewing the implementation of the obligatory work service. You know it is forbidden to avoid work!" he zealously explained, stretching his body and head to show off his uniform and power.

"Well, I'm sorry, but I can't apologise for Christian!" Mother returned to him boldly and Winter giggled, but only for the second before Christian's angry glower.

"I'll give you something to be sorry for, you filthy cunt...!" he jerked out, offended at Mother's words, and raised his hand to hit her with his usual ease. The *Milice* officer immediately restrained him.

"Please, please. There is no reason for tension. The girl just has to go to work. Here and now, all four of us will come to an agreement. There is a job opportunity for her with you, Carole. Christian and I have already talked to your boss at the cabaret. Otherwise, I'll have to take her with me. Factories in Germany are in great demand of strong, young workers!"

They all turned and looked at her, Jules, Christian, Mother, three pairs of eyes spearing her, each with their own intentions.

"If you dare touch her, I'll kill you with my own hands!" Mother warned emphatically and stepped between the two men and her daughter, resolutely giving Jules and Christian a good push back to show she was deadly serious.

It was a decisive move: from one moment to the next, the room turned into a battlefield. Mother was fighting with Stepfather, while Winter was struggling to escape Jules's forcible drag towards the door.

"They'll take care of you nicely where you're going, little shit!"

He struck her down and Winter fell to the floor. But as soon as Jules came to lift her up again, she scratched him on the face so hard she nearly pulled his eye out. Infuriated, she then turned against Christian, who was exchanging ferocious blows and vile words with Mother.

"Bastard, you did this!" she screamed and jumped onto his back, grabbing him by the neck.

Winter's attack surprised Christian and gave Mother the chance to kick him in the groin. He squirmed with pain and fell down, cursing and swearing, while Jules was looking at the two women uncertain who to deal with first. He chose Mother. But Mother was stronger than she looked. Jules's scraggy figure could hardly deal with her. Then, in what seemed to be the right moment, Winter grabbed a bottle of absinthe, patiently awaiting on the table to be used properly, smashed it on Jules's head and knocked him unconscious. A moment of odd silence followed. Winter and Mother faintly smiled at each other. It was a temporary victory.

"You have to leave!" Mother moaned, grabbing Winter by the hand and pulling her towards the door. She snatched Winter's worn handbag from the coat rack and shoved it into her arms, pressed into her daughter's reluctant hand however much of the household savings she could quickly lay her hand on and desperately begged, "Go now!"

An eerie gravity was keeping Winter transfixed. Some coins slipped from her fingers and tumbled across the floor, resounding like shellfire. "... Mum...!"

But Christian was coming around, threatening furiously that he would show them. Mother gave Winter one last imploring look; she held her daughter's cheek for a brief second. Then, she banged the door shut and stayed alone to face Stepfather's barbarity.

The fight rampaging behind the closed door brought Winter to her senses. Like a prisoner before an open and unguarded cell, she climbed down the stairs, jumped out and ran relentlessly until the end of the street, and then until the end of the next one; away from the neighbourhood and unstoppably away from the district.

"Mum...!"

Tears flooding her eyes, the image of Mother's self-sacrifice felt as heavy as an iron ball inside her. An acute pain in her chest was screaming of her heart's protest: what was she doing? where was she going? She halted with her back against a weathered wall, and panting for breath, she fainted.

2

All alone

"You are okay now! I found you unconscious near *Saint-Georges!*"

She opened her eyes to a dark atmosphere; the images were blurry, her throat dry and sore. She felt relieved when a hand lifted her up and gave her a little water to drink. She tried to smile. The word 'Mum' was the first thing she wanted to say, but she could only make a few awkward winces.

"You want to say something?"

Hearing the voice a second time, she realised it did not belong to Mother. A surge of anxiety attacked her, and she blinked to clear her vision and better see the person leaning over her. He was a young man with hazel eyes, shades of gold and green inside them, alternating with the darkest brown she had ever seen. She wondered if she knew him, but was soon certain she did not.

"You are okay now!" he told her again, and Winter noticed the tender smile on his rosy lips. "You looked in such need for sleep, I just couldn't wake you up!" he remarked and ran his fingers across her forehead, pulling away a tuft of her hair, looking deep into her eyes with the language of the warmest affection.

His fondness alarmed Winter. She had learnt from experience to distrust first impressions, especially the good ones. She shifted a little and sensed that the stranger was holding her in his arms. His embrace was pleasant, generous and inviting, and it had a welcoming fragrance reminiscent of something she could not define. She could easily give in to this perception of closeness, respond to it with all her desire for comfort and reassurance, and yet, it was exactly why she felt she had better keep her distance.

"Are you sure you can sit up?" he asked when she tried to move away and she nodded, so he helped her sit on some soft bedding. "I know what you need right now: a hot drink!" he stated with another auspicious smile and got up to reveal the taut and supple form which perfectly accorded with the vigour of his hug.

She watched him as he was preparing a brew at an age-old camp stove and his every move kept transmitting that feeling of close acquaintance, like a friend of old who had suddenly and most unexpectedly returned and he was familiar, even though too much water had gone under the bridge and too much of life had intervened for them to maintain their former state of companionship and understanding. He turned to her with those hypnotic eyes and she quivered.

"You're still in shock! You were as cold as death when I found you!" she heard him say, and, despite evading direct eye contact with him, his voice had the same unsettling effect.

Truly, something had died inside her, she painfully thought. Because her life might not have been a bed of roses and *Rue Goubet* might never have felt like home to her, but it was the home of Mother and the twins –and they were her family. The security one feels in a family even in the most adverse circumstance: that was what had died for her that night.

"It's almost ready now! It'll make you feel better, I promise! And then, you might decide to speak to me!"

It was a bizarre place where he had brought her. The air was dense and smelly; the walls were moist, with no natural light; she assumed it would be somewhere underground and wondered ominously what kind of man would live in such a place. An oil lamp, shedding its dim light from a nail on the wall, projected the young man's shadow on the opposite side of the small chamber and it looked as grotesque as a figure of horror cinematography. Winter was appalled, but just as magnetised.

"We're in the sewers!" he explained in the most natural tone. "It's not a nice place, but it is safe!"

He brought her a mug of the steaming brew and went back to the stove to get one for himself. Instinctively, Winter waited for him to drink first before she herself sipped at it. She could not tell what the brew was, but she had to admit that it did make her feel better. The young man came and sat next to her.

"I'm René. René Martin. I'm from Lille." he announced, and she preferred only to nod, glancing at him out of the corner of her eye. "And you?"

She could feel the heat of his gaze on her hair, on her temple, on the root of her ear; the line of her jaw, the curves of her lips, the tip of her nose; her cheekbone, her eyelashes, her lips again. And she sensed the exact expression on his face, some kind of longing and demand, a hungry impulse strenuously subdued.

She implored for his mercy with a piteous look, and he returned a lenient smile for an answer. He got up and walked away to an unseen corner, bent and picked something up: "You don't have to hide from me!" he claimed. "I know you are not one of us!" And as he turned around to reveal her handbag and Father's scrapbook in his hands, Winter broke out in a cold sweat and felt pervaded by the deadliest of threats. She saw him thumb through Father's scrapbook, his features painted with a kind of wistfulness: "I know some English, but poetry...! Even in French it's a real puzzle!" he admired, switching to her language, which he spoke decently, although strongly marked by his native tongue. Winter felt little relief.

Then, a photograph fell out of the pages of the scrapbook and she jumped up to catch it, as if it were a fragile, valuable object. The young man lifted the photo off the floor and stared at it silently for a while.

"Your family?" he presumed and Winter only replied by looking at him ruefully.

It was the old photo of the family in their garden in England.

Climbed up onto Father's back, there was little Winter holding him tightly, her arms wrapped around his neck and her legs hooked firmly to his sides. A sad memory speared her inside: the warmth of Father's back on her girlish bosom, the strength of his arm holding her, while he squeezed Mother's hand ardently onto his lips with his free hand. On the lovely spring day this photo was taken, and she could not have been older than seven, they had spent a playful morning in the garden and then had the most delicious barbeque for lunch. At tea time, a photographer was passing through the neighbourhood, with his camera and tripod on his back, advertising his trade. He was called upon to take the shot and the moment was made immortal.

"I lost my family in the bombings!" the man said, and Winter peered at him with profound sympathy. "I also had a brother! He was killed in Spain!"

She lowered her eyes in sorrow, herself feeling the heavy burden of loss. He came and kneeled before her, carefully leaving her belongings in her arms. His expression was filled with endearment, his eyes were soothing and encouraging.

"You can talk to me!" Warmth emanated from his voice. "You're safe here!" There was a curve of pure sweetness on his lips. He brought his fingertips to her cheek to caress it and, as she defensively flinched, he whispered: "Don't be afraid!"

His burning eyes spoke so loudly. Such an intense feeling, as if she were someone he already knew, a face he yearned to see and long awaited. Winter recognised this heart-aching nostalgia, the stabbing pain only an unhealed wound could inflict.

"My name is Winter... Pale!" she barely uttered, and he smiled, happily nodding like a child having just been offered a beautiful gift. He took her hand and squeezed it passionately against his chest.

"Winter Pale!"

They gazed at each other, safely surrendered to the sensation of this peculiar bond which was sometimes experienced with complete strangers: a bond rooted deep in the past, long before they started remembering, before they were born. They smiled.

"Are you in trouble? Are the Germans looking for you?" he enquired and Winter shook her head negatively, for a moment reluctant to say more.

"I couldn't stay at my house anymore; I had to leave ...!" she said with the heavy fog of the previous evening's memory covering her face.

The young man seemed to understand: "You're all alone then!" he concluded, giving the fact that she was on her own from now on an insufferable, irreversible and definite substance.

"Yes! I'm all alone!" she admitted in heartbreak, and a tear rolled down from her eye.

He came a little closer. Winter sensed that he wanted to put his arms around her and could not help feeling that perhaps so did she.

"I can take care of you, make sure you're safe!" he eagerly suggested, and she smiled hesitantly. "You shouldn't be alone out there! I have my way around these things; I can help, if you let me!" he insisted, and she showed both her gratitude and reservation with a glance.

"I..."

She felt so tempted to accept. For years she had been feeling lonely, but she was never alone, never had to face the dark and uncertain future ahead all by herself, this cold and threatening world with no one to turn to, her reliance on Mother's resolute character suddenly becoming so apparent that she doubted she had ever so much as attempted to decide anything for herself. He seemed like someone with enough human strength to take another under his wing and it felt like an attractive, promising prospect, but there was also this peculiar sting in her stomach, some kind of warning, and it was not that they were both alien to each other.

"I don't actually live here!" he most insightfully forestalled her, watching her eyes unconsciously scan the surroundings and reading the doubt on the expression of her face. "It's only a hideout; you know, for an emergency!"

"A hideout?" Winter repeated, and she was taken aback by the tiny sparks of red inside the pupils of his eyes, which stirred like a dark pool full of mysterious creatures. It did not take long for her to comprehend: "... The Resistance!" she mumbled in fear and awe.

He smiled instead of an answer and, in his smile, Winter read a spirit of sturdy independence, in his eyes, the bravery of a lionhearted warrior.

"You should rest a little more!" he urged her, taking the mug out of her hands, even though she had not finished the brew. "I'm going to make the arrangements for you and I'll come back to get you. Okay?"

She preferred not to give him a direct reply, but she obeyed his call to lie down, pretending it was all she needed. He caringly covered her with an overcoat and promised to return as soon as possible. Winter waited patiently for him to leave and then followed him closely. She had to muster all her courage to follow his footsteps through the labyrinthine tunnels of the sewers, staggering in filthy waters and trying to escape the rodents that were lurking everywhere. And the farther she went from the moldy shelter the generous Resistance fighter had offered, the more an inexplicable guilt burdened her.

When she saw the light again, it was a gray rainy day, but she felt thankful for the sense of cleanliness in the air and the smell of fresh moisture. Hidden in a remote corner, she watched her youthful benefactor cautiously wander off. She thought of how unpleasantly surprised he would be to see she was gone, and beforehand felt ashamed for his reasonable assumption that she had been cowardly and ungrateful.

She made way for an attractive woman in a fur coat to pass, prancing down the street with an umbrella in one hand. A man in a wool-felt trench coat and flat cap hurriedly walked across, holding a folded newspaper over his head as cover from the rain. A black limousine and a hooded jeep from the opposite direction crossed one another and their fully uniformed passengers exchanged greetings. Winter was standing by and this picture popped up in her mind, a picture of a painting which used to hang on the sitting-room wall at the family house in London, its short thick strokes seeming so clumsy and incoherent on the canvas when looking at them from up close, but moving back and away, how magically they joined into an overwhelming impression of the Houses of Parliament under a dramatically gray sky. In the painting of the world, she was feeling like a dot herself, only she would not be seen attached to anything, no matter the distance. She trembled, and it was not because of the cold. Once again, she thought of her underground saviour and wondered whether it was preferable to live dangerously in solidarity or safely in solitude. Safely? Could anyone feel safe being alone? she contemplated. She walked on with a numb feeling inside; the rain ceased to disturb her; it was all she had at the moment to touch her.

And the rain was dripping down on the surface of a large round pond, making countless circular shapes in the water.

"Not exactly the weather for a walk in *des Tuileries*, *Fräulein*! Mud is stuck all over your slippers!"

Behind the tulle of her hat, the elegant woman in a fur coat glanced at the eagle and swastika embroidery on the woollen gray sleeve that came to stand next to her. She took the handkerchief she was offered to wipe her shoes with and gracefully returned it once she was done.

"*Danke, mein Herr*!"[3] Then she went on her way, still prancing, despite the weather.

Skillfully tucked away in the dirty handkerchief, there was a brief note:

"Special Operations Executive[4]*, end of March, waiting for instructions.*
Liaison, code name 'Seamstress'.
Gaullist meeting, Quartier Latin. Date to be announced.

The Midwife"

A pair of black leather gloves folded the note back into four, hid it in the inside pocket of the gray winter coat. A silver cigarette case, a cigarette, match and light; smoke interwove with the fine threads of rain. There was heavy brume cloaking the *Tuileries* Garden, but, in the pale-hued solitary around, his was the darkest figure undoubtedly.

3

Like a doe

Deep in a calm stupor, a deafening wham startled Winter. Wandering around all day, just before dusk she had sneaked into a church and dozed off in a warm and quiet corner seat. There were moments when a tranquil mumble and heavenly plainchants accompanied her dreams, bringing back memories of a glorious past. The bang woke her up just before they were about to set off the fireworks for the 5th of November[5], and it took her a few seconds to figure out where she was. A woman walked down the middle aisle to the exit looking at her indiscreetly, and then Winter realised she was all alone in the church. Momentarily, she thought it would be a good idea to hide in a corner somewhere and spend the night there, but when she saw the priest coming down from the altar and towards her, she just jumped up and fled.

Hunger in her stomach, and the memory of the soup she had cooked at Stepfather's the previous day, made her drool. Outside a bistro window, she carefully observed the customers having their meals. Mother's savings would probably be adequate for one of those delicious-looking dishes, she presumed with her groaning entrails urgently pushing her to walk through the door. But the reflection of herself in the window convinced her not to: abandonment detests to be exposed to public view.

One street after another, no place seemed appropriate and hospitable enough to shelter her. There is no place like home, even a home as bleak and appalling as *Rue Goubet*, she pondered sadly, and Mother's image emerged in her mind, once again making her tearful. She could still go back, she thought, to Mother and the children, together they might find a way to get around Christian's vicious schemes. She halted. What was she thinking? Why was she fooling herself? There was no going back, not like this; she could never return, unless a winner.

She came to a main road that was unknown to her. She looked both to the right and left. The road was highly illuminated and, further in the distance, she could see several figures coming and going. Certain it was better to stay in the dark, she walked across into a small side street. There was a short uphill. Straight on, a few metres ahead, a paved clearing was visible. Generous electrical light was gushing from the corner of the square. A club of some sort, Winter guessed, and the music that started to play into the silence confirmed her thought. Its four-leaf window was red and gold and a wooden sign, floodlit by two yellow lamps, stated *'La Biche Dorée'*, the golden doe, with a gilded female deer posing above the letters.

"Whoso list to hunt, I know where is an hind,
But as for me, hélas, I may no more..."[6]

Father's voice sounded in her ears, clear like a fog bell signalling lost travellers to find their way. Perhaps it was an omen, she thought with expectation, and, as if hypnotized, she approached a little further. Then shrill female laughter shook her up and the ghost of Mother throwing crumpled sweaty banknotes onto the table restrained her. 'Leave now!' Mother had cried, and it was to keep her far and away from a place like this.

She turned around with a view to run off, but her heart almost stopped when she found herself face to face with a German officer. Standing in front of her in the pale light of the streetlamp, speechless and stern, with his gray woollen overcoat and the SS heraldry on the collar of his tunic, he was a sight which presaged nothing propitious.

"*Bonsoir, mademoiselle!*"[7] he said, speaking fluent French, and he pierced her with an enquiring eye.

Winter gasped. She knew she ought to reply and was horrified at the thought of how miserably poor her French would sound, immediately betraying she was a foreigner. She gulped and answered with a muttered 'Bonsoir!'

"You seem completely lost! Perhaps I could be of help?"

Winter understood that he was offering to help her, and she was glad that, this time, she could respond without words. She lowered her eyes to hide her agitation, shook her head negatively and, with unexpected courage, she turned her back on him and took a few steps towards the club, which seemed to her like the most protective place in the world at the moment.

"Don't walk away like this, miss!" he called at her and the tone of his voice had an instantly immobilising effect. "I'd like to see your papers, please!"

Her papers? she silently asked herself and images from the last two days immediately bombarded her, with her papers, however, to be found nowhere in her recollection. She prayed for her identity card to be in her handbag, where it should normally be, while a stray thought to her young rescuer stifled her breath and she stirred the contents of her bag with a terrible premonition.

"So long to find your papers! Perhaps you don't have any?" remarked the German in the kindest voice, manifesting the most polished sarcasm she had ever encountered. Winter's terror hindered her from even the slightest attempt to understand what he had said. She only understood she had to find her identity card.

"I ..." she uttered in her panic and immediately raised a dreadful gaze at the German, certain she had just signed her death warrant.

"English?" he wondered out loud in his own language and his eyes narrowed ominously, his well-groomed face emanating lethal tension.

"Please!" she begged and impulsively kneeled to grab the edge of his coat in a desperate appeal. "It's not what you think! It's not what you think!"

"What is your name?" he asked imperiously, strangely sounding like an excellent English speaker.

"Winter Pale! ... No, Dupont... Winter Dupont Pale..." She shook her head, struggling to clear her mind, regrettably recognising the danger of her own name. "Winter Dupont! Please...!"

The officer nodded, squeezing his lips together; he took her by the arm, forcing her to stand up and meet the blade of his eyes: "What is your purpose here?"

"... I..." Suddenly, she thought the club music played louder, the voices and laughter of its customers screamed the morbid silence out of the night. "I'm... I'm here for work..." she justified herself with the survival instinct speaking through her mouth. "Here... at the club... I came to work at the club. Please! ... It's not what you think...!"

Her lie made Winter feel completely transparent, and she thought the German's persistent gaze could see right through her.

"So you came to work at the club!" he repeated, and she could not discern whether or not he was mocking her. Then, he surprised her by releasing her arm and, although she felt like he still kept her captive, as if with heavy chains, only by the sternness of his look, momentarily she thought she might still have a hope to get away with it. "Very well, *Fräulein*, let's find out then, if you are telling the truth!" he decided and, with a resolute nod, he ordered her to move on towards the noisy building.

Stiff as a corpse, she had no choice but to obey his command, convinced she was walking on to her doom and feeling stupid about her foolish lie, as if the German would let her go without verifying her claim, as if he were as naive as her. Desperate, she looked at him out of the corner of her eye, a threatening shadow at a short distance, and she wondered whether she could sprint her way out: to run like the children did when the shopkeepers chased them, wishing she could be as fast as them, despite knowing it was useless, because she possessed neither their vigour nor their courage, but at least, if she tried, she might have the chance to die swiftly, painlessly even, with a bullet on her back, which, frenzied as she would be, she might not even feel. So pointless! she derided herself the moment they entered a narrow and enclosed courtyard leading to the club entrance, since it was too late even for that.

From the ground-floor window, the club interior, where fully uniformed military staff and citizens were having an orgiastic feast, left her with the impression of a slaughterhouse. The officer opened the door, gave her a slight push inside and she stumbled, her control over her limbs completely abandoning her. Only seconds later, a rather gross-looking man arrived to greet them. The owner, Winter thought, and, observing his round, well-fed figure, his particularly sharp eyes and obsequious smile, she immediately disliked him.

"*Sturmbannführer*[8] von Stielen! What a pleasant surprise! Welcome! I am always so pleased to see you, always so pleased!" the man emphasised and bowed several times, while glancing at Winter rather contemptuously.

"Cut the smooth talk, Pierre! What I need to know is whether or not this girl works here!" the German answered bluntly and straight to the point.

Winter was about to pass out from her anguish, but she managed to grasp the word 'work' in the German's utterance and was struck by the idea that, if the owner was not as despicable as he looked and had even the slightest intention to help her, then she would have to give him a clue in order to forestall his answers to any of the German's questions. The faintest chance to escape the terrible fate and the courage of one who has absolutely nothing to lose armed her with enough boldness to exclaim: "Sir, please..."

"Silence!" the officer hushed her strictly and blasted a look at her as dangerous as direct gunpoint.

"Please, *Herr Sturmbannführer* ..." the astute and perceptive club owner intervened with the most exaggerated faces. "This girl does not exactly work here. She came to ask for a job this morning and I told her to come back in the evening, but I didn't mean, of course, that she should show up in the dead of night!" And making a condescending gesture, he added in horrible English: "What time did I tell you to come, you fool?"

The officer looked at them both, one after the other.

"I guess you already know that the girl is British and can't speak a word of French!" he noticed with absolute disbelief.

The owner shrugged with indifference and shook his head, as if he were normally talking about the most ordinary matter.

"*Herr Sturmbannführer*, I was only doing a favour for a relative of mine, my first cousin on my mother's side, you know, her fourth brother's boy who studied abroad to be a doctor–I'm sure you remember me telling you about him! Well, he says he knows the girl, she's been here since before the war, they are hungry, the girl needs to work, etc., etc. So, I thought, it doesn't hurt to be of help if one can, and I said go ahead, give it a try, if she can do the job, what the hell, she can learn a word or two, after all we're not here to give lectures, are we? Hahaha. Please, *Herr Sturmbannführer*, I'm sure she can't be the first or the last foreigner to be stranded in our part of the world these days. Wouldn't you agree? But if you would like to take her along and verify her identity... or for whatever else you want, that is, I'm not the one to give you any instructions, heavens no, hahaha, I have no problem and no objection whatsoever. None! Absolutely none!" And he acquiescently bowed his head again and again.

The owner's unbearable babbling could hardly reassure Winter, who had only been able to understand few scattered, meaningless words. With her eyes fixed upon the owner's jabbering mouth, she had to rely more on the German's reactions for understanding, his deadpan expression, however, being of very little help. Then, miraculously, the officer distanced himself from her, and, looking at him with a spontaneous surprise, Winter felt as if a piece of her body were missing when the German's shadow stopped weighing down on her.

"No, that won't be necessary!" the German said, and Winter understood his French better than the owner's. "If you, Pierre, vouch for her... I'll take your word for it!"

"Well, I..." the owner exclaimed with the same shrug and head gesture as before. "Yes, I vouch for her!"

Sturmbannführer von Stielen looked at him ambiguously, the faint smile in his eyes showing his complete distrust. He merely gave Winter a glance of the same incredulity and passed by her in order to join the cheerful clientele without another word. Winter watched him go with a nasty shiver of relief.

"Come on, you good-for-nothing! Let's find you something to do around here!" shouted the owner with his broken English and, while his eyes were combing through the hall for precaution, he rapidly tucked a key into Winter's palm: "On the first floor, last door to your left. Wait for me there!"

The last door to the left on the corridor of the first floor at 'The Golden Doe' opened into a simple square room with a metal double bed. There was also a window with thick curtains looking onto a back courtyard, an oblong space with no access to the street. A small rectangular building with two narrow doors stood there, too. Winter looked abstractly, trying to overcome the shock, still unable to believe how lucky she had been to have slipped away from the German's claws. And she felt that a heartfelt 'thank God' was due, like the one which Mother insisted on saying with the patience of a saint. Perhaps there was, indeed, a God up there, perhaps He even liked her, she was keen to think. At that moment, one of the two doors of the rectangular building in the courtyard opened and a German soldier stepped out, buttoning up his trousers.

A second later, the door opened and the owner of the club hurried in: "I'm Pierre Morné." he stated seriously.

"Winter Pale" she introduced herself and immediately felt the need to add: "Dupont!"

Pierre Morné raised one eyebrow: "... Hmm! Come a bit closer, will you?" he requested, and Winter made a few tentative steps. "Are you in the Resistance?" he asked, and the question surprised as well as intimidated Winter.

"No!" she said in all sincerity, but all he did was, once again, raise his eyebrow. "I'm not in the Resistance!" she hurried to reassure him. "I ... I bumped into this German and I couldn't find my papers. I'm sorry, but it was the only excuse I could think of. If you would put me up just for tonight, I promise that tomorrow morning I'll..." she gushed almost without a breath.

"So, you are not in the Resistance!" Pierre Morné insisted in doubt, his frowning expression forcing Winter to summarise her entire situation in only a few sentences:

"My mother and I emigrated from England eight years ago! I have nothing to do with the Resistance, I swear it! I just had to leave my house. It was ... I just ... I had to leave!"

Winter looked at Pierre Morné's suspicious, almost hostile, face with complete dread. Not only did she not want to be thrown out onto the street again, she did not want to have to explain any more.

"I'm sorry, but you can't stay!" Pierre Morné disagreed, shattering her hopes. "I lied for you because I pitied you, but your story doesn't sound right and I want no trouble. Do you understand?"

Winter clasped her hands in a desperate gesture: "Oh, but please, sir, please, just for one night! I have nowhere to go, and I can't face that German again! I beg of you, I'll be indebted to you for life!"

Pierre Morné pouted and scratched his hairless chin.

"In debt?" he mumbled. "Hmm!" He looked at her from the top of her hair to every single detail of her face, to the sternum and the chest, from the waist to the curve of her thighs, the ankles and the tips of her dirty shoes. He looked at her from top to bottom, and from bottom to top again. "Hmm!" he exclaimed again and examined her with his eyes a bit more. "Well...! You may stay for now..." he finally declared with a tone forthrightly indicating he was doing her a favour. "But you will work!" he immediately clarified and found her gladly agreeing. "How old are you?"

"Just over twenty!"

He scratched his bald head and remarked that her age was good. "I guess you know what girls do around here!" he then added without mincing his words and causing an uncomfortable burn on Winter's cheeks. Pierre Morné opened his eyes wide.

"*Mon Dieu!*"[9] She blushes!" he spurted out with a laughter. "It's been a long time since I saw this!" And once again he inspected her, making a circle around her, as one would do to an item before buying it.

He gave her the clothes she was to wear, a fancy outfit with bows and ruffles, a red satin bonnet for her head. Then he ordered her to go down to the kitchen and eat well. When she finally made it back to the entertainment hall for instructions, she looked like a completely different girl. If she were a fast and good learner, she might just get along with the boss and continue to be granted the refuge he offered from this dark, cruel world. It all depended on Pierre Morné. He was the boss at 'The Golden Doe'. And that was the first and most important lesson that Winter should never forget.

4

The red

No sooner had Parisians recovered from the shock of the occupiers' settlement in the French capital than Pierre Morné, an unskilled, yet extremely perceptive and ambitious money-grubber, started his own business. As if he had lived through another occupation and knew exactly how to seize a hard times' opportunity, Pierre Morné set his very specific goals, centred all his attention on achieving them, and there he was, quickly transformed from a servile underling into an ingenious and crafty boss.

'The Golden Doe' was in no way as impressive as the cabarets of *Montmartre* or the *Champs-Élysées*, which excelled in the conquerors' preferences and were famous for their refined clientele, it was, however, located in a good spot near the *Place Pigalle*, considered quite commercial for this type of business, and it offered a wide variety of entertainment, as often advertised. There was a large hall for the bar, dance floor and stage downstairs, as well as a gallery with extra seats, which gave the space a rather theatrical feel. It was decorated to its owner's taste, with gold and red in abundance,–not very original for a nightclub many dared say, although not to Pierre's face. Even so, Winter could not fail to notice that the red at 'The Golden Doe' was not an ordinary red: it was not the bright red of poppies or the scarlet of the royal guards' uniforms, which she used to admire outside Buckingham Palace. It was a somewhat brownish red, dark, in the shade of blood...

Apart from work, the business also offered residence to its employees. Except for the members of the orchestra, who had their own house elsewhere, the staff occupied the two upper floors of the three-storey building. Each girl on Pierre Morné's payroll had her own space on the second floor, where small studio flats were established along a dimly lit corridor, much resembling a hotel. The boss, on the other hand, occupied the spacious apartment on the top floor, completely isolated from the rest. The first floor was empty of permanent residents. Winter always felt intimidated by the rooms on the first floor.

"Winter, are you down yet? You don't expect the dishes to get washed by themselves, do you?"

She scurried off to get the job done. When the boss gave an order, he did not suffer to be ignored. Soon, it would be four weeks since her arrival. She started off working for Pierre, thinking it would only be for a few days, just enough to do away with the obligation she felt for his help. Then, she would decide what to do. But she never got anywhere near making a concrete decision; she just stayed.

She was now a member of the small community that 'The Golden Doe' was and she had many obligations and few privileges. Pierre would not allow his employees to forget where their allegiance lay, so he would always find something for them to do, even on the one day in the week when clubs were closed, a recently issued order for which Pierre could not imprecate the Entertainment Control Committee enough for robbing him of an honest days' work.

The day went by exhaustingly and time flew fast, faster than when Winter was at *Rue Goubet*; she often missed those days of solitary reflection by the window,–at least then, she could relive the good times in a way, feel close to the past that defined her. She had not thought of Mother for quite some time and often felt guilty about it. But there was simply not enough time for remorse and all the time she could spare, she had to spend sleeping. Her body was tired and her thoughts were still. Sometimes, she felt she preferred it that way.

At 'The Golden Doe', Winter earned her first salary, which was no more than a few pennies, according to her skills, as the boss had made clear enough. Winter did not mind the peanuts she was paid; they were her own peanuts and nobody was going to ask her how she spent them or take them away from her. At Stepfather's, she was always answerable for what little she was given to manage, too little to provide for her family, and that was also something she had to account for. She only needed to take care of herself now. She hid what she could spare under a loose plank in the floor and frequently went back to see that it was there, the fruit of her labour, her own little treasure. When she had saved enough, she sometimes thought, there was also a debt to Mother and the twins she felt she had to repay. Perhaps then she could return to them.

Winter's first experiences as a waitress were quite encouraging. Most customers would be patient or even enjoy her initial clumsiness, but there were also some who took their authoritarian role very seriously. Winter gradually realised that there were tried and tested ways to deal with these people. A fully compliant smile or a cute gesture often saved the day when facing a customer's anger–she used to employ similar tactics with the shop owners in Stepfather's neighbourhood, especially in order to ask for credit. Eventually, she proved to have more flair for public relations than she originally thought. And she was a keen learner. On the job, it was impossible not to learn some elementary German, such as counting and making simple short sentences. The German language resembled English, she soon discovered, in vocabulary at least. This prompted her to take classes at the *Deutsche Institut*, where the girls had already been studying for some time.

There were another four girls working for Pierre Morné at 'The Golden Doe' and Winter found three of them quite easy to get along with, because they were kind, girls of her own class, who had experienced suffering and injustice from a young age, thus knowing enough about what it was like to be on the fringes of society. Michelle and Andrée were sisters–not blood sisters, that is, they had only been adopted by the same family. And yet, it was impressive how much they loved each other, no less than real siblings would. However, when the parents died, the couple's relatives hired lawyers to cancel the adoptions, because there was a rich inheritance involved, and, well, where there was self-interest, people always became less emotional. One way or another, the girls were thrown out onto the street and nobody knew what fate they would have met, until they were sheltered by a nurse from the orphanage, who was touched by their drama and soon became their next of kin–a reason the two girls called her 'aunt' ever since.

Georgette had come from the provinces, but she insistently avoided any specific reference to her place of origin. When they asked her about her story, there was an echo of bitterness in her words that could not be found anywhere in the narrations of Michelle and Andrée, despite their mistreatment. Georgette's family had been killed, and she had to flee, she said. Coming to Paris, she wandered here and there for a while, until Pierre took her in and literally saved her from certain death. Georgette loved Pierre and everyone could see that there was something very special about their relationship.

The fifth girl in the club, called Geneviève, was the singer, and she had a prominent role in their community. The girls did not like her, always calling her a snoot among other names, and no one really knew the story behind this beautiful curly-haired brunette,–ignorance giving food to the girls' imagination and fueling their appetite for gossip. Winter had to play along if she had any chance of being one of them. But soon she stopped feeling bad about it, realising that there was enough resentment for them lowly ones on Geneviève's part, as well.

Three of the people Winter liked the most in 'The Golden Doe' were the orchestra boys, such a dissimilar yet fully accordant triplet: Alain, Guillaume, Louis; double bass, accordion, piano. Alain was a bit of a ham. He did not seem to take anything seriously, though he preferred to call himself an incurable optimist. Guillaume was a charmer. He loved women and women loved him back, but, sadly, who he was really in love with was Geneviève; and did she make his life impossible because of it! Louis stood out from both his friends. He was earnest, romantic, educated and the mature way of his thinking fascinated everyone.

Winter found it very difficult to understand him when he spoke, but the way he spoke, the tone and character of his voice, the expressions on his face, the spark in his eyes, all made her listen to him, almost mesmerized. And then he played Chopin on the piano and he was wonderful and Winter listened and, listening, she learnt almost one by one most of the composer's *Nocturnes*.

The orchestra boys were unique at creating a cheerful atmosphere at the club. Winter knew little about laughing, but the boys brought a contented smile to her lips more and more often lately. One day, they urged her to sing along and even noticed she had a beautiful voice, making Winter as proud and happy as ever. A few moments later, however, her joy turned sour, as Pierre hastened to remind her she was not paid to have fun and she was specifically warned that she could find herself kicked out more easily than she could possibly imagine.

Pierre was the strict guard of the community. Georgette used to say that he was not as bad as he seemed, were one willing to look underneath the annoying surface, but Winter had her very legitimate doubts. To her mind, Pierre was a heartless profiteer who would sell his own mother if he were to gain anything from it. Sensitivity was not on the list of his qualities and he would do no favours, unless certain to get a bigger favour in return. He was as ruthless and cold-blooded as an executioner with his business. But if one played by his rules, they had nothing to fear. Pierre loved getting his own way, and he was much nicer to those who helped him get it.

Finally, there was Petit François, the eight-year-old son of a widow next door and the errand boy of the club. His mother would be forever grateful to Pierre for having him as an apprentice, but it was hardly out of Pierre's good heart. The boy would work more than his payment's worth, but he was granted permission to sell flowers for his own profit during working hours and Pierre rarely missed the opportunity to highlight the insurmountable asset of that: because the German customers had a commendable fondness for the laddie and the little fellow would go home every night with his pocket full of tips and chocolate bars, while there were also occasions when he would be offered entire baskets of delicacies and goodies which many those days would envy. And it was all owed to Pierre's generosity.

Generosity was the trait of Pierre's German customers on which he heavily relied to secure the supplies for the club. Of course, pulling some strings was not only necessary but also lucrative, since neither Pierre nor his suppliers could spurn a good deal. Whatever the means, the staff of 'The Golden Doe' never went hungry,–a scarce privilege in times like theirs. It would usually be some kind of soup or gruel made of vegetables or practically anything they could get their hands on, but they were often also treated to a piece of good meat, rabbit or game, a cause for a regular feast, for which Pierre would get all the credit.

The clientele of 'The Golden Doe' was mostly soldiers, the last cogs in the wheel of the conqueror's juggernaut. Unlike their high-ranking superiors, they were given limited options for entertainment, and, naturally, Pierre had managed to include 'The Golden Doe' on the white list after tough negotiations. Not that he scorned senior officers and prominent officials, but soldiers were significantly more convenient: they had fewer demands and tastes easier to please. However, those elect customers did not completely hold their old shack in contempt: *Sturmbannführer* von Stielen, for example, was a notable exception. There were plenty of new faces each night and there were the regular ones: Adolf Hörst from Radio Paris, Herman Weismiller from the Television Service with his girlfriend Marie-France, Stefan Schmidt from the guard at the Power Company, Klaus Molnich, the translator for the Central Intelligence Service... Assuredly, there were civilians as well, those who did not mind affiliating with the Germans.

Another bustling night at 'The Golden Doe' was just beginning. The tables were full, the gallery was crowded, customers were sitting at the bar and others were standing on the dance floor, shouting, laughing and ordering drinks, while ogling the waitresses and other people's dates. Here and there, loud singing voices would drown out Geneviève, who had long abandoned every intention of being artistic in her job, something Pierre had definitely had a hand in, repeatedly having ignored each one of her complaints.

"Winter, these beers go to table fourteen!" pointed out the boss, whose post was at the bar.

"*Oui, Monsieur*!" Winter responded and rushed into the packed hall carrying a tray of brimful glasses.

"Another three beers here, please, Miss!" a blonde soldier with clear blue eyes called to her, and she confirmed with a hand gesture, adding charmingly: "*Kommt sofort!*"[10]

On the way back, she was literally dragged onto the dance floor by a euphorically gleeful duo, one with a pip on his sleeve and another with a single chevron, who had apparently tired of watching others dance and decided to get a female dance partner for themselves.

"And she is a much better dancer than you, Fritz!" the single chevron said to the pip bearer, once he had stolen her from his arms.

"You kind, *mein Herr*!" replied Winter with her newly learnt German, and gladly whirled and fell backwards for him to show off to his friend. "But I must back work. You like more drink?"

Winter left the two men joyfully singing out loud, securing a fresh round of drinks for them which would make Pierre extremely happy, but the moment she turned around, she fell onto someone who had suddenly stepped in front of her, blocking her way.

"*Entschuldigung!*"[11] she uttered, taken aback by his bleary eyes, sunken into his face as if someone had pressed them in with their fingers. Without words, he made way for her to pass, tossing a coin he was holding, which he immediately caught without so much as blinking.

Winter's heart pumped alarmingly and an icy shiver ran down her spine. She went on her way, hoping to avoid him, but she was soon to find out he had, unfortunately, followed her to the bar. Out of the corner of her eye, she watched him talk to Pierre, and she knew what it meant. Her chest was hurting, her knees were trembling, and she prayed, she prayed for a divine intervention to relieve her of this bitter cup, which had eventually come out of its cupboard for her, too. When, a moment later, Pierre called her, she could simply not move, and, frozen from head to toe, she just gaped at Pierre and the almost inhuman creature with the dark red eyes that stood next to him. Then

Pierre called her again and, this time, his tone showed there was no more room for stalling. Winter could do little but approach.

"Seien Sie nicht traurig, Fräulein; wir werden sehr viel Spaß zusammen haben!"[12] the soldier said with a smirk, and having more or less understood what he had said, Winter felt sick to her stomach.

"I don't think so!" she heard her lips spontaneously utter and even she could not believe she had actually dared say so.

Pierre apologised a million times to the German on her behalf and, doing his best to keep up appearances, he pulled her aside to make sure he gave her a piece of his mind: "Look here, I made this clear to you when you came here begging me to take you in. So, don't give me that *'I don't think so'* horseshit and do what you must!"

"Why, Pierre, why?" Winter cried with a plea in her voice louder than any protest. "I didn't ask for more money, did I? Don't I always do as you tell me? Don't I slave all day to keep you happy, haven't I shown my gratitude enough? I will do whatever else you ask me, I swear it! I beg of you, Pierre, please, please!" And she imploringly grabbed his hand which, had they not been in public, she would not have hesitated to kneel before and kiss in submission, if that was what it would take for him to let her return to her work intact.

"Don't be stupid and let go! You are making a fool of yourself!" he blurted out and pulled his hand away, more embarrassed than her.

"I don't care!" blatted Winter. "Please! Don't do this to me..."

Pierre's anger seemed fused with emotions which Winter eagerly interpreted as ambivalence. It had never really been brought up, but, for an experienced eye such as Pierre's, it should be clear enough that she was a virgin and would not have the slightest idea what to do with herself in a situation like this; he might even be considering that satisfying this brute was not, after all, worth enough to corrupt a young girl like that. On the other hand, his practical mind would weigh the other girls' reaction, wondering whether any different treatment of Winter might raise a rebellion against him. But Winter was convinced that none of the girls, who had shown her such kindness, would have the indecency to protest, having been in her shoes and knowing what it would have meant to them had Pierre shown clemency and left them out of this shameful trade. Unfortunately, Pierre failed to meet any of her expectations.

"You can't play upon my feelings, so stop trying!" he stated bluntly, leaving Winter thunderstruck. "You will go with him, or else...!"

Winter was completely unprepared for such a response: "Or else, what?" she asked in a bewildered rather than confrontational manner. Nevertheless, Pierre took the remark no less than an insult, rolling his eyes and spitting feathers.

"Do you think I'm being cruel to you?" he hit out at her. "*C'est comme ça!*[13] The world is much crueler outside these walls. Make your choice!"

Pierre's words were like a punch in the face, and Winter stared at him, unable to believe that this was really happening. Her eyes glimpsed over Pierre's shoulder at that poor excuse of a man who meant to buy her, and the idea of his touch mortified her.

"Come on now! Don't take it to heart! It's not as bad as you think!" Pierre whispered, mildly pulling her by the arm to lead her to the drunken soldier's grasp and she felt like a lamb at the slaughter.

As they climbed up the stairs, all sounds suddenly went mute in her ears and the last thing she remembered hearing was her own self croak: "How can you do this!" And then, as if they were visions of somebody else, as if they were two people she did not recognise nor give a damn about, she watched an ill-matched couple walk down the corridor of their ruin on the first floor of 'The Golden Doe', the paradise of debauchery and abomination. A blood red haze encompassed their half-naked bodies as they lay on the lumpy mattress, she on her back, he on top of her, between her legs, which he held wide open with a rough, unkind grip. And there, on the ceiling, she observed the shadows, red and black silhouettes flirting and kissing with serpents' tongues, whispering mysteriously as they danced inside purple flames. Right where the ceiling lamp was suspended, a thick liquid was boiling in a red-hot cauldron, a simmering bloody red, splattering its dark stains on the walls, spattering onto the furniture, drenching the sheets, smearing her skin; her own condemned skin.

5

Cross-stitched

Late that night, Georgette found Winter deadly pale in the bathtub, with an ugly rash on her face, bosom, belly and thighs, while the high fever which burnt her up for the next three days gave everybody a good scare–even Pierre was scared, despite his whining that it was all a deliberate act to avoid doing her job.

As if in a dream, Winter remembered seeing the orchestra boys at her bedside speaking words of kindness; Michelle and Andrée with their considerate smiles; and, most of all, she remembered Georgette, her mild voice and tender caresses giving her a feeling of sisterhood: "Don't let them get the better of you, don't!" the girl would say in all her sweetness and warmth. "When I was in your place, my first reaction would be to hate myself. But then it all cleared up in my head and I said, it's okay, have your way with my body since you can, do what you want, do your worst; the time will come when all scores will be settled, in blood if need be!"

Exhausted by the fever, Winter was unable to understand what Georgette was saying about blood, but she guessed she meant the blood of her own horrible first time. And she felt tenderness and repugnance for this girl, only a couple of years older than her, who still refused to give up and surrender. Because she was only feeling helpless and miserable, knowing her disparagement was nothing but a common destiny for people like herself, unfortunate to be no more than mere commodities at the disposal of the ones with the power to control them. Nothing in life was given for free, and if they wanted to live, poor creatures like her, like Michelle and Andrée, like Georgette, like Mother, they had to pay with their only marketable possession, bargain with their face value and pay the bill in cash. What followed was a paralyzing sense of futility, evoked by a lack of uniqueness, even in pain. She was gravely disappointed, lost all meaning in things; but that, too, felt ordinary. After all, Pierre was right about one thing: there was nothing a person could not grow accustomed to. And the ball and chain on a prisoner's leg would soon become an integral part of their limb...

The bells of *Notre-Dame* rang a half hour past noon. Sitting on a bench by the river at the *Île Saint Louis*, Winter observed the passing of time in the water flow, in the flight of birds, in the travelling clouds. She found a rare serenity there; nowhere else in the city did everything seem so in place, so painless, peaceful and dignified. If only she could stay on this bench forever, become a piece of the landscape and share the happiness of being without cause and purpose, without means and necessities. If only, for once, living were easy and she could pretend nothing else mattered, but the beauty around, the breeze on her face, the velour-soft texture of memory in the pages of Father's poetry scrap-book. Like poems themselves, which served no life-support purpose, yet there was so much of life's true spirit in those lines, that suddenly everything was explained with no explanation at all.

"...And graven with diamonds in letters plain
There is written, her fair neck round about:
'Noli me tangere', for Caesar's I am,
And wild for to hold, though I seem tame."[14]

She turned the pages shut. It was but a short respite for the untamed doe, and she would have to return to her imperial cell without delay, especially if she wanted to be in time for lunch, because the kitchen closed at two o'clock and, after that, Pierre would allow no one to touch a single piece of bread.

She hurried to the underground station at the *Hôtel de Ville* and was piled into a crowded wagon. It was a long way to *Belleville*, where she would change to *Pigalle*, and she huddled her way to the back of the wagon, to be a little more comfortable. Looking at the adjacent wagon, she saw it was exclusively for Germans, and they were sitting in all their indulgence, a few empty seats here and there screaming of the injustice. But, of course, they were the conquerors and, by right of conquest, they were entitled to the best seats on the train, to priority on pavements and streets, at restaurants, shops and houses, and over the bodies and souls of those they subjugated.

Then, she noticed a low-ranking officer was watching her, and the moment their eyes met, he touched his double-breasted hat on skew-whiff to greet her. He was ugly, although objectively good-looking, and she quickly turned her eyes away, uncertain whether it was out of spite or out of fear, that he might get interested in her enough to follow her, find out what she did and be tempted to pay Pierre the agreed amount to buy her. She had become a shadow of herself, her only defense, and she might as well just disappear from the face of the earth.

Having to disembark at the next station, she pushed hurriedly to the door and stepped out with her head down–it had become a habit of hers to avoid looking at people's faces. Unfortunately, she stumbled upon somebody who was about to get on, so she had to raise her eyes.

"*Pardon*!" she muttered and immediately felt embarrassed, although not because of her bad French, as frequently. There was a pair of sparking eyes before her. What colour were they? Hazel eyes, she re-called. And they still shined with that light of self-assurance generated only by the experience of life's most relentless hardships. "...You?" she murmured, spontaneously changing to her native tongue.

"It's a small, small world!" he quipped with an ambiguous smile. The whistle for the departure of the train forced them to move further into the platform.

"I... I..." she felt the need to justify herself, but her mind had suddenly gone completely blank of excuses.

"Winter Pale Dupont!" he said, and Winter was baffled that he knew her full name, quite certain she had not been the one to tell him. "Your identity card fell out of your bag that day!" he explained, and Winter felt seriously doubtful. "I was hoping to see you again!" He stepped a little closer with the same presumptuousness which Winter so well remembered from their first encounter, and she backed off with a view to turn around and walk away. "Please, don't leave like this again!" he implored and extended an offer to a cup of coffee. "I think you owe me this much!" he insisted, seeing Winter's persistent hesitation.

The phrase 'you owe me' always had a decisive effect on Winter's opinions, making her practically incapable of refusing. She looked down, puckered her lips, and nodded.

"If you like..." she mumbled and was shocked by the sudden grasp of his hands on her arms.

"René. Say it, don't be afraid!" he urged her, looking into her eyes with his multi-coloured gaze, which stunned her into complete inability to react.

"...René!"

They sat near the station at a brasserie with a red tent. They were brought a hot drink, which they drank silently, staring off at the traffic outside the window. René could not take his eyes from her, but Winter deliberately avoided them. His magnetic aura radiated directly into her soul that same deeply disturbing familiarity, as if their destinies had been tied together like cross-stitch embroidery in some previous life, and now, having met once more, all the feelings reanimated, binding them with a clearly detectable, though undetermined, bond.

"Are you still all alone?" René asked.

She shrugged, looking elsewhere to ensure he would not be able to see her eyes. "I've found somewhere to settle in..."

"Somewhere?" he emphasised, causing her cheeks to flush with the fear that he might ask her to reveal more than she intended.

"Yes, I'm making a living!" she replied as evasively as she could and hurried to drive the conversation away from her person, asking him what he was doing.

"The same as before!" he willingly replied. "I have a small sewing shop at the *Galerie Vivienne*, near the *Palais-Royal*, if you know!" Winter declared ignorance. "If you had stayed that day, you would have learnt a lot about me!"

"I had to... I'm sorry!... You see..." Winter slurred her words in the most apologetic tone, but René showed no intention of hearing her explanations.

"No! I was more eager than I should have been, I know it! I probably frightened you off!" he admitted, leaving Winter speechless, never before having met such disposition for pardon. "I was really... I don't know how to say this... You are ... You are very special to me..." he continued with deep emotion and Winter could find no suitable response, so she simply watched his finger run about the brim of his cup. "I was thinking about you. That day, I couldn't return until quite late and something was telling me... I was sure you would have left!"

"So, you're not angry with me?" Winter dared to conclude.

"Angry?" René responded, surprised at the question and, instead of an answer, he reached for her hand,–a bizarre force preventing her from pulling it away.

"I feared you'd think me ungrateful, because you helped me and I..." she confessed encouraged by his attitude and raised her eyes to his deeply introspective countenance.

"When I found you that night, something moved inside me; I feel somewhat responsible for you..." he sincerely professed and, anticipating her reaction, he immediately added: "Don't take it the wrong way, it's just that... I'm interested in you... I'm really interested in you!"

He brought her hand to his lips and kissed it many, many times, looking at her straight in the eyes, and Winter quivered, because it was only disgust and hatred that she had learnt to feel at a man's touch and she had come to know of men to be cruel and unkind, claiming for their own, even by force, what they liked and whom. And he was doing just that, claiming her for his own without a shred of her consent, but she could hardly call him disgusting and she would definitely not find him appalling. René! As his name formed in her mind, she felt as though a spell had been cast upon her. And he was welcome, this almost impertinent stranger, with his burning palms all over her hand, his velvet kisses, the feverish want in his gaze. Her eyes were moist, adrift in their bewilderment, sunken in longing and despair. He smiled at her and slowly backed away, insightful and clement. They remained quiet for a while.

"... And what exactly do you sew at your shop?"

"... And where did you say you work?"

They impulsively laughed and Winter felt she could be a little more at ease.

"You first..." she urged him.

René explained gladly that, before the war, his father ran a pretty stable business of upholstery in his hometown, Lille. But then the war broke out, René moved to Paris, and later he opened this little shop, sewing and repairing deluxe linen, curtains and furniture fabric for the hotels the Germans had requisitioned. It was a business with no future, with demand having rapidly decreased as of late,–the turn of the war was already clear to those who had eyes to see. But he was content, in spite of it; he wanted little to do with living off their table scraps. He was at that point in time and history when he could do what he really wanted, fighting his bit to throw them overboard, helping to shape the new world of tomorrow...

Winter admired his idealism, but she also found it a little difficult to relate to. Because he had the opportunity for a settled life, the chance to survive without enormous sacrifices, yet he would risk everything for such an abstract purpose as 'the world of tomorrow'. What was that even like? she wondered. And how could he even begin to presume it would be any better? "Well, that sounds..." she hesitated, circumspect enough not to share these thoughts with him.

"You can only know what it's like once you're part of it! It's a wonderful, deeply gratifying feeling!" he asserted, looking at her in a way that was clearly inviting, seducing even. Winter's heart was fluttering like a fledgling trying out its wings; and she would eagerly get carried away by the fervent passion in his convictions, the shivering sensation of his breath on her ear, as he leaned over to add in complete secrecy:

"To them, I'm a miserable, pitiful wage earner. They see, and yet, they never look at me! But you won't tell on me, will you?" And moving backwards, he scanned her with his eyes shrouded in obscurity.

Winter's sentiment violently switched to a fierce alarm, which compelled her to immediately reassure him with an expressively negative head shake. His confessions flattered her, but the truth remained: the more she knew about him, the less secure they both were. Knowledge was power, and power meant responsibility. Ignorance was, in many ways, a guarantee. One could not disclose what one did not know, no matter how hard they were pressured. And while René kept talking to her as if he believed her to be of the same make, as if she were as bold and gritty against all fear and danger as he was, all she really wanted was for him to stop, because what he had already revealed to her was too much, too much for her to handle.

"Please! I can't listen to this!" she found the courage to interrupt him, knowing how cowardly it seemed, how demeaning and definitely unattractive, although completely open and frank, honest, even valiant, in its own peculiar way. With a stifling discomfort, she awkwardly stood up to leave, flabbergasting René, who sprang like a cat and grabbed her by the wrist.

"I've scared you. I didn't mean to. Please, don't go!" he appealed to her in the most steadfast manner.

"I'm late... I have to..."

"Wait!" he insisted, holding harder onto her. "Where can I find you?" Winter shook her head, deliberately avoiding his commanding gaze. "Will you come see me at the shop?"

"I don't know... I'm sorry..."

She broke free from his grasp and ran out of the brasserie, breathing in relief, as if she had been locked in a wooden box and, finally, someone had opened the lid. It had started to rain, but the rain was not the reason she walked fast. The station was near and, as soon as she got on the train, she could be safe again. Then, she would forget she had ever met this dangerous man and erase from her memory all she had heard and felt for him.

Suddenly, a strong arm took her by the waist, intercepting her hurried trade. She cried out, but there was no one around to hear. The arm pulled her firmly, although not forcibly, and held her against a wall.

"René?"

The darkness that surrounded him daunted her. His mask-like face was the most terrifying thing she had ever seen and his demonic eyes were debilitating. He was looking at her voicelessly, snorting like a wild animal after a long and strenuous hunt. And then, with a primitive urge and excruciating agony, he impassionedly enclosed her in his arms. With a flaming palm, he pressed her head against his chest and rubbed his cheek into her hair, breathing his roaring fire through it.

"Simone...!" an otherworldly voice escaped through his mouth.

Winter remained dumb and still. She even held her breath for fear that the slightest reaction on her part would provoke sinister forces within him. She heard the pounding of his heart, sensed the raging tempest in his spirit, and she was horrified, yet could not help feeling compassionate, as well as curious what suffering might have begotten this transformation.

Slowly regaining control of his emotions, René then pulled away, intently gazed at her half-opened lips, straight into her eyes afterwards, his shuddering breath on her face bringing about recurrent waves of tremor in her. Slowly, he released her, hanging his head down and painfully expressing his regret: "I'm sorry! I don't know what came over me!"

Winter was staggered, but instinctively nodded to grant him the affirmation he desired. She stepped back and supplicated his permission to leave, while he smiled bitterly.

"Come see me some day!" he almost pleaded, and, without response, she galloped away to the safety of the underground and onto the first train.

Still at the platform of Belleville station, a woman in a fur coat, engrossed in reading the day's *Le Petit Parisien*, looked up behind the birdcage veil of her fancy hat to watch the train leave. She folded the newspaper in haste, shoved it in her bag and rushed to the platform with the destination to *Châtelet*. At the central market of *Les Halles*, she stood by a street lamp, read the newspaper a little more and then threw it in the rubbish bin. She took a cigarette out of her purse, rolled it in her fingers, looking up and down the street for a light.

"Not easy to find good cigarettes nowadays!" a well-dressed man said in French, offering a smoke from his silver cigarette case. She gladly replaced her cigarette with the one offered and lit it off the match he struck for her.

"It's undetermined whether the girl is pregnant!" she said quietly, deeply inhaling and exhaling the smoke through her velvety red lips. "*Merci, Monsieur!*"

She opened her umbrella, briskly walked away in the increasing drizzle. In the rubbish bin, the day's *Le Petit Parisien*; among other things, a handwritten note was inside it:

"Region map with possible drop points of S.O.E.
Recent copy of Valmy[15] *Code "Seamstress": Hôtel Scribe*

The Midwife"

Printed on the kind of paper used to protect windows from air raids, the *Valmy* single page content was dominated by photographs from concentration camps, where German officers, standing next to mass graves, posed arrogantly. 'ONE AND ONLY ENEMY' read the main headline; then a couple of raindrops landed on it, dramatically spreading its ink.

6

The game of impressions

Despite the rain, Winter dragged her feet around the *Place Pigalle* for quite a while before finding it in herself to return to 'The Golden Doe'. She had promised to forget all about René Martin, to remove from her head his very existence and resume what she knew to be a quiet, uneventful life. But her mind had never been so disobedient, every single detail of her meeting with him replaying in it like newsreel footage on continuous play back. The name 'Simone' pestered her every thought, and she felt the green-eyed monster eating her up, for it was she, the mysterious Simone, who had stolen her own name from René's lips and it was probably her, precious Simone, that René was gazing at with his blazing passion. She remembered his eyes and trembled, the springtime rays of green in their honey brown, how they transformed from beaming sunlight to the ghastliest dusk. And yet, there was something irresistible about them, some obstinate determination having the power to rule over one's will, dangerously poised between gallantry and sheer brutality.

Utterly consumed by René's recollection, she had, naturally, been unable to do one thing right all night at 'The Golden Doe', and Pierre was fuming because it was, apparently, a third consecutive night that she had had no customers. Winter could not afford to worry about

Pierre. Next to daydreaming about René, concern was also added to her thoughts, concern about her own safety. What if he had been watched and someone had seen her with him? What if his own kind had seen her with him and regarded her as a threat? What if he had followed her and was reckless enough to show up right there, in the lion's den?

Suddenly, her foot got caught on something and, before she knew it, the heavy tray she was carrying slipped from her hands and smashed against the floor. A couple of drinks splattered on people sitting at the adjoining tables, causing their angered reaction, but her immediate and sincere apologies, fortunately, seemed to make up for it, one or two of them even becoming interested to see if she had been hurt. Mortified, Winter shifted her eyes around the hall to see the extent of her blunder. It was so noisy that few people would have been aware of the incident, if Pierre had not charged like a bull towards her, seeking to thunder out his stinging rebuke. The whole clientele and staff turned to see. Only the orchestra boys attempted to draw attention away by continuing to play some popular tunes, but their efforts fell flat since Geneviève refused to follow through, curiously standing to watch instead.

"I'm going to cut the damage out of your pay!" yelled Pierre, gesturing so intensely that he made a caricature of a man. Some even applauded because they thought it was an act of the club's entertainment program. "I've had enough of you, you worthless piece of shit! Now clean up your mess and get the hell out of here before...!"

Pierre screamed at the top of his lungs, making up reams of adjectives to bestow upon her, and Winter kneeled, pretending to pick up the broken glasses in order to hide her face from view. He had really become a spectacle even more than she had, but Pierre would rarely consider the consequences of his anger in advance. And he would have continued his reproach, heaven knows for how long, if someone had not stepped in and put a stop to it.

"You've made your point, Pierre! That's enough!"

Winter barely understood what had been said, all the same, she was spitefully glad to hear Pierre, suddenly, at a complete loss for words. As she watched his legs turn around and walk away, a vindictive smirk formed on her lips, which she carefully concealed before getting up to meet her rescuer.

"*Sturmbannführer* von Stielen!" she exclaimed and felt a snide satisfaction at the assumption that Pierre must have felt as powerless as an infant before the *Sturmbannführer*, even though she knew how much this moment of embarrassment for him would cost her later.

"I'm glad you remember me, Miss Pale!" the German replied, reminding her how well he spoke English, and gave her a temperate smile.

How could she not remember *Sturmbannführer* von Stielen, Winter thought, vividly recalling their dreary encounter which had led her to 'The Golden Doe' in the first place! Impulsively, she shivered and felt a disturbing squeeze in her stomach, where a sorely vexing question was now stirring: had she seen him at the club ever since? What a coincidence that he should choose this of all evenings to visit them again, advocated the skeptic inside her.

"Pierre overdoes it sometimes, doesn't he?" he commented and Winter agreed with a nod, wisely avoiding his gaze.

"Thank you for your intervention!" she said dubiously, and hurried to ask for his permission to be excused.

"May I...?" he suggested, with a minimal, yet decisive grimace. Winter gave her consent with another hesitant nod.

By the time they reached the bar, the incident seemed to have already been forgotten, and the club had regained its normal frivolity–fortunately for Winter, who hated being the centre of attention. When Pierre saw her arrive with an escort, he pouted and cast a malicious eye at her, but was restrained by the *Sturmbannführer*'s presence to only gnaw at his underlip. Eventually, he gave her another order to hand out.

Winter started out to do as the boss had bidden without objection. It was probably wiser not to let it go to her head that she had miraculously got away with her gaffe, since Pierre's anger rarely died out painlessly for the object of his wrath. Yet, the German's hand on her shoulder pinned her down, making both her and Pierre goggle their eyes in utter astonishment.

"This is disappointing, Pierre!" the *Sturmbannführer* stated, without hiding his acrid intent. "I've always thought of you as a brilliant businessman, but then you'd have to know your employees' talents and use them accordingly. So, I suggest you find something else for this girl to do, as waiting on tables is obviously not her métier."

When 'I suggest' came from the mouth of *Sturmbannführer* von Stielen, it had better be taken as a command and not a suggestion. Pierre gulped, but it was difficult to distinguish whether he had been offended or merely curious what the German implied and if there had been a profitable dealing that had escaped him, therefore depriving him of some rightful and deserving benefit.

"And that would be?" he asked, turning to look at Winter with a manifest doubt that there was anything she might actually be good at.

Sturmbannführer von Stielen did not bother to answer and pointed to the stage, where Geneviève had stopped singing and begun to exchange insults with some of the customers at the front tables, who seemed to disapprove by booing and even throwing their snacks at her. Then, she rattled out a curse, almost kicking in the face one of the protesters who was making deriding gestures, and abandoned the stage to run upstairs almost tearful.

The German turned to his interlocutors and scoffed a smile.

"I was talking to one of your girls earlier, Pierre! You know, that ginger-haired one!" he pointed out, turning his speech into English, so that Winter would better understand. Both Winter and Pierre realised he was talking about Georgette. "She said the girl can sing, so why not let her give it a try?"

"Hmm..." Pierre burbled, and an expression of long, hard thinking and swift, intricate calculation quickly followed his initial surprise. "Hmm..." he repeated and scratched his chin, apparently more and more warming to the idea. "Why not? I've heard you a couple of times and you weren't so bad!"

"But, I..." Winter muttered, rather reluctant to become entangled in this new, highly risky ordeal. "I haven't done it before... and well... Geneviève... she would..."

Pierre, however, was already persuaded and, hearing Winter's excuse, he flinched like something had stung him. "Geneviève! Who cares what she thinks!" he asserted and hurried off, ordering Winter to follow him.

Winter cast an uncertain look at *Sturmbannführer* von Stielen and could not help wondering about his intentions, putting her through this trial: was he trying to get her kicked out of the club? Because she might have learnt some of Geneviève's songs, mostly hearing her during rehearsals, and she might even have been offered a couple of compliments for her voice by the orchestra boys, but that was hardly an assurance that she could sing on stage, in front of people. Were she to fail, it would not be a simple misfortune; it would be a disaster and total humiliation. And the embarrassment she had felt at Pierre's reproach before would seem trivial compared to such ridicule. But, on the other hand, the singer's position at 'The Golden Doe' included privileges none of the other girls enjoyed and Winter would swear she had never seen Geneviève go upstairs with a man, even though she did flirt a lot with the customers during the intermissions between her performances. Well, if that were the case, then this was the opportunity of a lifetime. Why would *Sturmbannführer* von Stielen give her such an opportunity?

She had little time to speculate. Pierre rushed out of Geneviève's room fiery and masterful and he instructed Winter to wear one of the singer's dresses and, at least, try to appear decent–at which point, he looked at her from top to bottom, showing that he did not have great expectations. Inside the room, Geneviève had raised hell, kicking and smashing things, and when she turned her gaze to Winter, it was as if venom were dripping from her eyes.

"I'm sorry, Geneviève, I didn't mean..." Winter began timidly in her poor French.

"I wish you fall on your face, you idiot!" Geneviève exclaimed and, stoutly pushing her aside, she ran out of the room in blind fury.

Winter had expected Geneviève's angry reaction but felt annoyed by her attitude all the same. She entered the room and closed the door. At first glance, the singer's room was no better than hers, she scornfully observed. Then she opened the wardrobe and there it was, the basis for comparison: Geneviève had more than a dozen items of clothing, each of them more exquisite than the last. Branded or not, they were all extremely select and elegant, certain to make any girl look like a princess in them. A strong feeling of insecurity followed Winter's initial enthusiasm: she did not know much about fashion, she never could afford to buy expensive clothes, and the modish variety made her doubt her own taste.

Eventually, she surprised even her own self. And she admired the image in the mirror, but then she frowned, realising that a look like this meant full exposure, and the advantage of going unnoticed, which had been very useful to her until now, would be forever lost. Which was exactly why she had to succeed, she told her reflection, with a deep, fully determined breath. She would either make good or, the very next day, she would make her way out.

"*Mesdames et Messieurs*!"[16] Pierre would announce shortly after. "Misfortune and fortune are the two sides of the same coin; one flip and you turn from a pauper to a prince, or princess in our case! And so, I am honoured to present to you our magnificent new singer in her first performance in the world. Here she is! Exclusively for you: Winter Pale!"

Whispers and applause filled the hall, as the audience always showed an interest in something new. Quivering all over, feeling her mouth dry and her face blushed with agitation, Winter stepped onto the stage and bowed, throwing investigative glances at the audience in the packed hall and gallery, where many were almost hanging from the railings to see the stage better. She walked towards the orchestra and was encouraged to see that the boys did not seem at all anxious about the outcome of this venture. They agreed on which songs to play and in which order, and Winter took a few steps forward and stood, with her hands tied to her chest, in the middle of the stage, staring at the wooden floor. The orchestra began to play and her heart was beating so deafeningly that she could hardly hear the music.

As she struggled through the first verses of the song, twisting on her tongue, Winter dreadfully listened to the tremor of her amateur singing voice, and she was terrified that, any moment now, she would be booed as cruelly as Geneviève not long ago. She raised her eyes in dread, scanning the hall for people she knew, for support. Andrée and Georgette kept making encouraging nods, while Pierre looked impressed–well, he should be, at least, by the stunning difference in her appearance. Then she turned to the faces of familiar customers and was relieved to see they welcomed her anguished effort. In a corner far back in the hall, sitting alone at his table, *Sturmbannführer* von Stielen was gazing at her, serious and silent, drinking his ruby-red wine. Then he smiled at her, not a big smile of enthusiasm, just a faint extension of his lips.

And look! She had never realised how well she could actually sing. All she had to do was enjoy it and soon both tune and rhythm seemed to keep pace with her, rather than the other way round. She moved across the stage with grace, her arms and feet as light as feathers; she sang like she meant it and it was incredible what an engaging effect this sentiment had on the audience; confidence started gleaming like a thousand fireflies in her eyes; bold and assertive, her smiles could seduce everyone, because people always loved the most those who most loved themselves. As her singing was ending, the audience stood up and cheered and Winter would hardly be able to hold back her tears of joy, if not inspired by their request for more.

More? Yes, why not? she thought to herself. It was a leap of faith. And she had just started feeling like a believer.

At the end of her performance, the audience gave Winter several rounds of applause, whistling in frenzied cheer and tossing their precious money at her feet. The one whose excitement was really unparalleled, though, was, of course, Pierre, who did not neglect to remind everyone that he was the owner of this rare gem: "She works for me!" he exultantly cried out and urged everyone around him to praise and compliment his recently discovered treasure.

Finally, it was time for a spectacular exit. Petit François brought her his entire basket of flowers, offered by two kind gentlemen from a front table. As if she had been born for such expressions of admiration, Winter picked out two flowers from the basket, she kissed them and threw them back to the men, causing the envious cheers of those around them.

"Bravo! Bravo!" Pierre shouted, rushing to welcome her, as if he were afraid of losing her. "*Ma chérie! Mon ange! Mon trésor!*"[17] he exclaimed and gave Winter the heartiest embrace.

His entusiasm felt as insolent as the hundreds of names he had called her a little earlier for what was only a minor incident, and she was tempted to tell him to his face that she refused to sing for him again. If only she had the luxury of choice. But it was too important for her, this turn in her life, an opportunity she would not waste on any kind of revenge. And for this reason, she returned his embrace just as heartily and offered him her deepest thanks along with the stupidest, most pretentious smile.

At the boss's command, Petit François went on stage to collect the bank notes that still lay scattered there. And when Pierre counted the money and calculated the earnings of that night, he became even heartier: "How could I have missed discovering you earlier, *mon bijou*[18]*!*" he exclaimed.

At that moment, Georgette was approaching to offer Winter her congratulations, and she thought it appropriate to rein in Pierre's boasting, since she was the only one with such liberty.

"Hold your horses there, Pierre!" she said teasingly. "It was not you who discovered her!"

Winter hugged Georgette cordially and gratefully thanked her for the good word she had put in to *Sturmbannführer* von Stielen, which was the reason behind this unexpected fortune.

"Oh no! No!" Georgette impulsively refused any such honour. "You only have yourself to thank, because you did this on your own, and don't let anyone tell you otherwise–not even the *Sturmbannführer*, and definitely not this stubborn old coot!" she added and pinched Pierre's cheek as a response to his sulking face, a gesture which immediately transformed him into a docile child.

"Well, if a big-head like that puts in a good word for you, that must count for something!" intervened Michelle, who was just arriving along with Andrée to pay their respects.

"*Oui*, it was about time he did a good deep!" Andrée continued before giving Winter a wholehearted hug. "And I'm glad he did it for you, my sweet, because you deserve it!"

"I don't understand!" gasped Winter, completely overwhelmed by mixed emotions, while struggling to understand the speakers' French.

"You don't understand? What exactly do you not understand?" Michelle reacted with a sting of envy in her voice which she could not very well hide and turned to Andrée and Georgette with an exaggerated puzzlement. "Doesn't she know von Stielen is *Sipo*[19]*?*"

"Sipo? What does that mean?" Winter asked discontented at all these insinuations, which brought about unexpected discomfort and spoiled her festive mood.

"It means that..." Pierre interrupted, grabbing her by the shoulders to draw her away, "...that it is better not to have many dealings with him!" And resuming his irascible bossy tone, he called to the girls: "Off with you sluggards, always looking for excuses to laze about! Get back to work; people are thirsty!" And off the girls went, with no delay.

Winter felt an unpleasant fire burning on her cheeks. She might not know what Sipo was, but the sound of it was little better than that of Gestapo. And guilt and suspicion again overwhelmed her, losing her every bit of that lively excitement, which the reminiscence of *Sturmbannführer* von Stielen's rewarding smile evoked. She looked at Pierre out of the corner of her eye and felt completely distrustful of his unusual friendliness, beforehand bracing herself in view of the plans he had in stall for her this time.

"You're a little treasure!" he said and winked at her. "Forget about von Stielen! Besides, I don't think he stayed until the end! Look around! The place is crawling with fools for you to play on. And they will all be crazy about it, too!"

One disappointment after another, Winter thought, and the last speck of her previous contentment completely disappeared, when she realised that Pierre would simply not pass on the opportunity to profit even more from those aspiring lovers of hers, who would 'be crazy' about her and would be willing to pay whatever crazy amount Pierre required to sell her hide.

"You mean... customers?" she asked with clear distress and Pierre laughed victoriously, apparently finding the terror in her eyes and the thrall of obedience weighing on her neck very amusing.

"Well, I'll leave it up to you!" he exclaimed astounding Winter. "Do what you like!"

What she liked? Winter marvelled and, suddenly, her cheerfulness returned twice as breezy, and she could already envisage a future without indignity, where she could, at last, walk upright again and stop fearing other people's gazes. She stared at Pierre, thinking that he might not have been serious about what he said, forever profiteer and self-serving as she knew him to be; he might even deny his own words the next morning, making a scene that she had neglected to take advantage of her position properly. But, as far as she was concerned, the time of shame was over for her, whether it was with or without Pierre's blessings.

To Winter's surprise, Pierre denied nothing the next morning and the fighting spirit with which she had woken up, in case the boss tried to force his terms on her, went completely vacant. Only later did Winter understand that, when Pierre left the decision to her, it had in no way been on the spur of the moment. Because he was indeed a capable entrepreneur, thus knowing he could benefit more from a contented singer, who would make it her own business to keep his customers happy, and the truth was that as soon as Winter comprehended this simple but essential causality, she would give it her all.

Her new duties were clean and relatively painless. When she was not on stage singing, she would have to keep company to the most prominent of customers and make certain there was a considerable consumption of drinks. In their language, the word 'prominent' was used to describe the customers who would have anything close to a bucket of money to spend, and, beyond that, absolutely nothing else mattered: blue-blooded or common, of high rank or low, French, German or even a Jew–the latter, of course, in strict confidence–all were equally worthy of plucking. The first attempts, however, exposed the hazards involved in this expensively paid company, which only diverged from its old cheaper equivalent by a very thin line. Winter undertook the task anyway. If she so happened as to bump into a cretin, who thought he could get more than he had bargained for, she would craftily scold him, and if he were not intelligent enough to stop at that point, but recklessly kept laying his dirty hands on her, then she would not hesitate to discipline him, often with a resounding, greatly unforgiving smack. And she found it remarkable and extremely impressive that the more audacious her reaction was to whatever indignities her escorts should lapse in, the more compliant they seemed eager to become.

The new post offered Winter a steady salary for the show, half of her tips, and a small commission from drinks consumption, which was more than she had ever hoped for. Intoxicated by this completely new ability, for a short while, she could not resist a few expeditions to extravagant shopping, at least as regards goods that were not rationed; and she also bought the bicycle she had been dreaming of, which gave her an unrivaled sense of freedom, taking her on long rides around the city and helping her become more familiar with the place where she had lived for so long, but knew so little. Finally, taking the entire staff of 'The Golden Doe' to dinner at one of the restaurants which were thought to be beyond their reach, was a gesture much appreciated by everyone. She always paid in cash and it was unimaginable what effect the view of real money had on the willingness of employees to serve her. The Germans she knew would bow to greet her, address her with every courtesy, and Winter greatly appreciated the formal form of address in their language, which filled her with unprecedented self-esteem. She used to be a '*du*' kind of person before, but she was definitely a '*Sie*'[20] now and that would make all the difference in the world.

Naturally, there were no gains without losses. The change of status seemed to have also shifted the girls' feelings towards her, Andrée and Michelle's mostly. At moments of introspection, Winter could not help wondering whether it was solely the sisters that should be held accountable for this decline of warmth and congeniality, or whether she had played her own part as well. This experience obliged Winter to think differently of Geneviève, too, the girl who had seemed so estranged to them all. But who could tell for certain that her arrogant and contemptuous demeanor was not a defense mechanism against some deeply felt solitude? Geneviève, who refused to stay at 'The Golden Doe' after her position had been occupied, but perhaps not because she found it belittling to do anything below her station, as they had all rushed to conclude. Winter remembered her gathering her things without grief, as if there were absolutely nothing she would miss leaving, and retrospectively felt for her more than she had ever before.

Fortunately, there was still Georgette who had never ceased to be her amicable and cheerful self with her. Winter was sad to overhear the other girls call her a weathercock, an opportunist who took every chance she got to gain trivial privileges by adhering to those with power. But such a description had absolutely nothing to do with the Georgette she knew: the dear friend who selflessly stood by her during that dreadful time of disgrace, and sincerely told her that wise 'Don't let them get the better of you!' which proved to be more life-saving with each passing day.

There was Georgette and there were the boys of the orchestra. Guillaume often teased her that, because of her, he had lost the love of his life, but he almost immediately added with relief: 'Fortunately, there is a God!' Alain had promised to tell her a new joke for every new song she would learn, and, so far, he had never failed to do so. But Louis was still the one she was most fond of. He had always been there for her in a discreet way, which she could not say whether it was platonic love or brotherly affection: a feeling without a name, a form of communication that required no verbal expressions and a sense of intimacy that she had never shared, not even with Georgette, with whom she was the closest. Louis had been like this with her from the start and he had never made advances at her, nor had he ever acted in a way that insinuated he meant to. Of course, the girls jumped at every likely opportunity to imply that Louis had another preference in the romantic area, and they would mockingly warn her not to have such expectations of him. Winter had no romantic expectations of Louis anyway, and she thought of such remarks to be mean and hurtful, regardless of what the truth was. People always had the tendency to give names to whatever they did not understand, merely in order to stop being intimidated by it. None of them at 'The Golden Doe' understood Louis, even if they shook their heads in agreement when he spoke. Winter did not understand much either, but understanding him was not that important. Louis was like poetry to her: all she had to do was feel.

After all, Louis was the maestro of the band and Winter would spend hours with him building up her repertoire. They mainly played French and German songs, but there were also some written in the English language, with pure anti-Ally propaganda in their lyrics, which Pierre had insisted were included in their playlist for obvious reasons. Besides, what could be a louder declaration of loyalty for a British girl in the occupied city than to laud the conquerors in her own mother tongue? Winter had no intention of subscribing to Pierre's calculative logic, but she could hardly argue against it either.

She worked hard. It was not a minor effort to learn her songs, to memorise all these new words in languages that meant nothing to her, but the music somewhat reduced the difficulty and made things a little more manageable. When they said that music was a universal language, they were right, Winter professed, and her own experience had taught her it was much easier to remember something she had learnt through singing than anything she had to simply recite.

Between rehearsals, at lunchtime, or just before work began in the afternoon, Louis showed her how to play chess, so that he would have a companion to play with, since Alain and Guillaume were dead bored with it, whereas he completely adored it. In the beginning, all those pieces, with their predetermined movements on the black and white squares, gave her a headache: knights, bishops, rooks and the rest. The piece that fascinated her most was the queen. Being British and knowing a little about kings and queens, she had always admired the queens of her country's history–great ladies whose name remained engraved in collective memory, even more so than any king's, with the dreadful exception, perhaps, of King Henry VIII. And here it was, in this game of chess, where the king was a completely crippled piece, and even simple pawns seemed braver to her than him. Before that night when her life changed unexpectedly, Winter would say she was a pawn too, but she would say it more out of a sense of kinship to their sacrifices, when in fact she felt she had been nothing more than a king: forever hunted, desperate for others' protection, and taking only one step at a time, almost always in defense.

It was actually Michelle who had asked which piece she would say described her best, one day on the occasion of Pierre's absence, when she had sat around to watch her game with Louis. Michelle knew how to play chess, and so did Andrée. It was a shame that Pierre rarely allowed them the time to play, for they were great at it, acknowledged Louis, who also informed Winter that the sisters' foster parents were not only well-off but also cultured people, meaning to bequeath more than a fortune to their girls. Knowing this, Winter always felt self-conscious of playing should one of them be standing by; she was a clumsy amateur with no strategy at all and absolutely no competence in predicting the slightest move of the opponent. Nevertheless, the day Michelle asked her that question, Winter stopped feeling at a disadvantage. In the game of survival, more than any other, what counted the most was one's position: amongst the players, one had a chance to win, depending on the circumstances and one's own ability, but a piece was always under another's control, and even the most powerful piece, like the chess-queen, could be sacrificed by the player for the sake of winning. Well, since the night that Winter occupied the third most important place in the hierarchy of 'The Golden Doe', she had ceased to be a piece; she had become a player!

In the game of impressions, Winter was good, and she was a winner. She looked different on the outside and had put on a face that best suited her new appearance. Just like a painter with a brush and his palette at hand, a touch here, a bit of colour there, and soon the painting would change; no one could see what colours the canvas had underneath. The picture could fool everyone, and sometimes even the mirror.

Yet, there were nights when she felt discomfort in her beautiful new clothes, like that mythical hero and his poisoned robe[21]. Nights when she felt it like a mortal sin to enjoy herself so much on stage. And times when the extra money she earned weighed down like iron in her hand. Sometimes, she would stay awake until dawn sitting by the window, trying to recall things that were as bitter as they were sweet, things that used to be the very substance of her, which now seemed to disappear somewhere in the fog of her mind. And then, there was a void that seemed to devour her into nonexistence, and all that remained of her was a reflection, like a motion picture on screen, which would drop out of sight as soon as the projector stopped and the lights were turned on. She did not feel all that powerful then. More like a tree with no roots on the riverside, however proud and beautiful it might stand, which could easily be torn down by the slightest rainstorm and the first gust of wind.

7

The surprise tonight

It was early that day when Winter woke up resolute to spend yet another morning in the city centre, this time, however, not squandering her money on inessential luxuries, but with the view to buying food and clothes for her mother and the twins. She did not mean to take the presents to them herself, though; she would need a neutral third party, and Louis had offered to undertake the mission, much to her satisfaction, as he was the only one whom she fully trusted to keep her whereabouts and the way she earned her living a secret, especially if the person asking was a skinny vile-looking cad, who had absolutely nothing to do with his denotation: 'Christian'.

It was cold, but sunny, and the city was bustling with activity, determined to survive yet another period of hardship, as it had so many times in the past. At the grocer's, there was a queue of at least twenty people, but that would not discourage Winter, who had been accustomed to the task from the time when she lived at Stepfather's and was charged with all the chores, including queuing up for the rationed provisions. She stood in line and waited patiently, thinking of all the beautiful things she could buy her family to make them happy. Anything she might buy for Mother, Winter knew she would call it an unnecessary expense, but it would hardly be out of contempt; Mother had long wont to putting the needs of others before herself. The twins, on the other hand, would literally dive into the bags to see what was intended for them, and they would ask Louis where she was and why she had not been there in his stead. But it was not the right time yet, she said to herself wistfully. She would go back at some point, but not yet.

After they had moved forward a little and Winter had just passed through the door of the shop, two German soldiers crossed the threshold and casually bypassed all those who were waiting in order to go first in line. The people in the queue exchanged silent, displeased gazes, and some, too annoyed, even started muttering to themselves.

Suddenly, one man of those waiting in line left his place and moved towards the Germans. He decisively tapped one of them on the shoulder and bravely explained to them the meaning of the queue, pointing to the end of it to show them their proper place. The soldiers looked puzzled. They stared at the man and then at the long string of people extending far past the door of the shop. They whispered some German to each other and, with no opposition whatsoever, they left and went to stand at the end of the queue. People could not believe their eyes and some smiled, gratified by this rare restitution of moral order. Winter smiled, too, thinking that their times would never cease to amaze them with all their paradoxes. But before she could even finish her thought, the shop owner thrashed out from behind the cash desk and raised an angry fist at the man who had protested.

"What are you doing?" he reprimanded him. "These are the conquerors!" he said and ran to the end of the queue to bring the Germans back, doing everything he could to please them.

Outraged, the protester walked away from the line, murmuring some very unflattering comments. Not long after, a few others followed him, and soon almost half of the queue remained. Winter did not applaud the submissive attitude of the shop owner, either. Had she been French, she might have left herself, but now there was only one woman in line before her and she saw no reason she should spend another such time waiting in another queue. She shopped lavishly but treated the grocer in the most disdaining manner.

With her shopping bag full of supplies, Winter went down to *Les Grands Boulevards* to look for clothes. Having pulled some strings with her German acquaintances to gain the coupons for shoes, she then picked the warmest flannel coats for the twins and the most extravagant fur coat for Mother. She also bought thick socks for everyone and knitted gaiters with teddy bears, especially for the boys. All she had to do to complete her expedition was get the twins a toy, so she ardently set out for a set of marbles she had been ogling at the department store of *Les Grands Magasins du Louvre*, the multi-storey emporium right past the square of the *Palais Royal*.

'A small sewing shop at the *Galerie Vivienne*, near the *Palais-Royal*, if you know!'

It had been a long time since she had last thought of René Martin and many of her fears at the time now seemed exaggerated and ridiculous. Perhaps it was not a terrible idea to seek him out at his sewing shop; if there were enough encouragement, she could confide her thoughts in him and they would laugh about them together. He would see her so much changed that it would be impossible to resist her, and–why not?–offer her the embrace she so desired and felt so deserving of, instead of that faceless Simone, who must have hurt him immeasurably, if her memory alone could stir up such turbulence within him.

She asked a passerby for directions, walked down *Rue des Petits-Champs* and found the *Gallerie Vivienne*; it was a picturesque, covered arcade, decorated with colourful mosaics and arched glass roofs, which gently brought in the daylight, while several baroque style chandeliers and lamp-posts added enchantingly to the atmosphere. Different shops were established one next to the other: a tea-room, a boutique, a wine cellar, a bookshop, a barber shop, and, finally, at number thirty-nine, René Martin's sewing shop. Winter stood befuddled in front of the dusty shop window, frowning at the sight of the padlock at the door. Inside, signs of neglect showed the shop must have been out of business for quite a while. Could René have lied to her about it? Or could it be something worse?

"Are you looking for something?"

The barber from next door had come out and was curiously examining her. Who knows if he were not another squealer, offering his despicable services to God knows whom, no doubt for a proper price, Winter thought with enmity and hurried off, pretending to be indifferent. Coming out into the street again, a sudden feeling of fatigue took over, and she let the shopping bags fall to the pavement, suddenly losing all her nerve and drive for making her family happy with her presents and the promise that she would not forget them. Winter's sense of happiness had always been of a particularly volatile substance and it was easy for terror to instantly take its place.

"Winter!"

She flinched at the honk of the military jeep, which had stopped next to her, and shuddered at the idea that she might have to face any kind of challenge at that moment.

"Winter!" the man called again and stretched to open the co-driver's door, so that she would see and recognise him. As soon as Winter could clear her eyes from their panic, she saw it was Klaus Molnich, the translator for the Central Intelligence Service. She put on her most charming face with great effort and approached to greet him. "Where are you off to?" he asked.

"Well, I've been shopping, as you can see, and I was on my way back to the club!" she replied, and the German offered to give her a lift.

She hesitated for a moment, but feeling tired as she was, and thinking that the Intelligence Service translator might be able to tell her something about René Martin, she was persuaded to accept.

"We haven't seen each other for a long time!" said the man and Winter agreed, looking at him cautiously.

In his early thirties, Klaus Molnich was one of the most well-disposed customers of 'The Golden Doe'. He was gentle and kind, and, although he could not be regarded as a handsome man, there was a certain charm about him: he was wonderfully civil and he had never attempted to buy the affections of either her or any of the girls, as far as she knew.

"It is you who has burnt bridges with us, not the other way round, Klaus! Pierre keeps on and on about it: you've found better and we've fallen out of grace!" she deliberately jabbered, trying to give a playful tone to her voice.

Molnich laughed, looking completely unsuspecting of her despondence.

"You? Out of grace? As if that were ever possible!" he remarked and laughed again, before offering her a sincere explanation: "I've just been really busy and very out of pocket!"

"Poor you!" Winter exclaimed condescendingly and reached out to touch his hand in consolation.

Molnich smiled with sincere endearment, but he was, as ever, so noble.

"So, you've been shopping, you said?" he asked in order to make conversation and Winter hummed an agreement, thinking it was a perfect opportunity for her to ask about the burning issue.

"There was a cheap shop that sewed curtains there, in that passage– Lord, what's it called? I've been meaning to renovate my room for some time now, but from what I see, it's probably closed down. You may have heard of it, in that passage near the *Palais Royal*... Er ...Vernon? Voyance? ..." And she pretended to think really hard.

"*Vivienne*!" Molnich corrected.

"Yes, that's it! Don't you know everything!" she blurted with enthusiasm, once again reaching for his hand. Molnich glanced at her but avoided speaking and Winter felt the need to motivate him a little more. "It's so upsetting!" she sighed, sounding extremely disappointed. "I hate it when my mind is set on something and then it falls through. It's such a shame, because I've already bought the fabric for the curtains and now I'll have nothing to do with it!" she added and inspected his reactions out of the corner of her eye.

"Is it René Martin's sewing shop that you're talking about?" Molnich asked casually, and Winter found the fact that he knew the name discouraging.

"Whose?" she responded, allegedly puzzled.

"Martin. Did you not know?" enquired Molnich, and it was unclear whether or not he suspected something.

"It's the strangest thing about me, you know! I never forget a location, but I'm always terrible with the names!" Winter explained and let out a cackling laugh, which was, unfortunately, not as infectious as she had hoped. Then there was an awkward silence and Winter could not help feeling that they were both thinking about the same thing: René Martin.

"So, you've been visiting the shop often?" Molnich eventually broke the silence, and the tone of his voice alerted Winter.

"Oh, no!" she hurried to assure him and went on with a lighthearted chatter she hoped would be convincing enough: "Only once, just to enquire. I couldn't afford the renovation at the time, but I never, ever forget a good bargain!"

"And now that you can afford it, you came back for a small investment, right?" Molnich deduced, and Winter agreed with an innocent facial expression. "Well, I regret to inform you that this is an investment you won't be able to make, not for the time being, at least!"

"Oh! And why is that?"

Molnich shook his head in obvious disapproval.

"It seems René Martin is in trouble with the police!"

"The police? That's ...!" Winter blurted impulsively and not at all pretentiously this time, as confirming her suspicions meant she could easily find herself in grave danger.

"Unbelievable, yes?" Molnich concurred but seemed unwilling to say more. Winter felt the butterflies in her stomach fluttering so deliriously that it was impossible for her to settle for that much.

"Well? Aren't you going to tell me?" she provoked him only to receive a negative look. "Oh, come on, Klaus! You know I'm always dying for juicy gossip!" This time, Molnich looked at her affectionately and Winter now felt safe enough to push him a bit harder. "So, my dear Klaus? Will you leave me like this? In the dark?" she chirped and employed her best coy tricks to bring him round.

Molnich laughed, apparently enjoying their innocent flirtation: "What does your ladyship desire to know?"

Winter shrugged one shoulder and looked at him out of the top of her gaze.

"Anything! As long as it's fresh and spicy!" she replied, bringing about new laughter and a vivid excitement in his eyes.

"About René Martin?" he asked.

With a cute gesture, Winter responded 'Why not?' and Molnich returned to her a bright look and a smile of complacency.

"Well, have you heard of the *Resistance*?" he said and uttered the word 'Resistance' with its French accent to attach his contempt to it. Winter avoided answering and Molnich accepted her silence as denial. "They're a bunch of fools turning against us, when they should join us in the fight against the greater threat, the one from the East. Can you believe they prefer to play the Bolsheviks' game?" He turned to Winter and saw her looking completely stupefied. "I'm sorry! I'm sure you care nothing about the politics of this war, but it is so frustrating! For centuries, our cultures have been moving in the same direction, with some differences, yes, but minor, insignificant ones. And now they are siding with the savages who want to overturn the way of our thinking, the ways of our lives?" And as Winter nodded she did not have a clue what he was talking about, he continued with a condescending smile: "Anyway, apparently, *Monsieur* Martin has some involvement with this sorry lot; I don't know the details of the matter, but he wouldn't have fallen into the hands of the Gestapo if it were otherwise, would he?" He laughed rather cynically, but then he seemed to turn into himself and think out loud: "Many of us don't really like their tactics, there at the Gestapo, but it's undeniable how efficient they are! If a new order of things is to be established in this world, well, someone has to do the dirty work!"

Molnich's little speech would have left Winter completely indifferent if it did not remind her of the danger any involvement with René Martin pertained. She could easily lose all she had struggled for and the possibility of falling into the hands of the Gestapo herself, well, that was a harrowing idea of its own. She did not really care whatever order of things ran the world–she did not trust any government to know what was best for her and the people she cared about. But it was strange, another paradox of their times, that it should be within this kind of order that she had finally been a mistress of herself, to the extent that such a thing was possible for anyone these days, of course.

"What can I say! I, for one, am quite fine with this new order of things!" she declared, still amazed at the truth of her statement, and Molnich seemed to take pleasure in her remark.

As the vehicle turned past the *Place Pigalle* and came to a halt outside 'The Golden Doe', the passengers had resumed their cheerful mood and, hopefully, for Winter's sake, they would remember little of their uncongenial conversation regarding René Martin.

"I will be happy to see you at the show one night, Klaus! Your presence has not been missed by Pierre alone, you know!" she told him with her most seductive smile and offered her hand for him to kiss.

"I'll do my best!" he promised and waved goodbye.

Looking at the military jeep driving down the street, Winter was relieved that she could stop the acting now. She was feeling exhausted by this sense of threat and the strenuous effort to remember everything that had happened since her meeting with René which might menace her. The only association she could make was that *Sturmbannführer* von Stielen had been visiting 'The Golden Doe' regularly since. She had been spending enough time with him to discern his particular interest in her and she had been keen to believe it was owed to her new enchanting self. What did his interest really stem from? she could now not help but wonder.

Coming inside the club, she was surprised to find such quiet at a time of day when, normally, everyone should be getting ready to sit at the table.

"Pierre? ... Georgette?" she called out but received no reply. Just before she had reached her door, some strange knocks from Pierre's apartment startled her, and, soon, she would see the orchestra boys rumbling down the stairs, shortly followed by Pierre and Georgette. Seeing Winter standing in the hallway, they all seemed to be taken aback and Winter thought she caught Georgette throwing Pierre a dire look. Then Pierre made way to approach her and, holding her by the shoulders in the most affectionate manner, he gently guided her to her room.

"Well, well! How was the shopping? Got everything you wanted?"

Winter always felt suspicious of Pierre's friendly behaviour: "... It was okay!" she replied, glancing over his shoulder at Georgette first and then at each of the orchestra boys for some reassurance. "Won't you tell me what is going on?" she asked, seeing that they were all trying to avoid her eyes.

Then Louis laughed and soon everyone followed, laughing their heads off for no obvious reason: "Come on, Pierre, tell her, since she caught us red-handed!" he said, only to receive Pierre's most disapproving look.

"And spoil the surprise?" he disagreed and teasingly pinched Winter's cheek. "Go on! Rest now. It is going to be a busy evening. And don't bother to come down for lunch, Georgette will fetch you a tray, yes?" he urged her, leaving no room for further conversation, while pushing her inside the room and hurrying to close the door behind her.

"That's all I need! More snakes in the grass!" Winter mumbled once she was alone, and agitation stung her like a thousand pins and needles. As soon as she could process the idea more calmly, though, she felt more confident that it was probably the news about René Martin making her paranoid, as she considered it to be altogether unthinkable for Pierre to be involved in any anti-authoritarian action.

And, once again, René Martin was occupying her every thought, stirring up all kinds of feelings and millions of questions, a confusing blend of need, worry, fear and, definitely, lack of good sense. There she was, distressing about his welfare, when she should be more concerned about herself and what might happen if she were in any way found to relate to him. But if René had talked about her to the Germans or if they thought her to be involved with him somehow, wouldn't they have arrested her, too, by now? Wouldn't they have, at least, called her for a typical interrogation? They might have been waiting for the right moment, a cynic inside her stomach warned her; she might have been under surveillance the whole time–anything was likely. The only consolation was that, save for this day's incident, she had given little cause for suspicion and she would like to think she had been quite successful at pulling the wool over Klaus Molnich's eyes.

With a feeling she recognised to be more than sympathy, she wondered if René was still at the Gestapo or if Molnich knew about him because they had moved him to the Intelligence Service. Well, if that were so, it was also how *Sturmbannführer* von Stielen fitted into the picture.

Never having forgotten Michelle's remark, Winter had asked Georgette what Sipo was–Georgette always seemed to be very well informed on anything relating to the conquerors. So, Georgette explained to her that there was a Central Security Office, which included the city secret police, known to everyone as Gestapo, the crime police, Kripo in short, and the Intelligence Service, which had a broader and more independent role, often penetrating the jurisdiction of both the other two police services. And *Sturmbannführer* von Stielen was, of course, head of it.

He was not an easy target, even for her irresistible charms, she admitted. Getting to know him a little better, she had to grant him that he was pleasant and interesting company; he spoke English fluently and was also extremely educated on whatever gives a British person their Britishness. The major, as she had run the risk of calling him, assuming a certain amount of intimacy with him to which he had not seemed opposed, was notably intelligent, in a flattering way highly perceptive about her wishes, and the piercing way in which he often looked at her was something he and René had very much in common...

Late in the afternoon and not having slept a wink, she was getting ready for work when she heard a strange commotion coming from the hallway: steps and squeaks on the wooden floor, accompanied by low-pitched female voices and collusive whispers. Before she could overpower the tumbling apprehension, which gave her a premonition of danger, a loud knock on her door completely shook her up. She snapped the door open to see Louis. He had never had such a conflicting expression, as though he was trying to play a part he had not consented to, but was somehow amused by the challenge, which might explain the ill-defined smile on his lips. They went downstairs together, Winter cautiously following and ready for the worst.

They were all there, collaborators to the conspiracy of which everyone but her had knowledge of, simpering at her ignorance and the sickening dread depicted on her face: three beautiful young girls stood among them, three perfectly scandalous can-can dancers, their flouncy dresses with revealing bustier tops and colourful skirts, making them look like dolls having just slipped out from their boxes or posing on the shelf of a toy shop.

"They're our new girls!" Pierre announced proudly, while tapping the first of the girls on the back, urging her to greet.

The girls bobbed a curtsy and Winter laughed her angst away, admitting she found their greeting to be very cute, but she would be better off with just a handshake. The dancers did not understand English at all and a beguiling look betrayed their surprise at hearing a language they had never expected to hear.

"Would you, please, do us the honour, *Mademoiselle* Pale?" Pierre uttered in a theatrical tone and handed Winter a sealed bottle of champagne.

"Me?" Winter muttered, completely overwhelmed.

"Well, it was your success that made it possible to have them!" Pierre said with a displeased grimace, as if he had to confess to an ugly truth. But immediately, he laughed teasingly and his face shone with an honesty that Winter had never seen before and immediately made her feel guilty of all the bad thoughts she had had about him.

"Come on, pop the cork!" everyone entreated, and their impatience persuaded Winter to open the bottle and let the champagne sparkle out and fill the glasses.

Emotion and excitement swamped them that evening, as befitted a festive familial celebration. And when the new girls went on stage to demonstrate their dancing skills, no one doubted they would be a smash.

Another story of misfortune had caused the dancing ensemble to land up at 'The Golden Doe'. Two twin sisters at seventeen and an elder one, in her twenties, a mother who had died giving birth to the twins, a deceased father. And, as if that were not enough, the Germans had requisitioned their house, and they had to spend more than a month in a shelter provided by the Church. Then they crossed paths with Guillaume, who introduced them to Pierre, and such would be the happy ending of their sad story, or at least that was what the girls thought, but Winter could not help remembering that it was easy for the face of luck to change at 'The Golden Doe'.

Several days passed until the joy of this celebration faded; a celebration that warmed their hearts and brought them closer together with feelings of mutual appreciation and familiarity. For Winter, it was unexpected to share such feelings with any of the members at 'The Golden Doe', even with the boys of the orchestra and Georgette, who were her dearest friends, not to mention Pierre, whom until then she only considered a necessary evil. And, although she would never consider 'The Golden Doe' a home, she could not help but wonder whether it was possible to feel the strong kinship of family with people she did not relate to by blood, but with whom she shared a bond of friendship and heartfelt mutuality, which was equally powerful.

And her own family? she asked at moments of self-reflection. How all the more rarely were they recovered from her memory! How strangely distant their image seemed to be sometimes! When Louis had visited the family lodging to offer them her gifts, he had found no one there. Her offerings were returned, the food was consumed by the cohabitants of 'The Golden Doe' and the clothes were abandoned in their bags in Winter's wardrobe for dust mites and spiders to blanket, as they already had with her feelings. If Mother and the twins had left the hovel of *Rue Goubet*, it might have been for the best, she tried to console herself. Perhaps they had, somehow, got rid of Christian and moved to a more suitable place, she hoped against the devil's advocate in her conscience, who spoke words of doubt. Even so, Winter could never muster the courage to go and see for herself.

Day in and day out, she allowed herself to be absorbed into a compulsive routine which offered her the reassurance of a much-desired normality. She woke up in the morning, kept to her prearranged schedule; she had a few chats, a few laughs, a few dreams. She liked to dream; dreams were the one thing she had complete control of; she could make a dream of anything she liked and even if a dream could ever go astray, she would easily remedy it or even cast it away and start a new one.

She would often dream of René–her hands in his, her bosom pressed against his chest, his breath on her face, his eyes... Oh, the way he would dwell in her, watching her be, think and feel, little by little becoming an integral piece of her. It did not matter that she had had no more news of him or his fate. Of course, she had never dared make the slightest enquiry about him to the major, neither had she had the chance to fish anything new out of Klaus Molnich, since he had not visited the club since their last meeting, despite his promise. Had René been released from prison, would he seek her out? She was absolutely certain he could find her if he wanted to. And she? Did she want to be found? She could not say, but the idea of him being out there looking for her exalted her and gave her something to anticipate.

A loud knock on her door, together with Pierre's splenetic voice, brought her back to reality. She jerked up and pretended to correct her make-up in the mirror, while making up an excuse, should the boss feel inclined to slap her wrist for not being downstairs doing her job, daydreaming locked up in her room instead.

Pierre's entrance was furious and noisy: "Oh please, don't bother adorning yourself for us!" he blurted, full of grudge and hurled the large parcel he was holding on the bed.

"What is it, Pierre?" she curiously asked.

"For you!" he replied, squinting his eyes. "From von Stielen! He wants you to wear it and go out with him, he says!" he kept on with fury he showed no intention to contain.

"Out? How? And the show?" Winter marvelled with enough excitement to push Pierre's buttons even harder.

Huffing and puffing like a steam train, he started describing his encounter with *Sturmbannführer* von Stielen: apparently, when he showed up with his request, Pierre kindly explained to him that Winter could not leave the club before she had finished her performance, and if he wanted to take her out, he could do so afterwards or, at least, after the main part of the show, because he had to understand that Winter was there to do a job and that the club depended on her to do it. And he even proposed that they both stayed at the club, where they would be treated like king and queen, with the finest wine and the best snacks and everything, otherwise, he told him, he was sorry, the *Sturmbannführer* would have to wait. Then, von Stielen showed his true colours and grabbed Pierre by the collar right in front of everyone, howling like a mad dog: 'Listen here, you miserable, pathetic, little scoundrel: no one tells me to wait!' So, Pierre bit his tongue and came to bring her the parcel and the commandment.

Winter chuckled, absolutely certain that Pierre had amplified the incident in his own right, as she thought such behaviour to be very unbecoming of a gentleman such as the major.

"Come on, Pierre, don't fret about it!" she told him with a faint smirk. "You will pull through without me this one time. The boys will play, the girls will dance, you'll see, it'll all go smoothly!"

Pierre scowled down at her instead of answering, obviously considering her as impertinent as the German for being so eager to leave.

"Well, don't be late!" he warned her. "And listen! I don't know what he may want, but whatever he asks of you, don't pretend to be decent and refuse! I am in no mood to be marked down by him, got it?" he added before he went out thundering through the door.

Winter stared at the closed door coldly. 'Whatever he asks of you!' she repeated with aversion. What on earth had given him the idea that the major intended to ask her what he was implying? And yet, for so long, the major had been content to keeping company with her at the club; now, he wanted to take her out. One thing was certain: if the major had such a thing in mind, he would definitely not prefer to do it in the filthy rooms of the first floor like everyone else. But Winter felt inclined to believe this possibility was scarce. The major's civility was exemplary and far from what Pierre was able to understand.

She opened the parcel and admired the major's good taste in women's fashion. Having put on the dress, she felt bewitching and gloated over how expensive elegance suited her. She took her purse and fur coat and left the room with an air of magnificence. All eyes were on her as she dodged through the crowd downstairs, and she could even hear some customers rifling through their wallets, delving into their capability to enjoy the pleasure of her, but a surprise awaited them all tonight.

When she left the club on the major's arm, she felt like she was taking a gigantic step into the future.

8

Tread softly

Winter had seen her escort arrive at the club in his luxurious black car once or twice, but had never expected to find herself inside it with him; neither could she ever imagine in her first encounter with him that he might someday be radiating any other sensation than wild, deadly terror. The brim of his cap intentionally cast its shadow across his expressive eyes; his weathered face suggested something extremely amiable, despite its sternness. But then, there was the service uniform, a defining and determining factor. The protruding white line of his band collar shirt and the fine quality of the gray gabardine were making considerable effort to somewhat humanise the attire. They were struggling with adversity: the insignia on his collar–the SS rune on one side and four pips on the other; a three-coloured striped ribbon through the second buttonhole of his tunic; medals and badges with golden laurels, stars and swastikas; an embroidered cuff band on his left sleeve which read '*Das Reich*'. And it felt flattering, but also a little intimidating to sit right next to him on the back seat of the black limousine, a feeling she never had when they sat together at the corner table of 'The Golden Doe', which she considered her domain. At some point, between a can-can dance and a glass of champagne, he had told her that all he wanted was for her to be herself with him. Well, she thought, for good measure, tonight she would try to be more than that.

"You're unusually quiet, Miss Pale!" he noticed and Winter jolted and impulsively laughed.

"I' m sorry!" she apologised. "I was so absorbed in my thoughts!"

"Which you would not care to share with me!" he assumed, and she laughed again, a little more restrained this time, lowering her eyes in the most self-conscious manner. He observed the flush on her face and smiled, perceptive enough not to expect a response. He asked for her permission to smoke and she willingly granted it, espying his every move: how his fingers pulled the cigarette out of a silver cigarette case and put it to his lips, the casual way in which they held it between them. As he struck a match, the little flame revealed his fair eyelashes. He opened the window and threw out the match. He removed his cap and ran his fingers through his golden-brown hair: every moment more unexpected than the previous one. Winter wondered with excitement whether it would be her charming him that night or the other way round.

They drove through the city to the southwest. Beyond the *Arc de Triomphe*, the place was unknown to Winter. She thought she had got to know Paris enough riding around on her bicycle, but this region was too far away even for her insatiable curiosity. They crossed over the river to move through a piece of forested land, after which another densely built area followed. The buildings there had maximum three or four lines of windows, not as tall as the ones she was used to seeing within the city's *Boulevard Périphérique* and Winter asked if they were in some sort of suburb.

"Indeed!" he confirmed. "This is *Auteuil*; we just drove past the *Boulogne* forest. It's really quiet here, except for the days when there are horse races!"

"Are we going to see a race?" she continued in a relaxed tone, being rather intrigued by the possibility.

"No, we're going to my house!" he replied naturally, and his words banged into Winter's ears like a cannon, having a similar effect on her mood. She quailed into the seat, lowered her head and firmly closed her eyes, nodding affirmatively, as he added: "We're going to be completely undisturbed there!"

Thinking of her inflated sense of self-value when Pierre warned her about this, she simpered, and, for what it was worth, she might as well do as he had counselled. 'They are the conquerors!' she recalled the grocer from the other day, but it was not only for this reason that she felt in no position to deny *Sturmbannführer* von Stielen anything. She owed him; she owed him everything she had become or rather everything he had given her the chance to be. If he were there now, asking to collect his due, how could she refuse? Then, he would have every right to grab her by the collar and say: 'Listen here, you miserable, pathetic, little tart: no one tells me no!' She tried to sigh out her agitation, but her head was buzzing like a broken radio and her stomach had squeezed in like a fist.

Soon, they parked outside a well-maintained estate, whose imposing standing gave Winter an even more compelling feeling. *Sturmbannführer* von Stielen's influence in the conquerors' administration must have been even greater than she thought, if he had been granted a residence such as this, when even higher-ranking officers than him were just staying in apartments at the luxurious hotels of the city centre. The two soldiers outside their chevron striped sentry boxes on either side of the entrance indicated well enough that this was the location of a conqueror's establishment. The only discordance to the overall masterful impression seemed to be the woman who greeted them at the arched door,–a woman in her thirties, tall and slim, pretty much in the likes of Winter, save her conservative dark-coloured cardigan, the single pleat skirt and her groomed chignon of brown hair.

"*Bonsoir, Monsieur*!"[22] the housekeeper said with a gentle bow and the major called her by her first name: "*Bonsoir, Marie*!"

The housekeeper shut the door quietly; she took her master's cap and hung it on the hallstand.

"*Le manteau de madame?*"[23]

Winter gave the woman her coat with a groundless feeling of enmity, which she recognised as a reflection of her inner state. She kept her eyes low, her lips silent. As she followed the major to the house interior, she breathed deeply and forced herself to calm down. She had walked down this path before; at least this time the surroundings were better...

They sat in the living room; the heavy curtains were drawn, *for discretion*, the fireplace was lit, *for mood*; oh yes, the major had readied everything nicely. He offered her a seat on a spacious sofa and he sat in a comfortable armchair across from her. Had it been for a different purpose, it could have been a lovely evening, at a beautiful place, between people who actually felt fondly of each other. But now, Winter could hardly observe the rich decoration of old well-preserved furniture, vivid paintings and frames with photographs in timeworn black and white, the radio, the gramophone and records, the books and newspapers, the flowers in the vases, everything that made a room comfortable and warm. None of it impressed her; she knew what she was there for and it was not pretty.

"Marie will bring us some tea, unless you would prefer a drink" the major said drawing her attention and Winter shivered as she looked at him.

"Oh no, I have so many drinks at 'The Golden Doe'!" she replied, immediately regretting the spontaneity her anxiousness caused. "A cup of tea would be wonderful, thank you!" she added, to appear at least somewhat refined.

The major smiled in a certain way, which always gave Winter the confidence that she was dealing with a man who–if anything–had no intention of judging her. A devastating feeling of confusion overwhelmed her. The beginning of the evening had boded so well, the major had been decent, perhaps his mind was far from anything like what Pierre had suggested and it was nothing but his malice that ruined the occasion. As they silently sipped their aromatic beverage, the major felt keen to tell her it was pure Swiss mountain herb tea, sent to him by a close relative in Zurich, and she wondered if it were possible for a man as courteous as him to intend something so low. She looked at him and smiled, feeling a little warmer towards him.

"Your house is exquisite! And the area, too!" she declared, determined to save as much face as possible by engaging in some natural conversation. "But you're a little far from the centre. Wouldn't you rather be closer to your obligations?"

He shook his head negatively and stated in the most constant manner: "The centre of Paris is fascinating, but this is where I find peace and quiet. This is my home away from home!"

The ardency of his reply surprised Winter, who found it a little exaggerated for what she considered a temporary residence.

"Of course!" she felt the need to say, despite obviously being unable to share his opinion.

"Well, I own the house; it's not requisitioned!" he discerningly explained. Winter found herself even more amazed and made an expression to commensurate her thoughts. As the housekeeper entered the room to put another log in the fire, the major continued, looking at the woman with sincere gratitude: "As a matter of fact, I owe most of what this house is to Marie! She has been the most tentative caretaker for many years now!" And hearing her name in the impassioned tone of his voice, the woman dimpled a smile and her eyes sparkled.

Impressed by the major's genteel behaviour towards the housekeeper, Winter could not help gazing at the woman until she left the room.

"You seem very attached to your housekeeper!" she remarked, wondering if this woman was, perhaps, something more to the major, which could be a good reason he might not have a need for her ...services. "It's rather uncommon between employer and employee, wouldn't you think?"

The major agreed. "But Marie is not just a housekeeper!" he explained, arousing Winter's interest. "We've known each other for quite some time, since I served at the German embassy here, long before the war. I was only renting a room back then; Marie's parents were still alive. Honest, agreeable people they were. Sadly, things turned around badly for the family later, but for me, it was a unique opportunity to get a house of my own in this beautiful corner of the world!" Winter felt a familiar painful feeling flowing through her: the family house sold out, one's own home abandoned, pipe dreams in a foreign country, alien to anything familiar or dear. "I asked Marie to stay along," the major continued. "She could keep her house in a way, and she would take care of it for me. In fact, had it not been for her when the war broke out, it would probably have been burnt to the ground by those who knew it did not belong to French hands!"

"That'd be such a shame!" Winter felt compelled to comment, swaying between a sense of empathy and a strong dislike for the house-keeper, which grew greater the more the major praised her virtues.

"So, you can understand, Marie is more like a good friend taking care of us, both the house and me, than just a housekeeper!" he concluded, and Winter could not contain her impulsiveness anymore: "Please, don't say anymore! I'm so jealous of her!"

Winter's sincerity seemed to please the major, as was manifested by the touch of a smile on his face. Winter felt prompted to be even more forthright, helping to regain some of her sense of self-importance.

"Actually, I am extremely jealous of you, too!" she confessed amorously, and the major sat back in his armchair like someone who was about to enjoy a pleasant spectacle. "To be so privileged as to live in a house like this, well, what's not to envy? I mean the furniture, the carpets, the porcelain, the fireplace! What I wouldn't give to be able to rest here every evening, in front of the fire, just looking at it or reading a good book..."

"My favourite pastime!" the major concurred after a momentary pause. They looked at each other. They smiled. Winter felt her cheeks burn, but she preferred to attribute it to the hot tea and the warmth of the fireplace.

"Do you like books?" the major asked, spurred on by her last remark, and Winter felt swamped by a bittersweet emotion.

"My father had books at home and I had a couple of fairytale collections–naturally, most of them were about princesses and princes!

I enjoyed reading very much, but my greatest joy was when my father read to me, usually before bedtime or some evenings next to the woodstove, and others, warm summer evenings in the garden which smelt like heaven... He had such a beautiful reading voice, my father!" she reminisced with a cracked voice, touched because she could still remember the family home, after having for so long not had a single thought of home and family. She quickly took a deep breath in order to avoid becoming any more emotional. She looked the major straight in his eyes and let out a hollow laugh. "Yes, I like books. But I'm sorry I didn't have the chance to read more of them!" she stated, as if she wanted to give a completely accurate answer to the major's question.

He got up from his seat, urging her to follow. To the left of the curved staircase, a spacious corridor, gently illuminated by a background window, introduced two facing doors. He opened the one on the right and they entered the library.

It was hard to say whether it was the atmosphere of the room or its content that stirred up Winter's sentiment. A large low window, with a belly-style iron frame on the outside, allowed all the light of the night sky to enter. Beneath it, an inviting built-in sofa with plump cushions tempted the most reluctant reader. Two elaborate armchairs, accompanied by a low table with an old-fashioned reading-lamp, sat on an aesthetic mosaic, while a cast-iron stove aside filled the room with genial warmth and the musky scent of burning wood. And all around, the walls were covered with bookshelves, very few of which were left with empty spaces.

The major sat on the built-in sofa and, observing Winter's enthusiasm as she approached to look at the books, reviewed in his mind the contents of the Service's file on her: **Winter (Pale) Dupont. Father's name: John James Pale. Mother's name: Carole. Year of birth: 1923. Origin: Britain. Religion: Catholic Christian. Baptism Date: August 26, 1937. Naturalised in November of the same year, under the custody of one Christian Mattise Dupont. Residence: 6 Rue Goubet, Villette district. Education: elementary.** There was no record of registration or attendance in any kind of educational institution in France. Reports of her mother's employment at the *Hôtel Lutetia* described her as capable and skillful, well-educated and socially literate; she did not sound like a parent who would leave a child uneducated, it might have been different if they had remained in their own country, the major assumed.

"How old were you when you left England?" he asked and Winter replied she was twelve. "And what were things like after coming here?"

"I would say ...not very easy!" she answered with difficulty and the major read her emotional strain and avoided enquiring about her past any more.

"What do you like better, poetry or prose?" he changed the subject and looked content with Winter's answer: "Poetry!"

He pointed out to her that the poetry books were on the shelves to her left and she moved towards them. German poets occupied the most accessible shelves–their names and titles totally unknown to Winter. Some French poets on a shelf just above, one of them that she knew caught her attention: Guillaume Apollinaire. She smiled as she recalled the frequently repeated verses. Then she was glad to see there were also English-speaking poets, Blake, Milton, Shakespeare, Tennyson ..., she read fluently, not necessarily to mean she knew of them or their work. Suddenly, her expression shone, as if she had just come across some precious treasure. She distinguished one book and leafed through it. She opened the content page, searched in its lines and then turned the pages, stopping at the one she was looking for. She raised her eyes to give the major an exalted look.

"Listen to this!"

She approached and sat down across from him on the built-in sofa, read to him the verses about the heavens' embroidered cloths, the gold of day, the dim of night, the dearest gift for the one dearest. She was a poor girl, too, and she only had her dreams to offer.

"Tread softly" she read **"because you tread on my dreams!"**[24]

"Yeats!" the major admired with a tender smile. "You know this poem!"

Winter nodded proudly.

"My father often read poems to me! This one was among his

favourite! He said you don't need to understand poetry, you only need to feel it!" she confessed with clear eagerness to talk about her parent more, which the major welcomed with an encouraging nod. "He had a scrapbook where he collected poems he liked. It's the only thing of him that I still have with me. Losing him was very hard to accept, I thought I could somehow bring him back, even if it was only in my dreams. I learnt some of his most beloved poems by heart, repeated them night after night instead of prayer, thinking he needed some kind of call to know I was waiting. He didn't visit me for a very long time! And by then, I no longer believed in dreams, poems or prayers..."

Her eyes sank in the obscure dusk of memory and the tips of her lips hung in a downcast smile, like the one the sad white clown wore– heartbroken and disconsolate. Father's image came alive again: behind the workbench, his leather apron, nail and hammer, tack-tack-tack, three hits, and then he looked up: *"Where's my little flower? Come here, my precious blossom of winter!"*

"... Winter!"

She looked up in bewilderment, a panting breath, and her senses awoken like from a long deep sleep. The echo of her name was still on the major's lips and, as his palm lay warm upon her cheek, Winter wanted to turn and leave a kiss on the inside of his wrist, which almost touched the tip of her mouth. And then, she wanted to lean against his chest and rest, silently stare through the window at the night sky and let it blanket the chill of death inside her. The light of the lamp and the moon softly illuminated the major's face. There was something unexpectedly sensitive and reassuring about him. His eyes were blue-gray; never had she noticed their colour before, nor had she ever looked at them at such close range.

He gently removed the book from her hands, left it on the sofa, and stood up. Winter had to tilt her head far back to look at him. He offered his hand, she took it.

"Come!" he breathed and, as she rose to her feet before him, their faces near, this staggering sense of affinity infused her with warmth she would never have imagined feeling for him.

Returning to the living room, something felt changed between them. They sat in their previous seats and tried a little more of Marie's brew, but it had gone cold, and the major jested he never cared for ice tea, suggesting they switched to something stronger. Winter accompanied the major to a glass of aromatic cognac and a big sip of it was truly reviving. With renewed spirits and recuperated confidence, she held her glass and moved around the room to explore its charming corners. She admired the fancy little bibelots enclosed in a classic French display cabinet, played with the fringes of the shades on elegant table lamps and examined the paintings and photos on the walls. There was one particular photo she seemed extremely interested in: a couple with a little boy standing in front of them. The man was wearing a uniform, which, however, did not look like the ones the Germans wore these days, and the woman was a modestly dressed lady, with beautiful features and a maternal expression, the caring, loving and protective expression of mothers when they are around their children.

"My parents!" the major noticed approaching. "You know, my mother was like you, British!" he added in a natural tone and nodded with a smile to confirm his revelation at her clearly astonished countenance.

With an English mother, half British himself, Winter sensed a powerful uniting force between her and the major, now sharing a bond that could not be ignored or unbound by any power game, not even by 'whatever he asked of her'. Her heart fluttered, and she felt urged to turn around and fall in his arms.

"And this... this doesn't make you feel..." she preferred to say instead, but she was too overwhelmed to find the right words to finish her sentence.

"Torn in half?" he deduced. "Not really! My mother made a choice and she remained faithful to it. She never denied her origins and she was as British in her habits as she could get. But, she had married a German officer; she lived in Germany; and she raised a German child!"

Winter nodded in understanding, feeling sadly disadvantaged compared to the major, who had obviously grown up in a balanced environment, which disposed him towards becoming the steadfast character he seemed to be. She, on the other side, was deprived of any certainties only too early. She, too, had a family she felt proud of once; but her family was gone long ago, and, inside her, a crude emotion had replaced that self-assurance born out of a sense of belonging. An emotion strong enough to clip one's wings and tie them down to the murk of ambivalence and self-doubt.

"So, the boy is you?" she asked in order to stop her inner monologue.

A light laughter burst out from somewhere deep inside the major: "I always stood to attention in photos. My mother often asked the photographer not to warn us before the shot, so that he would have the chance to capture me in a more natural posture. I can remember one or two instances when he was actually successful!"

It was a curious image, the one of the little boy standing to attention; his hair neatly combed into a side parting; a white shirt buttoned up to his neck; leather breeches, leaving his bony knees exposed, while a pair of long socks covered his calves all the way down to the heavy-looking clean shoes. Winter remembered her own photo with her parents, which she preciously kept in the pages of Father's scrapbook. Two children more or less of the same age, two children so different from each other, with such different lives and such different destinies: these children were now man and woman, and Winter shuddered at the thought that the embrace which only the warm and generous familial love could deliver, she could perhaps ask of this man, without fear of his misjudgment or abuse.

She hesitated, and it was probably for the best. She moved a little further and distanced herself from the major's captivating aura, which only drove her to desires that could simply not be met. There was a framed papyrus in front of her that was printed in Celtic calligraphy. The major explained it was his degree from military school. Winter clumsily read his name in German: "Friedrick Radolph von Stielen!"

"*Friedrich Rudolph*!" he kindly corrected her with his distinct German pronunciation and his voice right next to her ear made her shiver. She closed her eyes, disarmed by the fervour of his touch on her arms, and wrestled with unexpected feelings, while he told her in an absolutely personal tone: "But you can call me Fred!"

She turned around to look at him. This was it then, she thought, and took the liberty to rest her hands on his chest and lean into him. She was ready to give in and, strangely, she did not feel so burdened by this obligation. Her eyes drew the outline of his mouth and she invitingly opened hers. It was his prerogative to choose the way, the intensity, even the meaning, and she would willingly follow through. Against her will, however, she stiffened a little as his hands slid along her arms and came up again strengthening their grip, but, almost immediately, she raised her eyes to his to reassure him she would not hesitate.

His face looked completely expressionless. When he pulled her away with a calm and perfectly controlled movement and left her standing there with no sign of sentiment other than his heavy breathing, Winter felt so ashamed that she thought all the blood in her body had flooded her cheeks and struggled to pour out from her burning eyes. And in her stomach, in her chest, in her baffled head, she was sorely aching.

"I didn't bring you here for this, Winter!" he affirmed, sounding inconceivably honest.

She buried her face in her hands and wished she would just vanish, so cheap and vulgar that she felt: "Forgive me!" she muttered, a sense of futility utterly nullifying any attempt to justify her contemptuous and pitiful self.

"Don't apologise!" he consoled her with a voice deeply immersed in his consciousness. "It is not your fault. It's all part of this damn game: one calls the tune and the rest must dance to it..."

In her confusion, Winter did not understand what he meant, but she felt it was not something she would expect to hear from the lips of a German conqueror. When the major claimed he was only interested in getting to know her, she did not know whether to feel reassured or terrified. She would love to accept that his upbringing and civility obliged him to avoid such discourtesy; that he was being kind because she was British, like his mother; or because he merely needed some sincere human contact, like many of those who dwelled at the top of any social pyramid. But how likely was that? she mocked herself, looking at him in the uniform which screamed for caution and explicitly warned her against any misconception of who he was. And he was the Chief of Intelligence, a trained spy who specialised in manipulation in order to get what he wanted. Now he wanted to get to know her. No doubt he wanted to make her trust him and tell him everything she knew. Then, that witling little devil in her mind insidiously turned her thought once again towards René. And it made perfect sense. It was so reasonable and so foreseeable that she felt entirely stupid to believe it could have been anything else, foolish to be so ready to fall for the major's trap. Apparently, little had she convinced Klaus Molnich with her act that morning, and who knows what tales René Martin had told about her while in custody...

When the major asked her about her life at 'The Golden Doe', whether she had friends or she felt lonely, she remembered René had asked her the same thing: 'Are you all alone?'

So what was loneliness other than the lack of trust? What was it, if not being unable to see the light in life and only know its darkness? What else was loneliness, but being bound by fear, many and various fears to be exact, all of which had the same result: to swaddle her feelings like a broken limp; to prevent her heart from finding happiness, the slightest hint of it making her suspicious; to handicap her hope for proximity, interpreting any kind of approach as a lethal threat.

She did not say these things to the major, and he did not insist; another time, possibly under better circumstances. For all she knew, he might not be one to give in to disappointment that easily. Or, perhaps, he had not yet got from her the answers he was looking for...

9

Hôtel du Louvre

A knock on the door abruptly woke Winter up and she raised her eyes to the window to see the sunlight streaming through the shutters. It was late morning, and she was still feeling exhausted. Her head felt like a pressurised container. Her chest was heavy and needful of repeated deep breaths. Second knock. She pulled the covers up to her neck and reluctantly called 'enter', only to see Pierre appear in unusually high spirits.

"There's my girl! A very good morning to you!" he cried out in an almost singing tone, which immediately alerted Winter: "What do you want, Pierre?"

Pierre grimaced with a simper, looking very pleased with what he was about to say:

"Well, von Stielen called. He sounded very enthusiastic about last night and he even apologised for the misunderstanding between us. He promised to be more considerate next time. Hear that? Next time, ha-haha! I knew I could rely on you. I always said you were my best girl!"

Winter was tempted to tell him to his face that he was a shameless liar, pretending to have the slightest appreciation of her, when all he cared about was that he had secured the major's favour and, of course, for a good price.

"I thought you'd still be mad!" she answered back, aiming to annoy him.

"Really?" Pierre grinned. "Don't you know by now when I mean what I say and when I don't?"

On the contrary, Winter silently argued; it was exactly because she did that she thought of him to be an opportunistic hypocrite: "Fine! Is that all?" she responded, deliberately manifesting her utter disengagement from determining whatever Pierre's personality traits were. Obviously, Pierre had yet another announcement to make.

"... Well, you know, I was thinking..." he started and Winter realised he was about to reveal the true reason for his morning charge. "... Since that, you know, with von Stielen, I thought I could introduce you to a couple of other gentlemen, who are a bit persistent..." he added rather hesitantly, seeing Winter's eyes heating up, "... But only if you approve of them, and they will be completely discreet, I guarantee!" he continued, vainly attempting to make the proposition more appealing.

Winter pounced out from bed in absolute fury: "Damn you, Pierre, if you ever say anything like that to me again!" she growled and her face breathed fire. "Don't you even think about it, do you hear me?"

"You will not speak to me this way!" he immediately retaliated, always short-tempered and presumptuous.

"I am not letting you do this!" Winter warned him, standing up on the mattress with indomitable fierceness.

"You are not letting me?" he scorned. "And who do you think you are? Did you think that because you have von Stielen run after you like a fool, you can do whatever you like? I am the boss here, get that? And if you don't like it, you know where the door is!" he threatened without a shred of regret and left the room, slamming the door behind him.

"We'll see about that!" Winter murmured and kicked away the bed covers in rage.

Later that day, she set out for the headquarters of the Intelligence Service. Without a second thought, she had decided to go straight to the major and ask him to intervene. She was going to teach Pierre a good lesson about who the boss was and she would do it as remorselessly as he was planning to drag her back into that filthy hell. It was impossible that the major would fail to understand when she explained it to him and he would not leave her defenseless at the mercy of Pierre Morné.

The Intelligence Service was in one of the most central hotels in the city, the *Hôtel du Louvre*. It was named after the Louvre museum, which was right behind it. Next to the *Palais Royal* and the *Comédie-Française*, and only a few steps away from the *Tuileries* garden, at the crossroads of the commercial and the historic centre, the *Hôtel du Louvre* imposed its five impressive floors on the area having nothing to envy compared to the luxurious hotels of *Rue de Rivoli* and the *Place de la Concorde*, where most of the German administration was established.

Winter had walked down Opera Avenue and passed by the *Hôtel du Louvre* several times, heading to *Les Grands Magasins du Louvre*, where she had often spent significant amounts of money on not-so-important purchases, but she had never been interested in finding out what was inside that building, which was heavily guarded and always seemed extremely busy. Standing there now, at the corner of the *Place du Théâtre Français*[25], observing the imposing structure, the Nazi flags waving on a long line of posts set up along the façade of the first floor, her heart was beating with a deafening pound and her mind felt foggy and much less certain that she could do what she had set out to do or that she even wanted to. All those vehicles and motorcycles, uniformed men and agents in civvies, resolute, purposeful, with their air of unquestionable superiority, gave her a sense of belittlement. What if her request offended the major? What if he found it trivial, if he scorned and laughed at her? Might there just be another way to overturn Pierre's plans without having to ask the major for help?

"There is none!" she decided and walked across the square with the determination that pressing need always evokes in people. "Good morning... I would like to see *Sturmbannführer* von Stielen!" she told the guard, using her best German and her cutest smile.

The guard looked straight down at her hands and, seeing that she was holding nothing, he gave her a condescending look–her charming face and coy attitude obviously had no effect on him.

"Papers, please!" he said and, fortunately, Winter understood. She took out the brand-new identity card, which she had reissued thanks to Pierre once she had settled in at 'The Golden Doe', and gave it to the guard in the most compliant manner.

"Do you have an appointment with *Herr Sturmbannführer*?" the guard asked as he was checking her papers, but this time, Winter did not understand and she gestured, explaining she did not speak the language. "If you don't have a pass, you need to have an appointment and if you don't have an appointment, entrance is forbidden!" the guard spouted and the only word Winter caught was 'forbidden', which sounded almost the same in both English and German. She looked around in frustration.

"Please... *Sturmbannführer* von Stielen to see!" she attempted once more, pronouncing the words one by one, but, again, the guard did not show any intention to cooperate.

"I told you, you must have an appointment or a pass! Take your papers back!" He placed the identity card back in her hand and showed her the way.

Winter looked down the street. She looked at the guard, then at the other guard, and even leaned over to look inside the hotel's marble entrance. She shook her head negatively.

"You not understand... I must *Sturmbannführer* von Stielen! I... I not speak German... do you understand?" she insisted, but the guard got irritated and pulled his rifle at Winter: *"Halt! Zutritt verboten!"*[26] he called and his reaction prompted the other guard to point another rifle at her.

"Bitte, bitte!"[27] she exclaimed and was terrified enough to turn around and flee, yet something was holding her back,–despair, which would only allow her to move a few steps away, with her eyes on the brink of tears and her mind at flank speed for a solution, because she could definitely not go back to the club empty-handed. Then she heard something from further away which sounded like her name and next followed an exchange of some unintelligible German between the voice that had spoken and the guards; Winter blinked several times before

she could clear the panic away from her eyes to see that Molnich, the translator, was among the speakers.

"Klaus? Oh, Klaus!" she called out and reached out to take his hand with the urge of a drowning person in sight of a floating ring.

Molnich gently wrapped her hand around his arm and smiled at her, which was apparently all the pass she needed to get inside. Winter was thankful, but, realising how helpless she really was, she had to admit that the once-too-many false proved sense of self-importance which had driven her to this eminently chimerical venture was, in fact, greatly contemptible.

"So, what are you doing here?" Molnich asked and Winter herself could not help but wonder.

She followed Klaus Molnich to the fourth floor, where the major's office was. In the waiting room, a young man was sitting plunged into a stack of documents, looking like he was zealously engaged in his work.

"Good morning, Peter!" Molnich greeted in German. "Is *Sturmbannführer* in?" The young man raised his eyes, glanced at Molnich, then at Winter, and again at Molnich. Finally, he returned to his work, showing little willingness to answer: "He is. You may enter, if you want, but I can't say about the lady!"

"That will be fine!" Molnich replied with plenty of self-assurance and turned to Winter, instructing her to wait while he talked to the major. "You're already here, so let's see how it goes!" he encouraged her with his humbly affectionate gaze, and Winter gratefully squeezed his hand with both of hers.

She watched him knock on the office door, go inside immediately after, and she remained awkwardly standing in the middle of the waiting room, nervously playing with the strap of her handbag. The young man raised his eyes again and stared at her for a few seconds.

"Please take a seat!" he told her and showed her the seats across the room to help her understand. She thanked him with a smile and sat down where he had shown.

The *Führer*'s enormous portrait on the wall added to Winter's agitation, the half-length depiction of him making him almost present in the room. The brown uniform illuminated him against the dark background, an almost divine figure at its birth from chaos, the red light which shone behind him, designating something magnificent and terrifying at the same time. He was leaning against the back of a chair with his left arm, where the Nazi armband was just barely distinct. His right arm bent, the loose fist against his waist, both meaningfully complemented the countenance of absolute rule, those eyes consciously looking into the future, the future of the people, the future of the world. '*Ein Volk, Ein Reich, Ein Führer!*'[28] was the title, and the exclamation mark was there to punctuate one's feeling: pure adoration and religious awe.

When Molnich came out of the major's office and Winter drew her eyes away from the portrait to look at his sympathetic face, she was almost shocked by the striking contrast. And she got the surreal feeling of standing between two different dimensions, two worlds looking at each other through a gruesome distorting mirror.

"He'll see you! You'll just have to wait for the meeting to finish, but that won't take long!" Molnich announced, and Winter stood up to shake his hand and give him an honestly warm embrace.

"Oh, Klaus, I can't thank you enough! It was so kind of you to help!"

Molnich confessed it had required little effort on his part, as the major agreed to see her as soon as he heard her name, and this was where the translator winked at her meaningfully. He bowed to signal her goodbye and expressed the hope of seeing her again soon. Then he left in a hurry.

Winter sat down again and waited, curious whether, and to what extent, the major's willingness to see her should encourage her. He was not just being polite, no, she could sense it. There was something other than common courtesy in his behaviour. She thought of the night before and felt that a man so insightful, with that certain soothing radiance which he beamed straight into her so effortlessly, could not just be employing tactics to accomplish a strategy; he would have to be... And she dug and dug into her mind for a proper adjective.

Suddenly, a woman rushed into the room and became the focus of attention. Her face expressed great distress and there was spasmodic energy and overwhelming determination in her every move. She kneeled next to the secretary and grabbed him by the arm.

"*Sturmann*[29] Schwarz!"

The secretary got up and nervously pushed her hands off him. He spoke harshly to her, while she begged him with tears in her eyes, and Winter understood that a name was insistently repeated in her desperate appeals: Nicolas. Not receiving the reaction she was hoping for, the woman then started deliriously calling out to the major. At that point, the secretary picked up the phone and gave a strict command. Only a minute later, three soldiers stormed in, grabbed the woman by the arms, and dragged her out by force. After that, the secretary took a deep breath, straightened his uniform and sat back behind his desk, glancing at Winter for a second, before he continued his work, as if not the slightest disturbance had occurred.

Winter clasped her hands together and shut her eyes, feeling the woman's pain as her own. Who knows what kind of misfortune necessitated her coming to beg for the German's mercy, only to receive his heartless refusal and find herself thrown out like a common criminal, she thought and, within moments, the short-lived previous optimism of hers went to rack and ruin.

Soon, the door of the major's office opened and about a dozen officers came out muttering to each other. One or two stood for a moment to look at the young woman sitting in the armchair and then walked away, following the others. The major appeared shortly after and, seeing him, Winter jumped up from her seat, ambivalent, but eager to meet with him again. Much to her astonishment, however, he merely cast a starchy glance at her and returned to his office, followed by his secretary, whose irritated voice permitted Winter to presume that he was briefing the major on the incident with the woman. And while she was standing there like a pillar of salt, her own despair started fluttering in her chest, stinging in her stomach, weakening her knees. When the secretary came out again to show her into the major's office, she was feeling no less anxious than a pupil at school having to stand up before a strict headmaster.

"Have a seat!" the major said, showing her exactly where he wanted her to sit. Winter approached and sat uneasily on a comfortable armchair in front of his desk, a beautiful piece of furniture with artistic marquetry and gold-bronze decorations. "I'm sorry you had to watch that scene!" he remarked in an uncommonly typical tone and Winter remained silent, not finding anything suitable to say. "We have dozens of unaware spouses coming every day, pleading for their husbands' release. They claim to have absolutely no idea about the tons of illegal material smuggled in and out of their homes and they expect us to believe it! Would anyone? Would you?" he continued in a torrent of resentment and challenged her with an uncommonly grating gaze.

The major's cynicism surprised Winter terribly, and she took a dreadful glimpse at him, as he was leaning back in his armchair, with a cigarette between his fingers, which he lit after long, careful consideration.

"Anyway, it's good that you came. You are, in fact, exactly the person I wanted to see!" she then heard him say in a completely altered mood, which maximised her confusion. "I spoke to Pierre earlier! I wouldn't like to cause you any more trouble, so I had to agree to his terms!" he explained, alarming Winter as to what he meant.

"Well, to be honest, that's the reason I'm here!" she said as cautiously as someone walking on dangerous ground.

"Oh?"

Winter braced herself and tried to portray the situation as best as she could: "Pierre thinks that, last night, you and I, that we..." she gulped and, fortunately, the major's side smile relieved her of the necessity to utter the exact words. "He suggested..." she went on with more and more difficulty "...he told me really that, since the start's been made, there are... there are also others who are interested!"

The major nodded with a hum, and he stood up, leaving his cigarette burning in the ashtray. He walked to the window, put his hands in his pockets, and looked outside quietly.

"And you?" he asked seriously. "Are you interested?"

Despite her dejection, Winter mustered the strength to get up and approach him. She even found the courage to stretch out her hand and touch his arm, squeezing her fingers onto the machine-embroidered eagle and swastika on the sleeve of his tunic.

"How can you ask me that!" she smothered, but there was no reply from him. She looked up and saw his eyes dark and impervious, and she feared she had been too bold and perhaps even insolent. She removed her hand, stepped back and finally returned to her seat, falling into it like a lifeless body. "I can't go back to that! I will have to go away, leave the club! And I will; there is no way I can do this again! It's just that... I don't have anywhere else to go. For the first time, I have my life in some kind of order. I'll lose everything. But I really can't go back to that..."

Her voice was constant, plain and weighty, as the presentation of solid facts usually is. And, in the silence that followed, the ticking clock sounded as though it had already begun the countdown to her fall. She could see herself picking up her things and walking out the door into a big, voracious nothing, having nothing to expect and nothing to hope for, and she remembered Geneviève, felt what she must have felt and knew she would leave the same way, without goodbyes, no tears, too desperate to waste any time or effort on them.

The knock on the door was a welcome sound and the major's '*Herein!*'[30] left a familiar hue in her ears, painfully bringing in mind that intimate feeling she thought they had shared the night before, but it must have been all in her imagination, in her hunger for human contact, a hunger obviously more insatiable than his could ever be.

The secretary appeared at the door, uncertain whether he could speak freely in front of the visitor. He requested the major's permission with an eye gesture, and, once it had been granted, he announced: "The prisoner is ready to be released at your command!"

The major's boots were heard creaking on the floor and soon hushed, as he stepped onto the thick carpet. He took his place back behind the desk, picked up the cigarette he had left in the ashtray, saw that it was burnt out, and put it back again. He breathed in and breathed out; he tapped the index finger of his right hand on the file folder which lay on the desk in front of him and silently read the dark-coloured label on it:

'Code: Seamstress'. Then he gaped at Winter, who speechlessly sat and discreetly avoided looking around, fully aware of her precariousness. "Give it five minutes and then have him released!" he said stoutly, and the secretary saluted and left to carry out the order.

Those voices in the language of power, Winter thought, and felt like a beggar, a waif and stray at the mercy of the mighty, the conquerors, the major, Pierre –they were all the same; and, for a moment, she was overwhelmed by the spirit of rebellion those lionhearted outlaws seethed at, only to be masters of their own fate. She raised her eyes to the major and saw he was looking at her, a hard look with a completely tamed blue-gray storm inside it.

"Yes!" he eventually conceded. "I will talk to Pierre! You needn't worry!"

He came to her, gave her his hand to help her up from the seat, and left an almost imperceptible kiss on her hand. Then, he opened the door and escorted her to the exit, leaving no room for anything more than a typical thank you and goodbye.

"Bring me the file of Nicolas Giroux!" the major ordered his secretary, once Winter was gone. He returned to his desk, lit another cigarette, and, as before, he came to stand by the window. The view always had a soothing effect on him. Far away at the northwest end of Opera Avenue, a flock of birds flew up from the imposing rooftops of the *Palais Garnier*. The green dome between the golden sculptures of Harmony and Poetry invigorated the dull landscape and contrasted with the gray sky. In the wide, treeless avenue, people and vehicles moved up and down like industrious ants. At the intersection of the avenue with *Rue Saint-Honoré*, some drivers were trying to take priority by honking their horns persistently. And outside the *Comédie-Française*, two women were vivaciously chatting. Soon, there was Winter.

An annoyingly ambiguous feeling had settled in Winter's chest when she left the *Hôtel du Louvre*. The meeting had ended up the way she wanted. Nevertheless, she was feeling just as discarded as a pair of old shoes. Across the square, the woman who had been forcibly thrown out of the major's office was still standing by, her agony written on every glance and every head turn, some fruitless hope misguiding her that there was still something to look forward to. What could she possibly expect? What in the devil's name was she thinking?

A man crossed her line of vision and in the instant that the woman was out of her sight, Winter sensed how fugitive and transient it all was and she felt desperate and lonely. Then something sparked in her mind, like a sudden revelation, an intuition or understanding of some sort, and she turned her head in the man's direction –his hurried stride, his lowered head, his hands safely hidden inside his trouser pockets. She did not have the time to wonder why this figure seemed familiar to her before a stimulating, reviving shiver swept through her body.

"Monsieur Martin!" she yelled *"Monsieur Martin!"* and ran fast to catch up with him. The man would not halt. "René!" Hearing his name, he stopped, turned back, looked at her coming close. "Hello!" she smiled at him, but immediately frowned, seeing worn-out marks of abuse on his face. He did not speak. "It's me, don't you remember me? My God, what have they done to you?" And she irrationally felt at complete liberty to reach out to his face and touch the sore spots.

He pushed her hand away and pierced her with his eyes.

"Oh, I remember you! I remember you better than you think!" he whispered, and this blend of wild passion and blind anger in his voice apprehended Winter.

"I came looking for you at your shop. It was closed. When I found out about you... It's not my fault... What you told me... I didn't tell anyone, you have to believe me!" she spurted with all the compulsion of a defendant wrongly accused.

He raised his eyebrow and narrowed his eyes. "Is that so?"

"Oh, but I swear it!" she wheezed, never having expected that she would need to prove her innocence to him. "Please, let's talk!"

"No!" he flatly refused and turned to walk away.

Winter had to overcome her bewilderment quickly in order to run after him and grab him by the arm.

"Listen to me, please! It wasn't me! I didn't betray you!" He nodded with clear disbelief, which hurt Winter's feelings deeply. "René, please!"

she begged and hearing his name, he looked at her,–his name and look together, making a disarmingly overpowering combination. "I work at 'The Golden Doe' in *Place Pigalle*" she told him breathlessly, and, finally, felt some encouragement from the intrigue in his eyes. "Please come and see me! Say you will!"

"I might!" he replied and brought his face only a breath away. Winter shuddered because she thought he would kiss her, but then he turned to her ear and hissed: "Aren't you afraid now? Have you realised where you are?"

And as he distanced his face and looked at her, there was something like vindictive satisfaction on his face, mixed with voluptuous self-indulgence, sensual, almost sexual. He smiled sideways, turned around and walked away, leaving her frozen to the pavement and terrified of even the slightest move, as if she had stepped onto a landmine.

René Martin wandered around the city long before he set out for his neighbourhood. By now, it was already getting dark, and he always felt more at home in the shadows. He came to a building whose cracked peeling paint and weathered windows would never suggest it could actually be someone's dwelling. There was a long open-air corridor behind the door to the street, a beat-up iron door with glass panels at the end of it and, beyond that, an outworn wooden door would open with a key stowed away inside a crack in the wall. Behind it, a flight of creaky stairs led down to an abandoned wine cellar. He took the rusty old oil-lamp which hung there and lit it. He had not gone down but a few steps when he heard weapons being cocked and the warning: "Don't move!"

He calmly extended his arms to show that he was unarmed and trudged all the way down the stairs into the cellar, looking for the person who had spoken.

"René?"

"Son of a gun, I told you he has nine lives!"

Weapons were put aside, genuine laughter filled the room, and three cordial embraces came to welcome him home with the joy inspired by the return of a lost comrade, with the relief and hopefulness a good omen brings in times of fear and misgiving.

"Tell us what happened! For so long now, we've been dreading the idea of a rat in our midst!"

They poured him a glass of strong wine and sat down around the square table, where they had often drawn up their plans, not without dissent, but always with passion for their ideals of '*Liberté, égalité, fraternité*'[31] and the dream of a changed world, whether it be by government or by revolution. René enjoyed the taste of wine with the euphoria of heaven and unquestionably ranked it as one of the true benefits of freedom. His brutalised face hid in the dimness, but his eyes seemed to sparkle like a sword-blade in the moonlight.

"They had nothing against me. I knew they couldn't hold me for long!"

René explained that his arrest was completely accidental. He was walking along *Rue des Petits-Champs*, at a particular point where the pavement was narrow. From the opposite direction, an SS schmuck and two krauts in civvies were approaching. He later found out that the SS was a major named Blut, a nasty little creep who actually called all the shots at the Gestapo. Of course, he proudly disregarded them and made absolutely no way for them to pass. There were three of them and he was alone, but he still remembered their sour faces as he forced them to maneuver past him, an action he never regretted despite what followed. They called on him to come back and checked his papers. Then the SS 'kindly invited' him to escort them to their vehicle and from there to the Gestapo. That was it! The little devil kept him locked up for three days before he started applying his persuasive methods, as he called them. They included starvation and thirst, sleep deprivation and a proper amount of beating. People were like octopuses, the SS would assert. In order to tenderise them, one had to beat the living hell out of them. At one point, he revealed that he originated from a fishing village on the coast of the North Sea. 'Not bad for a wretched old peasant's child, wouldn't you agree?' he chuckled with overweening self-admiration. Right then, René had been unable to answer him. He came round the next day in his cell, sick to his stomach from the smell of mold, vomit and urine, and he remained there, hardly able to breathe for days he failed to count. Eventually, he was picked up by the Intelligence Service and stayed at the *Hôtel du Louvre* for another fortnight or so.

"*Sturmbannführer* von Stielen!"

René laughed and scornfully remarked that, compared to his Gestapo counterpart, this one was literally like a Sister of Mercy. He had his wounds taken care of; he gave him food, drink and smokes; he even asked him for details of his treatment at the hands of the Gestapo. Then von Stielen started the questions: about his profession, about his shop, his affiliates, and sometimes about his origins, his family and background, even about his love affairs, as if he were ever going to tell him anything about any of that. Day after day, he asked the same questions and got the same answers. In the end, René knew exactly what he was going to be asked and was quick to give his replies beforehand.

"You mustn't underestimate von Stielen! Beware not of the danger that you can see, but of the one you can't!"

René painfully resisted dignifying *Chopin*'s advice with some advice of his own. His little adventure had made him forget about this annoying know-it-all, the same conceited bourgeois he had always been, who never missed an opportunity to show off his wit and education. And, right there and then, he solemnly renewed the promise to himself that, if he had to fight to the last of his breath, it would be not only to expel the conqueror but also to safeguard society from the claws of such smug, conformist braggarts.

"By God, I don't like it at all that he's been such a regular customer lately!"

"Well, at least, let us hope it is Winter that he comes for and not anyone else!"

Now, this was the kind of talk worthy of René's attention. Avoiding any mention to the fact that the name 'Winter' was not unknown to him, he asked who Winter was and his comrades informed him she was the new singer of 'The Doe'.

"And are you certain she is clean? If she has such dealings...!"

René's question forced Alain, Guillaume and Louis to exchange inquisitive glances, but they all, almost immediately, affirmed that, under no circumstances could Winter be a spy for the Germans. René, however, seemed to have moved into another dimension, and they could not even be sure he had heard. He sank deeply into the shadows of his mind and darkness veiled him. They left him to drink his wine and have his smoke withdrawn into himself all he wanted. René was never the most congenial companion–the deepest of his thoughts always seemed to be immersed in the heaviest gloom. And, at times like this, none of his comrades felt too comfortable around him.

... Your eyes could no longer see. They didn't want to. They wanted to drown in their tears. And they were full of doubt: Who was I? What was I? Hatred roared; it blinded the eyes. If only you would hate me! If only you were blind and spared me the look of wonder in your eyes...

Our homeland was always a place of joy. It was not glamorous like Île-de-France, not wild like Normandy, nor prosperous like Grand Est. It was at the far-most reaches of the country, the garrison to the north, with forests and swampy plains, villages with white houses and tall bell towers. And it was the home of some of the most delicious cheeses one could ever taste, and taste them we did,–three small children hungry from playing outdoors all day.

How could I bear to look at you like that? What kind of pain might change a man this way? What beasts of hell might possess him, devouring a heart that used to be pure! It would be unthinkable to you. Impossible. You'd like to believe it was someone else, someone who looked like, but was not, me. You'd wish it; you'd want it; but it was no other! It was me!

When war was about to knock on our door, she said she wasn't afraid. She'd heard the elders remember the Great War, we all had, but she was not afraid. Because this army was strong and armoured; and we were the army: their husbands, their sons and brothers. She looked at me and called me brave, no grief in her eyes seeing me off to battle. She had faith in me and she'd wait for me; she knew I'd be back safe. I made her words my lucky charm, and they kept me alive.

The stool was creaking. Balance. You had to keep balance. Your legs were shaking. Your knees were weak. The more you stood, the smaller the stool was getting. Soon you'd have to stand on a surface no bigger than your palm. Your legs had to be strong. They had to endure this trial. Your legs had to endure!

The first wave of refugees arrived in mid-May. Thousands came from Belgium: by car, by bicycle, on foot; entire families with their belongings on their backs. Panic. That was the word for it. Wherever they passed, they aroused others to leave. Maman wanted to abandon everything and go; it was Père's decision to stay. Fortunately, there were still people like Père left in the land.

How much longer would I just be looking at you? It was a sick joke, you always thought my jokes were lousy! Like that time when I'd hidden in the kitchen cupboard to scare you and you'd dropped the copper saucepot with Maman's stew in it. And yet, I had the decency to defend you, tell the truth and take the blame, you loved me for it or so you said. This was another poor joke, the poorest of them all! I'd be standing there to catch you, when you could no more...

Our house bombed down, both parents killed. She always preferred the fields to the house, and they saved her. Saved: it depends on the viewpoint! She hid away for as long as she could, it was just a matter of time before they found her. They took her to the home of the Troussier family, none of whom had survived. Some officers were staying there now. Surprising as it might sound, they were kind, she said. They'd have her cook, clean and tidy. She didn't think it was much of a sacrifice in return for her life.

It was getting late; you were getting sleepy. It was enough already! The joke had grown cold. Soon, it would be me begging for your forgiveness! You cursed, you warned, you threatened. Then you regretted it, apologised, and begged. Either way, you knew I wouldn't listen. Your cries could tear down the walls, they echoed in the wilderness. My name on your lips! Your voice in my ears! Simone! You should have kept your eyes open, your legs still. Just a little longer... A little longer... A little... longer...

10

In the realm of silence

Long did Winter's fears about that meeting with René outside the *Hôtel du Louvre* dwell, making her even more fearful of the completely impulsive and utterly stupid invitation she offered him to meet with her at 'The Golden Doe'. Had René actually taken her up on her offer, it could have been disastrous. But René never showed up and Winter was thankful almost as much as she was disappointed.

In early April, the air-raid siren sounded, finding Winter away from the club. She and others ran to the nearest métro station, which was packed with all sorts of people. They sat and waited. Some were looking at their watches every so often, some would smoke their cigarettes in small doses, some would try to explain the situation to their curious children, bringing faint smiles to some faces with the millions of their questions. Further away, about a dozen German soldiers had sought shelter along with the civilians. One of them approached to offer a piece of chocolate to a boy, but he cried and ran to hide behind his mother's skirt. At first, the soldier found the incident funny, but when he had to encounter the evil eye of those around, he took his chocolate, chewed it ostentatiously and returned to his own kind, who spared no exhibition of their icy contempt.

At 'The Golden Doe', the shelter was located under a hatch in the kitchen floor–a small space built for the water and sewerage facilities. Every time they had to go down, they could only compare it to a mass grave, and someone commented that if their building was ever bombed, they would be buried in there, no need for anyone to bother putting them in a regular grave. 'Poor business for the gravedigger!' Alain would joke and they all laughed, except for Pierre, who, if getting angry once for his shelter being disparaged, was twice as angry because he was superstitious and feared the effect of the other people's foul mouths. Winter was not afraid when they were all together. The idea of not dying alone made the thought of death more bearable.

She could not help wondering whether people would show the same solidarity with one another when the war was over. She asked Louis if he thought the times of peace would be simple, if there were such a thing as real peace. If there would not be another attempt to divide the world between the mightier, the rest of them remaining the same cog in the wheel they had always been, with nothing changed but the face of their rulers. Even a fervent advocate of freedom, such as Louis, did not believe that the end of the war would relieve the little people of their daily struggle. More had to be done, he would reflect, but the way was yet to be determined. Winter's mind often flew to René when Louis talked like this; only she knew what his way to change this durable and resilient status quo would be: by fire,–the element she thought best described him.

The evening was sweet, a sweet evening of spring. Under the dim light of the stage, she started her song, immediately carrying the audience away to sing along with her. The song was popular and not without good cause: it was the story of two people divided by war. And they would wait, wait and hope that they could ultimately meet again, perhaps under a street lamp, and, perhaps, its pale light would be enough to shine life back into the desire which the encompassing darkness of war obliterated.

Winter had to confess that, in spite of it all, she had truly and eagerly been waiting for René, feeling hurt that he never came, sad that he did not believe her. She wanted him. She wanted him to come for her, take her away; to be crazy about her, crazier than he had ever been for any Simone. And she dreamt he was so in love with her he could set aside all other battles, except the battle for their own happiness. It was a futile wish, but she wished it anyway.

When she stopped singing, a venerating silence spread across the hall, echoing the wistfulness for someone left behind, that someone who gave each one's life its true meaning, and, perhaps, some among the audience would even wonder what they were doing in a foreign country so far away from home, for what purpose and for what cause. And others would even try to wipe the soulful tears they cried inside, inside and not for anyone to see, because men did not cry, let alone soldiers. She signalled for the orchestra to start playing again, and the boys promptly responded with a brisk tango. Those nostalgic faces burst with liveliness and those hands, clenched together with suppressed sorrow, were revived and would clap with enthusiasm. Winter descended from the stage and took one soldier from a front table to dance with. Soon other couples joined in, and some customers, who did not have escorts of their own, invited the waitresses and the can-can dancers to be their partners, while others, who were just left on the shelf, started dancing with each other, making fun of the one who had to play the female part, and, on the gallery, where there was no space for dancing, some would hug or join hands to swing to the rhythm from their seats.

Winter changed partners three times during the dance, and the orchestra continued with a series of tangos for as long as the clientele grooved to the music. Then, in a swirl full of laughter and cheer, the grip of two strong and skillful arms drew her in. Her feet stamped and floundered helplessly; an astonished gasp escaped her mouth; and her eyes sparked a genuine surprise, which soon became a hungry welcome.

"Keep dancing!" he dictated and spun her away into his violent and demanding passion.

Winter gladly relinquished herself to him, with every bit of her he touched trembling and ready to explode. When he pulled her close, his blazing desire combusted the very core of her substance. She looked him in the eyes and felt his gaze pierce through her like a fiery spear;

his breath surged its tropical storm upon her face; and, as he held her, he bound her with a pair of flaming ropes: his arms.

And just when ecstasy was about to literally make her evaporate, both the music and dance stopped dead. Within an instance, her dancing companion abandoned her and disappeared into the turmoil of the audience's applause. Winter hunted for him with her eyes, but she saw Pierre charge against her instead, and, before she could speak a word of defense, he had already unleashed hell on her.

"Why all the fuss? It was only a dance!" she protested, more eager to locate the object of her desire than get into a pointless fight with the boss. "Look!" she told him impatiently and her resolve seemed to have an unexpected calming effect on Pierre. "I'm just going upstairs to change and I'll be back before you know it, alright?"

The introduction of everyone's favourite dance sounded and the dancing ensemble climbed onto the stage, manipulating their playful skirts, causing frantic cheers and unquenchable thirst from the clientele. Pierre had to return to his post. But, before doing so, he could not help but stand there a while and carefully investigate the hall.

Winter entered her room, still feeling drunk with excitement. He had come; he had come for her, she repeated in her mind, aroused to the bones. Little did it matter if it were only for one dance. One dance was all she needed to be happy for the rest of her life, she exaggerated, thrilled to bits and over the moon. Oh, but he would come again, she could tell. She had felt it in him, too, the same passion and want: the want for one another.

She took off her dress and threw it in the laundry basket. She went into the bathroom. The cool water on her skin made her feel good. She sighed over and over, reliving with the same exhilaration every moment she had spent with him, and she swirled across the floor while returning to the room. She kept on tapping her feet in front of the wardrobe, where she cheerfully looked for a new dress. Was it her imagination or was there really a warm radiance on her back, a certain heat wave, like a coal-burning heater on a cold winter night? she felt and instinctively turned to look. She was wearing little more than her underwear, but she could not say whether it was embarrassment that whooshed across her or whether it was simply pure desire. She stood confounded with the dress in her hands, looking like a model for photography, and only her eyes blinked to ensure that he was actually standing there before her, looking at her with his fierce, wolfish gaze.

"René!"

Suddenly, everything became insufferably tangible and concrete: René's presence, her semi-nudity and a devastating feeling of self-consciousness, none of which existed in her wild fantasies around a moment like this. She took a deep breath and hurried to put on her dress.

"Happy to see me, after all?"

"Of course, I'm happy!"

"That sour face could have fooled me!"

"You surprised me. And I had almost stopped waiting!"

She moved to her dressing table, where she pretended to look for something, when, in fact, she only needed to turn her back on him, for some unknown reason, feeling more secure to look at him in the mirror. The back-and-forth exchange between them and his tone disturbed Winter and seemed to shatter the illusion, which could apparently only be alive in the realm of silence inside her mind. His reflection in the glass seemed to fill the entire room. And he had something incomparably attractive, but primitive, undisciplined and threatening at the same time.

"I like it when you're not expecting me!" he smirked, making Winter feel very uncomfortable. "And I like you better as you were a moment ago, naked from pretense and armour!" And uttering the word *naked* with emphasis, he brought an uneasy flush to her cheeks. Stiflingly still, she saw him walk towards her; when he stood behind her and brought his hands to her arms, she was breathless. With a steady move, he turned her around to face him. He took her arms and wrapped them around his neck. His palms spread across her back and squeezed her onto him, while bending over to kiss her with a pair of soft and moist lips that seemed able to break all resistance in her and completely swallow her.

Daunted and overawed by his audacity, Winter managed to pull away and distance herself from him.

"Please... I just wanted to assure you... that I'm sorry for what happened to you and I was not the one to blame. It's wrong to believe I'd betray you. I'd never... I couldn't!" she stuttered, avoiding his gaze, which probed into her, skyrocketing her nervousness and apprehension.

He examined her carefully, her face, every inch of her trembling body: "Oh, you couldn't, could you?" he dashed against her with a cynical smile. "And why not? You don't exactly show any loathing for the Germans! Certainly, any information like this would motivate them to reward you well, and, from what I see, you are not doing so badly!" he added with resentment Winter could never have imagined in her daydreaming about him.

"How can you say that!" she exclaimed with great disappointment.

"Is it not true?" he challenged her.

Well, obviously! Winter secretly agreed: a former prostitute dallying with the conquerors was no great guarantee of loyalty. Hell, if it were not her own self they were talking about, she might have doubted as well.

"I know how it looks!" she confessed, feeling deeply ashamed. "But I'd never stoop so low, not for any reward; there is more integrity in me than my appearance suggests!"

He nodded in affirmation, but the asymmetrical shape of his lips manifested his complete disbelief: "Still, you were at the Intelligence Service that morning!"

"... I was coming back from the shops. I can afford to visit the expensive ones now, you see. And *Rue Saint-Honoré* has plenty!" she lied with perfect agility, and, slightly exasperated, she concluded: "I don't even know where the Intelligence Service is!"

"And I hope you never have to find out!" he replied with unspeakable bitterness.

Winter looked away sadly. For some irrational reason, love was always believed to magically overcome all obstacles. And, although she could not in full awareness declare that what she felt for René was love, had it been the other way round between them, she would definitely have believed him with no questions asked. When she looked his way again, she was astounded to see a face completely changed, beaming with tenderness, a bright face like a summer moon. He came closer; he took her hands in his, warmly and softly laid his burning kisses on them.

"I'm sorry!" he whispered. "Forgive me, if I hurt you! I just needed to know I could trust you!"

Winter got little reassurance out of this revelation. In her dreams, René's feelings were confident and valiant and his highest ideal was to share his life with her in a peaceful place where they could live their untainted love. He did not play games with her, justified or otherwise. And he did not require proof of her trustworthiness, because he trusted his faith in her.

"You needn't apologise or try to convince me" he attested, bringing her palm to his face, needily enjoying her guided caress. "I knew from the start it wasn't you!"

Eventually, Winter was feeling rather offended. Knowing that she had no involvement in his arrest but making her feel so guilty just the same! How could he be so cruel?

"... Yes, I was looking for an excuse to see you again...!" he said in response to her unstated question. "I wanted you to tell me where I could find you. I wanted you to ask for it!" He brought her hand to his lips and left a wet mark on her palm. "Tell me how you wanted to see me again! Tell me how you need me!" He leaned over once again to kiss her, she resisted, he tried to force it, she pulled away. René glared at her, with her back turned on him, looking like a frightened little bird. "First, you invite me. And then, you reject me!" he accused her, starting once again to approach little by little, step by step. "I expected more of you!" His burning palms touched her gently on the arms, fervently ran all the way down to her thighs, to come up again to her waist and round it, delicately pressuring her onto him. "... But I guess you still have a lot to think about!" His whisper in her ear was like electricity. "Until then..." He took a handful of her hair, inhaled its fragrance. He raised his eyes to meet hers in the mirror and his image behind her resembled that of a predator ready to jump onto his unsuspecting prey. Then he smiled. He moved away swiftly, reached the door. "We'll see each other again soon!" he said and Winter could not help wondering whether it was a promise or a threat.

II

On truth and lie

Sturmbannführer von Stielen was drinking the red wine the ginger-haired waitress had kindly just served him and was tapping his finger to the rhythm of the music, observing the surroundings: the dancing on stage, the orchestra, the waitresses coming and going at the bar, where Pierre seemed uncommonly agitated this night. The club was packed; the atmosphere exuberant and gay; officers, soldiers and civilians, all an intoxicated tangle eager to escape from reality into a more spirited version of the world.

"Your date is not here yet, *Herr Sturmbannführer*?"

Petit François stood with his innocent face and his basket full of flowers, fearlessly looking at the major. He smiled: "I'm afraid not, François. It looks like she stood me up tonight!" he joked, stroking the boy's buzz cut hair.

"Will you get her a flower?" Petit François asked, extending a small bouquet of lilies and wood violets to him.

"To be stood up and still get her a flower, well, that's too generous, is it not?" the major went on in the same humorous spirit. "But not at your expense, little fellow!"

He took a banknote out of his pocket, wrapped it in the boy's hand and winked at him. Petit François left satisfied and dived into the crowd to sell his flowers to others. The major's gaze followed him.

At that point, the two low-ranking officers at the front table, who had been dancing and singing out-of-tune so much for so long, finally sat in their seats. It was then, when a familiar figure appeared in the major's field of view: **René Martin, code name: Seamstress.** Well, a suspicion not substantially confirmed yet, he corrected himself. All the same, it was a strange coincidence that he should show up at 'The Golden Doe' ... or, perhaps, not strange at all. René Martin walked away, having to pass by the bar, where Pierre looked exceptionally irritated to see him. In fact, the ginger-haired waitress, who was just returning with her tray and noticed the rash on his face, was worried enough to run to him and enquire after his health. Pierre talked enraged, and his words made the girl dreadfully turn in the direction where Martin had gone. Pierre then seemed to have swallowed his tongue, and the major sensed it: he was dying to look his way and see if he was looking back at him. Only seconds later, Winter came down from upstairs, dashing as usual. As soon as Pierre saw her, he ran to her furiously and the way he talked to her was not kind. Winter looked unpleasantly surprised. She turned her eyes towards him somewhat alarmed, which, however, did not stop her from setting out to meet him at his table, graceful and lightsome as ever.

"*Herr Sturmbannführer*, good evening!" she greeted with an affable smile, and the major got up and courteously kissed her hand.

"Please, have a seat!" he offered, and Winter sat, seemingly with no concern.

"Did you have to wait long?" she cared to ask.

"Long enough!" the major replied in a way that did not sound at all encouraging. Winter contained her agitation and pretended to be unaware of the innuendo.

When the major suggested they leave, informing her he had made a reservation for them elsewhere, Winter was happy to accept, eager to leave the club in case René returned for any foolhardy reason. The major could not help noticing that, despite his usual self, Pierre seemed just as eager to see them off.

They arrived at *'Chez Pierre'*, a place of fine dining exclusively for the conquerors' elite, which connoted anything but resemblance to 'The Golden Doe' or its owner. Winter no longer lacked the confidence to stand decently in a chic restaurant such as this, but the presence of so many high-ranking officials did have a rather intimidating effect. Besides, the menu was entirely in German and, raising an eyebrow, Winter had to admit that she could hardly recognise six words in it. The major gladly offered to choose something for her.

She was brought a juicy fillet of oven roasted meat with thick gravy accompanied by a sort of potato dumplings, they called *knödels*, while the major had a simple *lapin a la cocotte*, the famous French rabbit stew. They also drank a bottle of dry red wine, which the major requested with its name and date.

The major had excellent knowledge of wine, which was owed to a family tradition. In fact, there had been good wine at every family dinner for as long as he could remember, and his father had always been an enthusiastic collector of rare wines. Winter was interested in hearing more about the major's past, and he said he came from a family with a long military history. His father was a major general in the Great War and before him, his grandfather and great-grandfather were also men of the uniform. This, naturally, meant a rather strict upbringing. His father was largely admired for his discipline and intellect, and he was an unrivaled role model for young Friedrich. He died in the trenches of the Marne in the Great War while the major was still a cadet at military school; it was his decisive step into adulthood, the experience which defined the man he grew up to be. His mother passed shortly after. Then, he spent a time with his aunt in Switzerland, perfected his knowledge in foreign languages and studied law, a qualification which granted him a place in the diplomatic corps and a few years of true bliss in the French capital, which he loved as much as home.

Winter confessed with sorrow that her education was only basic, and made a rather unconvinced gesture instead of an answer, when the major remarked that education did not always make a person great. She raised her glass, drinking her wine silently, observing the irregular figure of her dinner partner through the glass and wondered what he actually wanted, evening after evening meeting with her, exchanging life stories, becoming strangely familiar...

Putting her glass back, she noticed two officers sitting at a table behind the major, a square-faced one with the figure of a wrestler and one who was the exact opposite, a scrawny obnoxious type, of those one would want little to do with. Apparently, the two of them had been watching her and the major, because when they saw Winter look at them, they both sent her way entirely impudent grins.

"Well, I think your peers over there would have a different opinion!" she commented with a great dose of self-sarcasm.

The major turned to see who Winter was referring to. He slightly stood up from his seat to greet them, and so did they. Then the major turned to her and said with a perfectly ironic smile: "I can assure you, these two display the same disdain for anyone they set eyes on, even each other!"

At the major's remark, Winter lightheartedly chuckled, but when he explained the big man was *Standartenführer*[32] K., the senior commander of the Security Police and, officially, the major's boss, while the other was his sidekick in the Gestapo, *Kriminalrat*[33] Blut, the right man at the right place as his name suggested, 'blut' meaning 'blood', Winter had to admit that she found nothing amusing about mocking two of the most dangerous people in the city. The major agreed rather reluctantly. It was deeply disturbing, he contemplated, that such individuals would find themselves in positions of power and influence. He recalled that when he was requested to join the Waffen-SS on his return to Berlin after the battle of France, the very hearing of the second synthetic had caused him an impulsive desire to refuse. In the *Wehrmacht*[34] there was little respect for the SS and it was not due to prejudice. However, he was persuaded that the armed division of the SS was a select military unit formatted for special operations and tough missions. And it was true, that his men had fought bravely, and no one would dare say that these men were in the slightest likeness of cretins like Blut, who had climbed in rank simply by befitting a particular profile considered suitable for this role, while men like those he had fought side by side with were abandoned to the hell of the eastern front, where they had to battle more than other men; they had to battle the wrath of nature and God himself.

"Excuse me, I'm sorry to interrupt!"

The frost was exhausting. The German uniform was not designed for this kind of cold and we had been sent there completely unprepared, arrogantly dressed in our designer uniforms, only to meet the kind of ice that could freeze Hell itself. Woollen coats buttoned to the neck, noses red and running; he brought me a cup of hot brew and a dispatch from the fatherland, dreadfully waited to see my reaction to it. There was more and more bad news lately, but this time... God had, at last, cast His gaze upon us, even in that inhospitable land of the damned. I thought of my friend in the High Command with relief and gratitude, and I was glad to share the news with my soldier, who could hardly believe it.

"We are moving? ... "

I nodded at the memory of colourful images and joyful times. A life so fulfilling, condensed in just a few years! And in the years that followed, like the blink of an eye, an entire lifetime had passed by!

"... Don't you want to know where to?"

Oh, but he didn't care where we were being sent. Like myself, he only wanted to get out of that cursed part of the world. I told him in small doses to feed his curiosity: "To France! To Paris!"

If he were not afraid that his dry lips would tear up, he would scream happily with mouth and eyes wide open. Instead, he licked his lips many times and only simpered. Happiness was shining through him! It shone brighter than the white sky that hung like a piece of heavy metal above us.

"... There are beautiful girls in Paris, aren't there, Herr Sturmbannführer?"

He was a twenty-year-old boy. His face was icy white, like everything around. Only his eyes remained blue, light blue, like the spring sky of the fatherland, like a cloudless Parisian morning, just before the smells of steaming coffee and freshly baked croissants claimed your undivided attention. I smiled at him, discarding the obligation to be stern which hierarchy dictated. I was feeling like a humble soldier myself–a twenty-year-old chap, just as impatient to leave that frigid hell. I patted his cheek; he almost cried.

"Yes, Peter! There are beautiful girls in Paris! Beautiful... and plenty!"

Peter's laughter echoed through the plain. It had been a long time since a sound like that was heard! Other sounds overwhelmed the inhospitable river bend[35]; sounds that stretched for miles in the vast expanse of ice, dispersing thoughts, feelings, our very souls.

"Go on! Go tell the others and ask the signalman to come! Let them know we're ready before they change their minds!" He flew like an eagle. Even out of fear for his life, I had never seen the boy run so fast.

The brew had iced in the cup. I could almost see my breath rime. The damn clock began its ticking again, shortly followed by the voice of the loudspeaker, that metallic flat voice with the indicative accent, which swept across the land, harder than the harshest winter.

Tick-Tock, Tick-Tock...

"Every seven seconds, one of you German soldiers dies!"

Tick-Tock, Tick-Tock...

"Surrender to the red lions!"

Tick-Tock, Tick-Tock...

"Otherwise, Stalingrad will be your mass grave!"

The major's narration moved Winter. She also felt warm enough to take his hand in hers and they remained silent with the feeling of touch and the aftermath of memory.

"But you are here now, you are strong and you have so much power!" Winter consoled him and the major replied that power was like fire: it had to be handled with care. "Oh, but a man like you runs no risk of being seduced by it!" she asserted spontaneously, and the major sat back and smiled.

"And what exactly is a man like me, in your opinion?"

Winter did not expect such a forthright question and was taken by surprise. She looked at him straightforwardly and felt she wanted to give him an honest answer. Of all the adjectives she could think of, however, none seemed appropriate to portray her true idea of him, without implying any kind of intention to flatter him.

"Well, you are..."

The timing could not have been better for the waiter to appear in order to pick up their dishes and bring a platter with cheese for them to accompany their drink. The major's eyes gleamed a smile and he poured some more wine into the glasses.

"Let's talk about you, Miss Winter Pale Dupont!"

Winter impulsively asked him not to call her by the name 'Dupont' and her request reasonably made the major enquire why.

"Because..."

Winter thought back. She would not know where to begin in order to explain how deeply resentful she felt towards that man, who officially called himself her step-father, but had absolutely nothing to do with a father, not even to his own children. It was a pity the twins had never met a father like hers used to be. How different life would have been if her father had been alive!

"My father was a shoemaker, the finest in his district," she recounted, with the voice of the warmest affection. "He loved his craft, and he was great at it–his reputation brought his little shop at London Bridge customers from all over town. And he had many friends. They often came to our house with their wives and children. Ah, those Sunday barbecues were like no other. Life was good for us then. We were so happy, it now seems impossible that it should last. And it didn't!" She paused and sighed, lowered her eyes and nervously played with the nails of her fingers. Her mind flew to that gloomy afternoon, when someone told them Father had died. All alone he was in his shop; it was a customer who found him lying behind the counter. The doctor had said his heart had failed him and Winter could hardly grasp the meaning of this phrase: how could a heart such as Father's have failed? What was to be expected of whatever was good in this world, if a heart like his could fail? "He was... he was the cornerstone of our lives, my father! When he was gone, everything fell to pieces... My mother tried really hard to keep things together, but she knew little about the business and soon that was lost, too. All we had left was the family house and my mother went out looking for work. Fortunately, she had some skills; she got a job in a trading company and we made a living. I missed my mother, because she travelled a lot, and I stayed with the family of my father's best friend. You see, my parents had no other family but each other and these people were the closest thing to it we had... They were good to me, they were! But, you know... a child always needs a family of its own ...!"

She saw the major nodding in understanding and felt curious in what way he found her story interesting, for what reason. Then she remembered the conversation had started at the 'Dupont' part of her last name. Surely, if Christian was the lowlife she knew him to be, it would not seem impossible that the major was not completely unfamiliar with this individual–perhaps it was really him he wanted to know about. Winter never meant any harm to others, but Christian, well, she would gladly see him rot in a German dungeon. A malignant smile came to sit on her lips, which soon turned rueful and grim. The slum of *Rue Goubet* seemed abandoned, Louis had told her, when he had gone, in her stead, to seek her family out. And she could very well never see them again, if they had moved away, God knows where in this vast city. She sighed heavily and prayed it would, at least, be for the better. "... My mother met Christian on one of her trips, Christian Dupont." she continued vaguely looking at the major who expected to hear more. "I didn't like him from the beginning, it's true, but he had my mother convinced he could help us, that he wanted to. I gave her my consent, and she married him. We sold the house, paid our debts, saved what was left for a new start. Christian was supposed to be running a small business in Paris; and so, we came to France!"

Her face twisted in a dark expression, anger mixed with sadness. She remembered these first few months of disillusionment, their struggle to keep their heads above water and to maintain their sanity, while nothing, nothing could mend their emotions, their regret of leaving home, their sorrow for the curse that had befallen them and overturned everything they used to take for granted.

"It wasn't long before both my mother and I realised Christian would be the doom of us. But it was already too late. We had moved away, our savings were gone, we were in a foreign country, and it didn't care much about us aliens. When he took us to live in that hovel in *Villette*, it seemed like our fate was sealed. The only exception was the time when my mother worked at the *Hôtel Lutetia*. But that didn't last long either. The war came, and soon, so did you people!"

She lowered her eyes to hide her ambivalent feelings and the hostility which impulsively sprang inside her against the major's kind, although not necessarily against him in particular–that was clear enough to her for some obscure reason. And yet, if the Germans had not come and her mother had not been dismissed from her hotel job, things could have ended up differently for her: she would probably never have left home, she would not have found herself at 'The Golden Doe', this new life would not have been offered and she would never have met René or the major. And how was that a good thing? she pondered in the most disapproving manner. She had saved her own skin and had completely abandoned a self-sacrificing mother and the twins, whose only resort for a tender hug and kiss goodnight was her...

"... Winter? Winter?"

She raised her tearful eyes to carefully look in his gaze. It was filled with sympathy normally nonequivalent to his function, which was something that always confused her. She was feeling an awkward obligation to tell him anything he asked for, but there was also something comforting about his interest in her. Rarely did she have the opportunity to talk about her past or about her feelings, and there he was, a major of the SS, yet sometimes she felt like she could just pour her heart out to him and not regret it one bit. Perhaps it was this strange intimacy between them. Otherwise, he was just great at what he was doing.

"You want me to go on!" she uttered in a rather dry tone and the major replied with an affectionate hum. "Why? Who wants to know?

Fred or *Sturmbannführer* von Stielen?" she asked with a boldness deriving from that same equivocal feeling.

Her question attacked the major rather unexpectedly, but he was used to maintaining his composure, so he leaned back in his seat and lit a cigarette, ambiguously asking in return: "What do you think?"

In her emotional turbulence, Winter failed to read the evasiveness in the major's reply and shook her head to declare ignorance.

"I don't know!" she murmured, deeply immersed in herself. "I'd rather not think anything! You can't be disappointed if you have no expectations!"

"That's true!" the major admitted, breathing out heavily. "But how easy without them to lose your way, take a completely different path than the one you initially intended!" he added with genuine concern.

Winter grimaced bitterly, deliberately turned her face away: "While I was still at home with my mother, Christian threatened to send me to work with her at the cabaret. You see, the cabaret may not have been the best solution, but it put food on our table, clothes on our backs, gave us treatment in our sickness, and my mother made the choice, that, one way or another, we should survive. She gave up every bit of herself for us, but she would never have it for me. When it came down to that, she'd rather see me gone; and that's how I left... Then, I found myself at 'The Golden Doe'. So, I think I know enough about how easy it is to lose your way, as I'm sure you'd agree!"

The major seemed to empathise, and he extended his hand onto hers, leaning closer to her, his smile warm, his eyes even warmer: "Don't bitter yourself anymore!" he urged her with a voice as gentle as his touch. "You saw the ugly face of life only too soon, but you stood strong, stronger than many. I admire you and respect you for that!"

His words made Winter quiver, and she gaped with astonishment, unable to find a proper response. No one had ever told her they admired her, and she had never felt worthy of anyone's respect. She had created an improved image of herself; could that really be enough for her to change what she had been? She looked at the major exactly as he was looking at her: a vocal and direct look. She had never felt powerful enough to look at anyone this way; anyone but him.

Their dessert arrived, forcing them to resume an appropriate distance. They drank the remaining wine without words and enjoyed a delicious *Rote Grütze*[36]. Then the major sat back in his chair, lit another cigarette and gazed at her from behind the puffs of his smoke.

"You spoke frankly, Winter, at least that's what I would like to believe!" he told her seriously.

"Of course, Fred!" she hurried to attest, but the stern expression on his face refrained her from any further effusive manifestations.

"So, I would like to be as frank and plain with you!" he continued and Winter nodded, feeling she should prepare to hear something rather unpleasant. "There is something troubling me, something you've never talked to me about; and I can't help wondering if it has been deliberate or not!"

Winter felt disquieted by the change in the major's tone, and an ear-splitting alarm started ringing in her head, which brutally dissolved all the proximity she had felt and replaced it with a nasty counterpart. Still, she quickly cleared her mind and appeared willing to explain anything he wanted.

"I understand full well that you are familiar with René Martin!" he stated with undisputable certitude. "What I don't know is the nature of your association!"

Although quite prepared for combat, Winter felt exposed to his bluntness. It was pointless to deny knowing René Martin, and she tried to remember the story she had told Molnich, the translator, quickly examining it for its credibility. No, the major would see right through such a blatant lie. A distorted version of the truth might be better, a version she would even prefer herself...

"I met René Martin when I left home. He found me unconscious somewhere in the street, he took me in, offered me a place to rest. And then we parted. Sometime later, I met him again at the train station, all by chance. We sat together, we talked. He said he had been thinking about me, that he liked me and, if I wanted to, we could ... But, you see, by then, I was at 'The Golden Doe' and it had been... I couldn't be with him if I didn't tell him the truth about me, but I couldn't do that. I never... I never quite knew how I did it myself; how could I explain it to another ... Then, one day, I stopped by his shop. It wasn't that I expected anything, it was just ... I was very fond of him. It had been impossible for me to think about a man without feeling disgusted, but he... When Klaus Molnich told me he was arrested, I was so upset I could think of nothing else for days. And when I saw him again, freed and safe from harm...I don't know what I was thinking; I actually think I wasn't thinking at all! I just ran to him, no reason, no intent... "

Winter remembered every single instance of her with René and admired how a few minor omissions and a bit of overstressing some aspects of the truth at the expense of others could alter the entire picture and change it into something so harmless, romantic even. She brought her eyes to the major's interrogative expression and felt sad and sorry. She wished she did not have to lie to him, but they could not both be winners in this game.

"He is your lover then?" the major deduced with a gravelly, toneless voice.

"No, no, we never...!" she hurried to assure him with a fearful laughter. "I never meant to suggest anything of the kind! I think it was more like girlish daydreaming!" she admitted, able to be honest about this part, at least. "But I guess I must have given the wrong signals. What he thought, what he said ...!" And, as if she had suddenly realised a tragic mistake, she added: "You saw him, didn't you? You saw him at 'The Golden Doe' tonight!" The major confirmed her conclusion with a nod. Winter smiled bitterly and regretfully left her head rest on her hand, heaving a sigh: "Oh, Fred!" She closed her eyes tightly, and this time it was not a pretense of grief that she felt at the thought of him forming a poor opinion of her or having little else to do but mistrust her. Then, she looked at him again and she sensed a strong attachment, which made her feel even more guilty, but more resolute about putting an end to his skepticism. "... He asked me to give up everything and go with him. I couldn't say yes!" she lied without blinking an eye. "I have a settled life, and he's been in trouble with the Police. I can't be part of this. I'm lonely so very often, but, more than anything, I need to be safe. He didn't like it, he left angry... I can't say I really mind!" She faintly smiled at him. She reached for his hand, squeezed it tight. "Forgive me, Fred!" she impassionedly apologised. "If I never told you anything about it, it was because I was afraid you might misunderstand! Our friendship is valuable to me! I wouldn't want to lose it!"

The major appeased her with a sympathetic smile. Winter's explanations made sense, the facts matched, her priorities agreed with him for the time being, so he chose to maintain a heedful attitude and avoid any more disturbing talk for the rest of the evening.

They were both caught unawares, however, as soon as they came out of the restaurant, where a captain from the Intelligence Service, one of the major's staff, had just arrived to bring some greatly disturbing news. Winter could not fully comprehend the conversation, but she did get one particular phrase: '*Klaus Molnich ist tot*'. If she had heard it right, if it were true... She looked to the major for confirmation. His face was dark as pitch, his eyebrows pulled down, his lips pressed tightly together. There would not be one muscle in his body that was not tense at that particular moment, Winter sensed, and she made a defensive step back, watching him unfold the piece of paper the captain had given him and read it only to become more infuriated.

Apparently, the captain had informed the major that there had been another attack and that Klaus Molnich was shot dead leaving his lodgings. But what was more, the captain had said, a little uncertain as regards his own good, bearing the role of the messenger to what would obviously mean as much as open war for the major, there was a note clenched in the translator's fist, a note addressed to the major, signed and sealed:

"*Mark my words, von Stielen. You will always live in my shadow.*

René Martin"

Winter looked at the major in bewilderment to discover that he was looking back at her with a cloudy gaze, behind which there was surely a thunderstorm raging. Then, he expressed a simple apology for having to leave her so suddenly and he entrusted her to Heinz, his personal driver, to safely return her to 'The Golden Doe'. Winter watched him rush off in the captain's military jeep and her heart pounded with the fearful conviction that, whatever had happened, whatever there was in that note, it could not but, somehow, involve her, too.

12

Skeletons in the closet

The morning sunrays, slapping Winter's eyelids open, only added to the discomforting feeling of an impending calamity with which she had fallen asleep the night before. She got out of bed reluctantly, washed and dressed herself mechanically. Her throat felt sore, her head heavy, and she doubted the coffee substitute they had in the kitchen would be of any relief. Downstairs, she found Georgette washing the dishes and Pierre tidying up the shelves. She was not in the mood for talk, but she asked, anyway.

"Where are the others?"

Michelle and Andrée had gone to see their aunt and would not be back until late in the afternoon. For the sisters of the dancing ensemble, it was their first day off, so they were probably also not expected to return before they absolutely had to. As for the boys of the orchestra, they would not show up for the usual morning rehearsal, because the bass and accordion needed repair, and Louis would have to stay home and go over some new musical scores.

Winter did not really care for so many details. She took her beverage and a piece of bread, and went to sit down by the window, hoping to feel better watching the sunshine and the street. To no avail. She went over and over the previous evening and the more she thought about it, the more inevitable it seemed that a catastrophe was coming, one of titanic proportions.

She was now certain she did not want to see René Martin again. This man was an explicit threat. And yet, she had dreamt of him for so long, there had been moments when she so intensely remembered his sparking gaze, his touch on her arms, the sensation of his face bending over to kiss her, that it felt like trying to rip off one of her limbs, should she attempt to draw herself away from him. He was like a catalyst within her–and he had tried so little. Imagine if René ever made it his goal to have her! If the major had not been part of the equation, everything might be different, she thought. She did not want to lie to him, and it was not because she was afraid of him. She did not trust him completely, but she was not afraid. René, on the other hand... He was a frightful man. He could erupt like a volcano and drag anyone in his way through his burning lava.

"What's wrong?" Georgette sat across from her. "You don't look too well!"

"I slept so poorly!" Winter confessed and sighed deeply.

"What's troubling you?" the girl asked with tender interest.

Winter shook her head and sighed once more. Georgette was a good friend, she had proved it many times. She wanted to trust her, open her heart to her.

"It's probably the news about Klaus Molnich!" she rationalised, very much aiming to convince herself above all others. "When someone you know dies, don't you feel like a part of you is also gone?"

Georgette seemed surprised: "We were all shocked to hear about it last night, but I never imagined you two were so close!"

"We weren't!" Winter hurried to explain, rather defensively. "But I thought well of him. And he was always very sweet to me!"

Georgette reached out and gripped her hand in consolation.

"Come on, no more gloomy thoughts! Let's talk about something pleasant! A boyfriend, perhaps?" she urged, poking her teasingly. Winter smiled with resentment.

"That's another disaster!" she muttered as if to herself.

Georgette gestured in surprise and Winter wished she had kept her mouth shut.

"Was there a liaison that went sour?" Georgette asked in a conspiratorial tone, which, however, did not feel encouraging enough for Winter to answer. "Was it Louis?" she insisted, only to receive an expression of vehement denial. "Another?" Georgette pursed her lips like a complaining child. "And you told me nothing!"

Winter shook her head and knew in her mind that it was greatly advisable to keep her worries her own, but she was in such need of comfort that she would clutch at straws in order to even lightly ease her anxiety.

"Tell me, Georgette, was the major here long before I went to see him yesterday?"

Georgette looked thoughtful for a moment and then she wagged a negation: "I don't think so! Why? Did anything happen?"

Winter sighed in complete anguish and shrunk into her seat, feeling threatened even to make the slightest hint of what was troubling her.

"Someone came to see me last night. He is... He was... I mean, it's a bit complicated...!" she began and felt bemused by the fact that she could hardly describe her relationship with René even to herself. "Anyway, there's been a terrible misunderstanding. The major saw him and I fear that he's got the wrong idea about the whole thing!" she carried on cautiously and Georgette smiled in confusion, gesturing that she did not understand. "Well ..." hesitated Winter, but then leaned over towards Georgette to whisper in strict confidence: "... the man who came to see me is not exactly on friendly terms with the authorities!"

"Oh!" Georgette uttered with a spontaneous frown. "Really, I didn't know you were involved with such people!" she added and pulled away in what Winter interpreted as marked disfavour.

"That's the point; I'm not!" she categorically asserted. "I never have been and I never want to be! But, you see? Even you misjudged me! I don't dare think what the major made of it!"

Georgette seemed to share Winter's worries momentarily, but then she read all the terror and remorse on her face and she smiled and took Winter's hands and affectionately caressed them.

"I'm sure the major is not one to rush to conclusions!" she reassured her. "Did you explain?" Winter nodded to confirm. "Then I don't think you should worry that much!" Georgette declared with certitude which Winter was eager to consider indisputable. She turned her eyes away and tried to recall the major's reactions to everything she had told him. Perhaps Georgette was right, perhaps he had believed her, perhaps he wanted to. "You really like the major, don't you?" Georgette said, leaving Winter rather astonished and embarrassingly bereft of speech.

At that moment, Pierre's unattractive call resounded from upstairs and the girl stood up looking at Winter with an intriguing smile.

"It's a funny thing, how you sometimes get what you need from where it is least expected!" she stated with a wink and hurried up to Pierre's apartment before he called her a second time. Winter watched her go and wondered whether the comment was referring to her and the major or to Georgette herself and Pierre, of all people.

Eventually, the talk with Georgette had been quite relieving, she felt. In fact, she was even in the mood for a walk. She went up to her room to get her coat, and, as she was coming out again, she almost fell into Pierre, who seemed to have been standing outside her door somewhat undecided.

"What are you doing there?" she asked with an impetuous laugh, but Pierre did not look at all amused: "Are you going out?" he asked and Winter responded with a simple nod. "And what time do you intend to come back?" he asked again and once more Winter nodded she did not know. "Well, are you going to be late or not?"

"What's with the questions, Pierre?" Winter defiantly scowled at him, sensing something extremely unpleasant about his insistence, which was enough to spoil her fragile positivity.

"*Bon sang*[37]*!* Can't I just ask?" he screamed, raising a fist at her, to which Winter was ready to answer back with all the invectives she could think of, and there was a long list of them. Luckily, Georgette jumped in to save the day, and, as she escorted Winter to the exit, she felt an explanation was due.

"Please, don't mind him! He's expecting extra supplies, and ... you know how he is!" she said, and Winter thought this girl would find an excuse for Pierre even if she saw him strangle someone with his bare hands.

"Well, tell him he's an idiot! The supplier always comes on Thursdays and not Tuesdays!" Winter remarked scornfully and minced her last words, bewildered by Georgette's shush gesture.

"That's not him! This one's black market! That's why he got rid of everybody today!" Georgette confessed to her in a whisper.

Winter found the explanation quite satisfactory and very becoming her idea of Pierre. She stepped out into the small yard which separated the front door from the gate to the street, brushing her coat with her hands, as though any association with Pierre's trickery was like a thick layer of dust on her, dust that she impulsively felt the need to rid herself of.

Dust particles were floating inside a beam of sunlight coming from the office window. The ticking noise of the wall clock was keeping a near-silent tune. Cigarette; match; inhale; smoke. The double ringing of the telephone disturbed the quiet. The sole of a neatly polished boot stepped onto the sunny circle on the thick Louis-Philippe Aubusson carpet and stood next to its pair by the desk, a beautiful piece of furniture with artistic marquetry and gold-bronze decorations.

"Ja!"[38]

At the other end of the line, a pair of juicy red lips rushed to their whisper: "The midwife needs the doctor! The midwife needs the doctor!" And two soft hands with red nail enamel on the fingertips anxiously squeezed onto the receiver.

"... This is the surgeon! I told you not to call..."

A quick breath and a pause: "We're in labour. The stork is arriving two days early. I had no choice!"

"One baby?"

Another pause for safety: "Two, with all their dowry!"

The cigarette tip sizzled; exhale; smoke.

"... It will be tonight then! Make sure the babies sleep tightly in their crib until then!"

Pause. A hurried mutter: "I'll do my best!"

A click ended the conversation. A little inactivity followed, one that usually accompanied a moment of careful consideration. Then, the steps moved towards the door.

"Get the car ready, Peter!"

No sooner had he crossed the threshold than the soldier called in the command. The black car was standing by on *Rue Saint-Honoré*, before he had even stepped out of the marble decorated lobby of the *Hôtel du Louvre*. He got in and the driver glanced at him through the rear mirror, waiting for a destination.

"To the Gestapo!" he said, sitting back in the leather seat and watched the springtime aspect of the city turn gray: from cloud to smoke, from fossil to ash, iron and shadow by the end of the drive.

13

Underground

People. People walking down the streets, just as Winter. People who lived for today uncertain of tomorrow, committed to one thing in the morning and decided on another by nightfall; unable to be their own masters even in their resolution, because there was always something mightier, and it was called the unexpected.

Having proved incapable of maintaining the elated spirit with which she had left 'The Golden Doe', Winter drew her attention to the colourless images of their times. At the bus stop, a queue of at least twenty civilians made way for three or four soldiers to board; around a stall, some men were bargaining the price for a pair of shoelaces; a well-dressed gentleman was carrying a gramophone, probably off to sell it at the flea-market of *Saint Ouen*, a man in a sandwich board was advertising the new film at the *Moulin Rouge* cinema; at the edge of the pavement, under the scrutiny of two soldiers, a woman and a child, an acrobat was balancing on a weird shape constructed with four chairs, placed one on top of the other; soon the soldiers exchanged money– someone must have won the bet. A military jeep roaring with its waving triangular flag reminded Winter that the colours dominating the city and their lives were restricted to three: red, white, and black.

Never before had she felt so disturbed by the combination of these three colours.

A honking vehicle having just passed by her gave her a good scare, and she came to realise her whereabouts, not at all surprised. The criminal always returned to the scene of the crime. Impulsively, she hid behind a wall of the *Comédie-Française* on *Rue de Richelieu*. The line of tricolour flags hailed their predominance, a strongly persuasive propaganda rally of its own, on the first floor of the *Hôtel du Louvre*. There somewhere, on the fourth floor, above the 'du' of the sign, was the major's office. And, perhaps, he was there at that very moment, meditating on everything that was spoken the previous night and everything that took place afterwards, and he might even retrospectively question his decision to release René Martin, should he, in some way, be involved in Klaus Molnich's death, of which Winter's instinct was categorical. So why did he decide such as this? Why did he set René Martin free?

She chose to walk an entire circle around the *Palais Royal* garden, rather than risk being seen across *Place du Théâtre Français*. Wandering around, she found herself in front of the fountain of *Saint Michel*, the monumental statue of the archangel Michael defeating the devil. Winter felt she could not have been the only one whose faith had been severely afflicted by the hardships of reality. At one time, people believed in and revered God, and they invoked His saints, angels, and archangels for help and support. These days, there seemed to be a much stronger faith in man's own powers, but, as exhilarating as the ring to it might sound, it had not led the world wisely so far. Winter could not help wondering whether it was faith itself, defined as the quality of complete trust and confidence, which suffered the most in their times, regardless of whom or what it was channelled into: contemporary living called mainly for action, any action; action and reaction.

At that moment, someone shoved her in his haste, and Winter added rudeness to the many flaws of the human nature. But, only an instant later, she felt utterly baffled, as, instead of hearing the expected typical 'pardon', she heard something else, something strange, echoing like an obscure English: 'follow me'. Frozen up, she observed the figure in the long raincoat and bucket hat, which had already moved forward several metres. Sensing her halt, the figure turned around, its hands tucked in the coat pockets, its face hidden behind a muffler, but the eyes... Winter felt she had no choice but to follow.

He was walking fast down the main road. Winter walked at the same pace. He stood at a bus stop. Winter also stood there, a little to the side. The bus came, he got on it, and so did she. They sat diagonally across from each other, exchanged only one glance. The route was long, unknown to Winter. Within seconds, he sprang up and got off, and she hardly managed to slip through the door. He walked on without looking behind, and she proceeded along. Suddenly, he was gone. She looked around for him, but he just seemed to have vanished. Her head was spinning, a chill ran down her spine. What was she doing there? Why was she putting herself at risk? Had she not admitted to herself that very morning that she did not want to see René Martin ever again? Then, he came up from behind, grabbed her by the arm and, through a rusty iron gate, he pulled her into a secret interior, somewhere underground.

There were several flights of wet, slippery stairs, followed by a narrow corridor, and then a sunless chamber. He struck a match and lit an oil lamp. Eventually, he took off his hat, muffler and raincoat to reveal himself in full glory. She looked at him and admired the power he ever had to bedazzle and dumbfound her.

"I told you we'd meet again!" he said, gloating over her stupefied look. "You didn't expect it to be so soon, did you?" He took a step closer, stood in front of her, pampered her like a child. "You did well! Nobody followed us!" he remarked and gave her a kiss on her hair as a reward.

"How can you be so sure?" she panted, still trying to overcome the shock and awe of his presence. He responded with a confident smile and leaned over to kiss her, as simply as if they had known each other forever and been lovers for all eternity. Winter was once again taken aback and slipped away from him for fear that a kiss would completely overpower her and give him a message of consent she was not ready to grant. He turned his back to her, presumably looking for his cigarettes in his raincoat pockets.

"I could not get you out of my mind for a single moment since last night!" he stated in a stinging tone completely out of character for the content of his words. "I know you met with von Stielen after I left. He saw me, didn't he?"

He glowered at her, and Winter could see the existence of a peculiar rivalry in his eyes. She knew it was pointless to deny it.

"Wasn't that your intention?" she replied boldly, something which seemed to please him: "Yes!"

His plain affirmation hit Winter like a brick wall. She would rather he had attacked her with all sorts of silly excuses, any of which she would willingly accept, were it to ascribe to him the attributes of a normal man, a normal man with whom she could measure up and confront with equal chances. Not René. He was deviant and unpredictable; he was exceptional and extraordinary. Oh, she could easily adulate him, if she did not fear him so.

"What did you tell him about me?" he asked with a voice of unspoken anticipation and she simply answered: "I lied!"

René's face lit up. His eyes sparked, and the flame of the oil lamp trembled ardently inside their overflowing mere. He drew on to her, engulfed her in his arms. He rubbed his cheek against her hair, let out a fervent sigh. His face was warm and mellow as he stared long at her lips and then he bent over only to brush on them the silken sensation of his breath. Short of hers, Winter lowered her head, and, as soon as she felt the slightest release in the tension of his embrace, she once again escaped his magnetic force. The ambivalence of her feelings was tormenting, the frailty of her will dangerous. She examined the surroundings for distraction: the walls comprised several strata of different rock and the stone filling looked damp and moldy; in hollows opened on the vertical surfaces, bones and sculls were piled up creating a creepy décor; the air was dense with a smell of death and decay.

"What is this place?" she muttered, with an ominous disturbance in her stomach.

"It's the catacombs!" he replied, with no affectation. "You've never been here before?"

The answer was obvious, Winter thought, and her intuition warned her against the artlessness of his remark. "These bones..." she gasped.

"They belong to the people the Germans have executed!" he stated with his eyes fixed upon her, as if the executioner had been her. She gulped down a reasonable protest and the burden of an inexplicable guilt deformed her facial features. His baleful approach frightened her, his razzing giggle confused her. "Actually, that's not true!" he condescendingly confessed. "But they could be!"

"It's not funny, René!" she reacted with a stir of anger setting her heart on fire, and the temples of her head shook vigorously.

René did not show any sign of contrition for his poor joke: "No, it's not funny!" he attacked her. "Those hundred thousand corpses your friends make every day would be lucky to have their bones found and piled up like this one day; most of them will end up in anonymous mass graves, if they are fortunate enough to escape the furnaces of the concentration camps." His words felt like a whip, and she squeezed into a corner to protect herself when she saw him approach again. "Is this what you want to be part of?" He reached for her and she recoiled in fear that he might hit her, but he only took her by the arms and brought her closer to him. "I know there is a fighter in you. I saw it the very first time we met and I see it now through the anarchy in your head, behind the panic in your breast." He dug into her hair with his fingers and the feel of it seemed to absorb him completely. "You had the courage to lie to von Stielen; you'd be surprised at how much more you can do!"

Winter felt that her courage at the moment only sufficed for her to keep breathing the stuffy air of this hole. Weak to the knees, she leaned against the wall to rest, but the slimy feel to it made her withdraw and put on a face of disgust.

"Can we go out, please? I can't breathe in here!" she begged him, but he seemed to take her repugnance as a personal offense.

"What? Too grim for your taste?" he gushed ironically and moved away as though it was her reaction that repulsed him, and not the setting. "Forgive me, I forgot you now go about with the *crème de la crème*[39]. I hope your masters are pleased enough to throw you an occasional bone!"

"Stop it!" She raised her eyes to him, hurt more than she was insulted. "How can you speak to me this way? What I do, I do to survive. What else is there for me?"

"There is me! I'm here for you!" Winter looked at him, eyes wide open. There was a kind of urgency in the way he came to her, a firm conviction in his hands, placing them around her face, and a touch of despair in his voice as he said: "Come with me, Winter! It may not be paradise, but we will be free. You don't know what it's like, you've never tasted it. I'll give that to you; I can show you how to make life worth living!"

How could she not admire him for the courage he had to define his own destiny! How could she not marvel at his self-reliance, his belief in himself, which was stronger than she could ever dare dream of! Winter's eyes welled up, and a strong impulse overwhelmed her to just say yes.

"... I have dreamt it!" she admitted with a bittersweet pain. "Of you and me, our life together. And I have longed for you, for your touch, your kisses to be a promise that everything will be alright! But, I know... I'm not like you... I'm afraid of death... I want to live..."

"Live? Live?" The frown on René's face designated an express denial, perhaps, also a hint of incomprehension: "How is it possible to live in this gutter?"

"You don't have to remind me all the time!" Winter protested, suddenly recognising her delusion to think that there could ever be any kind of future between her and René, so dissimilar that they were and so unalike that their view of the world proved to be. "I haven't made the best of choices, but I wasn't exactly given many options!"

René's eyes turned to her like a thunderbolt. "Well, you are given one now!"

Winter gulped down a sob and hung her head down, shaking it

many, many times, with an exhausting feeling of futility and the distress of one who has broken out of prison only to run into a deadlock.

"I'm not cut out for this sort of life. This path you're walking is not for me!" she maintained with all the sincerity of her broken heart and she even made a few steps closer to him, desperate for him and hopeless about it.

He backed away, his face an impregnable wall, his eyes as hard as a nail: "But you are cut out for the sort of life you are leading! Is that what you're saying?"

"In God's name, René, what do you want from me?" she cried out in shame and despair.

He bit his lip and his top teeth exposed all the negation in him: "I want you to know who I am! And love me for it!" he raged, making it sound more like a reproach than an appeal.

Still, something glinted in the darkness of Winter's disappointment. It was only a twinkle, yet, with it, even this horrific hollow could be transformed into the fairyland of her childhood stories. She felt powerless and completely unfortified before this all-mighty word. Love him! Yes, she could probably love him and, with the power of that love, she could drag herself with him to the sewers, the catacombs, even the grave. But that would be her. She had no idea what his love was capable of.

"...And you?" she asked eagerly, looking at him directly in the eyes."... Can you love me for what I am?"

René's cheeks were drawn in, his eyelids twitched and his eyes had an uncanny shine inside their molten iron. "You'll change when you get away from this filth!" he asserted through the steel fence of his teeth. "You made a mistake. You will correct it!"

She averted her gaze, with the weight of a dream forever lost pulling down the edges of her lips. And, perhaps, with a bit of resentment, that she did not feel the obligation to correct any mistakes. Little had life been kind to her, and she had seen its hard face only too soon; perhaps, she needed someone to admire and respect her for it, not someone who asked of her even more sacrifices. She widely opened her eyes and held her breath in terror of what she was thinking. God forbid, if René could ever read her thoughts...

Spurred on by her timid reaction, which he interpreted as a tacit approval, he came to her, put his arms around her and held her tightly in his embrace. His breathing was heavy and laboured, indicating an effort to harness the wildest of his sentiments. He brought his fingers to her chin, lifted it up, looked deep into her. Then he kissed her and this time she did not resist.

"It's alright!" he whispered to her, his lips leaving their passionate marks on her face, like the male animal marks its territory. "You'll see! You'll see I'm right..."

Winter did not know what she would see, whether René was right or wrong, whether she could change and become a completely different person for his sake. All she knew was that, right now, she wanted to see the light again. And when she felt the breeze of fresh air on her face, its vigour bringing strength back to her limbs, she did not care about anything; little could she remember what René had said or not said, when and with what words he had left her, or how she had found her way back from this edge of the world where he had stranded her. She could breathe. It was nice to be able to breathe–one only understood the value of whatever they arbitrarily considered their own, when they were close to losing it. Winter was just beginning to realise the value of breathing.

It was well after five when she returned to 'The Golden Doe' to find absolute quiet. The black marketer must have come, everything must have gone according to Pierre's plans, and now he and Georgette would be sleeping, not at all unlikely, together. Winter herself was feeling exhausted, but also too disquieted for a proper rest. She would gladly get out and disappear if there were a remote possibility to escape her troubles, if she believed there was anywhere on this earth she could find peace.

She was forced to get up from bed, long after the noise of the club had signalled the beginning of yet another night of false gaiety and artificial merriment at 'The Golden Doe', the one available substitute for the authentic meaning of life, whatever that might be. Well, perhaps René was right, and none of the so-called joys of life could be truly enjoyed without freedom, but Winter seriously doubted that freedom alone could be sufficient either. Because there was another condition that needed to be satisfied, one she could not put a name to, but she sensed it, it had to be like when knowing one is at the right place at the right time, a feeling of being at home in oneself. She had thought she would feel that way with René, but this day had proved she could never...

She straightened her outfit, took a deep breath and looked in the mirror: "Everything will be fine!" she murmured to her reflection, but it was not convinced.

Then the door of her room opened violently and two soldiers barged in with their weapons pointed at her. They pulled her out by force, shouting in their rough language: *"Raus! Schnell!"*[40]

A German officer was standing at the top of the stairs and, in her befuddlement, she saw about a dozen soldiers running down the aisle and up to Pierre's apartment. Down the main hall, there was complete panic. Furious voices, screams, people running. The girls of the dancing ensemble were crouching in a corner of the stage, while Michelle and Andrée were hugging each other, with Georgette at a small distance, giving them a grave look.

"Louis!" Winter saw a group of soldiers surrounding the orchestra boys and pushing them violently towards the exit, beating and kicking them in their attempts to resist. Then, one soldier hit Louis with the stock of his rifle and he fell down. They picked him up, his face covered in blood, and pulled him to the door, where another officer was supervising. Pierre was nowhere to be seen. Shots were heard from the upper floor. Someone fired a few shots among them in the main hall, as well. They all ducked down for protection. Between the front tables, behind the maze of the wooden legs of the chairs, Winter discerned Petit François lying on the floor in a strange position. She gasped and her eyes opened wide. Out of pure instinct, she escaped from the soldiers' grip and she ran towards the boy, repeatedly calling out his name. She knelt beside him, lifted his body in her arms; a blood-stained wound in his chest was draining the life out of him.

The little boy's body, Winter's screams, her tears, the blood on her hands, on her clothes, on her face, nothing moved her pursuers, who came up to her in fury to drag her away. They were all thrown in the back of a truck, silent,–not even the eyes could speak anymore. There were also two other men along with them, strangers, fair hair, fair complexion; they did not speak either, but they were the only ones with a straightforward gaze and a resolute expression, fully prepared for anything might come, even for the firing squad.

The basement of the Gestapo building was dark and smelt of death, like the catacombs where René had dragged Winter that very morning. They locked the girls together in a cell and took the men elsewhere. A skylight high on one wall brought a little night light into their prison. There was the sound of sobbing; long exasperated sighs; occasionally there would be creaking and banging, but there would be no voices, as though not a single human soul existed in this prison other than them. Georgette was sitting at a distance, near the door; her figure could hardly be distinguished in the darkness. Winter could not help thinking she was the only one to know how this had happened. The disappearance of them all that morning, Pierre's unrest, the two strangers. It all made sense now, and Georgette's part in it could not but be an active one. If only she could go to her, tell her a few words of comfort, let her know she considered her a friend and she would miss her. Unexpectedly, Winter's feelings were numb. She did not even feel fear anymore.

The clinking sound of the key inside the lock drew all their attention to the door. In the dull light of the corridor, a low-ranking officer with his double-breasted hat appeared, two soldiers following him closely. The officer ordered Georgette to get out. She got up slowly and crossed the threshold with her head down, too shameful or remorseful to turn back and look at the rest of the girls. The door closed again, and the key turned twice.

"Dear God, please help us!" one of the sisters of the dancing ensemble whispered.

After that, time passed even more slowly in the cell with the dark skylight. Glassy eyes, empty minds, paralyzed limbs. They did not know if it had been only a few minutes or hours since Georgette had been taken away. At some point, finally, a sound was heard. But it was horrible, a horrible sound that made them quiver. A human scream. They got up in anguish, grabbed each other by the hands. Their eyes could not see through their tears.

"We're all going to die!" Michelle cried and fell into Andrée's arms.

Winter wanted to cry too, but something eerie held back her tears at the last moment. She stiffened and backed up until she reached the cold and damp wall. She did not want to die!

The first light of day, which pierced the skylight, brought them no consolation. When they heard the key in the lock again, their agony instantly spiked. Who would be next? The officer with the double-breasted hat and the two soldiers came through the prison door again. The officer was holding a list and, without delay, he started calling out the names that were written there. The girls, hearing their names, got up, glanced at each other and approached the soldiers, certain of their ill fate. Winter got up, too, waiting her turn, but the officer finished reading without calling her. The girls were driven out, and the door slammed closed, leaving Winter alone with a suffering that was worse than dying.

14

The martyr

"Well, *Monsieur* Morné, you must be very comfortable in this position or you would decide to talk to us no?" The scrawny obnoxious figure, which would hardly get noticed but for the uniform and its overbearing arrogance, turned to his prisoner and sneered. "No?" he asked again with fake surprise. "By all means, *Monsieur* Morné, let us get you down! All you have to do is tell us a name. A name and your torment ends here."

Pierre Morné did not speak at all. His head hung only a couple of feet above the floor, his hands were bound with a rough rope which stretched all the way to his ankles, suspended as he was from a heavy chain on the ceiling, upside down like a slaughtered lamb. The officer lowered to one knee and tilted his head to one side to observe his victim's face,–a livid face where even the bruises were no longer visible.

"One name; or two, if you'd please!" the officer whispered next to his ear. Annoyed by Pierre's silence, he got up and struck him in the nose with the rubber truncheon he was holding. He paced around the room, patting his palm with the tip of the truncheon; occasionally, he hit it against the side of his boot and Pierre would flinch at the whooshing noise and slap every time, despite his incapacity. "I was thinking..." the officer uttered with pure pretense "...hanging up-side-down like this cannot be too healthy for a man. How long could it be before it becomes seriously dangerous? Two, three hours? A day? Two days? ... Do any of you know?" he addressed the two thugs he had with him, and when they answered with a negative expression, he turned again to Pierre: "You wouldn't have *that* information, would you, *Monsieur* Morné?" He shook his head to mockingly respond on behalf of his disabled prisoner. "Then I guess we'll just have to wait and see exactly when your eyes pop out of your head."

"Get me down... please!" Pierre muttered eventually.

"Oh, I would love to do that!" the officer replied with fake compassion. "But I'm afraid I need something in return." Pierre once more shut his mouth and his eyes in search of strength and courage. "So be it! I have plenty of patience and time, which is more than I can say about you!" the officer scorned and made himself comfortable in a chair, lit a cigarette and smoked it at his leisure. Tranquil as a dead man, he smoked the cigarette down to its butt; then he checked his fingernails for dirt; he blew some moisture from his breath onto the fingers of the left hand, polished them onto the fabric of his tunic. "It is a pity, though, that you should take all the blame." he expressed at some point, as though talking to himself. "A completely useless sacrifice! You see, your girlfriend has already told us it was you who called all the shots. And those chappies, your virtuosos I mean ... well, not very brave boys, I dare say!... Of course, you understand what that means!" He got up from his seat and came down to his knee again to make certain there was enough stress on his next utterance: "They are getting off the hook and you are getting the gallows!"

He looked at Pierre with the self-assuredness of a man who had put this tactic to the test a million times and had always proved it to be fully effective–one tended to get terribly sensitive against the betrayal of his own people.

"You must help me help you, Pierre!" he told him and his tone sounded almost sympathetic. "I know this is all nonsense, but if I can't prove it, I will have no choice but to lay full responsibility on you!" He put his fingers on Pierre's chin, bent over and looked at him with almost soft eyes. "You don't want to die, Pierre!" he whispered to him, absolutely certain of this universal truth. "You want to go home, return to your business, get your life back on track. Isn't that what you want?"

Pierre's tears were enough of a response–tears, which coursed down from his bruised eyes to the forehead and dripped on the dirty floor: "Get me down!" he muttered with his smashed voice.

The officer gestured at the thugs, ordering them to unhang the prisoner, and so they did. With his arms and legs still tied up, they put him in a chair and one of them even gave him a few sips of water.

"And now, I'm listening!" the officer stated with clear demand.

Pierre lowered his head and gulped over and over, panting: "It was not me, I swear it!" he wheezed. "I don't know what the others said and why! The boxes I brought in today contained food supplies, not weapons. And the men in the apartment are relatives travelling to Bordeaux. You have to believe me!"

"Ah, but I won't have any more of this bullshit!" the officer squeaked and landed a furious strike on Pierre's head with his truncheon. "If you think you can joke with me, I will show you! I will show you!" He made a nod to one of the thugs and he approached to cut the ropes from Pierre's hands. "The right one!" he ordered in a cold, flat tone.

Pierre tried to resist, but he had no chance against the huge and strong thug who had him firmly in his grip. The other one of the officer's sadistic buddies dragged a wooden table closer, on which the former placed Pierre's hand and trapped it between his palm and the flat surface.

"Dr. Metzger!"

A second officer in a white medical coat stepped out from a dark corner. He was holding a small leather doctor's bag, which he lay on the table and opened wide to expose its dreadful contents: forceps of different types and sizes, pliers and pincers, steel dissecting scissors and knives, syringes, thread and needles. Of all the items, Dr. Metzger chose a pair of pliers. He looked at the officer to get permission to continue and then, without the slightest sign of hesitance, he grabbed the little finger of Pierre's hand and uprooted its fingernail.

Pierre screamed in pain and terror, and the sight of blood flowing from the root of the nail made him nauseous. He leaned to the side and vomited. Disgust and contempt were traced on the officer's face; he took a folded handkerchief from his pocket and brought it to his nostrils, while the thug was lifting Pierre upright only to punch him so hard that Pierre almost lost his sight. He flopped down on the floor and the officer came to press the sole of his black boot on Pierre's face and rub it in his own spew.

"I'm giving you this last opportunity to give me what I want! After this, you'll be begging me to stop, but it will be too late!" he said with all his malevolence and nodded at the thug to put the prisoner back in the chair. They threw a bucket of water in his face and the officer lifted Pierre's chin with the tip of his truncheon. "So, I'm asking you again: who supplied you with the weapons and what was the plan of the two British?"

Pierre was shaking, but he did not speak, and the officer commanded that another nail of his hand was removed. Pierre's horror, his cries and screaming would crack even the hardest stone, but the German did not even have that for a heart. With his fingertips bleeding profusely, with a soul that could not stand any more torture, Pierre fainted.

The officer and the doctor exchanged glances. When the doctor made sure that the victim was still alive, he took a small bottle of smelling salts from the pocket of his medical coat, twisted its cap off and swayed it in front of Pierre's nose. Before long Pierre was conscious again and he raised his eyes to his torturers, saw his hand bleeding and groaned. His head hung forward, silent tears wept from his eyes and his trembling lips only opened to whimper his pain, as the doctor dusted a wound seal powder on his bleeding fingers. Subsequently, Pierre's refusal to grant the officer his wish was followed by the uprooting of three more fingernails on his right hand.

The officer exhaled in disappointment and shook his head: "Well, we could go on like this forever, but I'm already bored and running a bit late on my schedule. Besides, I think this one really means to keep quiet, Dr. Metzger. What do you think?" he asked the doctor, who gestured an agreement. "Then, he might as well have an excuse for it!" he continued, and the doctor nodded affirmatively once again.

This time, the doctor looked in his medical bag and picked up a pair of curved forceps in one hand and a thin dissecting knife in the other.

"Ready when you are!" he claimed in the creepiest toneless voice.

"You see, *Monsieur* Morné..." the officer explained to Pierre, "... if you do not intend to talk to us, there is a body part you don't really need!"

Before Pierre could understand what the officer was telling him, a skillful headlock by one of the thugs completely immobilised him. Realising what they were about to do, he let out a scream and flopped around like a fish inside the thug's sturdy grip, begging them to with slurred words, coming out from a mouth which the other thug opened wide with strong cruel fingers, begging them to stop.

"I warned you that you would change your mind!" the officer preached with false regret. "It's just too late now!" And with a sharp look he commanded the doctor to proceed.

Pierre's pleadings were drowned by the doctor's hand in his mouth, which was trying to grab his tongue with the pair of forceps. When he finally did, he pulled it out and bent over to examine exactly where he was going to cut with his dissecting knife. Scared to his very bones, Pierre peed his pants. As he saw the urine dripping under Pierre's chair, the German took a step back, careful not to get his boots dirty and, with an abhorrent gawp at his victim's petrified gaze, he signalled the doctor to halt. He bent down to the level of Pierre's eyes.

"Are you going to talk?" he hissed. With as much freedom as his entrapped head allowed, Pierre nodded positively and, through his wide-open mouth, he repeatedly groaned 'yes'. "This is your last chance!" the officer cautioned. "I'm going to have your tongue removed, and, after that, your ears, your nose and everything that protrudes from your wretched body until you die! Do you understand?"

Pierre needed no more warnings. Without hope of redemption, with the fresh taste of the most beastly horror, with no wish but for no more pain, he fessed up to everything that he knew. The officer took paper and pencil, recorded the information and only after he had been completely satisfied, did he finally inform his associates that their mission was complete.

"And now, I should let you ponder on how you are going to face your friends, knowing you have stabbed them in the back!" were the officer's last words, venomous like a snakebite.

Barely maintaining consciousness, just enough to be certain that his torturer had no intention of harming him further, Pierre caught on to the rushed entrance of a soldier, who came up to the officer and urgently whispered something in his ear. The latter nodded and turned towards the cell door, straightening his hair and clothes. He stood upright, his face filled with a completely self-indulgent expression; the heels of his boots stomped vigorously, as he proudly raised into the air a perfectly outstretched right arm and straightened hand. The commander of the Security Police and *Sturmbannführer* von Stielen entered and reciprocated the salute, although less fervently.

"*Herr Standartenführer*, allow me to report that we are now in possession of the S.O.E. full plan and we have the name of their liaison and weapons supplier!" the officer announced with the proper amount of smugness. "It appears he has his hideout in an old cellar in Montparnasse and he goes about by the code name 'Seamstress', not unfamiliar to us, is it?" he hinted, turning a contemptuous gaze at *Sturmbannführer* von Stielen.

The Sipo commander nodded with satisfaction: "What about the others?" he asked and the officer turned his face away and his nose up to say: "They haven't talked yet! But they will!"

The commander seemed content and prepared to make his leave, when *Sturmbannführer* von Stielen meaningfully cleared his throat. The former was then obliged to return and say, although with no obvious dictate: "The council has approved the release of the women! See to it before morning!"

"...All the women, *Herr Standartenführer*?" the officer asked, with dissatisfaction he did not consider necessary to keep to himself.

"All of them, Blut!" the Sipo colonel commanded and stepped out with no further explanation. The two SS majors were left staring at each other, as if fighting a duel merely with their eyes.

"I noticed you were not at all surprised by the reference to René Martin, *Herr Sturmbannführer*! I assume you already knew or are you still trying to get a grasp of the association?" Blut indicated with all his sarcasm.

"Please, have the prisoner's wounds properly taken care of!" *Sturmbannführer* von Stielen replied, purposefully ignoring the remark. "*Polizeiführer*[41] O. requested that all prisoners should remain in good condition in case they can be of further use!"

Blut glared at him with pure disdain. "Of course!" he uttered with a sideways smile and watched *Sturmbannführer* von Stielen leave, after which, he closed the solid iron door of the cell with a gentle, perfectly controlled motion. "Chop them off!" he ordered the doctor, with his bloodthirsty and merciless gaze piercing through Pierre. "And then, we will take care of them properly!"

It took both thugs to pin Pierre down, as the doctor apathetically carried out the order and cut off the wounded fingers one by one. The dungeon quaked with Pierre's screams; they penetrated the iron door, cracked through the basement walls and spread like smoke in the corridors of this tyrannical building, reaching the farthest, darkest of its corners to impress sheer terror on the faces of all who had heard.

15

End of an era

It must have been late in the afternoon when Winter had finally crashed out in her cell and, now, the clanging of the keys in the lock sounded almost disturbing. It was dark again. Time had passed in grueling, insufferable anticipation. For a while, a beam of sunlight reached the dark basement, drawing a luminous rectangular shape on the opposite wall; little by little, it lost one of its corners, slowly becoming a triangle, and then it grew smaller and smaller until it completely disappeared. Soon, the daylight faded, and she had been abandoned in that damp cell, never more terrified of what was lying ahead. She opened her eyes expecting to see the man with the double-breasted hat again, but this time there was only one soldier standing by the doorway before a senior officer appeared in the dim light of the corridor.

"... *Herr Sturmbannführer*?" she uttered wishfully. The figure stepped inside and approached slowly.

"Nice try, *Fräulein*! But I'm afraid not!" a voice sounded, and Winter affirmed it could never have belonged to major von Stielen for reasons far beyond the harsh German accent. The officer came closer and a ray of the evening light shone on him. Winter could not fail to remember him, that formidable character from *'Chez Pierre'* with the same disdainful face and snide look. "Allow me to introduce myself. I am *Kriminalrat*

Erhard Blut of the Gestapo. In fact, I *am* the Gestapo!" he announced pompously, taking as many steps as necessary to reach her and offer his hand for her to get up.

The appalling attitude of the Gestapo major enabled Winter to refuse his help and get up on her own, albeit with great effort.

"Such extraordinary self-regard from you all at first!" he mocked. "And then you start the begging!" He came nose to nose with her and she felt the touch of his breath, tangy and sour like acid. He stared at her, from the chin to the lips and from the nose to her wailing eyes. "I would really like to see you beg, *Fräulein*!" he smirked and, with an imperative nod, he ordered her to follow.

He walked ahead and Winter walked behind him, with the soldier at her tail. They moved along a narrow corridor with a line of closed doors right and left. Three steps up, and then another long corridor. A strong odour of decay and chloroform filled the air. On their way, a door to the right was open, and Winter impulsively turned to look.

On the back wall, a chained man was hanging like a hunter's trophy, his body half-naked, his chest scarred with whip wounds, a bruised face whose features had been terribly disfigured. His legs were too weak to stand, his arm joints ready to snap off the rest of the body, one of his hands wrapped in a bandage soaked in blood. His tilted head, only the crown of thorns was missing.

At the sight of what she identified as Pierre, Winter gasped in horror. She looked away, lips tightly squeezed, eyes that could not hold back their tears, but she pushed herself not to burst out in sobs, for she did not want to give the German the satisfaction of seeing her break. He bent over and conceitedly observed her expression.

"Upset, are you? Unfortunately, *Monsieur* Morné did not decide to be cooperative until quite late!" he remarked with the tone of clear warning.

Winter held her breath and closed her eyes for strength. God have mercy on her, she prayed, because only a divine intervention could save her from the hands of this devil personified. The soldier pushed her with his rifle to move on, and she had to come face to face with the

Gestapo major's sinister smile. He would torture her to death and enjoy every minute, she thought, and shuddered.

They stopped in front of a closed door, which the soldier hurried to open. Blut turned to her and smiled arrogantly. "Please, ladies first!" he said and gestured accordingly.

She walked into the cell with her head held high, resolute not to satisfy his desire to beg, not even if she had to suffer the same fate as Pierre. She was seated in a chair facing a white interrogation lamp, whose light hit her painfully in the eyes. She put up her hand for shade and distinguished the Gestapo major standing at a short distance, stiff and still as a stone pillar. Before long, the soldier came to tie her hands behind the back of the chair and Winter had to turn her head to the side to avoid the gushing light. The rope gave a burning sensation to her wrists, and she knew this was only the beginning of her torment.

When the soldier had taken his place by the door once again, the Gestapo major came closer to her, brought his hand to her chin and raised it up to his scrutinizing gaze. Then he took a handkerchief out of his pocket, licked one end of it with his tongue and wiped clean all the spots of dried blood still on her face, neck and bosom from the previous night. Though disgusted by the touch of his saliva on her skin, the sight of Petit François's blood on his handkerchief felt like hubris, and she pulled her face away with all the indignation his every move, gesture, even his very existence, whipped up in her.

"Please!" he reacted in a tone which had absolutely nothing to do with a polite request. "Let me take care of you! Rarely does one see a beauty like yours in these dungeons, *Fräulein* Vinter Pal Dupont!" he uttered and, with a tight grip on her cheeks, he brought her face back where he wanted it in order to continue his work.

Winter raised her eyes to him, her contempt and disgust measuring up to her fear, and the way he had vandalised her name gave her the courage to say in a daringly defiant manner: "My name... is Winter Pale!"

"Ah!" Blut exclaimed, seeming to be surprised for a moment, but then he smiled, as if he enjoyed the challenge, as though it was all a game to him, a game not worth playing unless against a worthy opponent. "So there is actually a spine in this one!" he commented with a sarcastic laugh and stood up straight, giving the impression he was going to abandon his loathsome occupation and go away. She did not even see it coming, his furious hand slapping her cheek so hard that it rocked her head and caused her to bite her lip. Her eyes welled up, sobs racked her chest, and she feared the bones of her neck would break at the force with which he grabbed her from the hair and pulled her head backwards. "I will teach you some respect!" he lashed out at her. "By the end of this night, you will have gained a completely different attitude, *Fräulein* Winter Pale!"

He left her in her terror and disappeared to a shadowy corner of the cell, his disappearance in darkness evoking the most horrendous premonition. The blow of the rubber truncheon against his boot whooshed a punch into her stomach. The buzz of the interrogation lamp drilled through her ears, its white light clouded her sight and her mind. Suddenly, there was a commotion. The soldier at the threshold of the cell door saluted somewhat startled by the unexpected visitor and a familiar voice ordered him to get out. Winter raised her head with a warm feeling of relief and tried to distinguish the whereabouts of major von Stielen.

The figure of the Gestapo major stepped out into the light. This time he did not bother to salute but came to stand in front of the major with the comfort and confidence of one who felt very much at home; he raised his cynical gaze at the major, with complete disregard for their height difference.

"Right on time, von Stielen!" he squeed. "This time I was expecting you!"

Major von Stielen returned a contemptuous gaze and, maintaining a perfectly calm composure, he pulled a sheet of paper from the inside pocket of his uniform, unfolded it and showed it to his face: "Been to Charlottenburg[42] and still not learnt how to read an explicit order, have you, Blut?" he told him strictly and Blut only responded with a smirk.

"What is she still doing here? And why aren't my prisoners ready for transfer?" he enquired in a strongly demanding tone.

Blut turned his nose up and let out a condescending sigh: "Such a waste of a good mind and proper training! I sometimes wonder if you really have your priorities straight, von Stielen; it would be a shame to discover otherwise." he overtly warned him and added with a raised eyebrow: "You can have your damsel in distress, *Herr Sturmbannführer*! But the British are not moving an inch."

Major von Stielen frowned: "And why is that? S.O.E. members are primarily in the jurisdiction of the Intelligence Service, are they not? Besides, I have already agreed with the *Polizeiführer* on this!"

"Oh, but this was before, *mein Herr*!" Blut argued with the same supercilious smile. "Your British are not new to our neighbourhood. There has been a warrant out for them since last August for railroad sabotage, and the first one to lay a hand on them will be me. But, please, have no worry! If there is anything left of them when I'm done, I'll make sure to send it to you!" And looking extremely amused by the situation, the Gestapo officer pulled out an order of his own and showed it to the major.

"This is nonsense!" he opposed, skimming through the document silently, with his face screaming of deprecation. "You cannot prove they are the same people!"

Blut sneered and gestured that he could not agree more: "This is my territory, von Stielen! Did you really think I would let you cheat me out of my own game?"

The major glared at him, rage and hate thundering in his eyes, but he constrained himself to a derisive nod, while Blut, almost intoxicated by his own arrogance, walked past him to head for the place where Winter was still seated tied up and dreary. Unable to understand little else but the aversion of one officer for the other, Winter instinctively leaned back as Blut approached for a most pretentious farewell.

"I promise this will not be the last time we meet, *Fräulein*!"

He took the few steps that separated him from the cell door, stood to look at his adversaries and left with another of his notorious sneers.

After that, an awkward silence prevailed. Winter's original relief dissolved with every passing moment, seeing that major von Stielen abstained from coming to free her. That damn white light–she could not see him clearly, if she could just glimpse his face, she would know what to expect. What if she had been wrong about him? What if he had not been there with good intentions but to continue where the Gestapo major had left off? A renewed terror attacked her, one she did not feel as strong to counterattack as in the case of the Gestapo scoundrel: perhaps he had learnt something more about her and René than what she had devised to tell him; perhaps, she had been followed to the catacombs, after all, and there was no dispute of such a fact, neither could it be manipulated in her best interest, especially after she had more or less assured the major that she wanted no part in René Martin's affairs. She had lied to him once; twice would be far too risky. And it would be just as undesired.

When his boots were heard creaking on the floor and his figure appeared in front of her chair, his countenance seemed deadly cold and remote, and Winter could hardly expect it was on account of the interrogation lamp. She shrank into the chair and lowered her head, ready to hear him come down on her with words of condemnation. Then, the blinding white light went out and, almost immediately, the ropes were removed from her hands. She raised her eyes to him with uncertainty and anticipation: "Thank you!" she gasped, carefully avoiding calling him by his name.

"You are free to go!" he announced without a trace of his familiar intimacy. He called at the guard and his presence added to the atmosphere of estrangement. Winter hesitated. She wanted as much as anything to get out of this cell, away from this building where death was lurking in every corner, but there was this feeling, obligation possibly, gratitude, but no, she was convinced it was more than that, an indescribable, undefined kind of need... "What's the matter? Don't you want to leave?" he startled her with his completely distorted voice. "Guard, escort the lady to the exit!" he commanded in German.

The soldier grabbed her by the arm and it grieved Winter to see there was nothing more for her there. She shut her eyes, struggling to subdue an overwhelming desire to burst out crying. Instead, she just followed the soldier out, no last words, even of goodbye, between them.

The night was dark, the street was empty; a pair of warm eyes fixed their gaze upon Winter the moment she came out from the heavily guarded gate: standing dizzy, looking lost and uncertain, screaming of grief and desperation. When she crossed the road and walked away, it was a definite, but fond, adieu. The eyes closed, relieved and sad, and when they opened again to look through the driver's rear mirror, they only saw an empty regard: their own. Yet they were swamped and restless underneath their incurious casing and they would weep, in fact, they would cry like a baby, once they were away in their solitude.

Soon, the car door opened and major von Stielen took his place in the back seat, immediately giving the driver the order to head for *Gare de Lyon.*

The lips were chapped, no red lipstick this time to fire up their seductiveness: "So, this is the end for the Midwife!" they uttered, squeezed tight by their sorrow.

"I guess it is!" the major replied with a frown of his own, the both of them sharing a feeling of regret, as if they had just finished performing a perfectly successful operation, only to find out that the patient had died on the operating table.

"Thank you for seeing that the girls were let go!" she remarked after a long pause with an attempt to smile, and she turned to look at him, his jaw muscles tightened, his eyes fixated onto a detail on the back of the co-driver's seat that only he could see.

"My part of the bargain!" he responded with his renowned self-command and hurried to light a cigarette, offering one to her, which she did not refuse.

They smoked silently, both with the somber sense of finality at its darkest hour.

"I saw Winter, too!" she said in a soft but careful tone and raised her eyes at him, once again hoping he would do the same. Unfortunately, he continued smoking without even glancing at her.

"I hope she didn't see you!" he uttered and concentrated on the cigarette between his fingers, as if he had never seen one before.

She shook her head negatively and felt completely discouraged to express what was troubling her inside. The major finally cast a grave look at her and then he reached into the inside pocket of his tunic for a thick envelope, which he placed in her uneasy hands.

"It's your new papers, your ticket, and some money for your fresh start!" he explained.

She thanked him with a nod, biting her lips, feeling her eyes inflamed and sore: "I thought I'd feel better after this was all over!" she confessed with a heavy sigh and the conflict in her tone attracted the major's attention. "I had sworn one day I would get even, but if you ask me now, I no longer know who I wanted to get even with or why. And I don't feel the slightest relief! I was angry, consumed by hatred–who did I hate? I don't know anymore! It's this damn war, what it does to people! If it weren't for those hotheads at home, things could have turned out differently for us; but maybe not, who knows? It's just... It's just not fair!" The major breathed deeply and resumed observing that inexistent front seat detail, secretly agreeing that nothing about this war could ever be regarded as fair, too much evil done, too much hatred having pervaded even the holiest of consciences. "So, my brother had studied veterinary science in Berlin–my father was a cowman, what was so weird about that?" she continued forcing the major to look and listen. "And, yes, he spoke excellent German, of course he did, wasn't that why he was positioned at encoded communications during the invasion? No, he had to be tarnished as a Nazi sympathiser, hanged from a tree as a traitor, my father shot for defending him. I can't even begin to recall how my mother and I were treated without fuming with anger... Well, I'd show them what a traitor looks like and what a traitor can do. For months, for years, I prayed for the opportunity to come; and then my prayers were answered!" She welcomed the major's compassionate gaze, but little did it console her; on the contrary, she felt even more frustrated and sorry. "I'm really not trying to make any excuses for myself.

I'm not looking for anybody's forgiveness! I'm just hoping that, one day, I will be able to put all this behind me. Forget it ever happened!"

The major firmly pressed his lips together and closed his eyes, as if in a deep conversation with the very core of his being. His voice was serious and solid and his countenance was filled with a clarity that only the absolute lack of delusions could produce.

"You will never forget, Georgette!" he told her weightily, but without an intention to cause her any more pain than that of the naked truth. "And the sooner you realise that, the more easily you will learn to live with yourself!"

The major's straightforwardness cracked the shell of self-restraint, which she had so laboriously maintained, and a silent torrent of long overdue tears poured from the well of her eyes. Tears of remorse for this game of vengeance and betrayal, which she had willfully agreed on, but which had long since ceased to agree with her.

The car stopped. Few people travelled at this hour. There was only one train leaving from *Gare de Lyon* to *Grenoble* and from there, several options, even Italy was not far, neither was the south sea. The driver got out to unload the passenger's suitcase from the boot and Georgette sat absent-mindedly staring at a middle-aged woman staggering towards the entrance of the station with a small trunk on her back, while a younger one, smart-looking in her expensive skirt suit, was following with a coquettish walk. Then, feeling a sudden spur of courage, Georgette turned all the way towards the major.

"If ... if you'd allow me, *Herr Sturmbannführer...*" He granted her permission to speak, and she continued with an almost imperative urge: "... I was wondering, what have you decided about Winter?"

Once again, the major did not seem keen to discuss the matter: "As you saw, she was released!" he answered reluctantly.

"Yes, I saw that! But, what have *you* decided about her?" she insisted. The major's glare was as clear as crystal a sign that she was almost overstepping the mark, but Georgette seemed too committed to her purpose to be inhibited by it. "I beg of you, don't judge her too harshly! She can be stupidly impulsive at times but, the truth is, she is only a frightened little bird!" she entreated him in all her tenderness and care.

Georgette's interest in Winter surprised the major, who looked at the girl skeptically, but soon softened his expression and even faintly smiled at her. "And what would you have me do?" he asked ambiguously.

Georgette lowered her head but sounded very decisive: "Help her!" she implored him. "All alone, what will become of her?" And her supplication was commensurate with the appeal in her gaze.

"Winter Pale could not have had a stronger ally than you!" the major remarked and Georgette bitterly shook her head to deny the honourable description: "Oh... but she could!"

They looked at each other meaningfully; they shook hands, exchanged wishes of good luck, and then Georgette got out of the car, picked up her small luggage, and ran through the station gate.

The major sat back in his seat contemplating Georgette's last words, most likely the words of atonement from a last-minute repentant seeking peace of mind. Perhaps! And yet, none of them had found any concrete evidence to prove Winter guilty–neither had Georgette, Blut, nor even himself. Not a shred of actual guilt, other than her acquaintance with René Martin: a nearly romantic almost affair, according to her side of the story. Still, there was something very annoying about that image of her running after him that morning outside the *Hôtel du Louvre*, an unwelcome, but largely expected, confirmation of a vague suspicion, which was impossible to ignore. And he had to discover the end of this thread all by himself because it had unavoidably woven him into its apparel; an unnamed material with properties of indefinite power and incalculable consequences; a material that could very well create a world as much as it could destroy it.

Leaving the Gestapo headquarters, Winter was feeling no less confused than the time when she left her mother and the slum of *Rue Goubet*, which she always remembered with a certain repulse and an irritating needfulness. It was at moments like this when she could not entirely reject the idea of returning to that so-called home of hers. But then, a stinging feeling of pride always seemed to interfere, and any notion of regressing to her former state of being was utterly disregarded. The future was there ahead, covered in its magnificent, mysterious haze. Her world had been built around 'The Golden Doe' and that world had been toppled like a house of cards, once again tragically revealing the ruling power of the unexpected. Or, perhaps, of the exact opposite: her worlds had always been prone to a precocious disintegration, worlds of snow that melted down as soon as they were touched by the first rays of sun. She felt small, a tiny particle of an immaterial substance, a ghost amongst the apparitions of those dear to her heart–Alain, Guillaume, Louis... She could not expect to see any of them again, could not hope that any of them would escape the ultimate end. And neither would Georgette ... or Pierre. She could still not believe his involvement in a cause so selfless and heroic. If one could not be certain even of the obvious, how was this life to be lived with? She sighed deeply, put her head down and kept walking; she had no idea where she was going.

But her feet knew better. She did not realise until she sensed a wooden feel to her legs, that she had been standing at the familiar uphill corner, where, for the first time since she had first laid eyes on it, the sign with the carved golden doe was obscure and obfuscated. She looked around, pricked up her ears. Absolutely nothing. How ironic, she thought, that no one came along this time to ask her for her papers, even though the curfew had long ago begun; no one to lead her, even unintentionally, in a direction; to show her, even with the gloomiest outlook, a perspective. She hesitated long, but finally found the courage to enter, the same dread running in her veins as when entering a cemetery at night. In the small yard that separated the gate to the street from the front door, the two bushy flower pots that decorated the entrance were lying on the ground with their soil half-spilled on the coloured slabs. She lifted them up, set them up straight. The double-leaf door was unlocked–but who would have locked it? she thought cynically. She went inside and closed the door, turned the key, which was, paradoxically, left in place, and locked up.

In the club it was pitch dark. She stepped inside carefully, as if fearing being ambushed by a deadly threat. The unusual disarray increased the feeling of dismay. Chairs and tables overturned–fortunately, someone had provisioned to remove Petit François's dead body and the howling stains of his blood. At the tip of her eye, there was the apron which Pierre used to tie around his waist. She picked it up, folded it neatly, put it where it belonged, on the bar next to the stack of empty trays. The stage was in complete chaos. Music sheets were scattered all over the floor, the instruments lying down like dead soldiers on the battlefield. The bridge on the lower bout of the double bass had fallen flat, the strings were loose and off place; the bellows of the accordion had been left agape, some rattling came from its insides when she picked it up. She held it from its bases, as she had often observed Guillaume doing, squeezed it closed. The air that whistled through it made her quiver: this was what she imagined one's last breath to sound like. She placed the accordion gently on Guillaume's chair, set the double bass next to it, to keep it company. She left the piano last. The fall board was up, the music rack broken; the bench was fallen back, its top wide open with the under seat compartment empty. Louis would tidy his music sheets with such care every night after the show was over. He carried the book with Chopin's *Nocturnes* with him always, kept it under the bench seat throughout the show, even though he knew he would never have to use it. This music was too beautiful for the product they were selling at 'The Golden Doe', but, perhaps, that was precisely why he needed it. 'Chopin is sensitive, but never mawkish; he suffers, and he is not afraid to show it!' And Louis would smile at her, his fingers running up and down the black and white keys and his eyes closed, drawing in the music, as if it were the very air he breathed.

She put down the fall board, leaned on it and cried. The curtain had come down; the show was over. The sunset of the glory days, the end of an era.

Heavily aggrieved, she found her way upstairs. There was not one door to the rooms of the first floor that was left unopened, many of the beddings thrown out in the corridor. The same mess could be seen on the second floor, the girls' things scattered here and there like ancient ruins. On the wooden floor, stuck in some out-of-the-way corner of the corridor, there was a pamphlet. She picked it up, entered her room, came close to the window in order to read it in the dim streetlight: 'Unite! Prepare! Fight!'–words she had often heard the orchestra boys speak off but had never put all the pieces together to see the big picture. She let the pamphlet fall from her hand, feeling coldly indifferent about these lofty ideals. Real life was very much down to earth, where some had to drag themselves through, while it was only a stroll for others.

Right then, she thought she heard a voice speak to her. She flinched and shivered at the idea that she had already started hallucinating, and instantly turned around to the direction where she thought the voice was heard, gasping at the sight of a silhouette moving in the shadows.

"Don't be afraid! It's me, René!" He came forth, and Winter could see that it was, indeed, him. The blood hammered against her temples and her sight briefly blacked out.

"How did you get in?" she exclaimed breathlessly and felt completely threatened by his presence.

"I came before you!" he told her and Winter noticed a rare nervousness in his voice. "I was waiting for you!"

"You're crazy!" she threw out at him, trying to shake off the thought of being caught with him and having to face the Gestapo major again or having to explain the situation to major von Stielen, at worst. René Martin shook his head full of self-confidence, his most endearing and most frightful trait.

"Don't worry, nobody saw me!"

Two steps and he was already close, his eyes glimmering with sexual aggression, his breath smelling of alcohol. Winter felt vulnerable but alert: René was dangerous when sober; she could not imagine what he was capable of drunk.

"Why did you come?" she asked with the exhaustion of a strenuous physical and mental effort.

"Mon cœur!"[43] he sighed and took her in his arms with the might of a gale-force wind. "I had to see you were okay. Those bastards didn't hurt you, did they?" The touch of his breath was intoxicating, the grip of his arms so restful. Winter raised her face up to his, showed him her hurt

lip, her eyes welling up at the recollection of the terror evoked by her encounter with the Gestapo scum. "Damn them...!" René muttered and squeezed her even more tightly. She let him hold her onto him, stroke her with his passionate hands, and felt his hunger for her like a miracle drug. "I was worried sick about you!" he admitted with a burning whisper. "As soon as I found out what happened, I ran for you. I was outside the Gestapo for hours. Early in the morning, I saw the girls leave, they scattered like lost sheep. When I didn't see you with them, my heart stopped. I didn't know where to look for you, couldn't tell if they had moved you away, I tried to follow the trucks that left the building in the afternoon, rushed back to my place, found it turned upside down, I knew it was over for everyone ... I came to hide here and wait for you; if you didn't show up in a couple of days, I'd break into every prison in and out of Paris to find you!" Winter looked in his eyes, touched by his sentimental exaggeration, and she rubbed her forehead against his cheek breathing in his intense warmth. "Please say you are happy to see me!" he pleaded with a voice deeply afflicted. "Tell me those savages didn't hurt you much. Did he do that to you? Von Stielen? I swear it, for what he did to you, I'm going to kill him!"

Winter turned her face away, her eyes filled with sorrow: "He let me go..." she mumbled uncertain how to feel, except for that depthless emptiness there was in the way they had separated.

René took offense in her words and the clear predicament in her voice.

"He let you go? *He* let you go?" he growled and shook her, as if to wake her from a long delusive sleep. "It was I who kept it secret about you and me. I made sure no one found out. He let you go because he didn't know. What in the devil did you think with your stupid mind?"

Winter wished she could find a single argument to contest him, but there was none, and her own doubt, her frustration and the fear of abandonment crippled any ability of hers to react to whatever René was telling her, to whatever René was doing.

"Rest, my darling..." he comforted her and his voice spread across her senses like a summer breeze. "Fret no more!" His caress all the way across her back seemed to infuse his reassurance into her. "You don't have to be alone in this struggle, let me be there for you!" He held her hands, brought them to his chest, pressed them in so that she could feel his beating heart. "Listen! Listen to my heart! Hear how it needs you, how it wants you! I want you. I want you like crazy!" He was a man like wildfire, his mouth a furnace of burning passion to which Winter had little power to resist: "Be mine, Winter!" he demanded with his forceful longing. "Be mine now..."

His hands started peeling off her clothes like the fire scorches the bark of the logs in the fireplace before charring them to the core. He pulled her to the bed, captured her with his weight and, as he thrust into her with his combusting desire, he whispered to her that she wanted him too, like he was trying to convince her. Winter did not need to be convinced; she just surrendered.

"Everything you had here is gone; you belong to me now!" he was raving through his unsated lust. "You're coming with me, you are. There's no one else for you!" His eyes glowed like torches, his face lit up like a fire devil. "You don't know him like I do; you couldn't! When he had me in his hands, I was this close to telling him: it's me! Remember? ... It's a small, small world..." René let out a pernicious laugh and Winter wriggled as far as his hermetic embrace permitted. "Hush now! I'll let you in on a little secret!" he sizzled sharply and held her even tighter. "I will never let you be his. Do you hear me? I am never going to leave you..."

Winter sighed deeply but had not heard a word. Drained from the recent trials, sedated by lovemaking, the warmth of the bed, and his humming voice, she had long fallen asleep.

16

At the turn of the tide

She woke up reanimated after almost an entire day of sleep. René was no longer with her. Before leaving, she could not tell exactly when, he had once again asked her to follow him. 'Everything you had here is gone,' he had said. 'You will come with me. There's no one else for you...' And that was probably true, but there was another truth, cruel and undeniable, that Winter was not brave; she feared death; she wanted to live. And René would hate her for it.

The days to follow made the forthcoming hardships clear, although the little treasure of her savings had, paradoxically, remained intact under the loose plank in the floor in her room. Her notable nest egg consisted of five hundred Reichsmarks or ten thousand French francs, but it was impressive how quickly it was spent on merely the bare necessities, when one lacked the skill and connections to ensure more favourable terms in acquiring them. She looked at herself in the mirror: fortunately, she was able to dress properly, so that she would, at least, not look deprived. The more decent and presentable one was in the street, the less likely they were to be stopped for their document verification. And Winter did not want to come against the German police ever again, nor did she want to leave any suspicion that she had no life or profession, since snoops dwelled in every corner and the obligatory work service was hanging like the sword of Damocles over her.

Her first thought was to look for a singer's position at another club. Soon, she had to admit how delusional she was to believe that such opportunities could appear twice in a lifetime. And she still laughed at herself, thinking back at the self-important attitude with which she had entered the first couple of clubs in order to sell herself as an artist. If she were interested in selling herself in other ways, then doors opened up more willingly, but Winter was determined not to stoop so low again, not until she had reached the point of no return.

Then she turned to the businesses in the city centre, hoping for a position as a shop assistant. However, the lack of sufficient knowledge of French was an insurmountable obstacle. After all, it would be extremely reckless of her to even attempt to speak the language without risking of being exposed as a foreigner. She even went as far once as to pretend to be dumb when she turned to a farm in the suburbs for manual labour. The boss had seemed overeager to offer the job to the poor mute girl, given she agreed to a few weeks' work trial. It was exactly this 'trial' her intuition warned her against, hence immediately crossing out the option.

Unemployed and having lost the privilege of a daily working routine, Winter had too much free time and her inactivity gave room to endless thinking, which almost always wound up in complete desperation and anxiety. Having eventually managed to overcome the nervous apprehension of everyone's absence, because of which she initially limited herself to her usual living space in the club, she later discovered that it was extremely fascinating and inexpressibly comforting to explore the rooms of 'The Golden Doe' to which she had no access before. In the girls' rooms, their things remained as they had been abandoned that night–none of them had returned, not even for their personal belongings, she thought bitterly. Not that they were of any particular value! A very unflattering winter hat that Andrée had made with her knitting needles, notwithstanding her sister's strict monitoring, of course, which would always lead them to long, foolish, vexatious quarrels. She also found Michelle's ring, the one she had claimed to have discarded, once the German soldier who had offered it to her in what he professed to be their engagement stopped writing to her, a few weeks after he had been dispatched to the Eastern front, from which he had promised to return and marry her. His love letters were burnt in front of them all at 'The Golden Doe' in retaliation and Michelle would declare that forgetting her was a crime punishable by oblivion. None of them dared say anything about the other, the most probable explanation for the soldier's absence of contact: it was always more bearable to be mad than sad. The girls of the dancing ensemble had brought along a suitcase dollhouse, which they were proud to show off for the rare furnishings and very real-life accessories it contained, including a fully equipped medieval kitchen, a richly dressed sitting-room with a burning fireplace and two exceptionally detailed bedrooms in eighteenth century royal style. Three little dolls lived in it, their wooden heads with real human hair and their wire limbs making them look so alive, but in a creepy way, too, Winter always thought. More intriguing than anything were the discoveries she made in Georgette's room. Stacked in a box well hidden in her wardrobe, there were several photos of Georgette and her family and Winter could not help wondering why she would not find a more accessible place for the photos of her home, her father, mother and, by the look of it, elder brother. She remembered that on the scarce occasions when Georgette talked about her past, there was always this obscure cloud in her eyes, like the memory of insufferable pain, which was more than mourning and nostalgia. Winter had never attempted to descry what it was, because, to do so, she would have to look deep into Georgette's gaze and that would probably mean that she would have to allow Georgette to do the same with her.

Last but not least, Pierre's apartment was a true apocalypse. By all appearances, his involvement in the affairs of the Resistance was neither accidental nor occasional. His apartment had at least three hiding places that could comfortably accommodate a man. Inside a secret room behind the fireplace, the walls were smudged, a sign of a make-shift printing press or duplicator, while underneath the marble top of a boulle marquetry cabinet there was enough hiding place for a radio or a transmitter. No matter how much hard evidence there was, Winter could still not believe how many of these things were happening right under her nose. Who knows what the truth behind the black marketer's story of that fateful Tuesday was! And Georgette had trotted out a lie about it so easily. Georgette, who had seemed appalled to say 'I didn't know you were involved with such people!' and it was actually her who was involved, too involved for her own good to be exact. As for the orchestra boys, she supposed she always knew that they had some kind of underground association–so impassionedly assertive that they often were, it would seem unthinkable for them to hold an impartial stance to the matters of the war. But for Pierre, she would swear blindly that he could have had nothing to do with challenging the authorities–in her view, Pierre was the most shocking revelation of all.

She would think of him every time she sawed, admittedly with great effort and plenty of injuries, another chair or table from the main hall to throw into the stove for firewood, because, despite the dawning summer, the evenings were still chilly and her frequently sleepless mornings even chillier. Pierre would have had a heart attack if he could see her, she pondered and the thought of him yelling at her inconsiderately destroying his slaved-to-obtain property almost amused her; almost, for her dominant sentiments were grief and hopelessness.

Away from 'The Golden Doe', the world seemed to have a better healing effect. The presence of the conquerors was overwhelming, but there would be a comical aspect to it, as well: every day, the prefecture workers, with their buckets of white paint and brushes, would struggle to erase the resistance writings on walls, on street lighting posts, on mirrors and tiles of the public lavatories; in *Châtelet* once, a man threw flyers with rebellious slogans inside a shop, and the owner, together with an employee and two customers, were awestricken and utterly undecided what was best, to call the *Milice* and report the incident or hurry to clean up every trace of the incriminating material before they themselves were accused of possessing it. Even so, life in the city always found its way back to whatever normality the times dictated.

One morning, the air-raid siren sounded again after several months, finding Winter in Pierre's apartment. She got the fright of her life and she ran to the window to inspect the sky, the street, the buildings all around: nothing and nobody. For a moment, she wondered if she were the only soul present in the entire neighbourhood. She rushed down the stairs to the ground floor, grabbed a piece of bread and a bottle of water and jumped into the shelter under the kitchen floor. But memory echoed too deafening down in the shelter, and the ghosts of those with whom she had once shared this hiding place came out from inside the walls and behind the sewerage pipes, touching her arms, her back and her hair, breathing onto her face, smiling and whispering that it was time to meet again. In the corner, next to the water pressure regulator, Pierre appeared wearing a new apron and a glowing yellow sign above his head declared 'The New Golden Doe'. Hands on his hips, red in the face, he started moving towards her, growing more and more gigantic as he was approaching, ready to devour and assimilate her into his incorporeal body.

She broke full tilt out of the hatch, pushed it closed, covered it with the mat and even dragged a table over it for safety. She had left her bread and water inside, but the hell with it! she decided. She would not go down there again for all the bread and water in the world; and she would never go down there again were a hundred bombs to drop from the sky and right onto her head. Before the siren had sounded the end of the alarm, Winter was already out in the street. She walked and walked her fright away and did not return until she was forced back by a heavy rain late in the afternoon. Nevertheless, she stayed awake most of the night, hearing the thunderstorm beat against the window shutters, and sleeplessly watching the thin line of pale and motionless light under the door, for fear of a shadow appearing in the corridor.

Although not having slept much, she felt very relieved to see the daybreak. Going to the kitchen to prepare a simple breakfast, she ensured to pass by the table over the shelter hatch from a distance. Eager to shake off all negative thoughts and feelings, she put some extra citrus molasses on her bread, one of the last delights left in the cupboards from the days of abundance bearing Pierre's signature. She almost choked on the last bite, however, as an unexpected knock on the front door chilled her blood. Goggled-eyed, she stood still, felt the panic roar in her ears, explode on her face and blur her vision. Quietly, she slipped towards the window to the street, pulled the curtain a bit and peeped outside. She could see no one, and there were no clues to betray the identity of the visitor; friend or foe, it would have to be someone who knew she still lived there and to know that it would have to mean she had been watched and the fact that she was completely on her own must have already been confirmed. Second knock. On the way to the door, she went for the kitchen knife, gripped on it, and prepared for the worst. She turned the key in the lock and opened the door only an inch, putting her foot behind it for more security.

"Good morning!"

"... Good morning!"

It was an ambiguous sentiment to see *Sturmbannführer* von Stielen at the doorstep. He was wearing a blue pinstripe suit, white shirt and tie, the civilian outfit completely altering his mien. Somewhat embarrassed, she made certain to hide away the knife before opening the door wide to let him in. He walked inside and it was strange, how congenial it felt that they should both be at the same place, although he stood there, looking around the main hall of the club silent, contemplating, perhaps, over its past glories, so pitifully and irreversibly gone.

"So, you have been living here alone since?" he asked, apparently concluding an inner thought, and the familiarity of his voice moved Winter.

"... I try to spend as little time inside as possible!" she replied, trying to be quick and exact in her answer as if she were taking a test where accuracy mattered or as though she were facing interrogation where the promptness and truthfulness of a reply could determine one's very fate. The major nodded with understanding and smiled–another sight she felt well-acquainted with.

"How did you do with the alarm yesterday?" he enquired again and Winter had to recall the ridiculous scene of her panic inside the shelter and admit with a self-reproaching sneer: "Not very well!"

She looked at the major, who once more seemed to understand. What was he doing at her door? she wondered. Was it genuine interest this time, or yet another tactical move? The major smiled, as though he had read her thought.

"As a matter of fact, I'm here to ask you to go for a walk with me, if you'd like!" he said, as always without beating about the bush, and Winter felt that... well, of course, she would–she would like that very much.

On the hill of *Montmartre*, it was a sunny summer day at its best. Colourful shops, open window shutters, people in the streets. But for the men in uniform, it would be easy to forget about the war, as this district of Paris remained so genuinely traditional and charming. The major adored Paris. It was obvious in the way he talked about it. There was a certain magic about this city, he noted, and, if one believed in fairytales, this was where a fairytale could come to life. Of course, these would be the words of an incurable romantic; but it was hard not to become a romantic in Paris. Winter did not know much about romance, neither had she experienced many romantic moments in her life, but she had always liked fairytales and she would love to believe they could become true. Looking up to see the Basilica of the *Sacré-Cœur* gleam in its distinct whiteness, they both shared an intuitive sense that this day was to be marked a shiny landmark for reasons other than the radiating sun and the warm weather.

"There is the *Notre Dame*. Do you see the two tall towers? The *Louvre* is a little to the right and this large dome in the middle is the *Panthéon*!" He came to stand behind her, took her hand and extended her arm parallel to his, guiding her in the correct direction to look. As if the panoramic view from the stairs of the Basilica were not enough, the closeness between their two bodies electrified Winter, and she felt thankful he could not see her blushing face from that point of standing. When he proposed to extend their walk all the way to the *Notre Dame* and have some ice cream at *Bertillon*'s, Winter felt like a spoiled child; it was a change she more than welcomed.

Winter knew the route from the *Place Pigalle* to the centre like the back of her hand. This time it was her turn to show him little corners of interest, which she had discovered during her many expeditions in these parts of the city: a perfume shop with extremely decent prices; a painter's studio with beautiful landscape paintings, one of which she had actually bought for her room; a charming covered passage, unique to pass time on rainy days; and, last but not least, your friendly neighbourhood cathedral at the Church of *Saint-Eustache*, where she was lucky once to attend a concert by a full orchestra–an experience of a lifetime which introduced Winter to another kind of classical music than the greatly personal music of Chopin that Louis often played for her on his piano. Eventually, Winter found herself very much drawn to classical music, although she knew very little about it. It was alright, however, she thought: classical music was probably the poetry of sounds.

The major agreed and commended on the ingenuity of her remark. He even informed her he had a decent collection of classical music plates at his house, which they could play on the gramophone one evening.

"That would be very lovely!" Winter replied with a smile of delight and anticipation she could hardly conceal.

They strolled along the banks of the *Seine*, long digging in the treasures of books, art prints and posters on the green boxes of the *Bouquinistes*[44]. At the flower market he bought her a small bouquet of sweet pea flowers, which she eventually selected after quite a bit of faltering, fortunately, much to the major's amusement. In order to avoid the Police Prefecture and its connotations, they made a small round and reached the *Notre Dame* from the back. Its garden was all green and bloomed, a paradise for sore eyes and troubled minds, but the music which was heard from somewhere nearby attracted their interest more. In the square in front of the cathedral, the municipal orchestra set below the statue of Charlemagne played music for strings, Mendelssohn and Bach. They stood to watch for a while, then they entered the *Notre Dame*, surrendering to its atmosphere of awe and mystery.

All the best stained-glass windows, and many of the temple shrines, which were of particular value, had been removed from the cathedral before the Germans entered Paris, safely stored somewhere away from the renowned Nazi greed for anything ancient and symbolic. But the beauty of the *Notre Dame* was not only found in her ornaments. It was in the way the light came in through the clerestory and rose windows, in the dark corners the monumental pillars and ornate arches created, in how the trembling candle flames illuminated the altars and tombs. The music from the square inspired the soul to broaden, the mind to pacify; the sacred mysticism humbled the voice to a whisper, exactly what man was before the all-loving, all-forgiving might of God, an ascertainment exhilarating almost as much as it was despairing. At some point the music stopped and the silence inside the temple was so imposing, that they did not even want to disturb it with the sound of their breaths.

In this atmosphere, the growling of Winter's stomach embarrassed her as if she had committed some despicable mortal sin.

"I think reverence and ice cream will have to wait until next time!" the major jested, and offered her his hand, suggesting it was time to leave.

Never before had the major been so open with her. He was always polite, thoughtful and understanding. But she had never heard him make a joke–she could hardly imagine him laughing his head off in a company of friends. In fact, it was extremely difficult for her to envisage him doing any of the simple things that people do every day. She supposed it was because of the uniform he always used to wear. When she was a little girl, she remembered once hearing her mother say that a book couldn't be judged by its cover. At the time, it had seemed like a strange notion and she had set her childish mind to recreating the book covers of all the books she knew to see the impression they would make:

The little princess[45] riding *Peter Pan's goat*[46] and the mice from *The tailor of Gloucester*[47] waving the flags of *The railway children*[48]. One thought that troubled her deeply was the austere cover of the Holy Bible–why could it not be illustrated in a way it would be so much more attractive to read? When she told her idea to her mother, the poor woman had tried hard to hide her laughter, being in the presence of the ladies of the Charity Commission, who had found it extremely offending and disrespectful to talk this way about the good book. And yet, it was not long before Father had actually dug out a most wonderful illustration of the Bible stories in verse[49], which she gladly not only read but also memorised. She glanced at the major and impulsively cracked a smile: civilian clothing was a remarkably more suitable cover for this book, she pondered, or, at least, it was so much more appealing to her.

They sat for lunch at a nice bistro on the *Île Saint-Louis*. They ordered a vegetable beef stew cooked in beer and, as *hors d'oeuvres*[50] , they were brought a tray of snails in garlic butter. Winter had never eaten snails; the mere thought of them disgusted her. The major, on the other hand, who loved them, did not force her to try them, but when she saw how much he enjoyed eating them, she succumbed to the temptation to pick one. And she was very surprised to see that, if one could overcome the psychological barrier of eating a crawling black slimy thing, snails were actually a delicious food–apart from its nutritional value.

By the time they had started the second carafe of homemade wine and Winter's cheeks had begun to adorably blush from alcohol and merriment, a loud argument coming from the kitchen disturbed the high spirits of the restaurant habitués. Soon, the noise was transferred to the street, where a most aggravating scene unfolded: a member of the *Milice* had just arrested a man, who looked more obstinate about holding on to the fabric bag in his arms than concerned about his own safety. The owner of the restaurant soon joined, scowling at the man with the bag and, before long, hurling loud insults and curses, as he saw the offender was stubbornly unrepentant.

Oh Mum, my Mum!

Winter felt tearful, her heart was sad, and she was relieved that the major's apology for having to leave her alone for a while came at the right moment. She wiped her eyes and nose, took a deep breath, and continued to watch from the restaurant window, wondering how the major's interference would end the quarrel.

Both the man of the *Milice* and the restaurant owner started talking to the major simultaneously, but he hushed the *Milicien*[51] and allowed the restaurant owner to carry on explaining, which he did emphasising with angry gestures. At one point, he grabbed the bag from the offender's arms and stirred its contents to display a loaf of bread, some fruit, a handful of legumes. Such a pity, Winter thought hostilely, because when he took their order he had seemed like a truly amiable person; another hypocrite, she concluded and felt a strong dislike towards him. This feeling made her even more curious about the major's stance–would he, too, be a disappointment? She observed him closely: there was an idea of tolerance in his expression when he was looking at the offender, a shadow of contempt when addressing the *Milicien*, who was eager to swagger in front of the offender, but submissively stoop before his German superior. The offender had his eyes turned away and remained completely silent. He only raised his gaze to the major when he addressed him, and his words must have been of the same substance as his eyes: grieved and bold, with the pride of those who yield neither to man nor to fortune. The major gave an order to the uniformed man, immediately crushing his manifest resistance to it, and merely gave a disapproving glance at the restaurant owner, who was forced to leave the scene with the fabric bag in his hands and his head lowered. As the offender was being taken away, hands tied behind his back, but an expanded posture, the major stood and watched thoughtfully, before returning inside.

"What will they do to him?" Winter asked once the major had sat down at the table again. He stared at her vaguely, then he felt compelled to take on a dutiful look.

"Offences cannot be left unpunished!" he uttered in a deadpan voice, which did not accord with the sorrowful shadow in his misty look. He drew his attention to Winter and saw her face ablaze, her eyes weepy.

He took her hand in comfort, urging her to tell him what she was thinking.

"When I was at home, I often wondered what happens when someone is arrested for theft!" she confessed sadly. "My little brothers had been lucky, and we never had to find out. I didn't want to believe anyone would dare harm two five-year-old children for a reason as petty as this, but only my heart knows how I trembled every time the night fell and they still hadn't come back..." She peered at the kitchen door, felt resentful. "Would it be too much to spare, a loaf of bread and a handful of beans?" And to show her contempt for the restaurant owner, she pushed her plate away, refusing to continue eating his food.

The major did not rush into a reaction, obviously having diverse thoughts about the matter himself: "I cannot tell you, Winter, that you're wrong!" he eventually admitted, fully aware of the consequences of his words. "But imagine the chaos, were one allowed to steal a loaf of bread and a handful of beans from the other!"

Winter conceded with a reluctant nod: "Yes, but a hungry belly has no ears, and I'm sure it has no reason either!" she remarked with disarming simplicity, which she immediately regretted, thinking she might have been too disobliging, even offensive towards the major. "I'm sorry, I didn't mean to say that you..." she tried to compensate.

"There's no need for an apology!" he interrupted her, and Winter worriedly inspected his face for any signs of vexation. Surprisingly, he did not seem at all irritated or snubbed, but he sat back in silence and fixed his gaze on his glass, which he soon took and completely emptied its contents.

In retrospect, Winter reproached herself for her spontaneous absence of reserve with the major, a mistake she acknowledged to repeat with no good sense at all, considering who and what he was. But who and what was he, really? she could not help doubting. She had often sensed he was definitely a book not to be judged by its cover, but what was written inside that book remained largely hidden between the lines, and it was hardly guaranteed she would be allowed to read them or that she would have the insight to conceive their meaning. She had high hopes and absolutely no expectations. There was an obscurity in his eyes, which reminded her of the crystal ball a wizard had in his tent at a spring fair back in the times of her childhood bliss: if she looked hard enough, he had said, she could see her heart's desire. But even that was not clear to her: knowing one's heart's desire was never a simple task.

They finished their meal a little hurriedly after that. They silently walked around the *Île Saint-Louis*, and they stood where the river split in two to embrace the *Île de la Cité*. The surroundings were calming, but Winter's cheer was evidently gone. The smell of the river reminded her of her walks on the banks of the Thames. Father would let her run ahead, always faster than everyone else, always impatient. She was too little to understand the meaning of happiness, yet she was so happy. Where had this feeling strayed away from her? How could she ever get it back? she wondered with painful longing.

Before dusk, the sky had got heavy again, portending another rainfall and the prospect of spending the night alone amongst the ghosts of 'The Golden Doe' gave Winter a growing bitter feeling. She would cry if she did not feel obliged to comply with formalities and she wished she had the nerve to ask the major for comfort. But the major was the major, regardless of whatever cover he was wearing, and she was... Well, she was... she was definitely stupid to believe he could be anything but that.

"You should hurry! It looks like it's going to pour!" she told him, struggling with a conflicting urge to put an end to this chimerical anticipation of God knew what, because she certainly did not. But then he astonished her, and she was confused by the simple, honest truth in his voice, and the warm, inviting light in his look as he said: "I'm not afraid of the rain!"

They remained quiet, their eyes searching into each other for words unspoken. And when they kissed, it felt like a kiss they had both desired for a very long time.

17

Chantilly

She felt the change within her strong, a change in many ways different from before. All of a sudden, a face she had thought long gone reappeared: it was the girl with long blonde braids, with the vivacity of youth and hopefulness, the one who climbed onto Father's back pretending to be the warrior queen she had once admired as a statue[52] at Westminster Bridge, the one who would promptly get into a fight with the neighbourhood boys only to prove that war was as much a female as it was a male game. She would sometimes wink at her in the mirror, pump up the blood in her veins, and remind her of what it meant to be alive, what it meant to face life without fear. In her heart, she felt the warmth of the summer sun; a sun of the present, not the pale sun of dreams and recollection, which she struggled to keep bright, so that she would not completely lose herself in the dark. And its shine was coming from the inside out, not the other way round, like it used to.

She could discern a familiar, yet foreign feeling. People were used to recognising themselves through certain constants and usual recurrences. She always thought of her life as a circle. Similar things, same pattern in other places, with other faces. What would happen, she wondered, if the circle broke? What was this new shape? Where did it lead to? What happened to the contents of the circle when its protective perimetre was no more? Would she cease to be the person she was when she was no longer the same as before? That was probably not possible, she thought, because even in the simplest of minds, there was this human power called memory. And she remembered, she remembered everything. Never before did she remember so vividly, never before without a mournful taint. Because she was just finding out, there was another way to reach those parts of oneself where memory was dwelling: with a tender embrace and leniency, just like a loving parent.

It had been a long time since anyone had shown her this kind of tenderness, but he did, the major, *Sturmbannführer* von Stielen. One of the first things he cared for was that she stopped living preyed upon by ghosts, strongly insisting she move to more suitable lodgings. Hence, he secured her a modest but comfortable penthouse at the *Cité Berryer*[53], a charming residential and shopping complex built around an open-air passage, just steps away from the *Place de la Madeleine*. The people there were quiet, tending to their little shops, minding their own business–no one could tell whether they were indeed well-meaning or just capable liars. Thus concluded for Winter the days of 'The Golden Doe'. It was not without hurt that she left the place which had marked her so deeply, but she decided, after long consideration, not to take anything with her as a memento. She was determined to start anew, leave the past behind–this chapter of her past at least.

Her new apartment was very much to her liking, being in the city centre and very close to the *Hôtel Du Louvre*. The living space was more than adequate for a single resident. It was furnished elegantly with fabrics in earthy colours, which Winter found very heartwarming. There were two windows in the sitting-room, one overlooking the shops in the passage and one to the street, *Rue Royale*, a short but busy street, given it ran between the *Place de la Madeleine* and the *Place de la Concorde*. So, even with nothing better to do, Winter was certain never to get bored, just looking out of the window. In the bedroom, there was only an ample skylight in the roof, providing plenty of air and beautiful light, day and night. It was enchanting to lie there when it rained.

She tidied all her clothes in the commodious wardrobe and drawers;

she filled the small but functional bathroom with her fragrant soaps, lotions and cosmetics, equipped the kitchen with jars of jam and honey, groceries and spices. In the dining area, the major had sufficiently replenished the contents of the art nouveau cocktail cabinet and Winter regularly called upon it for a snifter, especially on a chilly evening. When she and the major were together, they usually drank wine. He often came to spend time with her at the apartment; it felt so homely to be there with him.

He took her everywhere a socially up-to-date *Parisienne* should be: to chic restaurants and *salon de thé*[54], to art galleries and entertainments, as well as to the fashionable soirees the Press Office held twice a month, where there was always abundant food and dancing. They once attended a horserace at the *Hippodrome de Longchamp*, where she even won a couple of bets. At the equestrian club in *Bois de Boulogne*, she was persuaded to try riding a horse. After three failed attempts, Winter declared that horses and she were definitely beyond each other's comprehension.

The major was good for her, and it was not only because of the comforts he could offer. He never overstepped the bounds of propriety, never asked for compensation, it was almost too obliging and Winter often felt the need to give him something, too, in return for his kindness.

"Don't ever show me gratitude!" he told her once, and she was quick to misinterpret his words. What was wrong with gratitude, she objected, it only allowed the one who expressed it a sense of fairness and balance. But the major had nothing against gratitude in general; it was Winter's gratitude he did not want.

One Thursday morning in the beginning of August, he instructed her to wake up early and dress comfortably. He came in his civvies, driving the black car himself, and he persistently refused to reveal anything about their destination. Winter was intrigued, but she was not afraid–he had more than earned her trust after this long. This long? It was only a few weeks and yet she could not have felt closer to him than if she had known him for years. It always amazed her how it was possible to feel this way about certain people: René, Louis, and now the major. She turned to look at him driving the car and a familiar doubt ran through her: the doubt of reality.

Soon, they were away from the city, driving north into the country, where vast farmland and forests would alternate with charming small towns and villages. Winter was thrilled; she had never been outside of Paris, and when she and Mother had travelled from England, she was too young and too much in pain to appreciate the value of a landscape. The countryside was serene and beautiful, as was everything natural and untouched by man. She lowered her window and breathed in the fresh breeze, feeling almost intoxicated by it.

"It's wonderful! Devine!" she exclaimed with a beaming smile which enormously gratified the major.

"I know what would make our trip even more pleasant!" he remarked to attract an inquisitive glance from her. "Some music!"

Winter agreed with a nod, but shrugged to show she did not care about the lack of this little luxury. But the major was staring at her with some expectation and then she realised what he meant by 'music'. She was surprised and pealed a merry laugh to show it. She had never imagined herself singing again, she had not as much as even whispered a tune since the last time she had been on stage, and that seemed like centuries ago. It was like she had been returned a dear personal belonging considered forever lost and she felt daring. She started to sing the first tune that sprang into her mind and it enthused her to hear him catch up with her at the next verse.

This could not be real, she was thinking, this had to be an image from some newly conceived daydream of hers, a scene from a romantic novel or a film in the movies. Happy and carefree, as though the world around them had not been at war, and life was simple and certain. And yet, perhaps it was not so strange, after all, when, in the turmoil of fear, hatred and pain, people wanted to live to the best of their ability and, because of that, they ate as much as they could, drank more than their head could bear, took pleasure where they found it, they argued fiercely, laughed hysterically, loved and hated with passion, giving in to life in every sense, because tomorrow, this unknown and ominous tomorrow, this life of theirs might be taken away.

They entered a picturesque provincial town and drove along its main street: dense vegetation to the right, lovely little townhouses, and small shops to the left. Some locals stopped at the side and stared at the car, curious probably about the fact that it went without the usual military escort. They followed the curve and came across the tall statue of a nobleman on horseback in the middle of a small square. In front of them rose a giant arch, built out of aged stone, opening onto an expanse of green grass. The car jumped roughly off the old weathered slates of the street, which was designated by a long line of full-grown water-loving cottonwood trees.

It was then that Winter saw it: as if springing out of the pages of a fairy tale, majestic in the middle of its peaceful lake, the *Château de Chantilly*. Rooted many centuries past, the town of *Chantilly* was originally known for two things: the detailed handmade black lace and the grand royal stables, while, later on, its name was attached to what was by many regarded as the queen of whipped cream. The major thought highly of this *Chantilly* cream, behind which there was also an intriguing story. So, it was alleged, the cream was inspired by the ingenious *maître d'hôtel*[55] at *Chantilly* castle at the time it was owned by Prince de Condé, cousin to Louis XIV, who was king of France in a period often referred to as the 'Great Century' of French history. Apparently, there had been a three-day feast at *Chantilly* to honour the visit of de Condé's royal cousin, and the head chef was keen to satisfy the extravagant tastes of the so-called Sun King. Unfortunately, several mishaps at the banquet hurt his pride so deeply that he was said to have taken his own life. Of course, what might seem like an exaggeration in contemporary times could be better understood, if one thought that, in the seventeenth century, when French cuisine had already established a reputation in fine dining, it was no little deal to be the head chef of a *Château*, let alone serve the king himself. One way or another, the cream had become legendary and the taste largely justified its name.

"A whipped cream like none you have tried before!" the major affirmed and promised her fair share when they had some at the castle, which, as he explained, had been requisitioned by a friend of his at the Embassy and he was kind enough to allow them a visit.

"He has requisitioned the castle?" Winter exclaimed, uncertain which of all the information sounded most inconceivable to her. One thing seemed to be unquestionable, though: there was no beginning or end to human vanity.

From beginning to end, however, the *Château de Chantilly* was a true jewel. The elderly gentleman in the costume of a royal butler, who had arrived to welcome them, was kind enough to give them a small tour and show them the highlights of the castle. Apart from the turrets with pointed tops, gray roofs and domes, arched galleries and windows, sculptures and statues and hundreds of stairs that marked the exterior, the inside was stamped with polished marble in imperial colours and golden decorations, elaborate doors opening into labyrinthine corridors and countless rooms, while majestic staircases led to the even more magnificent chambers of their former blue-blooded owners. They admired the aristocratic furniture, the vivid paintings and silk-screens of hunting scenes, and they were dazzled by the crystal, bronze and golden artifacts which enlivened the space. There was a different hall dedicated to a particular collection of the castle treasures: hunting, armoury, porcelain and utensils, lacework, jewellery, trinkets. The major mostly enjoyed the library: over twenty thousand volumes, some of which were literally ancient, on two floors with shelves loaded with knowledge and art.

Then they were led to a drawing room with marvellous daylight entering from a patio door overlooking the gardens, and they were offered coffee with some round lace-shaped biscuits. On a separate plate there were fruit, strawberries and raspberries, very hard to find in Paris, very rare for the commoners, too. The famous cream accompanied the dish, two bowls full to the brim with pure white, thick, sweet and sour whipped cream, a mouth-watering sight, they both admitted. They put some in their coffee, dipped the fruit and biscuits in it a few times, but most of it was eventually eaten with the spoon. The major was right;

Winter had tried several kinds of whipped cream on cakes, tarts and other pastry in the city, but, in truth, none was as full in body and distinct in taste. Once she had finished her own bowl, the major allowed her to have some of his, but, with an almost rapacious appetite and completely disregarding every rule of the *savoir-vivre*[56], Winter just devoured it all, making sure to wipe the sides of the bowl with her finger in order to leave none to waste. The major was looking at her with a broad smile; he enjoyed seeing Winter so spontaneous and happy.

With their hunger satiated and their spirits high, Winter and the major wandered around, immersing themselves in the refined atmosphere of the castle, where it was so easy to lose one's sense of proportion. At the chapel of Saint Louis, they sat side by side at a bench observing the marquetry panelled altar and the facing stained glass windows depicting children of the royal family protected by saints.

"Are you Catholic, Fred?" Winter asked, once again realising how little of the essentials she actually knew about him.

He hummed in confirmation and Winter said that she and Mother used to be members of the Church of England, but when they came to France, they had no choice but to attend mass in Catholic churches. Eventually, they also had to get baptized into Catholicism, because, otherwise, they would not have been able to be naturalised–so, at least, had Stepfather claimed, who, paradoxically, did not miss any of the Sunday church services. Mother never bothered to verify whether Christian was telling the truth: they had to become French citizens, and, besides, she did not consider changing dogma such a mortal sin; to her, Jesus Christ was Lord to them all. Winter did not care whether they were Catholic or Protestant either, but she did care that they had renounced the faith bequeathed to them by Father–how much more of him would they have to give up, she protested inside, never revealing her thoughts to Mother in order to spare her the pain.

She sighed, and the major took her hand in his to console her, this sense of affinity giving her the strength and will to avoid all depressing thoughts. Immediately, she noticed that the chapel was very plain, much like Anglican churches, which were nothing like their imposing and sumptuous Catholic counterparts. The major commented that the Roman Catholic Church had been a State for many centuries and, as such, it not only possessed power but also extreme wealth.

"Has it always been this way, rich and poor, sovereign and subjects, leaders and mere followers?" Winter wondered naively.

"For as long as civilization as we know it has existed, I'm afraid!" the major affirmed.

Winter argued that she would like things to be different. She would like to see a world generously offered to all; a place for everyone to have what they needed, no more, no less, but what and however much they needed to live decently and feel satisfied. Then, there would be no misery, no envy, and no reason for one to turn against another, making animosity and wars completely redundant. The major smiled and called her ideas a beautiful, but utopian, dream. Winter did not know the meaning of the word 'utopia' but recalled often hearing it in the conversations the boys of the orchestra had with each other, frequently leading to strong disagreement and occasional quarrel. It would have to be a very strong word, Winter deliberated, and hearing it from the major's lips in this context, she feared it might be a word in the revolutionary vocabulary, for which she could easily be held accountable.

"Forgive me," she said and cringed in her seat, looking at him out of the corner of her eye to distinguish the slightest irritation in his reactions. "I did not mean to say anything specific, I just..."

He looked at her with a smirk and she deliberately left her phrase unfinished.

"Don't worry, I'm not here to question your social beliefs!" the major asserted, keen in his perception of her, as usual. "Besides, every intelligent person would agree that inequality is a source of unrest and antagonism! I just find the equality usually professed by the strongest of its advocates almost as dangerous as its complete opposite!" he explained, probably expressing a substantially processed idea, and much to Winter's confusion. "Speaking of which, however..." he continued in an ambiguous tone and a corresponding facial expression, which largely apprehended Winter "... I mean, if you were a rebellious element, would you tell me?" And the wrinkles on his forehead, together with his raised eyebrow, showed his doubt. Bemused, Winter tried to detect the gravity of his question and skimmed through her mind for a suitable answer.

"What do you think?" she replied as soon as she overcame her shock, choosing to be evasive, and the major cracked a meaningful smile, breathed in decisively and stated with incontestable certainty: "I think you'd lie!"

Winter was once again taken by surprise. "Do you really believe that?"

"I believe you'd be afraid to tell me the truth!" he answered without a shred of skepticism. And he was right, Winter admitted to herself, but it was unthinkable that he would think that and still maintain his goodwill towards her, not an SS officer assigned to dig out the foes of the Reich and squash them where he found them. She had long since stopped questioning his intentions, she trusted him; could she have been so wrong? "I'm teasing you!" he whispered in her ear, and it took her a few seconds to wipe the icy smile from her flustered expression. She complained it was not funny to tease her about things as serious as this, and he agreed and sincerely apologised. He did not, however, hesitate to confess that he often wondered about her: who she really was in her mind and heart. And to emphasise, he touched the temple of her head with his fingers and then the place of her heart.

Winter's agitation forced her to remove his hand from her chest and enclose it tightly between her palms.

"There's nothing to wonder about me, Fred! I'm just a girl trying to survive!" she uttered with an unpretentious admission and lowered her head with a feeling of self-consciousness, which prevented her from seeing the major's gaze, a bleak gaze shadowed by a well-hidden disappointment.

"And is this what you're doing here, with me? Trying to survive?"

She brought her eyes into his without reservation. She did not speak at once, but an answer had never been clearer in the way she looked at him: "No!" she professed, on one of the rare occasions when she could be so genuinely honest.

For a couple of moments, the major stared at her with deadly seriousness, but then his eyes smiled and, soon, his lips followed.

"But if it weren't so, would you then tell me?" he asked again, causing no less discomfort to Winter than before. This time, nonetheless, she was more inclined to believe in his good faith. She had nothing to fear, no, she could say in absolute certainty; she had no reason to hide from him, at least not here and not now. She shook her head and giggled.

"No!" she admitted, and the major nodded with a convinced smile.

They went outside and felt the vastness of the landscape completely open up their souls. The cool and green verdure was invigorating, the grass soft and moist, still maintaining the morning dew. So much life in this piece of green land: lush trees with robust branches traipsed by squirrels and housing birds' nests, rustling leaves letting through the sunrays and blue sky; rivers with small waterfalls, quiet streams and ponds, with long-legged waders probing for small invertebrates, ducks, geese and swans swimming gracefully, occasionally plunging into the water. On a dry bulge in the middle of a stream, a stubborn blackbird was hitting the ground with its tiny feet as if trying to level it, and next to it, underwater, various fish shook their tails to the surface, making deep wet sounds.

Winter felt she could stay there forever, and she protested sweetly when the major informed her they would have to leave soon, if they wanted to return to Paris before dark.

"Oh, but can't we, please, please, please, stay?" Winter begged in the cuddliest manner, eager to keep the fairy tale alive for as long as she could. After all, how often did one have the opportunity to be a princess in an actual castle?

"Where's my little princess? Where has the evil witch hidden her?"

The major simply had to give in to her longing and somehow find a way to please her. He left her alone for a while and, when he returned, he announced that, if she liked, they could stay until dark at the castle, but they would have to spend the night at the town inn and travel back to Paris early in the morning. Although her wish had not been fulfilled exactly, Winter was no less content, for which she felt she owed him a greatly deserving, sincere and sprightly hug.

They spent the rest of the afternoon sitting on some rocks next to a murmuring spring. Winter had enjoyed the gardens more than anything–yes, the castle had been great, so spectacular and impressive; but the nature around, that was unique. It was exactly what she would imagine Paradise to be, if there actually were such a thing, she said, giving the major reason to claim, that, if one were to accept religion as largely symbolic, abandoning nature might be precisely what the Fall of Man was all about, and that the Second Coming could, in truth, be the reunification of Man with it.

It gave Winter a sense of self-importance and value, hearing the major talk to her about such intellectual issues, but when he spoke about ordinary matters, like stories from his past, well, that was really when she eagerly took in his every word. As a child, the major adored gardening, he confided in her. He dug the soil, planted seeds, cared for the plants and they reciprocated his love by growing, blooming, and bearing fruit. Winter acknowledged that, although they had a beautiful garden in England, she was never apt to growing things herself. Watering was her favourite garden activity, but not out of care for the plants: she could play with the water all she wanted and get soaked through without the risk of being told off by Mother. The major could not help but notice how Winter had shown particular love for water in all its forms and she shrugged in declaration of complete ignorance why.

"Maybe because England is a country with a lot of water around it!" she plainly guessed.

"Or perhaps because water means life!" the major contended, and Winter felt it might indeed be because of that. She stared at him, sensing an almost magical rapport: who was he, she wondered, who could see so deeply into her, who could reach into her heart and touch it without hurting it? Who was he and what was she to him?

They said goodbye to the *Château de Chantilly* shortly after nightfall. At the town, the inn was a charming three-storey building with an attic, climbing plants perched on every flat surface and lush flower pots hanging from its windows. The innkeeper, a hearty, middle-aged woman with a provincial face, led them to their rooms, the best rooms in the house, besides the bridal suite, she claimed.

Finding herself alone again, it seemed to Winter that a whole life had been squeezed into that single day, a life as should be. She opened the shutters to let in the evening cool, bent over to the flower pots and smelt their sweet fragrance. She was almost afraid to admit how happy she was, how wonderful it all felt, the quiet street, lit by a couple of old-fashioned oil lamps, the inn with its fresh lawn and shrubs, the quaint little room with no electricity, which was so befitting the fantasy the entire place created. As in the times of princesses and princes, when all that was needed was a dark corner, a secluded hiding place, and, perhaps, the pale, but warm, light of a candle, to dream of their loved ones and secretly meet them to consummate their love.

She sighed and shivered. She could stay there daydreaming all night, but she did not have to, not anymore. She hurried to freshen up and go downstairs to the dining room, where the major was waiting for her, already sitting at a round table in a corner near the window.

"I'm afraid this is all there is for dinner!" he modestly apologised on behalf of the innkeeper, who regretted not being able to prepare anything else at this time of day and without electricity available. There was a large jug of creamy milk, a basket with a sliced loaf of bread and a cup of butter, smooth and shiny like silk.

"Hmmm, probably the best I've ever had!" Winter said, demonstrating her every intention of simply scoffing the food.

"My words exactly!" the major agreed cheerfully and prepared a rich slice of bread and butter and a mug of milk for her.

She gave her bread an enthusiastic first bite and then she put aside all reservations and dipped the bread and butter into the milk, chowing down on it and smacking her lips. Looking at her, the major laughed sincerely, but soon did exactly as she. No doubt they were hungry, but the bread was delicious, with that light taste of sourdough and its dense crumb, which made them completely disregard the fact that it was neither fresh nor crispy. The milk was so thick that they felt it forming a protective layer of fat in their stomachs, its mouth-watering flavour whetting their appetite. And then, there was the butter, a true gastronomic luxury, soft and luscious on the bread and sweet as sugarplum.

He asked her if she was satisfied and she replied there were no words to describe it. He then asked if she would care for a last touch of perfection.

"The way you've spoiled me, I'd expect no less!" she challenged him in the cutest way and was delighted to see the major come back to the table with a bottle of bold-red wine in one hand and two crystal stemmed glasses in the other.

They had their wine at a bench on the front lawn of the inn, under the flickering lamp consuming its last reserves of oil. They talked about the experiences of the day, and both of them agreed it was unforgettable. They sat in silence, a calming silence only broken by the sounds of the night and the gargling of wine as it poured into their glasses.

"So how much more of this wine is there left in the bottle?" Winter wondered at one point, feeling so mellowed she could hardly articulate the words.

The major took the bottle in his hand, turned it towards the light and shook his head.

"Not much, I'm afraid, since you drank it all!" he teased her.

"Me? Such a lie!" Winter protested, laughing. "What am I to hear next? That I'm drunk?"

"Are you?" he enquired with a frolic raise of his eyebrow.

She held out her empty glass, urging him to refill it. "Well, obviously not enough to forget that we'll have to get back tomorrow!"

He filled up her glass and poured the remaining wine into his. "Perhaps the last fill will help!" he told her with a smile. "Shall we drink to today?"

"To today!"

The sound of clinking glasses, a high pitch note in the afterglow stillness, awakened the voice of a night owl. The leaves rustled, and the wind shook the flower petals in the pots decorating the inn windows.

"The inn looks very much like my father's house in Germany!" recalled the major in a velvety tone. "Pots and flowers on the windows, all very similar!" Sweet nostalgia was reflected in his eyes, but Winter could not see it, having turned to look at the inn windows. "My mother used to make her own flower pots, you know!" he added, faintly smiling.

"You don't say!" she exclaimed in surprise and admiration.

He hummed and added: "All kinds of clayware! She loved pottery! ... She even tried to show me once!" He laughed heartily. "I was so clumsy! Absolutely skill-less!"

Winter looked at him, seeming unconvinced: "I'd never think of you as clumsy at anything!" she spontaneously reflected and he found her remark very touching, but he chose not to show it.

"You're not trying to flatter me, I hope, *Fräulein*!" he joked, and Winter did not hesitate to respond accordingly.

"I wouldn't dare! You've said you hate adulators!" He confirmed with a nod, happy that she cared to remember, and let her carry on with her childlike enthusiasm, which he liked so much about her. "...In our house there were large bay windows downstairs, marvellously extending the view to the front yard and letting beautiful light inside. My favourite place in the house, of course, was the attic. I could stay up there for hours, digging into boxes and old trunks, trying on my mother's dresses and shoes, pretending to be a princess, locked away in the tower by the evil witch, waiting for my prince to come save me!"

"Weren't you a little young for a prince?" the major bantered with her and she responded with a sentimental smile.

"My father was my prince!" she remembered with her eyes in the mist of yearning. "We would play hide and seek. I was terrified waiting for him to find me, and when he eventually did, there was so much screaming and shouting we were often severely berated by my mother. Then we would collusively hush one another and rest long into each other's arms..." Winter's heart pined for the tenderness of that embrace, but it was somehow a painless longing with nothing too harrowing or pitiful. Perhaps because she had drunk a bit more than usual and her feelings had been amplified by the alcohol, perhaps because it was a memory being shared or because the major's hand reached for hers and soothed her with his touch. "...I miss him so much!" she felt strong enough to admit. "I miss all of them. Mother, the twins ..."

"Have you not been to see them since you left?" he gently asked, and she shook her head negatively, this time with a shadow of guilt and remorse. "Why not?"

She squeezed her lips, made an expression of utter helplessness: "I'm afraid, I guess! ... Afraid that if I see them, if I hold them in my arms, I will never be able to leave again...!"

She turned to him to see if he was disapproving, but he looked as ever so understanding. How could he, she wondered, when she could often not understand herself? He ran his fingers through her hair and smiled, and she closed her eyes and enjoyed the caress, feeling like all the unanswered questions in her had been mollified and become harmless, making everything seem so simple, so effortless and undemanding. She drank the remaining wine in her glass and quivered.

"Are you cold?"

"... A sudden chill!"

Without a second thought, he took off his suit jacket and carefully laid it over her shoulders.

"Better?"

Winter nodded, speechless at the sight of his fingers loosening his tie and unbuttoning the top button of his light blue shirt: his Adam's apple; the curve of the back of his neck; the spear pointed collar showing the direction to the defined muscles of his chest; the gray braces with button loops which tamed the irregular creases of the cotton shirt fabric, intriguingly hiding underneath the waistband of his trousers.

She blushed, realising her thoughts, and immediately turned her gaze elsewhere, pretending to look at the courtyard, at the lantern that went out with a faint rustling sound, leaving them alone with the seductive sky glow... Suddenly, there was the gentle pat of a raindrop on her forehead and she winced. Another drop. She raised her face up and laughed with growing excitement as the drizzle turned into rain. Then she lowered her eyes, looked at him: his face so close, his eyes reflecting their bright gray shine. She was not afraid of the rain either; at that moment, she was not afraid of anything.

They shut the door of the inn behind them, locked it up, as if they themselves had been the innkeepers. They went up the stairs, their wet hair dripping onto the floor. On the landing, they were to separate. She pulled his jacket off her shoulders and silently returned it to him.

"Thank you for everything!" she said and her voice was warm, warmer than she could possibly think. He smiled at her, reaching for her cheek, giving her a persistent kiss on the lips. Then he stood to watch her make her way to her room.

The door was there, ready to draw Winter into loneliness again. But she did not wish to be alone. She turned towards him, still on the landing, his hand in one pocket of the trousers offering enough support for his suit jacket, and he looked like an ordinary man, not a major, not a conqueror, perhaps like someone casually waiting for a bus or a girlfriend to show up. And she felt like it was this way that she had always been looking at him, a man like any other, a man she could easily fall in love with.

"Stay with me tonight, Fred!" she invited him, and there was no shame, no fear that he might misjudge or abuse her.

With calm passion, he came to claim her mouth. And it accepted him, as if it had only been created for this moment. Her fingers eagerly felt for everywhere her enchanted eyes had reached before and whatever stood in the way of their longing, she did not hesitate to remove. His back was strong, with muscles willingly responding to her every stroke; a shallow dimple where the stomach joined the sternum; between the ribs and the broad bone of his pelvis, a piece of tender skin; a line of soft dark hair, descending from the depression of his navel, trailed over his abdominals to the nucleus of lust. And she wanted to touch him. Touch him, that's what she wanted. Because he was mortal, like the man next door, like a random passerby, like she herself was. His forty-three-year-old body did not inspire the virginal sensation of youth, neither was the path of its life a bed of roses: there was a bullet scar below his right shoulder and, next to the left nipple on his chest, the skin was badly scorched. This body was not unfamiliar to pain and it had often heard the horrific whisper of death, but it was robust and unyielding, vivacious and receptive to her. She tasted its salty flesh, breathed in its fragrance. She soaked into the fervour of its hands, genuinely male hands, experienced and able. And she wanted to feel. Feel him, that's what she longed for: because he was as vulnerable as she; he conquered and surrendered; two bodies fused together, naked, unguarded, entirely human...

18

Just another playtoy

The window was veiled with yellow organza, concealing enough for eyes drowning in their rage, appropriate to dress the view with their mood for conflict: yellow morning; yellow street; yellow people: a German and a girl. He was first to get out of the black car, opened the door for her, helped her out. They looked at each other long; talkative eyes, though lips silent. A kiss on her hand, a kiss on her cheek. She smiled, and a sunray beamed at her, which hid almost right after. He watched as she entered the building and there was a fairly human-looking face on him before he got back in the car and drove off. Dancing steps resounded up the stairs, brisk and cheerful with the unbearable lightness of a desire adequately fulfilled. A hummed song echoing into the roof; tapping shoes pirouetting at the landing; the key in the lock turning four times–time for the plain truth to be told and faced up to.

Winter was humming the lively tune, climbing the staircase, dancing to the rhythm, and, when she reached the landing of her floor, she tapped her shoes and performed a graceful pirouette. She turned the key in the door four times and entered; on her lips a smile as playful as the song. She left her purse in an armchair and took off her shoes, noticing there was still on them mud from the gardens at the *Château de Chantilly*. She chortled with excitement and let out a wistful sigh.

She was happy, she might as well admit it; and she could just crack up laughing, but stood up instead, with her shoulders wide and her head tilted backwards, breathing in deeply that unparalleled feeling of completeness she had actually forgotten when she had last felt it: probably a long, long time ago, before she even knew what it meant, before she could even realise it was there.

She smiled and headed for the bedroom, but the minute she walked in, she froze and the blood drained from her head down to the tip of her toes. He was standing by the window, looking outside, his back to the door, a back in full tension, like a string on a guitar strained to the point of breaking, his hands two tight fists, eager to unleash their savage anger at the first opportunity.

"So, you finally found the way back!"

The skylight in the roof, wide open, violently caught her attention. So becoming of him, she thought, intimidated by the skills and determination she assumed were required of a man, in order to find his way onto the roof of the building and, from there, into her apartment, creeping inside, as if he were a shadow from the most mysterious depths of this earth. She brought her eyes down at him again, feverishly digging in her mind for an answer befitting the content and, particularly, the tone of his remark.

"René!" was the only appropriate thing she could find to say.

Hearing his name, he roared like an enraged animal.

"I've been here all night!" he stated, affirming with his every word that he was pure danger. Winter preferred silence. "I was waiting for you!" he continued, making it sound like an accusation. He turned his head to the side but avoided looking at her. "Where have you been?"

Confused and terrified, she stared at him. Telling him the truth was out of the question, though she was certain he already knew. It did not strike her as a surprise that he had found her, neither that he risked his life waiting for her, knowing that she might not return alone. It was impossible to even guess his intentions–it was the most frightening trait of his, a man ready for anything, indifferent to the consequences his actions could have on himself or others. What did he want from her?

What did he want from her? It was the only question that mattered, but she did not have the nerve to ask it. She always felt so weak, so defenseless before him. What was it about him that devoured every bit of strength in her? she could not help but wonder.

"You were with him!" she heard him throw another accusation and this time his gaze was as condemning as a death sentence to a convicted criminal. "You spent the night with him, didn't you?"

Suddenly, she felt ashamed; a guilt for an unforgivable sin corrupted the stimulating memory of the night before. Her mind was ravished by images of women with shaved heads under the warning 'No collaboration' printed on posters randomly set up all over the city one day, before the Prefecture workers had the chance to pull them down. And she envisaged René gladly taking the task upon himself to rid her of her hair, a just punishment for this and her other despicable crimes against humanity.

"Spit it out then!" René shouted, and she flinched and impulsively made a step backwards, the bedroom door open behind her, an invitation to be bold, damned if she did it and damned if she did not; but there she stood, stiff as wood, unable for little else than to look at him spring up towards her and reach her with only a couple of strides. The grip of his hands on her arms hurt her, but pain felt so familiar, so much more familiar than happiness. "You slept with him, didn't you?" he insisted with a suffering voice, and Winter could see he himself was feeling deeply wounded. "Hell, Winter, why? Why did you do that?" she heard his cry and her heart melted in such sorrow and remorse, that she could look into his eyes and tell him all he wanted to hear, she could take him in her arms and hold him in comfort, promising everything would be alright. "Tell me the truth!" he beseeched her. "Did he take you by force?"

Every word and another nail in the coffin, another accusation she had no means to refute, but it was frustrating because she knew that what was done could not be undone and she did not even know if she wanted it undone, which added up to her guilt, entrapping her in an unbreakable vicious circle. Guilt and shame, nothing else in the human conscience could be more morally degrading; and she felt them both.

"Speak!" René's gaze was a wedge of hard metal in her eyes. He stood in front of her, the volume of his body awesomely imposing, his eyes two narrow holes into darkness, his lips a thin line of spite: "Of course not!" he correctly concluded out of her persistence to keep quiet. "He wouldn't take you by force!" With his look as rough as sandpaper, he scraped her from face to bosom, the coral-red frills of her shirt irritating him like a matador's flag. "He just bought you!" he insulted her with grinding teeth. "And you sold yourself of your own free will!" He nodded on her behalf, not anymore expecting a word from her.

But her heart was broken, and a plaintive protest arose in it against his reproof, arrogantly stemming from his severe, self-important single-mindedness. Was it really? she wanted to cry out. Had anything she had done so far been of her own free will and not a product of her life's misfortunes? Had she been able to keep Father alive, had she remained home, grown up in a different environment, under different conditions, had the war found her with her family where they belonged, who knows what might have been? Who knows what kind of person she would have grown to be, what greatness she might have been capable of? ... No, enough with the excuses, the critical part of her innermost self dared her. If she wanted to be frank and hope to redeem herself somehow, someday, she would have to admit: life was all about choices; and she had made hers. And there she was, there was René, and there were the ways of her life questioned, and the arsenal of defense for her was poor, too poor for a man as defiant, bold and brave as he was.

"What were you so desperate for? A man? The worthless comforts you have come to be so accustomed to?" he bawled out and grabbed her by the neck, bringing her only a breath away, and Winter was scared that he would try to force himself on her in order to get even. But he only pulled her aside, and pushed her against the wardrobe door, caging her with his sturdy figure.

Winter raised a weepy gaze at him and felt the sting of jealousy under his armour of fury and madness: "Please!" she was finally able to utter with a warm petition, appealing to the most ardent of his emotions, which she knew were there, because she had felt them, body and soul, when he had her in his arms and loved her. "Don't do this!" Because not long ago, the two of them had found a precious comfort in each other, valuable and cherished like a rare gem, on her part, at least; and she felt tender towards him, tender and sad. If only it could have lasted. If only they had not been separated by such deep an ocean of dissension, if only it had not been as different as night and day between them. She looked at him, remembering his flaming touch, his passion with the intensity of a storm, and could not but compare it to the major's calm. But would he have been calm if he knew about the night she had spent with René? It always was the need of lovers to feel unique and irreplaceable. And how much more important it must have been for a man with a heart made of fire such as René, as fierce in the way he loved as in the way he lived, feeling betrayed not only because he had been replaced by another man, but mostly because this other man was a most hateful foe. She raised her eyes to him again, overwhelmed by the desire to soothe him, her gaze imploring and inviting, but his was harsh and sharp-edged like broken glass, like a warrior's sword crushed in battle.

"You're not even much of a bargain! Second-hand and overused!" he lashed out at her without a shred of mercy, utterly demolishing her every hope for compassion. "To be honest, I don't expect him to get by the whole idea without a second thought. You've given him what he wanted; he has tried you out; you don't really think he'll show up again, do you?" Well, for once, this was where René was completely wrong, Winter proudly opposed. The major was nothing like he thought he was. He did not know him; she did; and the night before was the plainest evidence that René was wrong. He came closer and observed the daring certainty spontaneously flooding her eyes, and he sneered in response, whipping her with his cynical look. "Oh, so, you do!" He laughed scornfully. He laughed hysterically. He laughed, and laughing, he shredded her confidence slowly but surely. Because he was the devil, and the devil most delighted in the small undetected details; perhaps he knew something more than she did, as had so often, but in hindsight, been revealed to her. She looked at him, the way he mockingly shook his head, the way he contemptibly squeezed his lips, and she could not but doubt everything she thought certain–had she not already been convinced enough by the facts of life that there was no such thing as assurance? "You think you're someone special!" he snubbed, enjoying every bit of hurting her. "You're an idiot! You're just another playtoy for him! He'll tire of you soon enough and then what will you be?" He leaned over to her ear–his breath was like hot iron. "Nothing but a German whore! Whore! Whore!"

His scream made her shrink, horrified by the rampage boiling in his nostrils, the sparks flying out of his eyes, the swelling of the veins on his temples. With the fury of a rabid beast, he grabbed her clothes, blouse, petticoat, brassiere, and tore them open, exposing her breasts to his humiliating gaze. Instinctively, Winter tried to cover herself with her hands, but he pulled them away violently, warning her with a finger pointing right into her face not to try it again.

"What are you going to do now?" he hissed with a venomous voice. "Who's going to want you when you're thrown out like the garbage you are?"

His words were like a knife shoved directly into her heart; his spit upon her face the finishing stroke. Then he turned away and walked out through the front door, like a perfect gentleman. Winter fell to her knees, curled up on the floor, and, for hours, she tried to cry away the shame. But shame always works its way inside one's soul in its own time and in quiet. And René knew it; it was his intention. René was gone, but he had already contaminated her with his hatred.

19

A time of true miracles

The end of summer was an extremely eventful period. The air-raids intensified, as did the Resistance strikes and subsequent German retaliations, while, on a completely contrary side, exorbitant auctions were being regularly attended at the city galleries and people crowded for the races at the *Hippodrome de Longchamp*, when the dust cloud from the bombardment of the area was yet to settle. In early September, an explosive mechanism, triggered outside a governmental building, severely injured fifteen people, and, at the end of the month, a British bomber crashed right into the roof of *Les Grands Magasins du Louvre*, the famous department store in the heart of the historical centre.

Winter rushed there to see the astonishing sight, mingled with the hundreds of strangers who had been driven by their curiosity, once it was indisputably confirmed that it was only an isolated event and not a horrible repetition of last March's bombing. Ambulances, fire engines and trucks from the German Technical Service swamped the area, all the way from the *Palais Royal* to the *Louvre*; people with light injuries still remained in the vicinity; soldiers helped clear away entire boulders of cement and bricks, while others tried to keep civilians off the perimetre. Winter was one of those persistent ones the soldiers had to keep at a distance, but it was more than mere nosiness that had prompted her presence at the scene: the *Hôtel du Louvre* was next to the metre of operations. When she finally managed to descry the major at the junction of *Rue de Rivoli* and *Place du Carrousel*, she slipped through guards and obstacles, ignoring every warning to run to his embrace.

"You shouldn't be here!" he reproved, fugitively caressing her cheek with his fingers. "You have to go ..."

In the following days, they only talked on the phone. The convenient apartment of the *Cité Berryer* was only a ten-minute walk from the *Hôtel du Louvre*, but the major did not even show up once. Winter was starting to believe Rene's dire predictions were becoming true and, were it so, it would not impress her at all–every beautiful thing in her life had always lasted so little.

Lying in bed, long staring at the moonlight from the skylight, Winter realised that she was yet another night going to stay awake. She got up, went to the cocktail cabinet, chose the strongest drink and had a couple of shots, one after the other, welcoming the warmth of the alcohol inside her. She came to stand by the front window, impassively looked outside. *Rue Royal* was quiet. On the façade of the opposite building, shutters were all closed; all but one, on a top floor to the left, its curtain faintly blowing in the autumn breeze, a definite eye-catcher. Someone with enough worries to stay up like her, she thought, and her mind flew directly to René. Yes, René could very well be behind that disobedient curtain, spying on her and her every move with his piercing eyes.

A momentary fear overwhelmed her, and with a spasmodic move, she hid to the side. It was so stupid of her not to think about it earlier. Of course René was there, of course he was watching her and not only her. He had complete control over her; he showed up and disappeared as he pleased, adored and condemned her with the same ease, leaving no room for reasoning, for explanation at least, because his feelings were primitive and savage, and there was something so disarming about that, as there was something so devastating. She glanced at the window again with an ambiguous sentiment, a wish for him, a spurn, too. She stepped forward, more determined than ever, stood in the middle of the window, her body in tension, her head held up high. She stretched out her arms, a signal of surrender and provocation.

"Here I am, strike me, if you want!" she murmured and imagined René with a firearm in his hands, his eyes fixed on the target, the butt plate pressing against his shoulder, his finger on the trigger, ready for a single key blow to her head or to her heart, to better serve his purpose.

Nothing happened, and Winter soon put her arms down, sighing a deep, grave disappointment. Death was only a convenience, she pondered with a large dose of self-bitterness, and he would not relieve her of his presence that easily. She reached out and closed the shutters, immersing the room in thick darkness. She picked up a pillow and snuggled with it on the sofa, yearning for some comfort. The bedroom felt so inhospitable that night.

Her head was heavy, and her stomach was like a tight fist the next day. She warmed a little water, took a refreshing bath, but she did not feel better. It was almost noon until she recovered and managed to have a simple breakfast, accompanied by countless cups of tea. The major had once more not shown up and, this morning, he had not even called. She forced herself not to start the desperate internal dialogues that drove her crazy and tried to think rationally. The plane crash, the attacks, everything that being at war meant and was taking place right there, around them; things far more important than her and her insecurities were happening in the world, she could make no pretensions to being the centre of it. But there was this feeling inside, which was stronger than any logical conclusion: the feeling of doom.

She sat in an armchair and picked up a book, one that the major had spoken of so fondly: "*Das Marienleben*" she read out loud in German. "*The Life of Mary*."

It was a beautiful, leather-bound edition of thirteen poems about the life of the Virgin Mary, but it was nothing like what one would expect hearing this description. Winter had begun reading it in the English translations that the major himself had written, but now her German was improved–comparing it to the English text, she could read the original with a pretty good understanding of the association of words and meanings, thus being able to enjoy the poems and contemplate upon them.

She had never considered herself a very religious person, although her parents had not neglected to teach her reverence for God. She used to pray before bed every night as a child, but then Father was gone and she ineffectually prayed for his return. She knew she believed in God–John and Carol Pale's daughter could never be an atheist; it just seemed that there had always been too much on her plate to leave her any appetite for religion. God would usually feel so distant that she would nearly forget His entire existence. She had, hence, no expectation of her prayers being heard on the scarce occasions she did remember Him.

The Life of Mary evoked tender and familiar feelings in Winter. Rilke's Mary was not, as often depicted, a strict symbol of sanctification and endurance. She was a girl who was born one still night in a family whose old age had meant it was hardly possible that such a coming could ever be. She knew she was special, she felt it in the strange vigour in her heart. When the miracle happened and the Angel came, she blushed so shyly, because he was handsome–a handsome young man quaking her heart. And the more the Holy Seed grew inside her, the more beautiful she became and Joseph was jealous, knowing it was not him her beauty was owed to. And the Angel said to him: you, who take pride in your work because you can make boards from wood, can you really judge the work of Him, who makes wood grow leaves and flowers? And Joseph fell silent and realised he was too little to judge, not only the works of God but also of man. Then He came, who was not He for Mary, for He was her son. And she protected Him, the protector of all, she cared for Him, the healer of all sicknesses, and urged Him to His wonderful works, because that was what mothers did, they struggled to see their children thrive. Shortly before the Passion, Mary knew that Her son's fate was the Cross, and hers was insufferable pain. And she mourned for the cruel Will that made her a mother without a child and annulled Nature. **"You lie now across my lap, and now I can no longer give birth to you!"**[57] His Resurrection would not bring her child back to her, but it was a consolation to know that death had not prevailed over Him. And with the mercy of memory which God had bestowed on man, with the remembrance of this last vision of Him, of His touch on her shoulder, she would quietly close her eyes when her time came.

Winter's eyes filled up with tears. She was always tearful reading these verses, feeling so attached to the fate of Mary, perhaps because she herself had mourned someone she loved and had to keep him alive with memory alone. Mary had been the paradigm of benevolence in the face of the undeniable, unavoidable fact of life which death was. But she was one of the few, very few ones created in the image and likeness of God who managed to attain such magnanimity–Winter herself included.

She closed the book and left it on the table. She put on some music, held the rhythm with her fingers, tried to focus on it. She could not find peace. On the opposite building, all the windows now had their shutters closed. Which one was it that had brought such turmoil to her thoughts and emotions the previous night? she asked herself and sighed deeply, letting her head fall backwards, closing her eyes. René! René! René: how was it possible to even think of him after all he had said to her, after that humiliation, to which there was no precedent and no redress either. It was an outburst of jealousy, a voice protested underneath the crust of her skull. No jealousy justified this spleen, another argued from the depths of her stomach. She had provoked him with her silence. She might as well have told him a lie to reassure him, the voice in her head was groaning. She owed him nothing, the other one disputed.

At that moment, the doorbell rang, and all voices and all thoughts simply disappeared. The expectation for the one she was waiting illuminated her face and with a brand new, lively mood, she ran to answer the door. Seeing only the major's driver, she frowned in frustration.

"*Guten Tag, Fräulein*!"[58] the driver saluted with every formality and passed her a small white envelope, saying, as Winter roughly understood, that the major was sending her a message to which she had to give him the reply in order to convey it.

She opened the envelope with much reservation, considering these new ways of communicating with the major strange, to say the least. Inside the envelope, a card with the major's handwriting read:

"I implore your forgiveness for dispatching such an impersonal notice, and I'd be honoured if you would accompany me to dinner tonight. My driver will pick you up at 8.00 p.m. I'm looking forward to it!

Fred"

She smiled and nodded positively to the driver, saying in her best German that she accepted the invitation.

Being invited to dinner by the major definitely had a soothing effect on her anxiety, and the ceremonial character of his request was, in fact, somewhat intriguing, she eagerly thought, but returning inside, her eye fell on the telephone, and that ill premonition warned her against raising her hopes up too high. She approached hesitantly, picked up the receiver, and brought it to her ear: the telephone was dead.

She walked to the window again, looked outside more carefully; nothing seemed out of the ordinary. With telephones not working, who knows what calamity might have befallen the conquerors this time, she wondered, and immediately thought that if René could hear her talk this way, he would congratulate her, and he might even take back some of his malice against her.

At exactly eight o'clock in the evening, the doorbell rang again: a sharp short ring, followed by an exact same one. Winter was ready, looking her best, putting on her best mood, too–the perspective of a night together with the major had played an enormously prominent role in that. When she realised that the car was heading to the major's house, her enthusiasm multiplied. There was no better place for an intimate evening with him than the well-maintained mansion, which seemed so familiar to her, although it had been a long time since that night, when, with as much excitement as suspicion, she had first passed its doorstep. She remembered every detail: the garden with the stone path to the staircase, the red brick walls with the vast windows, the shining chandeliers in every room, the layout of the furniture, the pictures on the walls.

As the driver escorted her to the entrance, a woman opened the door, a woman in her thirties, tall and slim, with conservative dress, dark-coloured cardigan with a single pleat skirt and a groomed chignon of brown hair: the housekeeper. Winter had completely forgotten about the housekeeper, which was peculiar, because, as soon as she saw her, she immediately recalled how much she had disliked her. At the end of these thoughts, the major appeared in the hallway and his warm welcome diminished the importance of all else.

"Winter!"

She was relieved to see he looked tired, sleepless, his civilian suit making him look a man almost like any other. But he was like no other. Just like René, the major had something extraordinary about him, something impossible to overlook and not be drawn to; only, the major inspired a feeling of security, while René... Well, there was definitely no sense of security with René; there was just wild and hungry instinct...

They drank a couple of aperitifs, chatted casually, flirted subtly. By dinner, it already seemed as though there had not been a day since they had last seen each other and Winter felt she could safely put to sleep all her former fears about their relationship. When they moved to the dining room, Winter was pleased to see that her tableware was set close to the major's and not at the top of the table opposite him, as probably instructed by formalities. And their excellent food and more excellent wine were accompanied by a most attentive attitude on the major's part, which Winter could not fail to notice.

"Let us drink to the beautiful things coming!" the major invited her, raising his glass and Winter gestured 'Why not?', although she did not quite understand what exactly the source of his optimism was, but assumed it must have been something related to the war. "You know, Winter, I've been thinking much of you lately!" the major continued, changing into what she perceived as a gravely serious tone by which she felt greatly alarmed.

"In what way?" she motivated him, ready with his answer to condemn or acquit herself.

"If you are happy!"

She bit her lip and questioned every single of her recent actions, which might have given the major the idea that she was not happy.

"Why wouldn't I be? Not many girls these days enjoy what I have, what you have offered me!" she hurried to reply and looked at him with deep gratitude and invisible fear.

The major preferred to disregard what her gaze spoke of and looked at his glass, the brim of which he touched with his finger and ran its perimetre. Winter observed this movement and remembered that René had once done the same thing with the brim of a coffee cup. She shivered inside and drew her gaze away, feeling her cheeks burning up.

"... But what if you could have more?"

She brought her eyes back to him and saw he was looking at her with captivating sobriety that made her linger between guilt and anticipation. How could she deny having longed for words like this, but it was René she had wanted to hear them from–instead he had offered her nothing but disillusionment and pain.

"What are you trying to say?" she asked, and not for lack of comprehension.

The major smiled. He brought his palm to her cheek and came closer, the distance of a breath between them readying Winter for the sweetest passionate kiss.

"If you could have... a home?" he whispered affectionately to her.

Winter shuddered at the echo of the word 'home'. She had almost forgotten what home meant, what a home looked or felt like. The only home she had ever considered hers was gone along with Father, it had been buried with him in a cemetery outside of London, in a grave that would have withered after so many years of desertion. She remembered it like yesterday when the half-round marble stone was placed upon the grave, a few days after the funeral. Freshly carved, unblemished, its calligraphic engravings making the mournful pledge,

John James Pale
1882 - 1933
Husband and father
Goodbye, our beloved!
You will live in our hearts forever!

She closed her eyelids shut, and a tear rolled down onto the major's fingers. She felt embarrassed, sat back awkwardly, and hurried to wipe the tears from her eyes.

"I'm sorry!" she apologised. "Forgive me, please!"

He looked at her with sincere emotion. "I never want to see you cry again! I never want you to be afraid, feel alone or helpless!" He took both her hands in his and fervently kissed them. "Marry me, Winter!" he said. "And I'll make sure nothing is missing in your life anymore!"

Oh, René had been so mistaken about him, a triumph hailed inside her. Because he was a truly honest and caring man, more honest and caring than anyone she had known, besides Father. What could he ever want with her? What could she possibly have to give him other than shame and misery?

"This is... What you said is very sweet!" she managed to say with difficulty and hated herself for not being able to feel this sweetness.

"... But?"

As if by the most vulgar rejection, she got up from the table, eyes wide open to restrain the tears; and inside she was torn into pieces that could not bear the existence of one another.

"But you don't really want me, Fred!" she uttered bitterly. "You couldn't want someone like me, don't fool yourself! I've violated every rule there is, every moral law; I'm tainted in the eyes of the world, in my own eyes. I wish things had been different, but what I've done, I cannot take back. Neither can I say that, under the same circumstances, I wouldn't do the exact same things all over again. I'm alive and I won't apologise for it. I cannot change either!"

She buried her face in her hands and wished the earth would open up to swallow her. She would like to cry, but she thought it too cheap and shameless a manipulation even for the likes of her.

"I appreciate your intention to be honest, Winter!" the major claimed, and the creaking of his chair indicated that he, too, had left his seat. "But I didn't ask you to change, nor to apologise. I don't care what you had to do to survive. I never saw you that way, you know it!"

His hands rested on her arms, firm, but full of sensitivity, which gave Winter an even more resentful feeling.

"Yes!" she reluctantly agreed. "You've always been decent. You didn't have to and yet you've always treated me like a lady!"

She was feeling naked, her walk of atonement yet to come, a just punishment for an unrepentant sinner. Only there was no absolution for her no matter how many miles she walked amidst the most barbarous crowd howling at her: 'Shame!' For her shame had forever marked her like a branding iron, and there was no knife sharp enough to cut away this burn.

"I will not have you talk about yourself this way!" she heard him utter, but his contestation was like adding fuel to the fire of her self-indignation.

"It doesn't matter how I talk! How I talk doesn't change what I am!" she cried out and darted at him a hostile gaze as if it were he who was to blame, he and not her, or, to be more exact, he and not someone else, someone she had never dared confront, even though she would like to, even though she should. After this, they both remained speechless, and, in a while, the major walked out, leaving Winter standing like a pillar of salt in the middle of the dining room.

A cold shiver ran down her spine, sweat, and a sensation of her blood draining away from her body. Lonely and deserted, as if she were the only person left in a world burnt to the ground, that was how she felt. And she herself could hardly comprehend this whole attempt to discourage the only man who, for some strange reason, wanted her, what perverse satisfaction it could have been stemming from. What she would gain if he, too, abandoned her, other than prove her ill fate once again right, that very fate she claimed to want changed. But did she really? Did she really want anything changed or was she content being miserable because that was all she knew how to be? She watched the major move up and down in the living room, lighting a cigarette, pouring a drink, sipping it quietly, and she remembered the urge to seek him out on the day the bomber crashed, an urge so spontaneous and true.

He raised his eyes at her; they were sad but mild, with that empathy she often failed to grasp. He showed her his glass, half-full of the dark-coloured drink, asked if she wanted one, she answered she did. He gave her the drink, drank up his, took a few steps towards the window, and continued to smoke silently.

"I've always had great respect for people with knowledge and understanding of themselves, but, truly, this seems to go far beyond self-awareness!" he said thoughtfully, calmly observing the irregular shapes of his smoke. "So, either you're punishing yourself, which is unfair to us both, or this is all just pretext!"

Winter looked at him mournfully, a countenance straightforward and demanding of a sincere reply, but she had no idea either of directness or of honesty.

"Pretext for what?" she sighed in frustration and his answer was nowhere close to what she would expect to hear: "If you don't want to marry a German, you can say so directly. I will not be angry and you're not going to lose my favour!"

"Oh, Fred!"

As if a solid piece of ice had suddenly melted inside her, she was overwhelmed with sympathy and affection for this man, who may not have been torn in two–half German, half British–but he must have had his own share of ghost-hunting, some kind of pain or hatred crushing and swamping his soul. And she felt enough tenderness to approach and stretch her hand to touch his face, ready and eager to say: "I've never caused you to believe such a thing, Fred, that I mind you are a German?"

The major gladly admitted that was true.

"But it's different when we talk about marriage!" he argued with disarming sobriety. "An unattached relationship can always be justified by necessity or even fear. Marriage, on the other hand, requires consent. It's like making a public statement, openly choosing your camp!" He looked at her seriously, but with no evidence of reproof. "If you can't do that... I'll understand!"

His reasoning left Winter hesitant, and the major regarded her ambivalence as an adequate response. He put out his cigarette, let out a perfectly controlled sigh, and even smiled at her. Winter's expression was frozen stiff. She did not know much about public statements, but she did know that, if ever she was asked about the major, she would only be able to say that he had treated her more warmly than anyone, that he had aroused feelings she had forgotten existed and that he shone as the only light in the long darkness of her life.

"No, Fred! It's not that!" she told him and moved closer with a heartfelt need to reassure him, but was fully apprehended by the dark in his eyes, his tight lips, and the grim aspect of him she only remembered seeing on the night she was released from the Gestapo.

"Then what?" he asked with a sting so unlike his usual tone. "Or should I say, 'who'?"

Strangely, Winter did not feel at all threatened by the major's clear allusion to René. She did not want René, she could confess and feel the bluntness of this truth as hard as steel. René did not want her either; he hated and despised her, and that was all she needed to remember of him. She did not want René, she could declare to the world and speak from the bottom of her soul. Wanting him was equal to suicide. And Winter wanted to live. All she had ever done was because she wanted to live.

"Nothing and no one!" she boldly stated and decisively took his hand and clasped it to her chest. "I'm not very proud of myself, Fred! But with you, it's somehow like none of it matters. Because you're... and I..." She looked into his eyes with a pious scream for hope. "Promise me you won't regret it. Say you'll never let the past come between us. Can you do that? Can you?"

The forthrightness in his gaze was frightening, but his face was calm and still like the surface of a quiet lake. He breathed in and he breathed out, deeply, peacefully: "What I can say, Winter, is that I love you enough to try!" he said with all the gravity evoked by this kind of commitment.

There was always a magic power in the word 'love' which Winter thought to be mightier than any shadow or fear. And she had always wanted to love and be loved, and now one part of that desire had been fulfilled. A thought sprang into her mind that had René given her a similar reply, that morning in the catacombs, she would have become his–right there and then, whatever the cost and consequence. Such were the games of fate and the irony of life!

> **"...She understood it later**
> **how it was her who had pushed him off on his path:**
> **for he was already performing his miracles,**
> **and the sacrifice to come was now inevitable."**[59]

20

Cinderella

Ever since she was little, she had been dreaming of a day like this. When lying in bed at nights, blissfully surrendered to Father's narrations, the poor orphan child whose fate was to be a princess always bore no other face but hers. She was too young to know what it meant to be with a man, but she would dream of her prince youthful and charming, his shining armour, a white horse, and only one desire–to put the crystal slipper on the foot of his beloved: her.

Now she was all grown up, wise enough to know that, when a fairy tale came to life, it was impossible to escape certain alterations. A prince could be forty-three years old, born in Augsburg, Bavaria, and his kingdom might not be a dreamland, but the Intelligence Service in the darkest of realms this or any imaginary world had ever seen. Instead of a white horse, there might be a black limousine; an SS-uniform in place of an armour. In real life, her prince's name was Fred; he was a German conqueror. And to become a princess next to him, she would have to do more than just put on a crystal shoe.

There were some hardly insignificant prerequisites for a woman from the occupied territories to marry a German officer, not to mention an officer of the SS. Fred had not been well informed and this critical detail had escaped him that, before any other considerations, a future wife of an SS officer had to prove her allegiance to the Führer and take the sacred oath. It was an old acquaintance who had hastened to break the news to her, the man from the Gestapo who actually *was* the Gestapo, the man who was, unfortunately, also the right hand both to the chief of the Security Police and the *Polizeiführer*; and he was the one whose discord with Fred meant he would do everything in his power to make this certificate, signed by the regional SS leader which was necessary by *RuSHA*[60] to issue the marriage license, as hard to get as possible.

Thus, she found herself once again in the building of *Avenue Foch*, a top floor office this time instead of the dungeons. They had said the oath had to be memorised and recited in German, but they had decided to do her the courtesy of being able to read it, so young that she was in their ways, and so pretty: they could not find it in their hearts to see her embarrass herself with linguistic inadequacies. She did her best to read it properly, to read it proudly; they would not get the satisfaction to see her feel small for just a few lines of words:

"I swear by God this sacred oath..."

Polizeiführer O. congratulated her that she was now one of them and she had to say it was her honour. The Sipo commander merely shook her hand in what was obviously a mocking silence, and *Kriminalrat* Blut did not fail to remind her that he had foreseen there would be a change of attitude in her–and what a change it was! Even he could not have hoped for a greater transformation. It was a miracle that she did not faint or vomit at that very moment.

Fred stood speechless near the door next to *Oberstleutnant*[61] von H., an old friend of his from the Military Command, who had actually mediated to the *Polizeiführer* in the General Commander's name, to even consider agreeing to such a marriage. Too much intrigue and the balances to keep so delicate, he confided in Fred, who restrained himself merely to an affirmative nod with eyes expressing the deepest sorrow.

When they left the Gestapo headquarters, Winter was feeling as if something had really changed about her. As if her hair had turned a little blonder, her skin fairer, and she felt white like snow and cold as ice, a perfect specimen of the Aryan race. She told Fred she needed to be alone for a while and he did not object. He did not even ask her where she was going. He gave her a kiss and let her go. He could not be sure she was coming back and, for a moment there, neither was she.

She walked and walked driven by this strange feeling, a kind of loneliness one gets when standing in the middle of a contemptuous crowd, facing thousands of indicting fingers. And she knew exactly where she needed to be, to whom she felt she owed a sincere apology. The key of 'The Golden Doe' was safely kept in the usual hiding place, under the once tufted green flowerpot at the entrance. The inside was dark, the stage and musical instruments quiet, but if she listened hard, she could hear them, the voices of those who had made this dreadful place worth living in, their screams of justified anger and biting reproof.

"Please, don't hate me!" she begged.

Michelle and Andrée turned their backs to her; Alain and Guillaume looked away; Pierre whispered a curse, threw down his towel, and went out banging the door; and there was none but Georgette who gave her a comforting smile and a meaningful wink: 'People sometimes get what they need from where it is least expected!' she said, and Winter burst into sobs and felt even more lonely and inconsolable. The first notes of a sad Chopin waltz[62] hurt her to her inmost depths. She turned to see and there was Louis, sitting at his piano, his fingers dancing on the keys, his eyes shut, breathing in every note, like it was the very air he lived on. 'Dance!' he told her and she stood still, her feet transfixed by guilt and heartache. 'Dance!'

She dragged the first hesitant steps on the floor: step back, side step, close, step forward, side step, close; step back, side step, close, step forward, step forward, close; shoulders, head and turn; up and down and turn. And as the dance carried her away, whisk after whisk, from one end of the dance floor to the other, with light steps, smooth shoulders, head in the direction of the turn, they were all alive again, Pierre's bar, the hall and gallery crowded and noisy, the girls with their fancy frills and red satin bonnets, the dancing ensemble ready in the dressing room to spread craze with their provocative skirts. And on the stage, there was her, doing what she loved, the boys budging up for her so that she would stand out and shine–Alain, Guillaume, Louis ... oh Louis with his wisdom, always full of hope and understanding: step back, side step, close; step forward, step forward, close...

When Fred and she met up again and headed home together from the *Hôtel du Louvre*, they both made the unspoken promise never to talk about the events of this day. And, at the first opportunity, Winter threw the key of 'The Golden Doe' in the river.

The wedding was arranged to be soon and with the discretion that befitted Fred anyway–a close circle ceremony at *L'église Notre-Dame d'Auteuil*, as far away from the busy centre as possible. With few selected guests, on Fred's part, including his aunt from Zurich, *Oberstleutnant* von H., who had generously offered to give away the bride, and Peter Schwarz, the young secretary from the office and Fred's protégé. Two of Fred's old colleagues from the Embassy, along with their wives, who lived in their neighbourhood, were also invited and the best man would be Karl Freier, a childhood friend, the renowned 'little rascal', recently having been transferred from Italy, largely because of Fred and the *Oberstleutnant*'s intervention. On Winter's side, there would be no one–the bride was all alone in this world and that was enough of a story for the people in Fred's circle to know about her. Nonetheless, strictly out of consideration for Fred, who had made the suggestion completely unsuspected of her resentment towards the housekeeper, she had settled for Marie as her maid of honour.

It was not for absence of desire that Winter had rejected the idea of her own people attending the wedding, even despite Fred's insistence on her mother at the very least. There were certain things that reason could not explain and emotion could not either, and Winter had sensed it, more instinctive powers were at play, more compelling, overmastering all others. Yet, she was tempted one day, took the *métro* from *Michel-Ange Molitor* to *Gare d' Austerlitz*, and, from there, by another line, to *Ourcq*–a long journey into the city, from one end to the other, just as it had been with her life. The change in the environment, as soon as she got off the underground, hit her like a punch to the stomach. It was a cloudy day, but the gloom all around was not owed to the weather. She had conveniently forgotten the gray buildings of her old neighbourhood and, even more so, she had forgotten its gray people. Her clothes were too nice and overly expensive, her hair too freshly styled, and the hat too exaggeratedly coloured for this corner of the world. She hid behind a wall and waited for three women with frayed coats and huge cloth pouches on their backs to pass by. Suddenly, it felt impossible for her to take another step. She rushed back to the underground and returned to the city centre, among people who looked a little more like her. But her reflection in a shop window looked back at her, laughing at this superficial sense of self-importance. She had promised never to return, if not a winner, and, frankly speaking, she did not feel like one.

Once she got home and Fred asked her why she had come back fruitless with her eyes swollen and dreary, she blatantly lied that her family had moved away and she had been unable to find them.

"I'm sure I can work something out with the municipal services!" he offered with no less willingness than if he were looking for his own family; his determination scared her and she reached out to him, desperately grabbing his hands, begging him not to. He was surprised, by all means he should have been a little appalled too, but then he understood, as he always did. He hugged her silently, held her long and tight, and she was so relieved it almost felt sinful.

Then his aunt came, Aunt Martha, as she insisted on being called; a meek and generous woman, speaking her language, having similar homeland images in her memory. Oh, she could easily be loved by Winter like a mother, if only the very idea of mother did not hurt her so damn much...

There was a piece of actual fairytale in the wedding preparations, however, and it concerned the wedding dress. Fred had been happy to be obliged for that purpose to an old acquaintance from the Embassy, whose girlfriend was an esteemed *haute couture*[63] designer. A woman personifying elegance and femininity both, and a strong personality with a controversial reputation of her own, she was an excellent morale booster for Winter on this occasion, making those couple of appointments for the fitting with her at the Ritz a true taste of dream.

Fred and Winter both agreed there would be no flamboyant decorations in the church, and, instead of the church organ playing Wagner's wedding march, there would be a string quartet to play Pachelbel's Canon[64]. After the ceremony, there would be a small reception at home and Fred ordered an enormous cake, with a newlywed couple of solid sugar on top. Karl Freier promised to secure two crates of good champagne and Marie... well, Marie took on the prime task of cooking for everyone. When Winter was informed of this, she could not help thinking of the *maître d'hôtel* at the *Château de Chantilly*, and what his ambition to impress had led him into. God forgive her, but, any such mishap happening to Marie, it would not distress her one bit, were it not for Fred, who thought highly of her and cared for her, like a loyal friend.

Last, but not least, there was the selection of the wedding rings. Winter had never been much of a jewellery enthusiast. She had never owned any valuable jewellery, neither had she ever seen enough impressive jewellery in her life to develop a liking for it. So, when they went to the goldsmith, she was initially somewhat indifferent–she did not really care what the rings looked like; she did not want anything too extravagant on her finger and she definitely had no criteria to question the rings' quality. But when she saw them ready, she could not help smiling, a feeling of tenderness overwhelming her. They were two plain gold rings, but they had their names engraved on the inside, along with the date of their union: 24 October 1943.

It was a sweet Sunday morning. Winter was so nervous, her feet trembled and she held onto the *Oberstleutnant* with a firm grip, fearing she would stumble and fall into complete ridicule. He was kind, the *Oberstleutnant*, smiling to reassure her everything was going to be fine, and she was thinking of Father and she was missing him so, him and Mother and the twins, wishing life had turned out differently, but no!

It was better this way, better for her, better for them and, undeniably, better for Fred.

He was standing at the centre of the altar, dressed in his brand-new uniform, and his eyes were shining. Karl Freier whispered something to him and he smiled and he looked so handsome and so happy. Winter had this rich tulle veil hiding her face, and she was thankful, for her spirit was heavy, despite the wonderfully light silk dress and the brilliant impression its snow white must have been making. Her heart was pounding; her heart was aching; her eyes were joyful, and they were weeping; she was feeling blessed; she was feeling cursed; she was hopeful and frightened to the bone.

Fred, who had believed in and accepted her with all her blemishes, who had raised her to the pedestal of his heart and he was good, so good for her. And she, who could not say if what she felt for him was anything more than gratitude–gratitude, which he hated, and admiration, which he despised. Coming to stand next to him at the altar, she prayed for the strength to prove herself worthy of this love and, even out of gratitude and admiration, that she might be able to be good for him, too.

'A good beginning makes a good ending' people often say and Winter paid close attention to all the minor details that could foretell what her new life as *Frau* von Stielen would be like. In the early weeks of the long-lasting marriage, the newlyweds' house was bombarded with a flurry of gifts, greeting cards and telegrams from friends or acquaintances of Fred's–indeed, Winter's German vocabulary on wedding wishes grew sufficiently after this experience. It seemed like an overlong celebration and Winter felt as if she were trying to balance on one side of the scale all alone, while, on the other, there were the hordes of people belonging to Fred's social circle, people who had absolutely no attachment to her and were not necessarily well-meaning either.

Winter's fear that she might never integrate into Fred's world, but forever be regarded as an intruder who used every vicious means known to climb the social ladder, was not always unfounded. Fred's circle did not consist of saints and angels; there were, in fact, several gossip lovers with hardly any discretion, who would seldom hide their wonder that such an esteemed officer had ended up marrying a girl nobody knew anything about, other than she was surely not of noble descent and she had no man of the uniform for a father, neither a politician, scientist, wealthy merchant or income earner; a girl who, aside from her many other flaws, was not even German. What could he possibly have seen in her, they shouted with caustic doubt, in a woman who was certainly young and beautiful, but was also a foreigner and too lowly for his station. It was rumoured that she was a gifted singer, but she had never been seen singing at any of the prominent stages in this city. And who knows what other 'gifts' she possessed and how she had used them to wrap *Sturmbannführer* von Stielen around her finger!

She spent many vigilant nights devising ways to once again win the game of impressions and preparing for the worst, the case where the naked truth about her past came to light. She had never known such anger, an anger that devoured her from within, until she felt sick, burst out in temper tantrums or became completely withdrawn, all for seemingly insignificant reasons, then feeling even more deficient and hostile. Fred would often be the recipient of this bitterness. She had thought he would always be a step ahead of her, making certain to protect her from her blunders, protect himself and his reputation, for that matter, but that was a role Fred did not seem interested in. What was he trying to do, throw her into the arena and see how she would escape the lions? But, no, that would be so unlike him, so unlike the way he had always treated her. They were peculiar, his ways with her, and she would feel so ambivalent, helpless even, but somehow also obstinate not to give in to despair.

One morning at breakfast, there was a ring from the doorbell. Marie, who was about to serve them their coffee, left the coffeepot on the table, approached the dining-room window, pulled back the curtain and looked to the front door. Seeing that the gate was still closed, she walked to the hall, where the intercom device was set, exactly at the moment it started ringing.

"Parcel? What parcel?" she asked in the proper tone and with the proper look in her eyes. "Very well, once you open it and it's safe, send the man on his way, and bring it in!" she ordered like one who knew well how to handle every household occasion.

Winter was watching with distinct interest, trying to hide her envy of Marie in an expression of apathetic contempt; so, as soon as Marie walked out of the front door to receive the parcel, she hurried to take the coffeepot and serve the coffee herself, making certain to attend to Fred better than the housekeeper. She got up, gave him a light kiss on his temple and roughly imitated Marie's moves, going to look outside from the dining-room window.

"All this trouble for a parcel!" she exclaimed in a sour tone, ready to launch an appropriate verbal attack on Marie the moment that Fred triggered her. "What could there be in it, for God's sake? A bomb?" And she turned around with an arrogant smile, only to stumble onto Fred's expression, which showed that what she was joking about could be an improbable possibility, but a possibility nevertheless.

Winter frowned. She had always felt so secure with Fred that it had never occurred to her there was ever any danger for them other than her past. And she was only just realising that there was an entire world out there, a world against them, full of adversaries ready to strike them down at the first opportunity. What would she do if all these enemies suddenly attacked them? How would she stand by the man she had chosen to be with, who would undoubtedly fight to the last drop of his blood? She looked at Fred and, strangely enough, nothing seemed more important to her at that moment than his presence in this room.

"It's only standard procedure" he remarked with a smile, before sipping some of the steaming coffee she had served, and Winter observed every detail of his moves with a sense of urgency, as if it were important to remember, in case she was ever deprived of the opportunity to see them again. "It's very kind of you, thank you!" Fred told the housekeeper, once she was back and handed him the parcel.

Winter approached with mixed feelings, watched Fred unfold the contents of the parcel, something like a long piece of red fabric.

"Another gift?" she assumed and Fred nodded 'probably'. When he opened it up, a smaller piece of cloth slipped and fell on the carpet. Winter bent down and took it. Unfolding it, she was surprised to see it was a pillowcase. But what was that? In the middle of the all-red fabric, there was a white circle and, in it, a black swastika. They both looked at each other, none of them seeming happy with the sight. While Fred was looking for a card from the sender, Winter unfolded the big piece, which was a bedsheet of the same pattern.

"There is no card!"

Winter felt very uncomfortable. 'Deluxe linen, curtains and furniture fabric for the hotels the Germans have requisitioned...' she recalled with a quiver and she searched in Fred's eyes to find out what the source of their gloomy shadow was. Then she burst into laughter, a loud roaring giggle at the verge of not being funny at all, and Fred cast a hazy gaze at her, exchanging uncertain glances with Marie, who had invented an excuse to remain in the room and record the curious incident, naturally making her own assumptions.

"I bet..." Winter spluttered in her hilarious laugh "... these are the kind of sheets the very dear to us both *Kriminalrat* Blut sleeps in every night!" And shaking the sheet out towards Marie, she forced her to make a few awkward steps back. Evidently annoyed, Marie placed some dishes on her tray and walked out, leaving Winter with a feeling of victory against her first opponent. She turned to Fred, reached for his hands, and brought them to her chest. "Think, my darling, this might be as close as he could ever get to a warm home bed!" And she started once again with a strident cackle, while Fred took her in his arms, looking, out of the corner of his eye, at the red mass on the floor around their feet, like an otherworldly creature, horrible and dangerous.

The best place for Winter to hide from her fears and insecurities was the house library. She sat on the built-in sofa by the window, remembering the first time she read Yeats to Fred. 'Tread softly' said the poem, and, sometimes, she felt like she had been stomping all over not just Fred's but also her own dreams instead. She studied meticulously. She loved literature, but also found history and geography fascinating. She had an appetite for learning and she had a reliable learning strategy–she always started with what was more familiar to her and then expanded on the most interesting related topics. Fred often commended her on her inborn learning talent, and Winter felt proud and flung herself into studying with even greater zeal.

At an art auction on *Les Grands Boulevards* once, Winter was unlucky to be seated next to two O.T.[65] officers, who did not miss out on the opportunity to demonstrate their eruditeness, allegedly to help her choose between the items being auctioned, while audaciously waiting for her to make a mistake, which they could later divulge to their coterie. At one point, a pair of Rococo-style armchairs was being sold, and the officers rushed with all their arrogance to explain to Winter what the distinctive features of this style were. She nodded and listened to them without interrupting until they had finished.

"Indeed!" she remarked with her eyes directed straight into their faces without a shred of intimidation. "Really, did you know that, when Rococo style was in fashion, it would more likely be called *'Augsburger Geschmack'*[66]?"

The bumptious officers were astonished and blabbered something so that they would not look like fools. Still, from that moment on, they did not dare offer their 'assistance' anymore.

Above all, Winter's best time at home was definitely when Fred was there. It always amazed her how much they had to talk about, how many stories to share, and Winter always felt closest to Fred when he narrated stories from his childhood and youth. Most of the children in his neighbourhood used to take part in the Peace Festival parade in early August, an event eagerly anticipated for the traditional costumes they wore and the banners they held, three times taller than they were, which had often been the cause of screamingly comic scenes. Karl Freier and he had almost grown up together–two years younger than Fred, and an only child himself, he lived next door, and the two of them were more or less like siblings. One night, they agreed to exchange places at each other's home, pretending to their parents that they did not understand the difference. The parents were initially surprised, but tacitly decided to play along with the boys' game, who were happy with the successful trick, until Karl's father, who was no less a practical joker than the children, forced Fred to get up in the crack of dawn to mow the lawn in the backyard, a long prearranged task there was no way to get around. Ever since, Fred had insisted the scheme was a premeditated crime conceived by Karl Freier in order to avoid the chore, for which he was deservingly accredited with the nickname 'little rascal'. On his first leave from military school, Fred had gone to see that impressive Fokker triplane with the unique climbing and turning ability on display at the city airport, the mere sight of it elevating his desire to become a pilot, despite the stated fears of his mother and the recommendations of his father, who preferred the earth instead of the air. A little later, news of his father's death arrived from the French front. Winter would often think that, had things been differently related to Fred's father, he might just have decided to go after his dream to fly; but, then, he would have taken an entirely different life course and their paths might never have crossed one another. Why did things happen the way they did? Oh, it would be so romantic to think it all happened so that the two of them would meet and end up together. Only she did not believe in huge universal conspiracies and she was not feeling particularly deserving of one, either.

Besides books, Fred also had many records, and his wondrous competence to remember where and how he had acquired each and every one of them, made a great impression on Winter. Sometimes, they played popular dance songs and stayed up late, rocking to the rhythm under the orange-yellow light of the fireplace. When they wanted to reminisce, they would play classical music. Fred's preferences were in Bach, Händel and Purcell, Arcangelo Corelli, Telemann, and Jean Philippe Rameau; Winter had no objection to baroque, Händel's *Sarabande* and Vivaldi's *Four Seasons* were among her best-loved pieces, but then she would go for Mendelssohn's violin and orchestra concertos and Liszt's *Preludes*, followed by Brahms's *Hungarian Dances* as an eventual emotional vent, while she would always listen closely to the Elizabethan era pavanes. Both of them were extremely fond of Chopin. Listening to him, Winter would sometimes talk to Fred about Louis.

Then it was time for the night to take over. For a girl who had been introduced to lovemaking under such inappropriate circumstances, being with Fred was the perfect remedy for the healing of all wounds. Winter was realising that making love was more about communion than it was about any carnal satisfaction. The desire to explore the body did not originate from mere pleasure, it was the pleasure that materialised in the need for close contact, while knowing one was being loved was the most stimulating aphrodisiac. And it was not only touch that made mating so enticing: there were whispers and breaths, murmurs and silences, the rustling of the sheets, the labial consonants of separating lips; there were fragrances and inspiring aromas, the awakening incense of the human skin, with fading traces of musk and jasmine, memories of primeval affect, sensuous and soothing; and there were impressions and images, the outline of the body, an aspect, a curve, the shadows swaying in the dim light of a storm lamp on the nightstand. It was nothing like the cheap substitute they sold at 'The Golden Doe'. And it was not like those inflamed hours she had once spent in the arms of René Martin, faded away like an old photograph in the sunlight.

When Fred was not with her and Winter did not feel like reading, she sat outside in the garden, breathed in the vivacity of the greenery and sometimes took care of the plants–there was a yellow climbing rose she was especially keen on, which she often pruned and dead-headed. Occasionally, she would go for walks, preferably with the new friends she had made in the wives of Fred's neighbouring old colleagues, who had sincerely welcomed her in their company and seemed to find having in their midst a member of the opposite war camp extremely engaging. They were a curious trio of frenemies, for which reason they referred to themselves with the euphemism 'the frio'. As expected, none of these ladies spoke any English, while their French was at an equally miserable level–no systematic learning of the language, only what they had picked up empirically from their stay in Paris. And, as Winter was just beginning to understand German a little better and speak it with many shortcomings and inconsistencies, the way they talked to each other was literally no less than a Tower of Babel. Quite remarkably, however, they not only managed to communicate but also enjoyed this peculiarity, where conveying their meaning meant they had to use vocabulary from all languages, as well as gestures and grimaces, and lots, lots of imagination.

It was greatly encouraging and important endorsement for Winter to be part of this joyful 'frio', going together to social gatherings, to the shops or for a treat at the local or city centre patisseries. Around the market of *Auteuil* they made friendly acquaintances with the local people, who had the kindness of being friendly and talkative, although they would certainly see the wives of their German conquerors with, at least, some suspicion. Among them, Winter had distinguished the family of the shoemaker, *Monsieur* Leon. He was a father of four and he had the same trade as Father.

Winter no longer felt alone or helpless and it had been a long time since she had last cried. Fred had a unique power to shrink her most monstrous pains and fears into harmless insignificance. And it seemed easy, much easier than she had initially expected, to live with him, because she was... and he...

That night, *Sturmbannführer* and *Frau* von Stielen were invited to one of the many receptions organised by the conquerors, as if they had been living in times of peace and prosperity. In the company of their friends and neighbours, Fred and Winter enjoyed the pleasant conversation, the abounding drink and the music performed by a small orchestra, consisting of strings, a piano and a tenor. It was actually he, for a while now, who had drawn Winter's attention away from the bold jokes a gentleman in their party had been telling to everyone's amusement. There was a brilliantly shining timbre in the tenor's voice, the melody was brisk, but also melancholic, and Winter had been able to distinguish the frequent repetition of the words '*Herz*' and '*Schmertzen*', which she knew to mean heart and pain: a pain in the heart,–it was almost inevitable that she would notice.

"Fred!" She gave him a gentle nudge on the arm and he turned to her with an enquiring smile. "What is that he is singing?"

Fred listened carefully for a moment or two.

"Oh, I think it must be one of Schubert's songs written on Goethe poetry!" he replied and listened a little more. **"Now I must dress in fine clothes from the wardrobe, because there is a feast today; but no one suspects the pains that tear me grimly in my heart of hearts ..."**[67] he recited in a free translation. "A bit sad for the occasion, isn't it?" he added with a beam of tenderness in his eyes outlining her face.

"It's beautiful!" she whispered, enthralled by the song and the scattered words she could understand from the lyrics, promising to look up the poem in Fred's library and learn it by heart.

Then they were approached by a couple, a rather mismatched couple, according to Winter's first impression. The lady, a woman who looked about forty, was a scandalous figure–pretentious outfit, intense makeup, an air of absolute self-indulgence. Slicker than her escort, the woman hurried to greet before he did, and, to everyone's surprise, she addressed Fred first and foremost, resting her cheek on his and giving him an air kiss. It was a gesture Winter did not feel particularly happy about.

"Friedrich, *mein Liebling!*[68]" the woman exclaimed in an inappropriately intimate tone. "Will you not introduce me?" And she hung herself on his arm, leaving everyone stunned, including Fred.

"Well, of course!" he replied, sounding and looking somewhat embarrassed, while he discreetly slipped away from the lady's grip. "May I introduce my wife Winter!" And addressing Winter, he said in English: "My dear, this is Mrs. Ingrid Beltzer ... an old friend!"

Mrs. Beltzer seemed to know some English, because upon hearing the words 'old friend', a brash smile spread on her lips with the bright red lipstick.

"Pleased to meet you!" Winter uttered in her best German and shook the woman's hand most unwillingly.

"Oh! Isn't she an angel?" Ingrid Beltzer ejaculated and, ignoring every sense of propriety, she shamelessly examined her from head to toe.

"And Mr. ...?" Winter responded, ostentatiously disregarding the woman, which, she was satisfied to descry, made Mrs. Beltzer absolutely furious.

"Stein, Madam! Kurt Stein!" the man responded politely and bowed.

"You are a merchant, are you not?" Fred rushed to comment.

"That's right, sir! Mostly iron goods for the time being. It's an honour that you know of me!"

"I've heard you are opening a factory now, somewhere in Freistatt?"

"Actually, we are already established in *Český Krumlov*. It's an affordable distance from Bohemia, hopefully allowing us to expand to its crystal glass sometime soon. We've been in operation for almost nine months now!"

"So, are things going that well?"

"We trade anything there is to trade, *Herr Sturmbannführer*, from pins to cannons!"

Fred's conversation with Mr. Stein somewhat alleviated the initial tension, and Mrs. Beltzer, who obviously expected to have the undivided attention of everyone, and, doubtlessly, Fred's in particular, was now standing exasperated.

Winter was completely indifferent to the discussion, exclusively consumed by the question of what kind of friendship the ... adorable Mrs. Beltzer and Fred used to share, which gave her such liberty as to call him 'sweetheart' and embarrassed him to the point of indisputable self-incrimination. Winter found herself before a most unexpected revelation: a feeling of possessiveness she had never before experienced with such intensity. She remembered once resenting the reference to an unknown Simone, and, every time she saw Fred with Marie, unquestionably, she felt a very unpleasant sting of rivalry. But right now, the idea of an old relationship of Fred's was confusingly irritating and also somewhat exciting in a strange way. She did not need proof of how much she cared for Fred, but the spontaneity of this sentiment made her feelings towards him seem a bit like... being in love. She turned her eyes onto him and impulsively smiled, right at the time when the orchestra entirely changed the genre and started to play a jaunty tango. Resolute not to leave things to chance, especially seeing that Mrs. Beltzer was hanging on Fred's slightest expression of interest to snatch him from her, Winter felt daring enough to invite her husband to dance. And so, they started to move in the eight-count walking steps they both so much enjoyed, extending only a cursory farewell to the incongruous couple, who immediately began to quarrel, as hapless Mr. Stein had the doomed inspiration to invite his escort to the dance floor. Winter watched the two of them for a moment, but was quickly fully drawn into her partner, whom she regarded as the most attractive man in the hall at the moment.

"So, how is it that Mrs. Beltzer goes around together with Mr. Stein instead of a Mr. Beltzer?" Winter could not help asking and Fred smiled expressively.

"She was most unfortunate in her marriage, I'm afraid!" he replied in a lightsome tone.

"Oh!" Winter fired off, momentarily surprised, but obviously with little empathy for the woman's misfortune. "Well, I see she has wasted no time replacing the poor late wretch!"

"Do I notice a slight dislike for Mrs. Beltzer?" Fred asked, in the mood to tease her. Winter squeezed her lips and determinedly shook her head.

"A great dislike!" she corrected him and he laughed.

"Would it be arrogant on my part to assume that... you're a little jealous?" he humorously continued and, this time, Winter overstressed her previous gesture.

"Most arrogant!" she noted, and he laughed even more heartily. "But so true!"

They smiled at each other, the upturned corners of their lips and the crinkles around their eyes telling each other the words they wanted to hear. Nothing too showy, nothing too loud. No uncontrolled outbursts of passion were ever to be expected from him, but little did it matter to Winter; for, in her experience, volcanoes impressively erupting might make a breathtakingly spectacular sight, but, eventually, they left behind nothing but casualties.

21

The Satin Slipper

On the first of December, the *Comédie Française* featured Paul Claudel's play *The Satin Slipper*[69], an expensive theatrical production with a live orchestra and a great number of actors and dancers. It was a drama, although with several comical elements, and it concerned a forbidden, unfulfilled love.

In view of their invitation to the theatrical performance, Winter had sought a copy of the play in Fred's library and had asked him to read her the most important points of the plot. Greatly surprised, she found herself identifying with the heroine in ways she hated to admit. So, when Doña Prouhèze took off her satin shoe and placed it in the hands of the Virgin's statue in order to hinder herself from the urge to join with her illegal love, while praying for strength to honour those who loved her, Winter could not but close her eyes deep in emotion and imagine herself saying the exact same prayer.

The story was long and dense, the set had to be changed every now and then and the use of such complex and unusual constructions for it resulted in the play being performed with two extended intermissions, one at the end of the 'First Day' and one at the end of the 'Second', which completed the first and longest parts of the performance. During these intervals, the theatre foyer would fill with exaggeratedly cheerful people, dressed in their best clothes and desperate for an opportunity to discuss and associate.

"Well, that pantomime with the shadows of man and woman seemed a little overplayed to me!" remarked one gentleman of the party, *Herr* Ludwig.

"My dear, you need to be a woman in order to comprehend this; I bet what you liked most about the play were the scenes of battle and shipwrecks!" his wife objected and everyone chuckled.

"It was actually very moving, this mourning of the double shadow, which did not belong to either Prouhèze or Rodrigo, but to both lovers, united for a single moment in all eternity!" exclaimed Uma, the third member of the notorious 'frio'.

"One moment and never again! It's tragic, isn't it?" *Frau* Ludwig commented ardently and clasped her hands to her chest to emphasise the depth of her feeling.

"And yet, this unique moment is perhaps better than never!" Karl Freier supported in a rather light tone, taking a big sip of his ruby wine, which he made certain not to part with on any given occasion.

"Women, my friend, love everything and always" the first gentleman intruded, speaking like an expert. "It's their fragile nature which seeks security, and all this, of course, has to do with the maternal instinct and procreation!"

"No offence, *Herr* Ludwig, but you should not underestimate the maternal instinct!" Uma balked at his remark. "I'm sure all of us here would gladly grant the male gender unquestionable superiority in strength and intelligence, but I would ask you to consider how often in nature, as you say, the female proves durable, adaptable and not at all negligibly combative, where her family is threatened!"

"Well, that is exactly why our *Führer* has ordained the *Mutterkreuz*[70], which praises the contribution of the German mother to our glorious cause. In fact, I'm hoping our darling Gretschen here earns her silver[71] one, pretty soon!" Ludwig replied and wrapped his arm around his wife's shoulders, causing her a shy blush.

"My dear colleague, you are talking about quantity! Yet Uma spoke about quality!" disagreed *Herr* Stobe, father only of three, whose wife, therefore, did not qualify for any medal.

"You, honourable Madam, will surely take the lead from us all! So young and adorable–with all due respect, *Herr Sturmbannführer*–I believe you have the Golden Cross already secured!" *Herr* Ludwig exclaimed, eager to express his esteem in Winter and, thus, please Fred.

Fred leaned into Winter's ear to explain to her what had been said, but Winter smiled and took a bold step forward, having already understood most of the conversation.

"I honour my beloved husband, *mein Herr*!" she asserted, impressing everyone, even Fred, with her conviction. "And I will be happy to make him proud with as many children as God gives us!" she continued in such a sweet and humble voice, that no one cared about the mistakes in her German.

Herr Ludwig bowed respectfully, and the others nodded and smiled approvingly, while Fred embraced her gently and softly kissed her hair.

"Ladies and gentlemen, I think there will be plenty of opportunities to discuss *The Satin Slipper*!" he said, proposing another glass of wine to the party.

"But, *Herr Sturmbannführer*, you have not told us what you think about the play!" Uma Stobe politely protested with her seemly, yet explicit, admiration.

"Frankly, I am more touched by the existential dimension of this love..." Fred temperately replied "...a love which is not attainable, neither sanctified nor pure, in the sense we usually mean it. It is completely human and almost divine, it is intertwined with pleasure, but also with its denial, and the way in which it is associated with pain, with the symbol of the cross, clearly refers us to a Christian redemption, from martyrdom and death to resurrection."

"Would you, therefore, say that Doña Prouhèze and Don Rodrigo will end up together and live happily ever after?" Gretschen Ludwig asked lightheartedly.

"I would say that we should not rely on such a superficial

expectation, dear Mrs. Ludwig; I don't think such is the meaning of this play!" Fred replied with a kind smile. "After all, if the characters only desired the consummation of their love, they would simply bypass every obstacle, they would be together from the very first scene and the play would end very quickly. Therefore, I believe, their issue is not practical; it is moral. The distance that separates them is not metric; it has to do with their very existence as human beings and as creatures of God. Of course, as human beings they have the right, and perhaps the obligation, to respond to the call of instincts, listen to the desires of their bodies and emotions; this is, indeed, the essence of all humans, and it is, also, the distinguishing difference between them and other living beings, which, despite having instincts, needs, preferences, and even some feelings, do not have the slightest awareness of them, because they lack this consciousness, which we might otherwise call morality. Thus, we come to the crucial matter of the characters' existence as creatures of God. As such, they obey another call, longing for a different kind of satisfaction–moral, spiritual, religious, if you will. And if we accept that this human transcendence is valuable enough to be quite rare and not readily available, for that very reason, my most respected lady, and in order to give a simple answer to your beautiful, romantic question, I would say, no, I regret to tell you that Doña Prouhèze and Don Rodrigo will not live happily ever after in the way you hope; they cannot, because what they seek cannot be fulfilled in the earthly human context. And as the Moon aptly remarked in the last scene before our intermission, '**man and woman could not love each other anywhere else other than Paradise**!'[72]"

Gretschen sighed in despair and there were also a couple of insufficiently hidden sneers in the party.

"I'm afraid I didn't have time to warn you not to invite Friedrich into a philosophical discussion!" Karl Freier joked, and immediately addressed Fred to add intently: "No offence, my friend, but Mrs. Ludwig would have been content with a simple 'yes' or 'no'!"

"Anything but, *Herr* Freier! These are extremely interesting thoughts, which are definitely going to give our view of the play an entirely new perspective! If you'd please, *Herr Sturmbannführer*, I would like to hear more!" Uma contested with genuine interest.

At that moment, the theatre bell rang once, a signal that the last part of the play would begin shortly, and the discussion had to be interrupted, as they had to return to their seats. Winter took advantage of the last minutes of the intermission to withdraw to the ladies', but she had to wait a while, so she stood in front of the mirror to freshen her makeup and straighten her hair. Most of all, however, she wanted to look at herself and say how proud she felt, that a girl having practically grown up in a hovel and become an adult in a dive, could make an entire party of respectable people utterly approve of her. And the warm shine in Fred's smiling eyes was an additional, most gratifying, reward.

Soon, one toilet was vacant and Winter took her turn. She was completely alone when she came out to wash her hands and feared she would be late and the play would have already started by the time she returned to their loge, although she could still hear noise from the foyer and was certain she had not heard the theatre bell ring a second time. She wiped her hands quickly and made haste to return to her seat. But, as soon as she opened the door to leave, she gasped in terror, having to encounter an unknown face, sweating with adrenaline and fear.

The man, who could not be over fifty years old, unshaven, with a wrinkled forehead and sunken eyes under the brim of a woollen flat cap, pushed her aside and rushed into the ladies' room with his rifle swinging behind his right shoulder. He tried to open the window that faced a gallery of the *Palais Royal* and, in his attempt, the flat cap he was wearing fell off to reveal a bald head with a crescent of gray hair. The window would not open, but the man did not quit: he broke the glass with the butt of his firearm and climbed out. Seconds later, a second man followed, wielding a luger pistol, and immediately a third one came after him, the youngest of the three, standing back to their cover, ready to shoot at anyone following with the machine gun he was holding firmly in his hands. He turned to his escape like the others before him but halted the moment he saw Winter, and she froze; she felt a tingle run through her from the abdomen to the neck, and she leaned against the door casing completely helpless. His face was blazing with the thrill of the pursuit; his hazel eyes were piercing into her unguarded gaze; his rosy lips half-open were spewing his fiery breath onto her; and then, a twinge of regret sealed this dangerously alluring mouth again, the liquid shine in his eyes betraying an underlying suffering. Before Winter could react, he passed her by and ran away. She turned to see him climb out of the window and disappear into the darkness of the night. The German shouts and gunshots, which echoed from the gallery outside, took a steely grip on her heart, but she was confident that they had not found a target on him. And without wanting to, she felt deeply relieved.

22

Fire at will

The execution of Judge Eichmeister in the *Comédie Française*, packed with spectators most of whom were Germans, alarmed the Authorities, which regarded the incident not only as a warning for the impending trial of the 'twenty-three terrorists'[73], but also as an attempt to ridicule them as conquerors. Few were capable of such a daring venture. And René Martin was one of them.

All of a sudden, old dusty ghosts sprang from the sealed chest of Fred's conscience. Winter claimed that she had seen none of the revolutionaries in the theatre; that, as soon as she realised there was something going on, she hid in the toilet and, when she heard the window glass break, she believed it to be her end. And she cried, she cried with actual terror, while, the little she slept the entire night, she remained hooked on him, unwilling to move away even an inch. And yet, Fred could not help but doubt that Winter would admit to seeing any of the perpetrators, and even more so, that she would admit to seeing René Martin.

Winter did not expect to see René again. Her new life had no place for him and this recently improved self of hers had squeezed him into a small invisible corner of her heart and an even smaller one in her mind. But now he was back, she wondered if she had ever really let go of him.

When his eyes looked at her, she felt naked, just as that evening at 'The Golden Doe' after a stormy tango in his arms. And when his breath touched her face, she could not help but remember its fire, its sound in the silent night, its taste. She did not want René, she did not want him, she was certain it was not desire, it was something else that bound her to him, something out of this world that she was powerless to rule. Something she feared would take more than Fred's love to be defeated; it would take a sacrifice ... her own.

When, unusually, Fred returned home for lunch the next day, Winter was as relieved as she was aggravated to see him. At the table, she notably talked about every irrelevant issue she could think of, and she drank glass after glass of wine, which seemed like the only thing able to calm down the recurrent waves of her agony. Her thoughts were at a loss and so were her feelings.

"Will you stay or do you have to go back to the *Hôtel du Louvre*?" she asked at coffee, and she was completely undecided which of the two she preferred.

Fred came to stand by the fireplace, finished up his cigarette, and threw the butt into the fire. "I have to go back!" he replied, tight-lipped like all lunchtime.

"Can I come with you?"

He turned and looked at her hard, a deep ambivalent look.

"It will be safer for you to stay home right now!" he eventually said with a gruelling gentleness, but seeing the faint expression of irony which impulsively sprang onto her face, Fred's features stiffened. "Is there something you would like to share with me?" he asked with an unexpected disaffection, which confused Winter on the more.

"I don't know what you're talking about!" she answered back in a totally disaccording tone.

"Is that so?" he scoffed at her. "Let me enlighten you then: René Martin! Does the name ring a bell?"

Winter responded with a snub and felt a wild anger burning up inside her, which even she did not know from where it originated, but it was definitely not from her better judgment.

"What sort of game is this you're playing with me?" she reacted.

"I'd ask you the same!" he countered, and Winter felt as if he had hit her right in the face with his fist.

There was silence; an ill silence, feeling like plague. Fred nervously rubbed his face with his palm. He approached, put his arms around her; he bent over and breathed through her hair.

"Winter ..." He let out a controlled sigh, closed his eyes, and brushed his face against her forehead. "Winter ..." he repeated painfully. He let go, took a couple of steps away, then turned towards her again, carefully examined her with his eyes. Hers hid in their mist, an inaccessible wall and an appalled expression repelling him with spite, contempt even. "At some point you will have to talk to me; you will have to tell me the truth!" he challenged and pleaded with her at the same time.

She smirked, and her gaze arrowed at him its bitter dispute. "Truth? What truth?"

"About René Martin!" he burst out, momentarily catching Winter completely by surprise. She felt defenseless; her heart was pounding, her cheeks flamed up, her ears had that hissing noise which was driving her crazy. Fred felt, knew, saw through her, and she was exposed because she was guilty–a guilty, ungrateful liar. Fred came up to her, took her by the arms, and forced her to face him. "Did you see him at the theatre yesterday?" he demanded, and she returned to him an expression of discomfort. "Did you?"

Completely muddled, she was tempted to answer him with a simple 'yes', but then she would have to do a lot of explaining. Only, there were no explanations, none she could think of anyway, because to explain there would have to be some kind of reasoning and what she felt for René was like a tangled ball of yarn–hell, she even doubted any attempt of hers to explain could even produce the slightest coherent speech.

"You're hurting me!" she cried like a trapped animal. His eyes speared her, his touch burnt her.

He gave her a petulant look and let her go. He went to the cocktail cabinet, where he poured a hefty dose of cognac into a glass. He snarfed it down and poured a second one, which he also threw back.

"If you were innocent, you would give me a straight answer! But you're lying, Winter, you're lying!" he spouted and banged the glass on the bar, struggling to contain this intolerable mixture of rage and letdown inside him.

She hid her face in her hands and shook her head. She had to find a way to reassure his well-founded suspicions, but the idea of an outright lie was killing her. She was just standing there–her frustration eliminating any chance of a calculated reaction, and the suspicion that he was not asking her for the truth out of duty, but out of a need to believe and trust her, struck her down without pity.

"Your accusations are completely unfair!" she protested with a greatly illegitimate grievance, which added to her feeling of entrapment. "You promised you wouldn't let anything come between us. You promised to put away the past, never let it come back and haunt us. What's changed? Where is this love of yours, which would be enough for you to try when it's needed?"

He made a sudden move towards her, but immediately disciplined his reaction, his clenched teeth being the sole manifestation of his fury. "I'm asking you a simple question; a simple question which requires a simple answer. Why won't you answer?"

"Because it underestimates me that you even ask!" she declaimed, incapable of finding a better way to defend herself than an open attack. "Why give you an answer, when your poisoned mind already has all the answers you want to hear? Go ahead, say what you want to say and then pass sentence, too, for whatever it is you think I deserve!"

He looked at her. He looked at her with bitterness and sadness. The muscles of his face were twitching, a spike of resentment was stinging from behind his eyes. "Rest assured, that is exactly what I intend to do! I will not let you mock me like this anymore!" he uttered, with a toxic hue in his tone.

"Really? Mocking you, am I? Of course! Why should I deny it?" she answered back in a state of delirium. "Each time you leave, I run off to René Martin's hideout so that we can mock you together, I admit it! Do you want to hear more?" She was yelling in complete frenzy. She was brutal and cynic, almost sadistic, and she did not recognise herself, neither could she restrain it: "Would you like to hear that I sleep with him, too? Or that I sell myself to his friends for a little extra dosh?"

Hearing her last words, Fred jumped at her in fury and grabbed her violently by the arms. Winter was frightened that he would hit her and she screamed and beat him on the chest with her fists, wriggling as a fish caught on a hook; and the more she thrashed at him, the tighter his grasp and the sorrier his gaze. Then, he just let her go and, stumbling, Winter clumsily fell back on the soft sofa cushions.

His groan banged into her head like a canon and the sound of breaking glass hurt her hearing as if a bombshell had exploded in her ears. She looked up: he had thrown all the glassware of the cocktail cabinet on the floor, his head hung down, his shoulders going up and down to the pace of his wailing gasps. Suddenly, she came to her senses and everything seemed unbelievable, so unbelievable she did not even feel it as real.

"I'm sorry! I don't know what I'm saying! Please, please, forgive me!" she muttered, and she leaped to her feet in despair, making a few anguished steps toward him.

He shook his head heavyheartedly, looked at her with blurry eyes. "Your lying and deceit must give you such a sense of triumph, don't they, *Frau von Stielen*! Do you think I'm stupid? Do you think I don't see the guilt in your eyes, in your actions? Or do you think that I'm so madly in love with you that I can't see through your lies? I'm only sorry for one thing: I truly believed you could be honest! But you've made a fool out of me for the last time!"

His words fell as heavy as stones; and his eyes were overcast looking at her, before he turned around and left the room with big resolute strides. The door slammed and then silence prevailed, dead silence, like the one that dominates the battlefield after a ceasefire. She stood in the middle of the room, never having felt so uncertain; the walls were closing in on her and she was suffocating. An eerie sensation forced her to turn her head towards the dining-room door: the housekeeper was standing there. And if a gaze could be deadly, hers would certainly kill Winter instantly.

Fred was like a raging bull when he left; his pride was wounded, his heart was shredded, and he was angry, not only at Winter, but mostly at himself. Because he had had René Martin and he simply let him go. Of course, at the time, it had seemed strategically more fruitful to set him free, as Georgette Douffet had not yet identified René Martin as their S.O.E. liaison and the person with whom Winter had met at Belleville could not yet be related to the code name 'Seamstress'. Tragic irony all at his expense! And Winter's part in it? That was the real question! He knew from the start that she had lied about how she arrived at 'The Golden Doe' in the first place–Pierre had offered an alibi to a stranger, a British stranger, but that was not enough to incriminate her. And he had searched everywhere, God and the Devil both knew how hard he had looked for evidence of her guilt, but then, perhaps, his feelings had overmastered his judgment, perhaps the evidence had always been there, under his nose, and he had lacked the clarity to see it. Now, for all his doubts and conflicts, he had to dig out this vermin and crush it.

Officially, it was the Gestapo who was charged with the task of coordinating the search for Judge Eichmeinster's killers, and *Polizeiführer* O. had issued the explicit order: 'I want them alive.' On his own initiative, Fred had put all his informants and undercover agents on their own search. He asked for a list of the Gestapo attack points and compared it with one of his own, which included all the place names that had emerged from time to time in his searches for S.O.E. If Pierre Morné's team and René Martin worked together on the foreigners' special operations, it was not unlikely he could be found at any one of them. And he swore he would clamp down on Martin so tight, that he would not even dare so much as blink, let alone resurface. But, somehow, that was not enough. He wanted him and he wanted him now.

Thus, he ordered his secretary to assemble two patrols and inform the driver that he was going to take part in the search for the criminals personally. They started at the *Canal Saint Martin*, scouring the entire open air section from *Villette* to the *Gare du Nord*, and for the underground part, four boats were commandeered, after every boat owner in the area was first thoroughly interrogated. In complete darkness, Fred and his men covered a distance of about one and a half miles, from the tunnel entrance at the *Place de la République* until the canal surfaced again close to the *Place de la Bastille*. Apart from the 1830 revolutionaries' remains, kept in a crypt under the base of the July Column, their search yielded no result, other than to agitate his soldiers, who looked at their commander utterly bemused, wondering what he might have been offered which was so obligating, or what absurdity might have possessed him, to drag them to such extremities.

The sewer network was the next target. From *Madeleine* to the *Place de la Concorde*, they combed the sewer section, using a floating scaffold towed by chains attached to the walls of the tunnel. In some places, behind large-diametre conduits and tanks of all sizes, there were narrow platforms leading, through damp corridors, to sunless chambers, some of which still had warm signs of use. They walked along the stretch from the *Quai d' Orsay* to *Pont de l' Alma* and emerged at the area of the *École Militaire* with plenty of loot–documents, maps, and sabotage material. But the people had escaped, and it was the people that Fred wanted madly.

It was almost dawn. Just before twilight, the night was always at its darkest. Fred and his men looked like ghosts, smudged and filthy, tired and disgusted, but full of fierce determination. He spread the map on the bonnet of the service jeep, which was waiting along with the trucks for the troopers at the predetermined point. He was about to order the group to head for the catacombs of *Montparnasse*, when suddenly his eyes fell on the name *La Mouette* on the map. It was an underground station in the *Passy* area, where a few months ago his informants had noted increased mobility by the members of an organisation led by a former French official named 'Max', and it was not that far from his house. If René Martin actually had any 'business' associations with Winter, or if, at best, he only wanted to stalk her, he should be somewhere relatively close. This time, he was certain that he had hit the nail on the head. He gave the order and everyone followed with willing readiness. After the canal and the sewers, the underground network seemed to his soldiers like a walk in the park.

The raid on the metro tunnels was divided into four groups. The first two were led by Captain Gruber together with Staff Sergeant Brandt, and headed for the main metro line to *Rue de la Pompe* and *Ranelagh*, while the other two were led by Fred and Lieutenant Mann to follow the passage to *Boulainvilliers*, and split at the suburban railway line. Fred's unit had not walked more than a hundred metres since they split with the lieutenant when they heard a barrage of gunfire. They turned back and ran in a rush of adrenaline. The young lieutenant was lying dead on the tracks of *Boulainvilliers*. Two more soldiers had been shot down a little further away. They swooped on, exchanging fire with three of the revolutionaries, who were trying to escape along the line to *Henri Martin*, while the dawn had already begun to break and the lifting of the curfew would quickly bring the first trains back to the tracks. At one point, the fugitives climbed an iron ladder. There, one of the rebels, a one-handed middle-aged man, was hit. The other two, younger and more agile men, raised a manhole cover and rushed into one of *Rue Octave Feulliet*'s side streets. Amidst a pandemonium of gunfire and shouting, the Germans followed, with Fred and three other men crossing the street to cover the opposite corner. During the exchange of fire, Fred's two men were killed, and he was hit in the left arm. The gunfire stopped and Fred was certain that the rebels would attempt an escape. He was alone now, with another soldier across the street, but gave the order to attack, grabbing the machine gun from the dead soldier next to him. They dashed with furious screams. One of the rebels fell, while the other reflexively turned toward his pursuers and started firing again. It was dark, but the intensity of the moment had rocketed all senses into fierce hyperarousal, and Fred could discern the fugitive's face.

"Martin!" he screamed resounding louder than the hammering of the firearms and ran towards him, defying danger and shooting like a frantic madman, until he completely emptied his shell cartridge. Right then, a group of soldiers ran to his aid and quickly reached and passed him, firing non-stop. He ran behind them for a while, with his pistol ready to aim at his mortal enemy, but it was too late. With an acrobatic maneuver, René climbed up a wall and, from there, onto a rooftop and disappeared.

Fred swallowed his failure, blind with hatred. René Martin had proved to be more capable than he was; René Martin was winning the game against him hand by hand, as if damn luck favoured him and him alone. But it was not over, not yet, he swore with stubborn conviction, determined to break him, even if it was the last thing he did.

He and his men reassembled at the trucks. They had suffered several losses, but at least the mission was not a complete fiasco: half a dozen prisoners had been captured, as Captain Gruber had unearthed some more of these swine at *La Muette* station. Among them was a fifty-year-old man with a crescent of gray hair. Fred knew who he was. He was Andres Jérôme, a popular name in the German roll of outlaws. A baleful smirk spread on Fred's lips, as he felt he had finally been handed an ace. Andres Jérôme had a daughter, a girl in her twenties, whose name often accompanied that of René Martin's in his research. Father and daughter: it was an unbreakable bond and a pretty good reason for Fred to trust that at least one of them would have to cooperate, for the sake of the other.

23

On rewind

She opened her eyes to see it was already dark. Isolated all afternoon in the bedroom, Winter had, after some time, fallen asleep and deep sleep had made her completely lose sense of time. She got up with weak limbs. On the nightstand, the clock read a little after eleven. Confident that the housekeeper would have retired, she wrapped a woollen shawl around her shoulders and went downstairs. It was all as expected. The fire was still burning in the fireplace, but no one was sitting in the armchair in front of it. No one was waiting for her and she had no one to wait for. On the cocktail cabinet, the glassware had been replaced, a fresh bottle of cognac stood there screaming. She poured some generously into a glass, took it and went out into the garden. Now and then, a few clouds high in the sky hid the quartered moon; the moonlight spread a luminous veil on the tops of the winter greenery, but it was dark, pitch dark at the base, on the ground, where she felt she had always been crawling. She drank a mouthful of her cognac. It tasted sweet and strong, yet it offered little consolation. When was it that she last sat on this bench together with Fred, rested her head on his shoulder and talked with him for hours? These rare moments of happiness, which she so foolishly failed to appreciate.

From outside the gate, the melody of a harmonica, soon joined by a youthful singing voice, lured her close and she stood near the gate to listen.

> **"How I would like to go to her**
> **If the way was not so far**
> **If the way, if the way, if the way was not so far..."**[74]

She closed her eyes, slow and bitter tears rolled down. How songs spoke the truth in such simplicity, if only people could be as bold as songs in candidness. The harmonica played its melancholic melody a little more and then the song stopped and the voices outside the gate became a wistful murmur. Winter felt so lonely.

Unconsciously, she found herself in the sitting-room again. She had a second drink and then a third. She was dizzy, but not as much as she wanted in order to stop feeling. She looked at the bottle of cognac: so refined and expensive, she could not help but wonder whether it was purchased or it went with the house, which, had it not been sold to Fred, might very well have been given to him as dowry, Marie's dowry. Marie and Fred. Everything in this house belonged to the two of them. She herself had nothing, she was an intruder, at best, a visitor. She forced herself to get angry. Anger was always a good antidote to sadness. And yet, she had something that was so tangible, despite not being material: she had the moments she and Fred had shared, beautiful precious moments, so many of them in such a short time; moments that she took for granted, blinded by pride to recognise their value. With ingratitude adding up to her guilt, Winter concluded that she had more than earned the way things had turned.

Like a shadow, she finally crawled back to the bedroom. She lay down, but was scorned by sleep, just as by everyone else that mattered, including herself. She sat up. She looked through the mirror at the dark window and her even darker apparition. It was far too late for Fred to return home. He might not come back the next day either, or the day after that. She was alone in a house that was not even hers. She felt like she had no place there, and a sense of being unwanted generated in her the desire to leave. But where to? Who in the world would shelter an outcast such as her?

In a corner of the bedroom, Fred's clothes hanging from the stand screamed of his absence: if Fred never returned to her, she would miss more than just a place in the world. She got up, took the clothes in her arms, deeply and painfully breathed in their scent. It was impossible to think she would never again see him wear these clothes, which transformed him from a soldier into a man, only a man, a man who loved her. It was unthinkable that he would never again lie next to her in bed, inconceivable that he would not wake up with her, getting up to put on his uniform while she looked captivated, observing every detail about him and his every move. She, on the other hand, had always been so decently granted room to her shyness or, perhaps, it was no shyness at all, only the terrible fear that, if he saw her fully naked in broad daylight, he would see through her and realise how undeserving she was of him.

Then she thought she heard a creak outside the door, a familiar creak that his steps made on the wooden floor, sometimes before daybreak, when he returned from a night shift on guard.

She began to laugh, laugh hysterically, and propelled Fred's clothes up with insane enthusiasm. A fool, a fool, she was such a fool! Always so susceptible to despair, always inclined to give in to the gloomiest thoughts, to the most bleak probabilities. Of course he would not return with a night shift on guard and of course he would be on guard, every single German in Paris would be on guard after what happened the day before, and it was to be expected, because there was war, and they were the conquerors and there were rebels out there fighting against them, it was war; it was war ... and she was grateful for it.

When she opened her eyes again, sunlight was rushing in violently from the window, where she had neglected to close the shutters the previous night. With only her clothes and the woollen shawl around her as she had fallen asleep, she felt the stiffness of the night cold in every muscle and her joints were so tight, she thought, at the slightest move, they would break. But the worst of all was her head and stomach. She should not have drunk so much, but then again she should not have been so sad, either–grief always made alcohol even stronger. She looked at Fred's side on the bed, which was completely untouched. Fred had not returned from any night shift on guard, and this could be nothing but discouraging.

She washed and dressed with no care about her appearance–a beautiful decorative wrap was completely useless to an empty package. Emptiness echoed inside her like a bottomless well. She walked down the staircase quietly, standing at its base with a desperate hope of hearing a sound that might indicate Fred's presence. Quiet. A few seconds later, the housekeeper showed up coming from the kitchen with a full breakfast tray: coffee, milk, bread and butter, jam, sweet pastry, fresh orange juice. Marie stared at her for a while with the same scornful arrogance as the night before. Then, she moved on to the dining room, saying *'Bonjour, Monsieur!'*, and began to serve breakfast at Fred's place at the table. Winter leaned over the railing of the staircase bewildered, but full of expectation, which quickly turned into astonishment and wonder: there was no one in the dining room other than Marie.

Mystified as if she had seen a ghost, Winter ran to the front door, grabbed her coat and rushed out, feeling the cool air give her a reviving slap on the face. At the gate, the guards greeted her formally, with their voices having no trace of the sweetness she had heard the previous night.

She walked around like a stray dog. Everything seemed familiar and strange; meaningful and insignificant; gray and colourless, horribly depressing and cold. The bench, where she usually sat in the park of *Sainte-Périne*, was empty, but she preferred to sit under the trunk of a plane tree instead. She caressed the soft grass with her palms, combed it with her fingers and she was infused with its moisture, relieved with the sense of its touch. She closed her eyes and fell into soothing inertia, a quiet little death; it was a thought she did not fear as much as that of loneliness.

"How I would like to go to her
If the way was not so far..."

With the song drilling her brain, she lost sense of her body, dispersed into a non-physical dimension, where only sounds existed: a bird chirping on a branch, a bug buzzing nearby, the plane tree leaves rustling, a car engine revving up, shouting children from afar. A light-coloured shadow spread under her eyelids, which soon turned to red, then some shapes danced into it, squares and circles and thick lines, which slowly started becoming darker, until they sank into a solid black. In a while, the sounds also drowned in silence.

"*Madame*! *Madame*!"

"She's dead!"

"No, you fool, she's breathing. Look at her chest; it's going up and down!"

"She's *Sainte-Périne*!"

"Haha! I told you to stop reading those tales before bed!"

"She won't wake up!"

"Shhh! I'll check her temperature!"

"Let's get her purse!"

"Shut up! We don't steal purses! I'm going to chop your hand off if you try!"

Two voices so delicate, like singing blackbirds, and something like a touch on her face made her darkness shudder, two images arising from it: two boys, identical like drops of water, two boys, blossoms of youth, infants in the cradle of life, with their smile, with their tears, with the glow of the sun on their tender faces. A powerful force pulled her out of the trance and back to reality. She opened her eyelids, heavy and sore, slowly raised her head. Two children, thin as rakes, one taller than the other, standing to attention two paces away, spoke with the language of their sparking eyes. The knit caps over their shaved heads and their jackets buttoned up to the neck would hardly offer the warmth they needed on this cold winter morning. She lowered her gaze to their tweed shorts, long socks and worn-out shoes.

"A franc, *Madame*?"

The tall child extended his hand and the younger one immediately imitated him. Winter felt a smile on her lips, but she doubted if they had made the slightest contraction. Stiff as a brick, she gruellingly stretched out her hand and the boys took it, each of them clinching it with both hands, soft, warm hands, despite the hardship. They helped her up, tilting their heads back to look at her. She felt like she wanted to embrace them, she even raised her arms a bit in order to do so, but she did not dare: so empty and frozen, she would probably appall them, frighten them away. She sighed, and the air in her lungs gave her a sense of endurance. She opened her purse, picked out two large banknotes, made two rolls out of them, put a roll in the hand of each boy. The children's faces brightened up; they glanced at each other and uttered two uncoordinated Thank you's, without even so much as looking at their benefactress. And then, they turned around and ran away, with all their might, perhaps, to a vicious father, who would be happy tonight and would spare them the evening spank.

Winter stood still, watching the boys' flight until their figures became a dot in the landscape. She felt an unexpected consolation and unusual clarity as if she had suddenly gained all the knowledge in the world. This time she did not stop anywhere from *Ourcq* to the *Villette* cemetery. With the feeling that not a day had passed, she walked down the road, where one cold night she had fled like a mouse, and her entire life up to that point in time rewound like a film reel, making it uncertain whether she had actually lived any of it or she had just woken up from her collapse at that weathered wall and still had to run away– unless she decided not to, unless she was brave enough to go back and help Mother kick out the two bastards who thought could intimidate and threaten them. There they were still: the cooper and the tailor and the fancy curtains on the windows of *Madame* Folie, who was once a great theatrical actress. And the grocer, *Monsieur* Luart: 'Come and take what you like, *ma douce*[75], and we'll find a way to settle the bill!' How much would it have cost her then for two handfuls of beans, a bag of flour and half a bar of soap! How much that it was not worth paying to feed and wash Mother and the children, when a little later she gave it to Pierre Morné's customers, only to save her own hide. She smiled bitterly. The door was closed at *Le Cordonnier*[76] Étienne, the old geezer who chased away the children playing outside his shop; and around the corner, at number 6 of *Rue Goubet*, the shutters were sealed at the spinster's windows, behind which *Mademoiselle* Fanny used to sit for hours, taking notice of everything, and if she so happened as to recognise her, she would definitely have all kinds of offensive adjectives to tell her widowed sister about the prostitute's daughter.

Looking at the six-storey building where she once used to live, Winter felt an acute pain in her chest and her knees weakened from breathing discomfort. The front door was corroded and wide open, as always. The entrance was just as miserable and dirty. On the first flight of stairs, the fifth step was still missing and now the eighth one was half-broken: the little devils must have been playing with the bats on the stairs again! Anticipation filled her throughout and she tried to dispel the feeling of evil created by the eerie silence around. On the third floor on the left it was, behind that over-worn wall: her house; where her brothers would shutter all sadness with their laughter; where Mother would dissolve all pains in her powerful embrace; and everything would seem possible again and all problems would be solved. Perhaps Christian would also be there: 'Well, well, well! The little princess has come back with her tail between her legs!' But, right now, it might be healing for her to see even him.

The door was completely dilapidated and Winter feared it would tumble the minute she touched it. Her heart ached when she compared this shack to Fred's beautiful mansion, but she quickly banished all thoughts and breathed in and out several times for courage. Finally, she knocked on the door. Instead of an answer, she heard some voices from a nearby floor. She reached over the door casing to find the key, which was still there as it used to be. She opened the door with great care. The inside was completely dark, and the air was moist and stale,–she had to grope her way around, stumbling on things a couple of times.

"Hello? Anybody?" she called. No answer. "Mum? Michael? Benjamin?" Fear overran her, that, perhaps, her family had indeed moved away and no longer lived there. "Mum?"

It was then that a sound reached her, like a painful groan in the dark depths. Using her memory, she found the way to where Mother's bedroom once was. She pulled aside the damp curtain and saw a woman lying in bed.

"... Mum?" she asked in doubt.

"Who is it?"

Winter recognised the voice, but could not believe the abjection of the woman she was looking at, the quiver in her spine forewarning her of a certain misfortune.

"... Mum, it's me, Winter! ..." she uttered, unable to hide her frustration.

"Winter?"

At the bedside table, she found a candle crammed into a bronze candlestick and a box of damp matches next to it, just barely capable of lighting the candle.

"Your daughter!"

Were it the candle shadows or an unrecoverable tragedy that distorted the figure of the woman she remembered with haughty beauty and youthful freshness, little difference would it make to Winter, who looked pitifully at the rags covering Mother instead of a blanket and observed her expressionless face with undesired gloom.

"Winter!" Mother exclaimed mournfully and turned her eyes on her, with a contraction testifying they wanted to cry. "... My sweet girl!" she whispered, and it took her a lot of effort to drag her hand over her daughter's and let it rest there.

Mother's touch, cold and weak, accompanied by the complete abandonment in the surroundings, shocked Winter, whose troubles suddenly left an impression of absolute insignificance.

"What's happened to you, Mum? Where is everybody? Where are the children?" she asked with little hope of a promising reply.

The question seemed to cause Mother more pain than the misery of her body. She brought her hand over her eyes and covered them, beginning a dreadful moaning, which panicked Winter, because she thought it was her last breath. Then, she realised this was how Mother was crying now and an awful helplessness paralyzed her inside. She took Mother by the shoulders, carefully, as though touching something fragile and likely to break at the slightest pressure.

"Mum, where are the children?" she repeated slowly, word by word, as if Mother had not understood the first time. "Michael and Benjamin?"

Mother stopped grunting and cast her gaze to the stains of dampness on the ceiling.

"Gone!" she curtly replied, pinning an expression of disbelief and denial on Winter's face.

"When will they be back?" she insisted, refusing to accept any other alternative to the meaning of the word.

Mother said no more and Winter's blood pumped inside her head, causing excruciating pain in her temples. For a moment, she thought she would faint. In her mind, a flood of assumptions, images and thoughts twisted together with memories, creating a tangle she was unable to put back in order and even more unable to consent to. She turned her head to look at the large room where she and the children once slept. But they could not have died, a voice inside her reacted incontestably. In a little while, Michael would walk to her with his cards in hand to play snap with her and he would argue with Benjamin, who wanted her all to himself. Last time she saw them, they had promised her a pair of stockings, like the ones some girls at *Oberkampf* wore, which they tied high under their skirts with laces hanging from their... And they laughed looking at each other in a conspiratorial way and poked each other meaningfully, and when she asked them where they had learnt such mischief, they would not tell her, and they would keep on glancing and poking and laughing until their bellies hurt. No, it was not possible, her heart protested, and she turned to look at Mother tearful, ready to tell her that she had lost her mind, that illness had disturbed her ability to distinguish the truth and it was only fear, her constant fear about the twins' health, after their last serious fever, which had cost her a fortune in cash and an entire self in dignity.

Mother's gaze on her, marked with longing and despair, forced Winter to push aside whatever feelings she herself had, in order to be strong for the sake of Mother, this poor, afflicted creature who had endured a lifetime of struggle with adversity and had understandably got tired, wanting to let go and yield.

"It's alright, Mum!" she found the strength to say and caressed her forehead and hair with care and affection. "I'm going to be here for you from now on. And I'm getting you out of here! Even if I have to carry you on my shoulders, right now, I'm getting you out of here. I swear it!"

Mother's plucked eyelids blinked repeatedly, and a forgotten expression of tenderness meliorated her face. With unexpected vigour, she extended her hand to her daughter's cheek: "How you have grown, how beautiful you are! ... And such nice clothes!" she murmured and touched Winter's soft coat. "... But you remembered your mother! And you came back to see her! ... You have always been a sensitive child, Winter! ... And now you're a woman!" Mother's cracked eyes finally shed a few tears.

"I'm married now, Mum!" Winter hesitated, but impulsively smiled. "To a kind and well-to-do man!"

"Oh!" Mother exclaimed and her grief subdued and her voice warmed up. "God bless you! ... At least, now I know ... one of my children lives happy!"

"Oh, Mum!" Winter cried, feeling guilty and ashamed. "I wanted ... I wish I could have... Please, forgive me..."

"Winter, my sweetie ..." Mother interrupted her with that tone which always had the power to impose on every fear. "It's not your fault ... It's not your fault! ..."

Winter was appeased and eager to accept Mother's forgiveness, and she took Mother's hand, caressing it dearly, kissing it again and again.

"Tomorrow," she promised with the will to atone for all her failures, as a daughter, as a sister, and even as a wife. "Fred and I will come and pick you up in the car! ... We'll be together from now on and everything will be alright, I promise!"

Mother's eyes shone for a brief moment and Winter's heart fluttered hopeful again, perhaps even strong enough to fight away that annoying fear tirelessly threatening to stab it.

"Oh, Winter, what a gentle thought!" Mother whispered while her gaze blurred, her smile faded and her face turned towards the dark wall. "But you needn't worry about me! I'll be fine! Antoinette comes now and then to keep an eye on me! Do you remember Antoinette?" Indeed, Winter remembered her. She was a courageous middle-aged woman, the only friend of the prostitute in the entire neighbourhood. "You and your husband shouldn't bother!" Mother continued, and little by little, the tone of her voice also changed into something formal and distant. "As soon as I'm better, then... What will your husband say to see your mother like this..."

"He's going to say you're the bravest woman he's ever seen!" Winter declared with undoubted confidence and hugged Mother with so much love, as if she were the mother and unfortunate Mother were the baby. "I'm not leaving you again. Ever! Ever!" she swore in tears and touched Mother's forehead, Mother's cheek, Mother's shoulder, Mother's hand.

Mother smiled with dry eyes, squeezed her daughter's hand: "It's enough that you came!"

Winter took a deep breath, tamed her emotions, gave Mother a resolute nod to reassure her. Perhaps Mother did not believe she was coming back; but she was; none of them could afford any more losses. She opened her purse, took out the thick roll of banknotes she had in it, fixed it into Mother's apathetic fist.

"Give this to Antoinette. Have her prepare you a proper meal! And tomorrow, first thing, we're coming to get you ... or even tonight, if Fred can make it!" She smiled at her warmly, bent and kissed her forehead, caressed her hand. "Promise you'll be here!" she asked, giving in to that persistent, unexplained premonition.

Mother gazed at her child in silence, and then she nodded. Winter was relieved. She got up and turned to blow out the candle on the bedside table, but Mother stopped her.

"Please! Leave it! I want to look at you as you go!"

Winter did not object. She said goodbye and repeated her promise to return the next day. Coming out of the shabby building, she stood to take a breath of fresh air. Her heart was heavy, but she was encouraged by the idea that, at least, Mother could be offered a more dignified life in the future. All that remained was to convince Fred. But it was absolutely impossible that he would deny something like this to her, even after they had so foolishly quarrelled. She felt positive. Fred's feelings were tender and strong, they would get through this ordeal. Fred would be as good to Mother as he had been to her, and perhaps, perhaps Mother could visit Aunt Martha, stay with her for a while, the both of them finding comfort in each other's company! She almost laughed propitious and cheery, gladly surrendering to the over-optimistic prospect. Yes, the time to put an end to all their suffering was long overdue. Together as a family, they could eventually forget the past and live happily ever after.

24

Smoke and clouds

It was not the first time Winter had set out for the *Hôtel du Louvre* with almost unjustifiable certitude of a favourable result, her confidence shrinking dramatically the shorter the distance to her destination became. The image of abandoned Mother was a dreadful reminder of a greatly undesired, yet not completely impossible, future, and she knew she wanted, she needed to see Fred for reasons far beyond Mother's situation.

On the fourth floor, she was sincerely welcomed by the secretary, which gave her a sense of courage, but he got up and hurried to open the office door for her before she had the time to brace herself and settle down to an appropriate introduction to what she had in mind.

"*Herr Sturmbannführer* is waiting for you!" he told her and Winter felt puzzled, but she was already in front of Fred, same as a defendant before the judge.

His full attention was drawn to a voluminous pack of documents, which he read and signed. "Have a seat!" he formally offered, without even so much as looking at her, and she stood motionless, nervously loosening and tightening the strap of her handbag.

"Peter said you were waiting for me?" she finally managed to say just to avoid the annoying quiet.

"They called from the lobby!"

She nodded and approached hesitantly, standing in front of his desk like a soldier awaiting orders. He looked up sternly, showing her the chair with his eyes.

"I did not come to sit!" she gasped.

"Then? What did you come for?"

She lowered her head, biting her lip. Her presence alone was enough for Fred to know her intentions–Fred, who understood her so well and always read right through her, but that was when he cared and wanted to, neither of which seemed very obvious right now.

"I've been meaning to apologise about yesterday!" she explained timidly. "I'm sorry, Fred, and I'm begging you to forget what happened and what was said! It was a terrible, terrible mistake."

He leaned back in his chair and stared at her coldly, that resentful shadow over him being the saddest spectacle she had ever seen, an image totally unbefitting of him, and she knew she was the reason for this repulsive transformation.

"Forgive me!" she uttered painfully and was no longer referring to the incident of the day before.

Fred got up from his seat with his still very much unabated fury; he went to stand by the window; the gray view was not enough to calm him down this time.

"It's easy for you to forget, isn't it?" he unkindly challenged her. "One night alone and you were terrified you'll lose it all. You feel remorse because you realised you're walking on thin ice. And you come here with your humble apologies in order to manipulate me once again!"

"No!" she protested with the fervour befitting a matter of life and death. "Say what you will! Punish me, humiliate me, if it'll make your anger go away, curse me, hit me, whatever! But ..." She came closer, focused all her attention on his shoulder as if that were her only source of strength. "... don't say that my apology is manipulation. And don't say that the fear that brought me here is so cheap. Yes, I am afraid, but it's not because ... I'm... For me, you're not..." She reached out to his arm because a touch could often speak so much more properly than any words, but his face became distorted and his hand cruelly removed hers and kept it away. He shocked her. Could it have actually come to this? That he should despise her so much as not to even allow her to touch him? It took her a couple of seconds to put the pieces together: "My God! You've been hurt!" she choked, but he turned to look at her completely indifferent to the terror that ripped her apart and the feeling of helplessness that crushed her. "You could have been killed!" she murmured, horrified. "And I'd have no idea!"

Fred walked away with a mask of disbelief for a face; he stood over his desk, took a cigarette and lit it.

"I had a rather unfriendly meeting with some acquaintances of yours last night!" he divulged with overflowing sarcasm, but she remained completely unmoved by his insinuation, only able to think how easy it was for her to lose him, another irreversible loss with the sign and seal of her undeniable guilt. And that image of him froze her blood, lying dead in a coffin, a white, freshly carved stone set in the ground, making the horrendous pledge,

Friedrich Rudolf von Stielen
1900 – 1943
Husband and nephew
Goodbye, our beloved!
You will live in our hearts forever!

"Go ahead, then! Ask away!" he spurted out, bringing her back to just as painful a reality. "I know you're dying to know if your little darling was among them!"

She looked at him with her disoriented expression, her grief-stricken gaze, only to meet his most biting rejection.

"I *am* sorry about what happened, Fred! I wish I could do something more than apologise, but I can't!" she asserted, and he returned to her an ugly sneer.

"Of course!" he rasped. "And then, you will have once again fooled the naive husband, so that you can go about with your work completely undisturbed!"

"With René Martin!" she deduced with a bitter smile, his expression being enough of an answer and a cue that there was nothing else to be said between them. A contraction in her forehead and her burning eyes warned her that she could no longer hold back her tears. And she had to leave before he could see it, because, for him, it would only be manipulation. She walked to the door, resolutely grabbed the door handle.

"If you love your life, you'd better not be with him when he falls into my hands!" were Fred's last words, hurtful like a knife stabbed in her back.

As she opened the door, it startled her to find herself face to face with Peter, and he seemed just as surprised and even more confounded than she was. He stared at her for a moment, then looked over her shoulder at his superior, who was standing by his desk with a cigarette burning between his fingers.

"*Fräulein* Marguerite Jérôme is here!" Winter understood he said.

She walked by him, without greeting. She took a glimpse of the girl sitting in all her comfort in an armchair there, a girl almost her age, accompanied by an officer, and the sting of jealousy pierced her heart. She rushed out to the staircase, fled downstairs like an unearthly menace chased her, and she was unable to detect Fred's nod to his secretary or the fact that the young man willingly obeyed and left the office after her. Her limbs felt weak, her mind and eyes foggy.

Panting and sweating, she huddled between the stalls at *Les Halles*, the hustle of the market exacerbating her frustration. She was pushed, given the evil eye, and, at a point, she was even berated, because she stumbled on a woman and threw down her shopping bag. As she was walking out from the marketplace and into *Châtelet* square, she was nearly run over by a *vélo taxi*[77] and both driver and passenger gestured at her offensively. She looked at them riding away and thought she saw all her hopes and dreams crumbling under the four wheels of their vehicle. When she reached the *Île Saint-Louis*, she slumped down on a ledge, the same ledge where she had more than once sat, always heavy with an unbearable burden. And it was at a time like this when she had run into René and they had sat together at the brasserie with the red tent,–his eyes, his touch, the name of that Simone, the beginning of her downfall and ruin.

This was it, then! And with her face buried into her hands, she felt finally permitted to cry. It was all over for her and Fred, and it seemed unbelievable, completely unimaginable how something so trivial had the power, in just a moment, to turn an entire world upside down and break it to pieces. There was more than enough regret in her, but it was pointless because the past could not be undone, and it felt utterly incomprehensible, what she did, what she did not: so what if she had told Fred she had seen René at the theatre, what more harm could have been done, what could have been more damaging than this constant hide and seek game, that she loathed, but felt compelled to carry on playing? Yet, she did not tell him when she should have, God knew why she did not tell him when she should, and now it was late, too late to admit it. And Fred knew; he always knew something more about her and René than she imagined, and perhaps he even knew why she did not tell him, but that hardly relieved her of the obligation to be honest with him, as he had been with her. *Oh, Fred!*

And yet, she had believed it for a while, she had believed Fred's love could endure. Because she had felt its strength, the same strength transfused into her, erasing the signs of depravity from her body, giving her a sense of worthiness and the entitlement to state what she wanted and claim it. And what she wanted were those moments with him, when they sat together in front of the fireplace, Fred in the armchair and she at his feet, on the soft thick carpet, her head against his knee, his fingers in her hair, talking, reading their favourite books–Fred would often read the newspaper–, and their glasses of cognac warming on the fireplace mantel, because 'this is how its delicate aromas are released'. And she had felt that there were joys in this life that did not require great sacrifices. Like one evening, when she had cooked that onion soup with melted cheese, which Pierre so proudly prepared for them at 'The Golden Doe' and was a true remedy for the winter cold, and she would swear she had never been happier than when Fred tasted it and sincerely approved of it. A simple, painless happiness! And she also recalled Marie's long face, when she had been kicked out of the kitchen and, later, had to admit, in Fred's presence, that her soup was an honestly decent effort. A small victory and a sentiment so fulfilling! Marie would be celebrating now, confident that she had regained her throne in *Sturmbannführer* von Stielen's household. *Oh, Fred!*

Then, it seemed as if there were nothing else to mourn for and she remained apathetic and cold, watching the ripples of the water on the *Seine*. She started counting, one ripple, two ripples, ... a hundred thirty-six ... two hundred fifty-one ..., until she lost count and she began to count the birds, but was soon unable to keep up, because some birds left and came back again, as did people sometimes, but sometimes they did not. Then, she focused on the fishermen along the opposite bank: how they threw the line into the water, how they spun it back on the spool, who caught fish and how often. She remembered the summer baths in the river–some fixed parts of the establishment still stood on the bank below the *Hôtel de Ville*. Fred was an excellent swimmer; he had technique, speed and beautiful movement. Despite coming from an island country, Winter could only barely float and pull a few slow and inelegant strokes. He was so superior to her in so many ways it had only been a matter of time before he would also realise it, and, even though he loved her enough to try, acknowledge that a man could only for so long keep trying to no avail.

Suddenly, the noise from the street caught her attention. Heavy trucks were speeding towards the north and, from afar, the bells of fire engines rang with urgency. What would be the end of them all? She tried to shake off the evil presage pursuing this question and a strange feeling urged her to get up and follow the commotion. She crossed *Pont Marie* to the *Marais* and from the *Place des Vosges* to the streets of the old Jewish quarter. Complete wilderness prevailed. This neighbourhood was dead, its life drained for a purpose as obscure as it was vile. It was the essence of this war: total annihilation. And she felt like a victim, as well as a perpetrator.

At the *Place de la République*, the atmosphere was dense, the air smelt of burning wood and moisture. The horn of a fire engine behind her made her flinch, and she stood at the side to watch a second fire engine rush by, followed by a truck and two German service jeeps. One of the latter braked abruptly a few metres past her, drove backward, and halted right in front of her. The rear door window was lowered and a familiar face appeared.

"*Frau* von Stielen?" the voice called in wonder.

"Karl Freier!" Winter exclaimed and poised herself to hide her disposition.

"Are you alright? You look faint. How did you get here? Would you like me to drop you off somewhere?" Karl Freier offered with honest concern, in his decent English. Winter straightened her hair nervously, seeing him get out of the car and approach, while she was digging in her head to find an excuse for herself.

"I took a longer walk than I expected, but I'm fine, thank you. It's probably this suffocating atmosphere! What is going on?"

"There's a huge fire, almost an entire building block at the *Villette* cemetery." Karl Freier explained, discreetly observing the paleness on her face.

At Karl Freier's utterance, the image of a lit candle on a bedside table came and stuck like a crooked nail in her mind; a withered body lying in a sick bed and a soul deprived of hope, who had long abandoned the desire to be salvaged: 'I don't want to be a burden. What will your husband say!' And, within a single moment, the day turned to night, and she almost passed out into the arms of Karl Freier, who instinctively sprang to her aid, his firm embrace, his tender face, his carefully attentive touch causing her the deepest suffering, for she was aching for another, but he, too, was gone like everyone she cared about, like everyone she loved...

"Come, let's get in the car! I'll drive you to the *Hôtel du Louvre*. There is always a doctor on duty and Friedrich will probably still be there!" Karl Freier caringly urged, and his words were enough for Winter to forcibly bestir herself.

"No, no!" she reacted strongly against the idea of once again facing

Fred's resentment. "I just felt a little dizzy. I'm fine now, really. I've walked long, haven't eaten much either. I'll just sit somewhere for some lunch." she added decisively, faking a smile as best as she could. "Did you say the fire was at *Villette*?"

"It is." Karl Freier affirmed and, seeing that Winter was not willing to accept his help, he immediately resumed the appropriate distance. "It has spread quickly, and it's yet to be determined how it started, but some stated the first to burn down was a six-storey building opposite the church. They are now trying to extinguish the cemetery. Can you imagine the horror?"

Winter nodded vaguely and turned to somewhere she did not have to look at anything specific. Karl Freier stood there, undecided for a while, but eventually backed off and returned to the vehicle.

"Forgive me, but I have to go!" he said hesitantly. "A fluent speaker of French is required for the inquiries!" He got in the jeep and closed the door, looking at her with clear reluctance to leave her like that in the middle of the street. Finally, he formally bid her farewell and turned to the driver: "*Rue Goubet!* And hurry!"

After that, everything went mute for Winter. Beneath her trembling feet, the ground became a fluid mass in which she began to sink. This swamp had already covered her up to the knees when she bent her head to look. From a disgusting hole in her abdomen, her entire self was pouring out onto the asphalt. A brutal shiver swept over her as if her skin desired to part from her. A thundering roar from the sky called for her eyes to look up at the gray clouds, which began to quickly gather over the city and soon started to pour. The rain was battering her face. No one could tell if she were crying. The rain was a good thing. It would help put out the fire. But even if it soaked her to the bone, it would not be able to extinguish the blaze in her heart.

25

The fruit around which it all revolves

"Good evening, Marie!"

Marie waited patiently for him to come through the door, take his cap, gloves and heavy woollen coat, and made a casual remark about the cold, seeing him breathing into his hands and rubbing them together immediately after. He gave her a tempered smile instead of an answer and hurried to the living room.

"*Madame* is not here, *Monsieur*!" Marie stated, diligently tidying his clothes, without caring to hide her disapproval.

Fred nodded, humming a deep sigh; he unfastened his pistol belt and put it away in the chest of drawers next to the hallstand, then walked back into the living room, closely followed by the housekeeper. He unbuttoned his tunic, undid the first buttons of his white shirt, and generously poured himself a drink.

"If I may, *Monsieur*, you must not drink on an empty stomach!" she uttered in a tenderly caring manner, while helping him to take off his tunic. Seeing two small irregular stains of blood on the left sleeve of his shirt, she let out a horrified gasp. "Goodness, *Monsieur*, you are hurt! Shall I bring the first aid kit?" she proposed with clear worry.

"Don't bother, Marie! It's only a scratch!" Fred said but immediately reconsidered. "On second thought, I'd better have the bandage replaced; it hasn't been changed since last night!"

The housekeeper hurried to fetch the first aid kit from the bathroom and, returning, she found Fred already sitting in his armchair by the fireplace, undoing the buttons of his shirt.

"Please, allow me!" she eagerly volunteered.

She removed the stained shirt, leaving his upper body exposed to the light of the crackling fire and her impatient eyes. She knelt at his side, gently touched the skin around the wound and noticed that it was, fortunately, not swollen. With a pair of scissors, she cut the bandage, which was soaked in dry blood, put iodine on a piece of cotton and cleansed the wound. She then placed clean gauze on it and tied it firmly with a new bandage. Finally, she helped him put on a fresh shirt.

"Perhaps a little dinner now, *Monsieur*?" she urged, gathering up the items she had used into a basin.

"Thank you, Marie, but no!" Fred responded, sounding rather preoccupied. "Just some coffee, if it isn't much trouble!"

He sat back in his armchair, feeling overwhelmed by the fatigue of the last two days. Too much had happened and there had been enough anger and sorrow to wear out even the sturdiest of characters. He looked deep into the flames of the fireplace and felt Winter's absence like a hollow in his soul. Normally, she would be there, sitting on the carpet at his feet, her head against his knee, his fingers through her hair. It was too late for her to be outside on her own–that was if she were on her own! he corrected himself, with spite and doubt still powerful enough to get the better of him. He wondered if she had heard the terrible news and, if she had, why she was not there to seek consolation in him–he would not deny it. But, of course, there was no way she would know that! He had treated her harshly; too harshly for both their good.

Marie soon brought in the coffee with some pastry she said she had baked only that morning, but Fred ignored not only her remark, he ignored her very presence, until he remembered to ask: "How long has the mistress been gone?"

"Since morning, *Monsieur*!" Marie replied, serving him the coffee, and Fred missed noticing the contempt in the housekeeper's eyes.

"Did she say where she was going?"

"She did not, *Monsieur*! Is there anything else I can do for you?"

And since Fred did not answer, Marie left him alone with his thoughts.

The day was full of unexpected emotions. It was a shock to hear where the fire was, to read the name 'Carole Dupont' on the list of victims. Winter had told him her family had moved to an unknown address, which was the reason she had brought no one to the wedding. Another lie. And yet, there was absolutely no doubt in his mind why Winter would lie about something like that, and, if he wanted to be completely truthful, he knew it all along that she was lying, even then he knew. He had failed to show enough sensitivity on this issue, regarding which Winter might not have had the courage to ask him for much. The result was disastrous.

At the site of the fire, the images surpassed the most morbid imagination: there were only a few scorched brick walls remaining of the burnt buildings, the interior floors, stairs, households, along with the people in them, all a gray dust cloud that smelt of death. Testimonies described human torches rushing out from the flames, running in screams to embrace the terrified eyewitnesses. Some of them landed on piles of rubbish, igniting new fires, while others did not even have the chance to leave the flaming buildings, or, perhaps, they did not want to. At the cemetery, the tombs with wooden crosses would now shelter anonymous corpses; monuments, headstones, all severely damaged, and even the soil was covered with a brown-gray crust of ash and decay. Bystanders, charred people, staring at the houses they no longer had. If they had escaped the fire, they would now have to face a bleak reality. He signed a personal warrant for the provision of food and clothing for the destitute addressed to the local municipal service. A generous gesture some were eager to commend. But he felt it was more like bribery to a guilty conscience.

Winter must have heard the news, he assumed. Karl Freier himself informed him that he had told her about the fire, but he could never have imagined that her mother lived there. Poor girl, Karl had said with sincere sympathy. And he, the man who claimed to love her, had been only ruthless to her.

The truth was not yet clear in his mind. All he knew for certain was that there were things he could not live with: that, being in the Resistance, Winter may have only married him for the inside information she could get her hands on; that she might be in love with someone else, that specific someone else, who had, therefore, every reason to begin a personal war with him; that she might have been disgusted every time he touched her, running to her true love to cleanse herself after...

He rubbed his palm on his face, recalling the surprising conversation he had with Andres Jérôme's daughter in the morning. It was surely a convenience having someone else decide for you, at least for as long as you had no serious objections to their choices, the young woman had said, guiltlessly admitting to a kind of opportunism. At first, in fact, the revolutionary ideas her father represented seemed fascinating, sometimes going to such extremes, as the desire to burn this world to the ground before creating a new inspired one. But, being the daughter of a rebel, conflict was inevitable. Life underground had taught the passionate teenager disobedience, and it had been long since her father's ideas ceased to appeal to her. You see, life had intervened; she was a young woman now, she did not want to spend her best years in hiding and, even more so, at risk of losing her own life. And, at this point, as impressively learned as cynic, Marguerite Jérôme quoted John Locke as to her right of rebellion: 'one principle upon which this very country was founded!' she declared, apparently having no reservations about siding with her father's enemies! It was her own rebellious manifest, which, like any combative action, unfortunately had its collateral losses. And now that her arrest gave her adequate cover to disappear from the Resistance circles completely unsuspected, all she wanted in return for her cooperation was a one-way ticket to Flensburg, her mother's ancestral village in northern Denmark. There was a whole other story there,–a banished adulteress, a girl growing up without a mother... Who knows what feelings were the ones actually prevailing in this young woman's heart, who chose to be regarded as a defector rather than a suffering motherless child!

If Winter had started a rebellion of her own, the collateral loss would be he and he could understand that, as a soldier and an officer, he knew the cost of collateral losses. He only admired how flexible human morality was, how fluid the boundaries of right and wrong for each person. The hero of a novel[78] had argued that the only reason man loved his fellow human was because he believed in the immortality of his soul. Consequently, while man was gradually losing faith in the immortality of the soul, the boundaries of his morality were becoming broader and broader. This was not unreasonable, considering that the more science and human achievements detached man from God, the more arrogant man grew. But, on the other hand, how was it possible for humanity to survive on such a selfish and petty motive as being good only to reserve a place in Paradise? Not to mention what hideous crimes had been committed throughout the history of mankind in the name of God–it was such atrocities that gave atheists an argument for the complete condemnation of any religious sentiment. And yet, it had to be a religious sentiment that separated man from beasts, a belief in a supreme being, an evolved spirit and a higher existence, not necessarily in the sense of an extraneous Judge God, against whom resistance would be reasonable in terms of justice like the one Marguerite Jérôme advocated, but in the sense of God existing within each person's heart and each person constituting the very substance of God.

This was all wonderful in theory, his more practical self contested. When it was time for actions to speak, everyone was more or less willing to turn a blind eye to whatever higher or evolved existence there was in order to accomplish the desired goal. He was no exception, for which reason he gladly gave Marguerite Jérôme the assurances she required and guiltlessly exploited the flood of her revelations.

First of all, seeing Winter, she did not recognise her and doubtlessly certified she had never seen her before. Neither did the name remind her of anything. It was only when Fred guided the conversation toward René Martin that *Mademoiselle* Jérôme could make the assumption about who Winter was. She remembered that, for a time, René Martin had his eye on a girl from Pierre Morné's club, nothing... professional, though, she could assure him, as the crush on her had obviously started before he had even found out she was working at 'The Doe'. It seemed, however, that the girl was poor at meeting his expectations, at which point she hurried to remark with a smirk: 'Fortunately for me!' And she added, somewhat wistfully, that the only thing she would miss from her life underground was the fervid nights she had spent in the arms of this willful man, with the insidious, but so enchanting character. Then, she validated her credibility with a series of addresses, names, schemes, and plans, which were first-rate material for the Intelligence Service.

Marguerite Jérôme's testimony was another indisputable confirmation of Winter's story, but, strangely, the more evidence he found of her innocence, the less certain he felt of it. After all, there was always the possibility that Martin and Winter's liaison was carefully hidden from everyone, their schemes being known to none other but the two of them. And then again, if Winter had been involved in the affairs of the Resistance, the name Marguerite Jérôme would not have been unfamiliar to her and it was logical to assume the young woman's presence in his office this morning would urge Winter to alert her associates. Instead, she just spent hours on the *Île Saint-Louis*, sitting at the same spot, occasionally breaking down into what could be regarded by a third party as very emotional tears. Could she have been aware of being followed, could her very presence at that spot be a signal to something, was he just being paranoid? Perhaps, Winter knew more about the affairs of the Resistance than Marguerite Jérôme, or, perhaps, she was confident that the people she cared about were safe from any of the deserter's revelations. The fact that René Martin remained uncaptured could not have been accidental.

He felt exhausted. He had done nothing all day but think and rethink, make scenarios and then reject them, build up a possible big picture and then demolish it. His doubts, which any logic might challenge, were so disturbingly powerful, exactly because they had nothing to do with logic: they were more like a feeling, a strong insuperable feeling. He breathed in and out hearing the sound of his frustration; he stretched his back into the armchair, the tension of his muscles was gripping. Then, he felt his toe press on something hard: it was the leather-bound volume of Rilke's poems, which Winter stubbornly aimed to learn to read and understand in German, because she knew they were among his favourite. He picked up the book to look at the page where it was left open.

"O Lord, give each person his own death
the death that comes out of the life he lived..."[79]

It was then that the key was heard in the front door. The door opened and closed slowly. Female footsteps resounded heavy on the hallway tiles; they halted, creating a moment of screaming silence, and they continued towards the staircase and up the first stairs.

"Winter!"

Winter had stood at the threshold of the living room, looking out over the armchair in front of the fireplace, where Fred's protruding arm indicated he was there. His presence offered her some reassurance but futility seemed like a much more powerful sentiment, and she wrapped and unwrapped the strap of her handbag around her fingers several times, so tightly she could feel the blood burning in her fingertips. Then she decided to continue on her way to the staircase, certain there was little else to say than the awful words they had already exchanged. His voice caught her on the third step. She took a deep breath and turned back.

"You're late!" he said without attempting to look at her.

"I didn't realise the time!" she answered in a barely audible voice.

"Where were you?" his next question followed and so did a serious, though milder look than she had expected. Winter's countenance was pale, her eyes swollen and weary.

"Walking!" she replied with great effort.

Fred got up and approached. He freed her fingers from the noose of her handbag strap, took her by the arm, brought her near the fire. He took off her coat, put her to sit in the armchair, and rubbed her stiff hands with what felt like an awkward caress. She looked up at him.

"... You've heard!" she concluded, immediately feeling stupid at the assumption that he, the Chief of Intelligence, might not have heard.

She lowered her eyes, pulled her hands away from his care, and laced her fingers together into a tight, unbreakable knot.

"I'm sorry, Winter! I truly am!" he uttered but, other than squeezing her fingers even tighter, she remained motionless and completely mute.

The change of disposition on his behalf filled her with grief and animosity. If it were out of decency, she did not want his sympathy, not even his simple human interest, and she definitely did not need his pity–her own self-pity was enough to last for the rest of her life. He was the only one left in the world for her, but she might as well be all alone than be a beggar for his feelings. She did not want any Christian, compassionate love, she wanted the primitive, selfish, even ignoble, love of man and woman, which was meant to satisfy not only the spirit but also the body, and would need no Paradise to be fulfilled in, only the earth, this petty earth where they all struggled to save their petty lives and their even pettier souls. Her body was aching for comfort, her heart beat to the top of the heavens, yearning for a touch on this desolate piece of flesh, which, however contemptible it might be considered for its base desires, was still what they had been granted to contain the divine gift of the soul. And this lustful, jealous, mortal flesh could not be satiated by pity, sympathy, or compassion; it wanted more; it wanted everything...

She turned her face away, pressing it strongly on her shoulder, her own arms giving her body an alien embrace, simultaneously building up an impenetrable fortification. Fred was unpleasantly surprised. The Winter he knew would fall in his arms crying, holding onto him with every bit of strength in her. But, apparently, she did not need him anymore. She had found consolation elsewhere. Possessed by egoism, he got up and walked away, clenching hands into fists and leaking anger from his airtight lips, his squinting eyes, and frowning eyebrows. He poured himself a drink, drank it up, felt his grip squeezing on the glass almost to the point of breaking it.

"Fred!"

His gaze on her cut like a knife, but it was immediately astounded by the sight of her, panting for breath, standing up with her shoulders in full tension, her arms slightly extended to the side, palms facing forward, like a body completely surrendered to the flames of an internal Inquisition; and these eyes of hers, mournful and utterly lonely, desperate and resigned, an admission to an irredeemable guilt, subscribing to be condemned and hopeless of salvation.

A few long steps and he was there, the force of his embrace almost painful; an invigorating, liberating pain that brought the feeling of life and silenced the death inside her. Like the sweet bread in a famished mouth. Like the spring of cool water to a thirsty traveller. Like the miracle to a bedridden invalid suddenly regaining the feel of his arms and legs, thus flinging into a frenzied dance, jumping and falling and rolling on the ground, because he was back on his feet, he could move and he lived...

26

A silent welcome

There was not one book in Fred's library that would cogently argue about the Afterlife. Winter spent hours and days in it looking for answers, but none would suffice to heal the loss of a loved one. She had felt this way before, only then she was a child and still believed in something, however unspecified. What did she believe in now? If she lived in ancient Greece, she would believe that, after death, people met again in Hades, good or bad regardless, and it was an idea most appealing. But the religion she was taught was not as magnanimous: the good and the bad were separated like wheat from chaff, and Winter could find no consolation in that. Because, if there were a Paradise, she knew Father, Mother and the twins would be there–innocent souls entrapped in suffering bodies. But if there were a Paradise, she would have no hope of ever meeting with them again: because if Paradise existed, then so would Hell.

Those nights she was constantly having the same dream. She was in the apartment of the *Cité Berryer*. It was windy and snowing heavily, but she was standing in front of the window, her arms outstretched, a sign of surrender and provocation. At the building across the street, all windows were wide open, their curtains furiously blowing. And she was waiting. Then she could hear a noise coming from the bedroom.

She did not want to abandon her waiting position, but the noise was compelling. Something like scratching on glass and light footfalls on a hard but thin surface. She would put her arms down and go to see without fear, although she knew she was about to face something eerie. Motionless in the middle of the bedroom, she carefully listened. The sound was coming from above, from the roof tiles. She would get up on her toes and open the skylight, hiding her face behind her arm to protect it from the sleet-like snow which suddenly charged inside. Then, a crow would fly in and sit on the bed's headboard–the bed sheets in disarray after a night of lovemaking with Fred. The crow would shake its plumage every now and then. 'Who are you? What are you?' she would ask and the bird would answer in a shrill human voice: 'Nevermore. Nevermore.' And it would cast a deep and penetrating stare into her eyes, piercing like his voice, devastating and impossible to look at...

She awoke in a sweat, and she was alone in bed–Fred had been assigned consecutive night shifts. The first time she had the dream, she immediately ran down to the phone and called the *Hôtel du Louvre* to hear his voice, a calm, patient, and fully rational voice, reminding her of the book she was reading that afternoon, a poem by Poe[80], and tenderly scolding her for not choosing some lighter reading in her condition. When she had hung up, Marie was standing at the door of her bedroom, which was downstairs next to the kitchen, silently glaring at her in her nightgown, clearly thinking she looked like someone having just broken out from an asylum for the insane.

It was incredible how life was so largely taken for granted. Things happened for no specific reason at all, there was no grand scheme behind people's coming to this earth, and they could die just as accidentally as they had been born. And yet, they lived their lives as if their time were infinite, with this illusion of eternity making them arrogant, thinking the things they needed would always be at their disposal, and so would the people they loved, waiting for this or that condition to be met before giving those loved ones the attention they deserved. If God actually laughed when people made plans, He would certainly have laughed His heart out at her.

But it was too late to repent, and those who could forgive her were no more. She could not even ask for God's forgiveness: they both knew she was not really sincere, that all she wanted was to get rid of her guilt, which burdened her chest, stealing her of vital breaths and leaving her with less and less strength to breathe every day that went by. But living organisms were created on the principle of adaptability, the books said, and Winter knew she would learn to live with less air, as subterranean creatures had learnt to live with less light, and some of them were blind or with atrophic eyes because they did not need them. Winter was hardly certain she needed to be alive at all–it would matter little to her, if she did not think of Fred a bit: this man, who, only God knew, what he saw in her and loved her. She had wished to be good for him, too; great disappointments that come with great expectations. She never used to have any expectations before him; sometimes she thought it had been easier that way.

Winter's grief had an unexpectedly powerful impact on the daily life of the *Auteuil* mansion. Her withdrawal made it clear that what gave the house its liveliness was none else but her passionate temperament: her steps on the floors, the rustling of her clothes, the songs she murmured, her lively speech, her explosive enthusiasm. Even Marie had noticed that the house had long been this calm. Fred saw Winter sink deeper and deeper into a bottomless ocean of gloom and pessimism. Losing a loved one often had such an effect on people, but Winter did not just have an expected reaction to the death of a loved one. She did not want to be redeemed. She sought pain, dwelled on and intensified it as if it were only this dark abyss where she could find peace.

Christmas was coming and Fred was afraid that it would be a time most difficult for Winter. A change might do her good, he thought, and he was, indeed, in no less need of a change than she was.

That cold and snowy morning, only a few days away from Christmas, Winter was standing by the dining-room window looking at the garden, fully regressed to that state of reminiscing which had carried her through most of her life after Father's death, safe, almost happy in her memories. And she would swear that, if she looked hard enough, she could see Father there, his full-length apron on, a pair of secateurs in his hand. Mother would be heard from the kitchen, asking for some spearmint to put in her meatballs, and the little girl with the blonde plaits that she used to be would anxiously jump around waiting for lunchtime.

"Winter, come sit with me!"

There was always a touch of regret and a load of despair when she was called upon to return to reality. She took a deep breath and found it very difficult to soften the expression on her face as she took her seat near him at the table, wordlessly watching him open the mail. He smiled and gave her a letter to read, but she could not smile back and she could barely extend her hand to take and reluctantly skim through the page.

"Let's go to Switzerland for the holidays, shall we?" he proposed with an eager whisper and she felt obliged to nod affirmatively, lowering her eyes to hide the dread in them.

The train left *Paris-Est* station in the early afternoon and by the time they had left *Île-de-France* it was already getting dark. They had a long night ahead–for safety reasons, the lights on the train would go out early.

Winter woke up just before dawn. Having had a few drinks more than usual at dinner, she had slept for hours. The train was chuffing monotonously and, outside the window of the sleeping car, it was slowly lighting up, revealing the beautiful scenery of a snowy forest under a yellow, orange and rose-pink painted sky. Sunrise. No matter what people did, sunrise would always come,–a rare certainty which added to Winter's sense of insignificance. Then the rails squealed, entering a tunnel, and she was startled and jumped up, almost hitting her head on the car ceiling. She climbed off her berth and saw Fred sleeping on his back, with one hand under the pillow. How guiltless must Fred's conscience have been for him to sleep in a position like this, whereas she always felt the need to sleep on her stomach, preferably hugging a pillow, as if to protect her chest from a bitter nocturnal foe. As she lay down next to him, she woke him up. Silently, he made room for her and turned to the side to cuddle her. His chest on her back felt warm, his slow breath through her hair soothing. Before long, she fell asleep again.

Shortly after breakfast, they arrived in Strasbourg. The route would then take them to Freiburg and from there, through Basel, to Zurich, hopefully in time for a late dinner at Aunt Martha's. Coming from the north, they were not fortunate to see the towering mountains of the Alps, which were synonymous with Switzerland in many people's minds. They were taking a lowlands course, where white valleys were masterfully decorated with winding rivers and picturesque villages. It was a natural beauty full of contrasts, wild, but serene, delicate, and elegant.

"A completely different world, isn't it, Fred?" Winter remarked, feeling the beneficial effect of the landscape, and he agreed. "It's probably because the war has not reached here!" she continued, leaning on his shoulder to sigh in relief.

And yet the Swiss had proved quite ready for war, Fred noticed, observing that, in his mind, Germany's attitude towards Switzerland had been one of the *Führer*'s smartest political and military moves: Switzerland largely depended on its neighbours for the importation of basic goods and raw materials, and, to get them, it was willing to make bigger or smaller concessions. Instead of making another enemy who would fight tooth and nail against it, the Reich had actually found in neutral Switzerland a covert ally. Winter felt frustrated, though not at all surprised, that there was no real neutrality in this war. One could not expect a glass of calm water to stand alone in the middle of a stormy sea, she said, and Fred seemed to like the metaphor.

At Zurich Central Station, *Hauptbahnhof*, their journey reached its end. They stepped down to the platform holding their luggage, and, when the driver kindly sent to pick them up asked to confirm their identity, they introduced themselves as *Herr* and *Frau* von Stielen, no rank, no salutations, no formalities–Winter liked this minor detail, which gave her the odd sensation that they could actually be two ordinary people, with ordinary lives and a nice, ordinary future ahead.

As the car drove through the snow-covered city to *Schweighof*, the little suburb on the foothills of *Uetliberg*, where Aunt Martha lived, Winter would try to discover on the way pretty-looking corners where Fred and she could create new histories, bold new histories, leading them as far away from the past as possible: Fred's aunt had dared do so, and it did not seem to have turned out badly for her.

Fred had explained to Winter that Aunt Martha was his mother's younger sister, who followed her to Germany when she came to live with her husband, Fred's father. She was a strong-headed young woman, enjoying challenges and adventures, who would stubbornly refuse to remain buried in the British provinces, as she herself often declared. During the Great War, Martha became involved with an official from the Kaiser's war council; they bonded closely and everyone believed their relationship would end up in marriage. And yet, suddenly, just before the end of the war, they separated. Aunt Martha came to Zurich and never returned, except for the few weeks between Fred's mother's illness and her death. She took Fred with her to Zurich for a while after that, and he loved her like a mother. Winter remembered how dearly Aunt Martha had welcomed her into the family, she still felt a little intimidated by the idea of being around her motherly figure, but there was also something comforting in the prospect of staying with her for a while. After all, she had worked miracles with Fred and he had not been spared the suffering of losing a family, either.

"Oh, please, do come in, do come in! I can't believe you are both here! Welcome! Welcome!" she repeated, delighted to see them and could not get enough of hugging and kissing them.

"It's nice to see you again, Aunt Martha!" Winter said with an ambiguous feeling, contrary to Fred, who, impressively affectionate, gave his aunt a long, powerful embrace.

"You seem to get prettier and prettier every time I see you! What's your secret?" he teased her, and she broke out into wholehearted laughter.

"Well, you!" she reciprocated. "Hasn't marriage been good for you! Every day I thank God for this girl, who lights you up!" she added and

Winter blushed and lowered her eyes, feeling weepy as Aunt Martha took her in her arms and stroked her hair and face. "You'll be alright, my darling, I promise!" she whispered sweetly to her and Winter smiled emotionally, for the first time with the feeling that there might actually be such hope.

Then, a well-dressed butler approached to take their coats and, in his turn, bid them a warm welcome. Winter was pleased with the butler's amiable attitude–nothing like the stiff formality of their own housekeeper–and, as she was handing him her coat and hat, she thanked him in German.

"You can speak English to Huppert, my girl" Aunt Martha intervened. "He's been hearing it for so long, he now speaks it better than an Oxford graduate. Right, Huppert?"

"Indeed, my lady!" uttered the butler as imperiously as would befit the most phlegmatic Englishman.

"How can you not love a man like this with all your heart!" Aunt Martha exclaimed jovially, reminding Winter how much the vivacious elderly woman liked to be expressive of her thoughts and feelings.

"Oh, but **'Never give all the heart for- love will hardly seem worth thinking of'**!"[81] Huppert recited with grand style and impeccable accent, pointing his index finger at Aunt Martha in a humorous warning gesture. And while everyone laughed, Winter was staring in astonishment, envious of the closeness the people in that room shared, the closeness that made them a family.

"Huppert and I were reading Yeats on my vacation from military school. Or should I say he suffered me reading, isn't that so, Huppert?" Fred joked, and the butler hurried to explain to Winter.

"What would you like to do, Mr. Fred, for a pastime, play some cards, maybe a little chess, a drink at the beer bar? No! Let's read, Mr. Fred said. But dear boy, this is not the way for a young man such as you! No! Reading it is, he said. What could a poor man like me do? I dusted the books off, sat with him by the fireplace and he read to me. Yeats and again Yeats! It was impossible not to learn every verse the man ever wrote by heart!"

"Come on! As if you didn't love every minute of it!" Aunt Martha exclaimed teasingly and ready for more revelations: "As a child, my poor Huppert was dying to go to Ireland and search for his own chest of gold. He had this Irish storybook, which had completely blown his mind, and he even considered changing his name into something extremely Irish, like Patrick or Cillian, didn't you, dear?" she chattered and immediately grabbed the butler by the arm, whimsically saying to him: "Please forgive me for spilling the beans, love, won't you?" And Huppert nodded 'perhaps' with an expression strongly showing he would forgive her almost anything.

"Well, for what it's worth, I think Huppert is a nice and decent name!" Winter contributed in a spirit of reconciliation.

"Oh but 'Huppert' is a name for dogs!" the butler cried out with pretend indignation and Fred hurried to explain to Winter that some neighbours had once been so imprudent as to name their white Swiss shepherd dog 'Huppert'.

Winter was amused, but immediately her attention was drawn to a clowder of cats, which barged in and began to rub at Aunt Martha's feet, meowing and purring.

"Which is why, here, we only have cats!" Aunt Martha stated and laughed out loud, lifting a fluffy cinnamon cat in her arms.

"These brats!" Huppert spurted out and hurried to pick them up, one by one, muttering to himself.

"Careful, Huppert! Your dislike for my kitties leads to very unpleasant associations!" Aunt Martha warned him playfully and mockingly shook the cat's front leg at the frowning butler.

"Oh, but enough of this joke, Auntie!" Fred stepped in with a smile.

"Don't bother, Mr. Fred. She knows who her pussies love the most!" Huppert declared and ostentatiously meowed and gestured to the cat Aunt Martha was holding, which did not take long to be persuaded to abandon her mistress's arms and follow the butler to the kitchen, along with the other cats.

"You little traitor!" Aunt Martha exclaimed with a shake of her head and a hearty laugh, taking her nephew and niece, as she called them, by the arms, and leading them to the dining room, where the table was already set for them. "Are you hungry? You must be hungry after such a long journey!" And as Fred and Winter confirmed they would have dinner with pleasure, Aunt Martha continued: "I hope you like our cuisine, dear! You see, the rationing has deprived us of great variety, but, for the both of you coming from so far away, and especially for you, my girl, coming for the first time, I promised no ration would get in the way!" she proclaimed with her torrential disposition and caressed Winter's cheek.

"You shouldn't have gone to so much trouble, Aunt Martha. After all, I'm not very particular about food, am I, Fred?" Winter replied in order to reassure her.

"About everything else though...!" Fred added with explicit disapproval.

"Fred!" Winter exclaimed, shooting at him with a look of surprise, surprise not at his disagreeable remark but rather at his naughty mood. He laughed and gestured in apology, while Winter remained pleasantly astonished. In Paris, Fred's position was always a factor largely dictating his behaviour, and, even with her, it was not always easy to shake off this role where he had to remain firm and composed at all times. With Aunt Martha, however, Fred was still the child of the family, a child with every right to be playful, frisky, even disobedient, a child likely to receive affection as much as reproof, since Aunt Martha did not seem at all intimidated by the fact that her nephew was now not only a fully grown man but also a major of the SS.

She glanced at him sitting next to her at the table and a strange sentiment whirled inside her chest: she was exhausted by the trip, amazed by her first impressions, and was actually starting to feel excited about the holidays to come, thinking it might be possible, after all, to recover from her grief, from the guilt surrounding it mostly, if there were people around still loving her, people who felt she deserved to be loved. She reached for Fred's hand and squeezed it softly; they exchanged gazes, and she smiled at him. Then Fred shone as if he had witnessed a miracle.

Aunt Martha had prepared Fred's adolescent room for them to stay, with a comfortable double bed, which had replaced Fred's old single one, being the only change in the space with so many memories for him. The shelf cabinet where his wooden constructions were being displayed was intact, and so were his works of art–a three-masted barque with white cotton sails; a nineteen twenties Mercedes-Benz with black buttons for wheels; an elaborate clock tower with an actual working mechanism; a red painted triplane model with the iron cross on both sides of its tail, like that 1917 Fokker he never became an aviator to fly. Winter discerned the nostalgia in his eyes, feeling a plural sense of complicity with him and a strong bond.

The morning that followed smelt of home and icy nature. Winter was awed by the sight outside the window, pulling back the curtains as accustomed to after getting out of bed. "Ah, it's snowing!"

"You'll catch a cold!" Fred whispered with care and came to place a shawl over her shoulders. Winter was pleased to feel the warmth of his arms around her waist.

"It's beautiful, isn't it?" she admired, and he shared the feeling with a hum.

Enchanting and wonderful, nature would fill their souls with its calm lightness. And it was so quiet they could almost hear the snow touching the ground. Then, a couple of men walked in through the garden gate, calling out Aunt Martha's name in an almost singing tone. Holding some packages in their hands, they crossed the garden and entered the house, talking and laughing cheerfully and loudly.

"Your aunt has guests!" Winter said with a smile as Fred stroked her shoulders and kissed her hair.

"Aunt Martha never seems to be left alone!" he remarked. "And yet, she's very lonely!"

"But I thought Huppert..." Winter argued, mostly out of a personal need to avoid anything even remotely related to loneliness.

"They're more like brother and sister, I'm afraid! Two bachelors abandoned in the care of each other!" Fred noted with some regret, and Winter felt sad. Because, if he had not come to complete and comfort her life, she, too, would have been utterly lonely and she doubted she would have had half of Aunt Martha's courage to live life to the fullest.

"Imagine if we could stay here forever!" she wished and turned around to curl up in Fred's arms. "We'd make a beautiful family, your aunt would not be lonely anymore and our children would grow up knowing nothing but love and security! Wouldn't you like that, Fred?"

"Of course, I would!" he uttered without hesitation and held her tight. "When the war is over ...!" he assured her but his words cut through her heart, filling her eyes with despairing tears. She pressed her face against his chest and inhaled the scent of him. She wanted to whisper his name a thousand times, stay in this warm and safe embrace for the rest of her life, and forget about the war and what else it could take away from her. When the war was over, she dreadfully repeated in her mind. This war had to be over soon; it had to before it was too late. "What is it, my love?" he enquired, reading through her heartsick silence.

She raised her aching eyes to his face. Just by looking at him, she knew he loved her, and she...

"Kiss me, Fred, kiss me!" She closed her eyes and drank balsam and nectar from his mouth. No shadow and no fear were stronger than what she felt for Fred.

A knock on the door interrupted their tender moment and Aunt Martha appeared at the threshold, staring at the embracing couple with eyes lingering between contentment and undefined sadness. Then, she apologised with a chortle and informed them merrily that she was going to spend the morning at the *Lichterschwimmen*[82] committee, but urged them not to let her absence refrain them from a walk in the city.

"After all, who likes to be a third wheel, right?" she teased them and left them alone sending from afar a very theatrical kiss.

They began their little tour around Zurich with the suburban railway, which got them as far as the central train station. First stop at *Lindenhof*, a small hill with a panoramic view of the city, and, coming down from there towards the river, they admired the ancient church of St. Augustine and the oversized clock of St. Peter's Church. The

Romanesque abbey of the *Grossmünster* raised its two eminent towers over the *Limmat*, overlooking the turret of the *Fraumünster* on the opposite side of the bridge. Winter thought the most charming area of the city was on this side of the river, a little further from the City Hall, which was built on the riverbank. It was *Niederdorf*, the medieval-looking old city with its little cobblestone streets and the iron shop signs depicting the object of their trade: a watch for a watchmaker, a shoe for a shoemaker, a key for the locksmith, some loaves of bread for the baker. And there were nice pastry shops, cafés, and restaurants with lacy curtains on the windows, quiet and peaceful, an ideal place to sit and chat with the locals while tasting their delicious treats. And only steps away, the lake extended to the edge of the horizon.

"Do you really think we'll be able to take that trip around the lake tomorrow?" asked Winter, gazing at the boats quietly moored at the dock, and Fred replied: "I'm sure Aunt Martha will move heaven and earth!"

Late in the afternoon, they ended up in the foothills of *Uetliberg*. Some cleared trails allowed them to walk through the snow-covered fir trees, the spectacular top being inaccessible at that time of year. There was a shelter there, which in warmer weather also served as a place of recreation, and the view was breathtaking, Fred informed her. In summer, one could see the whole city of Zurich and the lake all the way to the northeast, while to the south, on a clear day, even the peaks of the Alps could be distinguished. In winter, the landscape was painted with wild beauty in its icy stillness. But the season Fred liked the most was really autumn, the first rainfalls in the forest filling it with life–sounds and scents able to infuse the soul with their moist and stimulating freshness.

Winter listened to Fred ecstatically with an overwhelming feeling of completeness and togetherness,–comforting and awakening, unable to be contained in the boundaries of a simple body. They were standing under a tree with low branches loaded with snow. She raised her hand and shook the branch, causing the snow to fall onto their hats and coats. Fred was initially surprised, but not a moment passed before he retaliated with a handful of snow, which he threw at her, challenging her with his sprightly expression. They laughed with their hearts, threw snowballs at each other, they ran and rolled on the ground, coating their clothes with snow and wet fir needles. They lay on their backs, panting, looking for pieces of sky through the dense branches. Dusk was upon them and, every now and then, small birds would come to perch in the trees.

"I love you, Fred!" she said with a clear and fully committed voice. He turned his head to look at her, and she did the same. "I love you so much!"

He opened his arms, and she nestled in them; his face in her hair, his tight embrace, a silent welcome. Undisciplined to the words of the poet, he had given all his heart to this girl, against everyone, sometimes even against himself. And yet, he had the feeling that Winter had loved him since that first time they sat together on the library sofa, the same time he had fallen in love with her. People often sought love in words, feeling insecure when they were absent. But an expressed love was no more valuable than an unexpressed one, which was manifested in small undefined moments by indiscernible, yet determined and decisive gestures. He knew this now more than ever, now that Winter was telling him she loved him. But he had to admit, a sweet, heartwarming admission, that he had not been less happy with her when she had not yet uttered a single word.

27

Winter frost

Christmas Eve morning and the single boat sailing around Zurich Lake looked like the theme of a romantic painting, travelling smoothly along the verdant banks, adorned by intricate laces of snow. Beautiful houses with steep roofs and smoking chimneys, people shoveling the snow off their doorsteps and others coming for a visit with presents in their hands and merriment in their greetings. Here and there moored boats, which many lakeside dwellings used as a means of transport; and solitary fishermen, with their waterproof coats and hats, patiently waited, their rods outstretched, their lines penetrating the calm water; for them, neither time nor the frost was of any importance; they were part of the landscape, like the ducks, geese and all-white swans competing with them in fishing, each with equal opportunities of success.

Winter would assume by the look of the houses around the lake that the villagers prospered, much the same as in the city–she had not noticed signs of poverty anywhere she and Fred had been, while, in Paris, it was only a few steps away from the centre that complete destitution would reside. The kind of misery that follows people to their grave, name it as one may, hunger, disease, or despair. *Oh Mum, my Mum*! And she lost them all, one by one, the people she loved.

She turned to look at Fred in sheer terror. Aunt Martha was

chattering about the year when the lake was completely frozen and he had an intrigued smile on his lips. His arm was tenderly wrapped around her shoulders; she felt its weight, its warmth, its imperceptible convulsive movements–the arm of a man alive. She squeezed into him, but he did not realise. He brought his eyes onto her with a brittle laugh. Inside, Winter was shedding inconsolable tears.

They had already had a few *Schnapps*[83] on the boat and, when they returned home, Winter secretly had at least a couple more, while Fred and Aunt Martha were setting up a fresh, fragrant fir tree in a corner of the living room. She looked at them from a distance feeling like a child who was new to a company of friends, fearing they might not let it join in their games. Before long, Aunt Martha came to leave a complete box of fancy ornaments in her arms and Fred gave her the golden star, holding the stool for her to climb up and put it on the treetop. Then, Huppert appeared with drinks and treats for everyone, singing *'O Tannenbaum'*, immediately inviting them all to sing along. Well, all who knew how to sing *'Oh Christmas Tree'* in German, anyway.

At lunchtime, Winter drank even more–wine this time. She would empty her glass and either Fred or Huppert would fill it up again, festive and carefree enough not to keep count.

"...And, for the Christmas reception tomorrow evening, *Herr* Walther is sending his car for us, which is very kind of him, but we wouldn't have it any other way, would we?" Aunt Martha informed them craftily winking. "The other day I met *Frau* Walther at the market and she insisted I found a way to bring you to Zurich, Fred. You do know how highly she thinks of you, not to mention Elsa, who never stopped asking about you before leaving for Norway: Is Fred coming this summer? Is Fred coming for game and mushrooms this year[84]? Is Fred coming for Christmas? Fred, I said to her, is married now, and she is the loveliest creature, too!" continued Aunt Martha, and, at the end of her sentence, three pairs of smiling eyes turned to Winter, and she blushed and sipped on her wine a little more. "How long is it since they last saw you, love? Wasn't it last year before you left for Russia?" Aunt Martha kept on in high spirits.

"I dare say it's been at least since the beginning of the war!" Fred corrected. "Last year *Herr* Walther was in New York on banking business and *Frau* Walther had visited her relatives in *Appenzell*! As for Elsa, we met once in Berlin, sometime in '41, I believe. There was a trade exhibition of some kind, and she was most busy, as usual."

"Well, she has fortunately taken little after her mother! You know *Frau* Walther stayed at *Appenzell* during the whole time *Herr* Walther was gone, and I'm sure she didn't return home before he was well back! Anyway, we will be seeing them at the *Lichterschwimmen* tonight. Oh my God, Huppert! Please say the *Glühwein* is ready!"

"Ready and fantastic!" Huppert announced proudly.

"Huppert makes the best *Glühwein* in all of Zurich!" Aunt Martha ardently professed.

"It did seem to me that something nice was cooking in the kitchen this morning!" Winter noticed spiritedly and everyone looked happy with her intervention. "But you didn't bring any for us to try, Huppert!"

"Of course not!" Huppert responded pompously. "You can only taste *Glühwein* on *Rathausbrücke*, crunching on *Ingwerplätzchen*!" he added, particularly emphasising each of the German words.

"Oh, I get it!" Winter exclaimed with a sudden, remarkable jubilance. "You drink something better somewhere when eating something!"

They all laughed in agreement when Winter stated she thought no other language on the planet, other than German, must have consisted of so many compound nouns and so many consonants in a single word. And they reeled off simple everyday words, which sounded, however, like a tongue twister to anyone who did not have German as a native language.

"Frohe Weihnachten!"[85] Winter exclaimed, having rehearsed the phrase a million times in her head before uttering it.

"Frohe Weihnachten!" they all wished clinking their glasses.

The German-speaking majority considered it their duty to inform Winter about the *Lichterschwimmen* tradition[86], explaining that, on Christmas Eve, they gathered at the City Hall bridge, *Rathausbrücke*, to celebrate the lighting of the 'sailing candles'. It was accustomed to accompany this ritual with drinking *Glühwein*, an especially festive red wine, boiled with cloves, cinnamon, 'and lemon peels', Huppert added as the expert in this case, and eating *Ingwerplätzchen*, spicy ginger cookies, which were the best to bring out the aromas of the wine. Then Aunt Martha wistfully recalled a youthful Christmas Eve in Kent, when she and Fred's mother had drunk tons of eggnog, feasting their eyes on a distant cousin from some Scottish province who had arrived to captivate them with his primitive masculinity.

"Auntie!" Fred cried out with a jesting rebuke.

"What did you think, Mr. Fred?" Huppert frivolously remarked. "Whenever did your auntie seem like butter wouldn't melt in her mouth?"

Their laughter was so loud that the first time the telephone rang, no one heard it. And it was not until the third or fourth ring when Aunt Martha, Huppert, and Fred looked at each other in unpleasant surprise, knowing that Aunt Martha's phone never rang between one and five in the afternoon, a well-known whim of hers which everyone in town had accepted and revered. Completely unaware and unsuspecting, Winter was cheerfully explaining her favourite game of Christmas charades, where she and Father often conspired against Mother, but she was so crafty, they could hardly beat her even as such. Only when Aunt Martha got up from the table a little nervous, saying to Huppert 'No, stay, I'll pick it up!', did she realise that something unusual was happening, but she could not understand the reason for the strange agitation in everyone's eyes and was the only one willing to accept Aunt Martha's explanation that someone must have had a bit more to drink and forgotten the time.

As she walked out of the dining room and into the hallway, they all waited in complete silence to hear what would follow the typical 'Hallo!' of the answer to the telephone.

"*Warten Sie, bitte!*"[87] Aunt Martha replied in an unpleasantly hued tone.

She reappeared at the threshold of the dining room with clear frustration. She bit her lips, looked at Fred and then at Winter: "It's from Paris!" she said and clasped her hands tightly together. "For you!"

The certainty of an impending disaster struck Winter, impulsively thinking it was definitely this moment she had unknowingly been preparing herself for since the morning. She watched Fred leave his napkin next to the tableware, and he looked as though he had suddenly changed personality–his totally controlled moves, his overly-straight body posture, the severe face. His voice on the telephone sealed this unwelcome metamorphosis: "*Sturmbannführer* von Stielen!"

Winter jumped up from her seat and came to stand next to Aunt Martha at the dining-room door, so that she could see Fred talking on the telephone. But he did not say much; in fact, he was mostly listening to what the voice on the other end of the line was telling him. On a couple of instances, he glanced at Winter and, observing his facial features become more and more rigid, she could tell the news was not good. Finally, Fred put the telephone down and stood breathing heavily, his head lowered, his gaze deliberately turned away.

"What is it? What did they say?"

He looked up, stared at Winter for a few moments. An unaffected, penetrating look, that, had it not been for the alcohol she had consumed, might have made her feel very uncomfortable.

"I have to leave!" he said with his eyes fixed into hers, soon pulling them away over her shoulder to meet Aunt Martha's. "I have to go back to Paris!"

"No!" Winter instantly objected. "We can't leave now. I don't want to go back!"

"But there is no need for you to come along!" Fred explained, and if Winter could see beyond her own distress, she would be able to distinguish the struggle in his mind, and in his heart.

"I'm not staying without you!" she exclaimed, feeling threatened by the suggestion, throwing at him almost hostile looks.

"It's for the best, believe me; for both of us!" Fred insisted with exemplary self-composure, contrary to her eruptive disposition.

"I'm not staying!" she stubbornly protested, impelling him to conclude in an entirely overbearing tone as if he were commanding one of his soldiers: "Well, you are! And that's final!"

Winter glared at him with clenched teeth and then she turned around to return to the dining room, accidentally, but rather rudely, pushing Aunt Martha with her shoulder. Fred and his aunt exchanged meaningful glances, and it was not long before Aunt Martha took Huppert to the kitchen, allegedly to finish making the festive wine, and the two of them soon left the house with the excuse that they had to take the wine carboys to the City Hall.

"Why does it always have to end like this?" Winter uttered with heartache, desperate and tired, so very tired that she let her head fall onto her arm, hiding her face in the cavity it created with the surface of the table. And it was comforting, this little hollow which seemed enough to hold in it her whole existence, and she wished it swallowed her and rid her of the sufferings of her life.

Fred was standing by the door, gazing at her with his throbbing heart no less in pain than hers. But she felt far away, as though the distance between Zurich and Paris had already imposed itself on them. And so he sat there and stared, as she sat at the table and cried, but neither of them sought in each other the comfort they both so substantially needed.

When Aunt Martha and Huppert returned from the *Lichterschwimmen* event, Fred was alone sitting in front of the fireplace and drinking cognac, staring at the flames in a pensive mood.

"Winter has gone to bed?" Aunt Martha asked kindly and full of honest concern.

"She doesn't usually drink this much!" Fred apologised on Winter's behalf. But that was unnecessary. Aunt Martha understood Fred; she might not have given birth to him, but a woman could very well be a mother without going through the pains of labour. She came and sat near him, took his hand, left a firm kiss on the top of his palm.

"My dear, sweet Fred!" she whispered warmly.

"Forgive me, Auntie!" he felt the need to express his regret. "I know you've made all kinds of plans. I understand how you feel."

"Look at me, Fred!" she told him, and he spontaneously obeyed. "Why are you leaving?" she asked with the same candour that also characterised him.

"Berlin has ordered general mobilisation!" he replied hesitantly, averting his gaze, and Aunt Martha became alarmed and asked to know if he was going back to the battlefront. He shook his head negatively. "Frontline battles are hard, but concrete and honest!" he stated with almost eerie sobriety. "I have so often wished I was there again, at the front: a firearm in my hands and the enemy right before me. When you face your enemy like that, everything is simple, and you don't have time for second thoughts, there is no room in your heart for fear or doubt. You take aim and shoot! And you'll either kill or be killed!"

"God forbid!" Aunt Martha exclaimed, crossing herself and murmuring a quick prayer.

"It is not avoiding death that one should pray for, Auntie, but being able to live a decent, peaceful life!" Fred said immersed in thought, and Aunt Martha leaned towards him, grabbed his hand, and once more asked him as if looking for confirmation to an answer she already knew.

"Why are you leaving, Fred? The truth; why are you leaving?" Aunt's gaze completely saw through him and the resolve in her tone was inescapable. He turned his eyes towards the fire, sighed out his deep trouble. "Is it him?" she persisted, forcing him to face her again. His expression turned even darker, and he reached for his glass with a sense of urgency.

"He's been seen in Bern!" he affirmed with a voice full of distress and spite. "It is known these creeps gather there from all corners of Europe, making fools out of us, knowing we can do nothing about it. They cannot be touched. HE cannot be touched!" He had a big sip of his drink and immediately a second and finally he emptied the whole glass. Aunt Martha decisively removed the glass from his hand, she stood up, took the bottle of cognac away, and hid it in the cupboard.

"And is the source reliable?" she asked with absolute self-possession.

Fred nodded: "Blut would not lie to me about it!"

Aunt Martha came to the fireplace, set a cast-iron tripod in the flames, and placed an enamel kettle on it. Quietly following a familiar ritual, she brought the tea bag, pinched on a few tea leaves, and put them in the infuser, waiting for the water to boil to leave the infuser in the teapot.

"Blut hates you and he would say anything just to ruin your holiday!" she observed, calmly pouring the tea into elegantly embellished porcelain cups.

"I believe him!" Fred replied with a tone of significance.

"But you can't possibly believe he's here for her!" Aunt Martha attested as if to the most obvious truth, but Fred seemed too convinced of the opposite to take her word for it: "Do you know what Blut told me on the phone? 'Why don't you give some space to your wife? Aren't you curious to know what René Martin's next destination would be, were *Frau* von Stielen free to go about as she pleased?' Do you know what that means?"

"It means he's nasty and you're playing right into his hands!" Aunt Martha reacted, and they looked at each other long, but without animosity, no hidden thoughts, or ulterior motives. She came to him, squeezing both his hands tight between her palms. "My dear child, listen to me!" she urged him and tenderly caressed his face. "If you have to be in Paris for military reasons that have absolutely nothing to do with her, by all means, it's your duty and you should go. But if you're leaving because of what Blut told you and what he implied and whatever on earth he meant, then you should stay right here and not move an inch. Do you hear me? You promised to be with her for better and for worse, and now you are about to set a trap for her, but you must know, it is not wild and cunning prey that gets caught in traps, only the small and unsuspecting. I know you love her, but there is no love without trust, and you promised to trust and believe in her. Fred, if you let yourself just a few steps down into the abyss of doubt, there is no end to how deep it can pull you. Is this what you want for yourself? Is this what you want for her?"

"I want to know, Aunt Martha!" he objected painfully.

"And why is that? To appease your heart or your ego?" Aunt Martha concluded dramatically with a heartache that seemed very personal, much more personal than the understandable concern for another's welfare, regardless of how dear.

Fred stared at her mournfully and, full of tension, he got up and strode out of the room, leaving Aunt Martha alone, silent and glum.

She was right, his aunt, he thought as he was lying in bed next to Winter, sunk in her sad sleep. She had told him she loved him and he believed her and knew he had promised not to doubt her, but even if he doubted her, it did not really matter, because his love for her was more powerful than any doubt. So, why seek to discover a possibly unbearable truth? And equally so, why the hell not?

Oh, but simply because the truth was often hard to live with; and the truth, once revealed, could not be hidden away, set aside, or ignored. It was an enormous spotlight, impossible to turn off. Light gave the objective world its discernible quality and, set in the ranks of the visible, the world became somehow more manageable. But, sometimes, strong light also made objects look harsh and, sometimes, it dissolved their discreet lines. In the end, abundant light differed little from darkness–in neither could the true essence of things be distinguished. Because all essential things in life were not completely in light, and they were not completely in darkness; they were, probably, somewhere in between, in the shadows, which people dreaded and struggled to clear away. It was the way things were, and they could not but accept it.

He smiled bitterly. People were hardly keen on accepting things the way they were. They always needed to leave their mark, but that was not out of greed, as one would frivolously criticise: it was out of pure fear. Out of the fear that, perhaps, their own existence on this earth had no meaning, and so, they devised ways to prove their life meaningful. And the greater the fear, the more notable the evidence had to be, and some aimed for great achievements and some for great disasters, while others would be satisfied to overcome every difficulty cast in the way and they would throw themselves into the most demanding or risky situations, because every time they survived, they became stronger and felt they could cope with the mysterious enigma of living.

He gazed at Winter's sleeping fragility, wondering about the many ways in which she could be deceiving him and the also so many others in which he could expose her. If he wanted to protect her, yes, he would stay or take her with him. But he was leaving alone. Heart or ego, he needed to know the truth. It was an instinct telling him that, in this drama, there was a certain role for him to play, and this role he would play to the end.

28

The Grand Inquisitor

Winter woke up quietly to see the gray light of dawn coming in through the window. She turned her head and saw Fred lying in bed a short distance from her. Face up, eyes closed, arm under his pillow. His calm breath was barely audible. She felt a knot in her throat. If she had what it took, she would go to him that very moment, wake him up with whispers, caresses, and kisses, using every lure in her femininity to persuade him to stay; and if she were bold and determined enough, she might even succeed. They called them 'whores', the women who used their body to get their heart's desire, but she had been one, deservingly gaining the reputation, though never having possessed the grace. She would always wait for others to offer her what little they wished, while, if she ever really dared reach out for something she wanted, guilt and fear would steal away from her its very pleasure. And now that Fred was leaving, she was once again hesitant to claim him, although she knew it in her heart that, if she tried, if she did something, anything at all, it might change the course of fate, as it had been proven so many times in the past that, if she had tried, if she had done something, anything at all, some things could have been different and some people could have been spared the suffering, while others their lives.

"You're not sleeping," Fred's voice resounded, catching her by surprise. She looked at him: his eyes closed, his lips unmoved, his breath quiet–for a moment she even doubted he had as much as spoken.

"Neither are you," she uttered faintly. He opened his eyes, nailing his gaze to the ceiling. "You are still determined to leave?" she timidly asked.

"I'm afraid so!" he replied calmly.

"Please, let me go with you!" she implored him. He turned to look at her, a long and steady look, but then he returned to his previous position.

"I can't!"

Winter shook her head and frowned painfully. "I don't understand your persistence to leave me behind!" she cried, and Fred was silent for a moment.

"Certain things need to be done in certain ways, even if we don't always understand why!"

Winter's sigh sounded heavy, and she sat up with her elbows on her knees, her head squeezed between her agitated hands. "You speak in riddles! But you, Fred, don't speak in riddles!"

Suddenly, a sweet feeling replaced Fred's gloom, and he smiled. Because she knew this little truth about him and it was one of those little things to know when actually caring about another. He came, put his arms around her: "It'll be alright!" he promised and Winter was eager to believe him, because she needed to believe him and because she had, over time, gained the certainty that Fred always kept his promises.

They stayed in bed until late and then had a long breakfast, exchanging cheerful conversations with Huppert and Aunt Martha. Shortly before noon, Fred left and Winter was resolved not be depressed, and even enjoy herself in his absence–he would like that, he had said.

So, until their guests for the festive meal had arrived, she kept busy helping Huppert in the kitchen, playing with Aunt Martha's cats, putting flowers in vases, setting the Christmas table. When the Pfaffingers came, a well-off middle-aged married couple with their teenage daughter and a little later the Councilor of the Evangelical Reformed Church of Zurich joined them, there was no room for dejection, anyway: they were all so noisily cheerful, and, with Aunt Martha combined, they created a very stimulating company, to say the least.

"Well, to be honest, I've never quite understood what the difference between Protestant and Catholic is!" Winter admitted with striking vivacity. "In England, we belonged to the Anglican Church, and I had heard my father say that our church was the most Protestant of all Catholic and the most Catholic of all Protestant churches. My mother, on the other hand, used to say it doesn't matter which Church we belong to since we all share the same faith in God and Christ! I could never really tell which of the two was correct!"

The Councilor, who, unlike the rest of the guests, spoke no English, had to wait for Aunt Martha's translation, but he seemed pleased with the question, because, besides being a Councilor in their synodical church, he was also a teacher, and was very keen on catechism.

"Surely your mother's viewpoint was the most accurate!" he said with an approving smile and bowed his head in respect, which made Winter feel very proud. "The truth is that when the Anglican Church was first founded, it was not considered seceding from Catholicism, but only from the authority of the Pope. The matter in question was that each State Church should have its own autonomous head, which, in the case of England, was, of course, the King. Over time, however, and especially since the Elizabethan era, the Church of England leaned more towards Protestantism. Yet, quite a few of the Catholic practices remain, even today!"

"Baptism and Eucharist, for example, they are two rites every Christian Church practices, are they not?" Mr. Pfaffinger commented, eager to receive the Councilor's approval.

"So, what about you, Councilor? What exactly is this Evangelical Reformed Church of yours?" Winter enquired.

"Well, as our founder, Ulrich Zwingli, might say in contemporary language, if you want to know the truth about our religion, go to the Scriptures, the earliest and most fundamental sources of our faith. All else is pure human intervention, largely aiming to manipulate and control people." the Councilor replied again with great willingness.

"That sounds like a truly revolutionary idea!" Aunt Martha remarked after translating for Winter.

"Indeed, but what does it mean in practice?" Winter insisted, her experience having made her rather suspicious of highly appealing vocabulary.

"It means that tradition, dogma, and authority figures have no place in our faith. We don't need any mediator other than Christ to communicate with God; and our faith cannot be judged by the rules and regulations of any Pope or Bishop, but by our good works, our life of service out of gratitude to God and to the glory of God!" the Councilor fervently explained, only to be interrupted by the Pfaffinger daughter's comic exclamation: 'Amen!', which immediately attracted her mother's severe glare. Nevertheless, the Councilor continued, undaunted and impassioned. "Consequently, we reject teachings such as that saints or the Virgin Mary intercede with the Lord to provide people with God's grace and protection. In fact, Catholics even believe that the Virgin Mary rules together with her Son in the Kingdom of Heaven. But Mary was only a pure woman who conceived our Lord by the grace of the Holy Spirit, only because the will of God was that His Son came to this earth as Man!" he ardently concluded, while Aunt Martha kept interpreting for Winter in a low voice.

"I have read a collection of poems by Rilke, which refers to Mary this way!" she pointed out enthusiastically. "Would you say he was also an Evangelist?"

"I do not know of this poet, I'm afraid, but being as you say, I would be very interested in reading his work!" the Councilor replied with another of his approving nods and Winter felt, once again, proud of herself, stating that she could give him details of the edition in question.

"It's a relief that such freedom can exist in faith, Councilor, isn't it? Imagine the fear humanity experienced in the Middle Ages or the horrors of the Inquisition!" Mrs. Pfaffinger noted and the Councilor turned to her and nodded in the same approving way as he did to Winter before.

Unpleasantly surprised, Winter then observed that the Councilor moved his head the same way every time he was addressed, and she concluded that there was nothing really praising in his reactions towards her, just a kind of mimic spasm he probably suffered from even since childhood. And suddenly, all her enthusiasm waned and her confidence subsided and she felt like the emperor with the new clothes in that fairy tale, who was, in fact, naked, and ended up becoming the laughingstock of his subjects. Yes, she might have spent considerable time in Fred's library, perched on the shelves, searching, reading, becoming impressed. She had once been able to put some arrogant O.T. Germans in their place with this newly acquired knowledge, and Fred always listened intently to her when she talked to him about the things she was learning, paying attention, showing interest; Fred, who knew how to make her feel important and how to make this feeling last...

Winter was starting to feel annoyed by the conversation and the Councilor's way of speech until he started narrating the story of the Grand Inquisitor, which was part of a Russian author's novel[88]. In this story, Christ had returned to earth to remind people of the teachings of love and free will upon which the Christian faith was founded, but he was arrested by the Inquisition and was sentenced to burn at the stake the next day. The night before the execution, the Grand Inquisitor visited Christ in his cell to testify, in the most absurdly convincing way, that He was no longer needed because the Church was now in charge of the faith and no one could lead people into salvation better than it could. Because His sermons on freedom to decide whether or not people should give in to temptation were misleading and dangerous, and they threatened to destroy people's lives and deprive them of the security one feels in knowing exactly what to think and do in any situation,–instruction and guidance only the Church had, for so many centuries, so successfully provided. And people were content in their ignorance, while that absurd free will He was so eager to inspire in them would eventually lead them to ruin and unnecessary suffering.

The end of the Councilor's narration left all listeners thoughtful, while Winter and Aunt Martha exchanged glances for no obvious reason, other, perhaps, than a covert agreement that the Grand Inquisitor might not have been entirely wrong. Because, for an act of free will, a great deal of virtue and courage was required; and it was often easier to bear a burden imposed than a burden chosen.

Fortunately, there was little time to contemplate, since almost immediately after the guests had left, Winter and Aunt Martha had to attend the Christmas reception at the Walthers', a long-anticipated event, given the fact that *Herr* Walther and his senior position in the *Credit Suisse*[89] were highly respected in their own circle. The Walther house was located in the old town of Zurich, on the top floor of a stone building with long rows of green windows and a splendid view of the city and the river. Despite his status, *Herr* Walther was not at all snobbish; on the contrary, he was known for his simple and hearty character, a common feature of both him and Aunt Martha, which was why the two of them had become extremely close friends. *Frau* Walther must have been a little jealous of Aunt Martha for this reason, a sentiment unable to die out even after so many years of acquaintance. She was not bad at heart, only somewhat insecure, constantly in need to refer to her husband's and daughter's accomplishments in a way that implied she was the secret to everybody's success. Nevertheless, she spoke proudly of her daughter, Elsa, now thirty-eight and still a beautiful woman with the muscle of a vigorous and ingenious man. Her only regret was that she had remained unmarried, having, in fact, the lowest opinion of marriage as an institution purposefully detaining women from personal, social, and financial emancipation. She was in Oslo at the time, and, before that, in Copenhagen and Rome, and *Frau* Walther would hardly be surprised if she did not make a stop at Berlin and Paris before returning home.

"But we should cable Elsa that Fred is not here, should we not, Bruno? It would be such a shame that she should pass by Paris and not seek him out, thinking he is with us!" *Frau* Walther exclaimed with rather tactless enthusiasm and Bruno Walther had to clear his throat as a sign of embarrassment, while apologetically smiling at Aunt Martha and Winter, the moment his unbridled wife continued with disclosing details of Elsa's past with Fred, which, out of discretion, no one would talk to Winter about. Apparently, Fred and Elsa were close in age, interests, as well as opinions, and the intimacy between them extended beyond friendship, raising hopes to some, and to *Frau* Walther most particularly, that Fred and Elsa would, at some point in life, reunite. The news of his marriage must have come as a great disappointment to the elderly couple and they would certainly judge strictly whoever had taken their daughter's place in Fred's heart. In this case, the least Winter could do was to prove herself worthy of Fred and the high regard the Walthers' had for him.

"Fred has so often spoken to me about you! And Elsa!" she informed them kindly and was happy to see she had pleased the couple immensely. "In fact, he has also told me that story, about your cat?"

Truthfully, it was not Fred who had told Winter the story but Aunt Martha, who knew exactly how to handle *Frau* Walther and had been provident enough to forewarn Winter of the woman's often indelicate behaviour: 'If you feel awkward with her, tell her the story of the cat and she'll just love you!' And indeed, *Frau* Walther beamed with joy and emotion rehashing the same old story of Fifi the cat, who had climbed up on the roof tiles one morning but could not climb down again, being very much of a house pet, very lazy and dependent, with absolutely no flair for adventure. And Fifi meowed on the roof and watched the two women from below call and gesture at him to jump onto the window shutter so that they could catch him, and Fifi did nothing but sit there, look at them, and meow in distress. Had it not been for Fred, who was incidentally dropping by, to climb on the roof himself and bring Fifi back, the cat would probably still be there meowing. *Frau* Walther would never forget how terrified she and Elsa were to see Fred risk his life like that for the sake of a 'wretched old cat', but then she was so grateful for Fifi having been saved, that for a long time afterwards she did not call Fred by his name but called him their 'saviour' instead.

"Ah, Fred was ever so gallant, a true knight, was he not, Bruno?" she urged her husband to agree and she brought her handkerchief to dry her welled-up eyes.

"A true knight he was and still is!" *Herr* Walther consented, eager to add: "And now he has found his princess!" And he smiled generously and raised his glass for everyone to drink to Winter's health and to the newlyweds' happiness.

Then the formal arrival of a representative of the Social Democratic Party attracted the attention of most guests, the majority of whom were socialists and in opposition to the governing right-wing coalition. The recent election had designated the Social Democrats as the big winners, with a percentage of almost twenty-nine percent significantly elevating the party both in public opinion and public affairs.

After that, many discussions at the reception had a strong political tone. With bits and pieces of the conversations, Winter was able to understand that the common sentiment of the Swiss, even in the German-speaking part, was rather anti-Nazi, an attitude which had changed very little even after the bombing of Basel and Zurich by American fighters, officially recorded as accidents, of course. And so, to her mind, it probably explained why Fred had only put civilian clothes in their suitcase, and, thinking back, she doubted she had seen even a single German military uniform, although many Germans loitered around in Zurich. But in Zurich, she realised, so did various kinds of people, even Jews, who had been forced to abandon every part of Europe where the Nazis had trampled. Switzerland, she heard, had sheltered everyone, from ordinary citizens, who could not suffer Nazi terrorism in their own country, to intellectuals and artists, some of whom were persecuted by the Nazi regime, and others who would rather be in self-exile than be Nazified. And, despite having imposed some censorship measures, since, officially at least, the Swiss government was neutral, it was no coincidence that the Swiss radio was the only German-speaking broadcast service to criticise national-socialist practices and even air British correspondents. On top of that, theatres in Zurich had a reputation for staging anti-Hitler satire, which had never fallen out of popularity since as early as the 1930s. At some point, a more ardent anti-Nazi advocate even claimed that a very unpleasant surprise was to be expected by the *Wehrmacht* generals if they so much as attempted to make good on their threats and step foot on Swiss soil. And many at the reception enthusiastically applauded this statement.

Such publicly outspoken comments gave Winter a very uncomfortable feeling after a while. She would not call herself a Nazi-sympathiser, but the ardent anti-national-socialist sentiment of the gathering made her question her initial hope for this serene and beautiful place to be the home of Fred and her future. And that old sense of some inescapable dreadful evil haunting their life together overwhelmed and greatly discouraged her.

Shortly after midnight, Aunt Martha had retired to a table of bridge, and Winter, who did not care much for card games, had remained close as a spectator for some time, but soon preferred to sit in her own company by a window, where the snowy view was so attractively magnificent. She thought of Fred travelling alone and nostalgically recalled their journey there, which was full of anticipation, even some enthusiasm, despite her genuine reluctance to leave Paris in the first place. Life was a mysterious path, sadness alternating with happiness at every corner, just as darkness alternated with light at the turn of the day. Only sometimes the night lasted longer, so much longer it was an open invitation to all kinds of demons...

As soon as Aunt Martha found her a ride, with an acquaintance not minding a slight detour to *Schweighof*, Winter jumped at the opportunity to return home, to the solitude she had learnt to cherish. There was a feeling of unrest in her heart. She missed Fred, and she already felt as if they had been separated for ages. She treated herself to a glass of cognac and sat in front of the fireplace, which Huppert had made certain to fill with enough wood to keep the fire going. She remembered their fireplace in Paris and recalled the nights she had spent in front of it with Fred, many of which ended up in bed with him, eagerly making love. He would be at home with Marie from the next night on, and she would care for him like the 'good friend' he considered her to be. It was more than dislike that Winter felt for Marie. She did not think of her as a worthy rival. She envied her, nevertheless, because she had lived with Fred longer and there was a kind of bond between them, this 'friendship' and mutual trust, which she did not always feel as strong between herself and Fred. Besides, she had no doubt *Frau* Walther would not neglect to inform her precious daughter of Fred's whereabouts, and, during her absence, Fred might just find himself reunited with a companion, whom he had much to share with, and–why not?–much to expect from.

She got up, trying to sigh off the terrible burden in her chest, and came to stand by the window, idyllically framing the snowy garden. Behind the fence, the bushes moved almost rhythmically, like people in a primitive dance. She felt strange, fear, as though there had been a universe of invisible creatures glaring at her with their hostile eyes through the cracks of the fence, the gaps in the branches and the foliage. Deeply quivering, she took a defensive step backward and hurried to draw the curtains.

She returned to the fireplace, drank up the cognac in the glass, and poured herself another hefty dose. The fire was burning. It absorbed all her thoughts. The flames danced back and forth feeding on the thick logs, which, every now and then, would make a crackling noise, as if they wanted to scream they were still alive but were doomed to burn in the fire, like Christ in the story of the Grand Inquisitor. Another sip. The fire sedated her, paralyzing her mind, just as the alcohol did to her body. At one point, she felt the glass slip from her hand and fall onto the carpet. She did not have the strength to stretch and pick it up. Curled up in the armchair, she fell asleep.

And the flames continued to burn, flames that heated up an iron cauldron, large enough to contain a man. Inside it, a thick red liquid was boiling, stirred with the papal ferula the Grand Inquisitor was holding. On his shoulder, perched Poe's raven; every stir of the ferula and the raven would croak: 'Nevermore. Nevermore.' Then, two uniformed men arrived, whom Winter recognised as the O.T. Germans from the auction on *Les Grands Boulevards*, and they threw human bones and crushed skulls to fuel the fire. 'This bullet blew his head up. A single shot!' one Nazi said to the other, and Winter understood them perfectly, even though they spoke in German. She felt that she was holding on to something. She looked, and it was Fred's shirt, soaked in blood. There was a bullet hole in its upper right front and, on the left, at about the height of a man's nipple, huge burn marks were screaming of a deadly horror. She opened her mouth, intending to ask the Germans where Fred was, but instead of his name, another name formed on her lips: 'René'. She shook her head, and attempted to correct herself, but every time she tried to call Fred's name, it was René she called. The Grand Inquisitor struck her down with his condemning gaze and the raven on his shoulder croaked René's name. Her blood had frozen and so had her legs. She wanted to hush the damned bird, but she stood mute, pinned to the ground, terrified, and so, so ashamed...

She flinched awake with a gasp. She saw the fire in the fireplace go out and realised she was having a nightmare. Instinctively, she turned to the side and was surprised to see Aunt Martha knelt down next to her, silent, serious, and inapproachable as Fred was sometimes.

"Aunt Martha!" she whispered with a pounding heart.

"You fell asleep in the armchair and had a bad dream!" Aunt Martha expressionlessly replied. "You'd better go to bed!"

Winter nodded. Her limbs felt numb, just like in the nightmare, and, in her stomach, a sudden upset stirred up in her a frightful sense of menace.

29

A closely guarded secret

Aunt Martha was sitting speechless, remote and grim at the breakfast table, a rare, greatly alarming sight. They barely said 'good morning' to each other and Winter was certain she was due for a very unpleasant encounter.

"I don't understand how I fell asleep in the armchair last night. Not to mention the awful nightmare I had!" she remarked in order to make conversation, only to hit upon Aunt Martha's deeply discouraging stare. "I must have had more to drink than I thought! Alcohol always gets to me when I feel gloomy!" she continued with an instinctive urge to antecedently make an excuse for herself. Then, she began to tell Aunt Martha about her dream, at least to the extent she considered harmless. It had left a very disturbing feeling inside her and she was largely hoping that, if she shared it, any evil it might have been foretelling could be expelled.

Aunt Martha listened carefully. She did not speak; she did not even shake her head, as one normally does when listening to an interlocutor.

"Has Fred ever spoken to you about how he got these scars?" she asked, and Winter had to admit that Fred rarely spoke to her of his war experiences. He used to say that, one day, thousands of stories would be told about this war, each of them from a different perspective, and none of them absolutely true or absolutely false; because, for anyone having been in this war, no story would be able to give a satisfactory account, while, for anyone not having lived through it, no imagination could be sick and twisted enough to portray it. Aunt Martha smiled for the first time that morning, a tender motherly smile. "Yes, that sounds exactly like Fred!" she affirmed.

And she told Winter about that bombing in the spring of 1937 when Fred had been dispatched with an armoured unit in assistance of the Spanish Nationalists. They were battering against a Communist platoon when the bombing started. Fred had just shot down the Reds' artilleryman before a bomb exploded near them. In the chaos, he remembered hearing a chilling cry and a figure from the enemy camp jumped out of cover, rushing towards them, screaming and shooting like a mad dog. He hit Fred under the right shoulder moments before the total disaster. After that, there was deadly silence. The air smelt of destruction, everything was buried under dust and debris, an unworldly light was blazing down, devouring volumes, annihilating shapes. When Fred came around with a burning sensation all over his upper body, he saw someone standing over him: his face obscured by smoke and blood, the clothes disclosing he was not one of his unit. He asked for help anyway, but all he got was a pointed gun barrel, ready to give him the death blow. Fortunately, a squad of Nationalists charged onto the scene with heavy gunfire, chasing off the battle-hardened stranger. Fred was taken to a field hospital and, from there, to Munich. He had also spent some time with her in Zurich after his recuperation. He was the only one of his comrades who had survived that battle.

Hearing the story, Winter breathed heavily, her eyes watery, her face crumpled by a feeling that was more than pain. She did not know why this story sounded familiar to her, perhaps because in all war stories there was an abundance of the same horror. Once again, she marvelled at the grand conspiracy of the universe which kept Fred alive, so that she would have the chance to meet him. Could she really have been that blessed, or was there more to this story than she could realise, a warning signal that she did not have enough wisdom to discern?

"I can only thank God that Fred lived then!" she said emotionally and felt the need to reach out to Aunt Martha's hand and brace it. Aunt's hand remained completely unmoved in Winter's grip.

"Do you love Fred, Winter?" she asked with a straightforwardness that caught Winter off guard.

She looked at the woman who was next to mother for Fred and the first word that came to her lips was a simple, one-word affirmation. But she felt self-conscious about it, feeble before such an emphatic statement.

"Why would you ask something like that?" she uttered with a certain bitterness, which was primarily aimed at her own self.

"In your sleep, you were calling out a name!" Aunt Martha informed her, and Winter felt she had to ask, although she already knew the answer.

"What name?"

"René!"

Coming from Aunt Martha's mouth, René's name resounded decisively condemning. Winter lowered her eyes, clasped her hands, and squeezed them nervously. Finally, a reaction which seemed to have a calming effect on Aunt Martha's reproving attitude.

"Come! Let's take a walk!" she proposed with a sense of urgency, and Winter could not help but follow.

The day was cold but mild. It had stopped snowing and the heavy white clouds had thinned out, allowing a pale-yellow sun to shine behind them. They walked parallel to the suburban train line, silently as long as they were still within the residential area. Soon, it became obvious this was not just a walk, that there was rather a deliberate purpose in it, a purpose Winter was certain not to welcome: "Aunt Martha, stop! Where are we going?"

The woman who turned around to look at Winter astonished her with her affliction; as if she had consciously stripped herself of all conformity to the conventionally accepted rules of conduct and was about to purge herself of some unconfessed sin.

"I want to talk to you, tell you a story!" Aunt Martha announced emphatically. "A story no one else will hear after you! Not even Fred!"

Winter reassured her with a nod and felt certain relief, having expected a full-frontal attack. She followed Aunt Martha's gaze towards the snow-covered greenery and her thoughts ran to Fred, admiring how this beautiful landscape could fit as well in sorrow as in complete happiness.

"I guess Fred has told you about an affair I had with a German official in the Great War" Aunt Martha began, obliging Winter to withdraw from her memories to confirm her assumption. "Strange times they were, war tends to bring out the most peculiar character in people. When the world around you burns, you try to narrow things down, keep it simple and close to your own desires. Johann's and my desire was to be with each other; nothing else would matter. Being on the Kaiser's War Council, he was in no direct contact with the front. He was based in Berlin. In the beginning, we travelled for miles only to meet for a few hours; a night or two would feel like a lifetime. We would usually meet half-way,–those ancient Thuringian towns hosting us felt like the centre of the earth. At some point, I left Augsburg to move in with him. He offered me a job at the War Ministry, where I could translate documents to and from English. He trusted me and there was no reason not to: to each other, we were not foreigners, not opponents in any war. We had no homeland; we were the homeland of one another. It was so sweet... After Rudolph was killed, I had to return to Augsburg for a few months; my sister really suffered from his death, I think her illness was very much due to it. I don't know if you have any idea exactly where Augsburg is in Germany, but it's quite to the south, not that far from the Swiss border, at least not for someone who had travelled so much back and forth, like I had. At that time, an old acquaintance approached me. Until the war broke out, I had kept almost all my contacts from Kent and London, contrary to my sister, who had grown much attached to Rudolph and had little to do with the past. I wasn't as young any longer, but age does not necessarily coincide with maturity. I was impetuous, reckless and, at the end of the day, naive. I crossed the border secretly and met with him at some village on the Swiss side of Lake Constance. He was an old flame, and we had a couple of memories to share, lasting memories! Those were the good days, with not too much at stake! Little did we have to care about the risks of our impulses and desires; we used to laugh at the consequences after! He asked me to be a double agent. I refused. Yet, I helped him get fake papers to enter and walk around freely in Germany. Later, long after I had returned to Berlin, he came to find me. He wanted plans, maps, documents from the War Council. I was in dire straits, terrified that his identity might be revealed, that someone might be able to relate me to him. I could swear by the life of all I hold dear, I didn't want to give him what he was asking for. But, as long as he was moving around in Berlin, I was in danger. He promised to leave me alone if I helped him, so, one afternoon, I turned a blind eye at the office and let him take whatever he wanted. He was found dead before even having the chance to leave the city–a mutual friend was provident enough to alert me. The stolen documents were on him so I knew I would be the first and only suspect. I was terrified. I didn't so much care about my life, I cared that I would have to face Johann, look at him and confess to what I'd done. I couldn't do it. I left him a note that I had to see my sister urgently and I never went back. I didn't go to Augsburg either. I crossed the border and, after wandering for a while, I found myself here. It was more than a month before I contacted Fred's mother to tell her I was alright. She was upset because I hadn't been in touch for so long, but she knew nothing about what had happened; there hadn't been as much as a rumour of the incident and no one had bothered her looking for me. I never found out what had become of Johann. He did not seek me out, even after the war, and I didn't look for him either. Our story ended just like that: ingloriously!"

Aunt Martha put a dramatic stop to her story. She was able to keep her composure, but alas the heart which would not bleed with a secret such as that hidden inside. She raised her head, took a deep breath, and regained full strength, focusing on the issue at hand. She made two big steps towards Winter, gazed at her intently, sincerity and determination shining in her eyes.

"The reason I confided in you is because I wanted you to know you are not the first, and you will certainly not be the last, to find yourself in this position. It's so easy to get carried away, to become part of things you don't really care about. Our hearts and minds play awful games with us, and what seems completely insignificant today may become of gigantic proportions tomorrow!" She reached out for Winter's hands, held them tightly with all her motherly affection. "If this man does not give you something you want, if what he represents doesn't speak to your soul, you have to find what it takes to get him out of your life for good. Out of your life, before it's too late, Winter, for you and for Fred!"

Winter remained silent. She wanted to cry; she wanted to cry on Aunt Martha's shoulder, tell her everything and ask her how, how she could pull off this enormous feat of getting René out of her life. Many questions she had had from time to time about Fred's aunt had been answered. But now, other more compelling questions had been raised, concerning none other than herself–the hardest ones to answer. Yes, she loved Fred. And no, she did not want René. She was afraid of him, afraid he was too strong to fight back against. And she was afraid it was not even up to her to rid herself of him. She glanced at the woman, who was still lingering between her familiar, congenial self and that old one, who had ruined her best opportunity to be happy. She felt for her and she was sorry she could not do differently.

"I am sorry, Aunt Martha! I'm really sorry for the pain you had to go through!" she said, but there was nothing warm or comforting in her voice. "I sympathise and thank you for your trust. But you are wrong to parallel this story with Fred and me."

Aunt Martha gave her a sad look and smiled just as sad. "The name you were whispering in your sleep is not unknown to me! Fred told me everything about you before he decided to marry you!"

Although there was no tone of rebuke in Aunt Martha's words, Winter was unpleasantly surprised. If Fred had talked to his aunt about her and René, then he must have told her about 'The Golden Doe' and everything involved. She felt embarrassed at the thought that Aunt Martha knew, and, most of all, she was upset that Fred had exposed her secrets, even if it was to the woman he considered no less than a mother and it was only natural that, if anything troubled him, it would be her he would entrust it to.

"Then you must also know exactly how and when this story with René Martin ended!" she responded coldly. She turned her face away and her voice sounded harsh. "And that should be enough for you to stop accusing me of things that are completely unthinkable."

"I have neither the right nor the desire to accuse you of anything, Winter!" Aunt Martha exclaimed and tried to approach her, but Winter apprehensively moved away. "I only mean to help, give you this bit of advice I wish someone had given me back then. I want what's best for you; for the both of you!"

"How considerate!" Winter spouted and turned a poisonous look at her. "But I don't need your help or advice! I have nothing to hide and nothing to apologise for! What I understand is that you seek comfort; you need to prove your actions are not unique, so that you can better bear the burden of your conscience. Well, I'm sorry, Aunt Martha! I'm sorry, but I am not you!"

Before she had even finished her bitter lecture, Winter already regretted the words she so heartlessly spewed out at the woman who had only been kind and receptive to her. She knew she ought to beg for her forgiveness immediately, but felt trapped in her disgraceful impropriety, captive to her lies and secrets. When Aunt Martha walked away shattered, leaving her there, all alone, she sensed this might just be the proper state of being for her, no matter how she fooled herself there could be any other way. She walked on further along the snow-covered path,–the chill in her legs, the frost in her heart. Upfront there was a clearing, some benches here and there, and she would not believe there was someone actually sitting at one of them. A feeling of relief warmed her up a little; at least, she was not the only soul in the cold out there, without a place of comfort to thaw her inner snow. She came to sit at a discreet distance from him, indifferent that he was a stranger. In Paris, she had often seen complete strangers sit closely next to each other at benches, drawing in the heat from each other's body, strangers who became familiar after a while, because the body had this unique property to generate honest, pure intimacy. Thus seemed Winter's companion at this bench to somewhat elevate her gloom, although he sat perfectly quiet and hidden inside the fur collar of his leather trench coat and his fleece-wool winter hat.

"Merry Christmas to you!" she wished him in German. The man did not reply and Winter hesitated but considered a second attempt worth trying. "Quite cold, isn't it?"

The stranger got up and left without even so much as whispering a typical goodbye, and Winter was heartbroken. She followed the man's figure for a moment and then dragged her eyes around the punishing solitude, her heart aching for Fred and the basking sensation of his companionship.

They had been so happy with the little time they had spent together there–an evening, a morning, an afternoon. Time was of peculiar essence. An infinite number of thoughts could sweep across one's mind within a minute's time, and one moment, which was not but a tick on the clock, could last for a lifetime. Time could fly; time could stand still. But it was the good times that usually went by quickly, while pain and sorrow always lingered on for so much longer.

Her life had been full of sorrow; then Fred came along and, so effortlessly, she was happy again. But Fred was now light years away and she felt it would take her thousands of lives to reach him. He would always stay a little back for her, but for how long? It would probably be for the best if she made a turn and left before she had to watch him disappear into the horizon, and yet, she had no courage even for that. She only had the courage to behave odiously and hurt the people she cared about; to demolish what was good and worthy in her life and invent ways to become completely unworthy of it. She had the courage to justify the unjustifiable and the courage to blatantly lie and hide the truth from the one she loved.

From the one she loved... Was it really true that she loved Fred? What was love, if not trust, and she did not trust him enough to reveal her secrets to him. Unlike Aunt Martha, Winter had not really committed an offence, but was keeping silent not as reprehensible? Was hiding the truth from him not deserving of his anger, of the disappointment in his eyes, perfectly legitimate to ask with their devastating silence how she could have so gruesomely betrayed him? Facing up to this horrifying reality, well, that would be the true meaning of love and that its unquestionable proof.

The pale sun could no longer be seen behind the heavy sky, which had lain low, as if it meant to cover the earth and its transgressions. It would snow again soon. People would stay indoors. The second day of Christmas was also a festive day. It called for family gatherings and intimate company around a joyful table. She had spent the previous Christmas at Stepfather's, once again alone: Mother had been as good as absent for most of the time she was at home, as if home were no more a place for her–her soul had been kept captive in some bleak room of the cabaret. And the twins, the twins used to leave from dawn to dusk, eager to bring their father the desired penny. On Christmas Eve, after putting the boys to bed, having given them nothing but a piece of bread with some oil and sugar for a festive dinner, she had retreated to the broken window where she had her mattress and watched the snow fall on *Rue Goubet* almost all night, while Stepfather and his gang played cards until morning. And so she was here, in this place with the insufferable beauty, as lonely and desolate as ever.

Sooner or later she would have to go back to Aunt Martha's. She was ashamed to look at her, but she had nowhere else to go. And she had this dreadful premonition about Fred, her guilt bearing inconceivable terrors in her head. It was impossible for her to stay away from him throughout the entire holiday. She could rebel and leave that same day, go back to Paris, even if Fred had expressed a desire for the opposite. She would say it was her decision to return and he would have to respect that. She would show him how much she had missed him and he would not be able but to forgive her disobedience and happily take her back. But even if he did not, it would still not matter–she would rather be with him and punished, than obedient and far away. Perhaps all it took for fate to change its course was for her to make a decisive move; something; anything; an act of free will.

With her senses in full arousal, she then noticed there was a piece of paper, folded in six, left next to her on the bench. She took it assuming it must have fallen off the stranger, and she looked around in case he could be seen somewhere in the vicinity. With the simple thought that the note might contain a name or a phone number, she unfolded it,–a plain piece of notepaper with no distinctive marks. At a first glance, she saw it was a letter. When she looked properly, she found out it was written in English.

'My dearest Winter,' she read and felt puzzled until she realised it was addressed to her. But she did not know anyone in Zurich and, instinctively, her eyes were drawn to the signature at the bottom of the page. It was then that her hands paralyzed and the beneficial vivacity she had experienced only moments ago just evaporated, like a volatile liquid in a boiling state. The letter was signed *'René'*.

She raised her head again, looking for him in a cold sweat. He was nowhere around, but the very thought of him sitting next to her was greatly disturbing. The note in her hands, with his handwriting and signature, was incriminating enough, and she immediately crumpled and hid it in her fist. He was there; he was stalking her even there, so far away and after so long. What nerve and folly! And what useless bravery! René, René, René! Dwelling so deep inside her, an almost invisible presence, and a stowaway in her life...

She was relieved to see Huppert open the door to Aunt Martha's house, and she doubtlessly intended to go upstairs, avoiding any contact with her for the time being. But she was standing near the dining-room door speaking on the telephone and she decisively nodded to Winter to stay on.

"...I'm so sorry you had to go into all that trouble, sweetheart!" she said and gestured at Winter to approach. "Don't you worry about us, we're just fine!... Oh, yes, a wonderful time! Winter, as well!... Of course, she's here –she's been dying to talk to you! Here she is! Ta-ta, love!"

Winter took the receiver rather reluctantly. Fred's voice through the line gave her a feeling of proximity, which stung in her heart like a thorn. When she put down the telephone, she looked up towards Aunt Martha with a feeling of utter helplessness. Aunt Martha came and engulfed her in a warm and generous embrace.

The following days went by in passivity and silence. Winter would stay in the bedroom most of the time, although she slept very little. It would be long after dusk when she would finally come down to the sitting-room for a glass of cognac in front of the fireplace, lost in her thoughts, which were scattered and incoherent, like a sick person's delirium. The only thing that seemed unambiguous was René's letter, his words which she had almost fully memorised and from which she could not escape, even if she ran off to hide at the edge of the world.

'Do not be surprised by these lines...' he wrote. *'... It was the only safe way for you to hear from me. Do not even be surprised about my presence. I'm always close, regardless of you knowing. It's been a long time for you; for me, it's been only a few moments. You would probably think that I've forgotten you; you might even think that you had forgotten me. But you remember. You remember how our bodies merged, how I was holding you in my arms, the taste of my mouth, the smell of my skin. You remember! That's why you still look for me in your thoughts. Wherever you are, you still look for me and you can sense I'm there! At some point, you'll learn to see past the surroundings and distinguish me. When you're ready to be mine again. And this time completely!*

I was blind with jealousy that last time we met. I was blind with jealousy when I found out you married him. I sent you that distasteful wedding present to spite you. I'm sure you knew it came from me. But I'm also sure you would never lie down on those sheets, not even out of obedience to him, obedience which he demands of you to have you. The thought of him touching you drives me crazy. No woman has ever inflamed me like you do. And that means a lot to me, a lot that I could only speak to you of holding you in my arms, because only in this way would you understand.

I want you to know I've forgiven you for denying me. I've even forgiven you for marrying that German. It's probably for the best. You're more strong-headed than you look, words would have no effect on you. Reality will show you how delusional you've been about him. Reality will manifest you can only be truly happy with me. With me, where you have nothing to hide and nothing to fear!' ...

On New Year's Eve Winter had to, yet again, follow Aunt Martha this time to the New Year's reception held at Mrs. Rupelt's, who was a member of the Government Council in the canton of Zurich and an invitation from her could simply not be declined. Winter cared little about high society protocols, but she was resolved to travel back to Paris the day after New Year's, thus, she could make no more excuses about being indisposed. She was, therefore, obliged to find herself, once more, in a hall full of people, carefree, merry people, against whom Winter felt a growing resentment. With no festive mood whatsoever, she spent most of the evening sitting alone near the window of a small balcony, with the intent of getting out of sight the minute a certain reckless figure might venture to make its appearance. Only the thought of him being somewhere around watching her made her a bundle of nerves and she ceaselessly scanned the faces in the hall, putting her patience to the test every time she confirmed that none of them belonged to him.

In a little while, the day would end. In a few minutes, the year would pass. Nineteen forty-three would farewell this world, heavy in events and emotions. Winter was uncertain if, for her, this year could go down as good or bad. She had experienced such pain, and, at the same time, she had been blessed with Fred's love. One thing was certain; it was a year of enormous change. She would have been happy just having survived another year, but that was before. Now, happiness had taken up a new face, bearing with it all sorts of new expectations, which, in turn, raised new fears and fostered new weaknesses in her defenses.

"*Schnapps*?" a voice uttered over her head.

She looked up with alarm, the blood pumping in her head until she realised that the speaker was unknown to her.

"Thank you, but no!" she responded, almost out of breath, and attempted a formal smile.

The man standing in front of her sent away the waiter he had brought with him and sat next to her, without having been invited. Winter frowned.

"Oh, but you don't remember me!" the man concluded by her reaction and portrayed his surprise with a corresponding facial expression. His English was just bearable, but it was not linguistic inadequacy that made his speaking feel so unpleasant. Winter replied to his remark with a negative shake of her head. "I am *Madame* Ditron's nephew! We were introduced at the Walthers' Christmas gathering!"

"Oh! Of course! Please forgive me; I'm always so bad with new faces!" Winter apologised as congenially as she could.

"I hope this is not the reason you are sitting here all alone!" the young man speculated in a tone she did not like.

"No!" she contested. "I've been rather unwell these past few days, and I thought it better to keep my strength for the journey home!"

"Indeed, I heard about your illness! But you are feeling better now?" Mr. Ditron asked with ostentatious interest, and Winter typically replied: "Yes, thank you!"

"You missed out on so many opportunities of fun with your illness!" he remarked. "I do hope you stay a little longer to make up for the lost time!"

"I'm afraid not!" Winter answered without hiding her impatience. "I'm actually leaving the day after tomorrow!"

"Oh, what a disappointment!" the man cried out dispirited. "I would really have liked to know you a little better!"

Winter smiled at him affectedly: "You might come to Paris, meet my husband as well!"

Mr. Ditron smirked in complete satisfaction; he would be one of those who liked to pursue goals of some difficulty, make the prize a little worthier: "Your husband abandoned you early!" he commented, and brushed an insolent gaze at her.

"My husband is a senior officer!" Winter argued, raising her face to look down on him. "It was his duty to return to Paris!"

"Poor excuses..." the young man contradicted and hurried to change the subject, before she had another chance to oppose him. "You know, if you stayed a little longer, I would be willing to keep you company. I'm very interested in... how do you say it in English... your kind?" Winter sprang up from her seat to show him her annoyance and Ditron followed almost reflexively. "Forgive me, I was talking about your profession. You were an artist before, of course, you married the respectable *Sturmbannführer*, am I right?"

"And where exactly did you get this information from, may I ask?" Winter answered with evidently restrained anger.

"Oh, but my aunt spends a lot of time in Paris. Henriette Ditron, perhaps, you've met her. She maintains a very close friendship with *Kriminalrat* Blut. You are acquainted with *Kriminalrat* Blut, are you not?"

Winter looked at him coldly and, with every bit of apathy in her, she turned her back on him and went out to stand in the middle of the small balcony, so as not to give him room to approach her again. He followed her to the balcony door and continued from inside the hall, showing he was not yet done with her.

"Do not abandon your interlocutor this way, *Frau* von Stielen. It is not polite!" he insulted her with his brazen tone.

"What do you want, sir?" she asked him with proud directness. "Because, obviously, you want something!"

"Do not get excited, please!" he advised her and smiled ambiguously. "I just wanted to assure you that being in a foreign place does not necessarily mean being... alone... if you know what I mean!"

Winter did not know if Ditron's words should enrage or make her suspicious. He was shameless, but his innuendos were not sexual. The reference to Blut was meant to connote something different, and Winter could only associate it with René, once again René, always René...

Then the guests at the reception began to count down the last seconds of the year.

"Ten, nine, eight, seven..."

Winter saw Aunt Martha from the back of the room, nodding at her to join her for the countdown, and she attempted to walk inside, but Mr. Ditron was standing spread-eagled at the balcony door, deliberately blocking her way.

"... Four, three, two..."

Then the lights went out. There was a second's silence and, once the lights came on again, a spree of excitement filled the hall, which Winter felt completely unable to share. The express dislike in her eyes was fighting an uneven combat with Ditron's impious impudence, when, somewhere in between the frenzied arousal, a voice, which had been trying to stand out in the noise, finally beat the merriment, and, hearing it, people would immediately hush and look at each other in fear and alarm.

"Paris! Paris has been bombed!"

Winter's anger was instantly replaced by frightful panic. Instinctively, she looked for reassurance in the most immediate gaze, but Ditron seemed to be taking pleasure in her dread. He was loathsome and detestable! Showing him exactly how she felt, she shoved him away and urgently ran to Aunt Martha.

30

The ice and fire

Valid news about the bombing did not reach them until the afternoon of New Year's Day. Apparently, bombs had been dropped on war material facilities and a factory of the Electric Company was also damaged, plunging the entire city into darkness. Telephone lines established near the theatre of the attack had been impaired, disrupting telecommunications for several hours. Until late in the morning, in Paris, they could only communicate through the local wireless network. No casualties were reported, but some resistance groups took advantage of the situation to hit individual targets, while anti-Nazi propaganda raged spreading the rumour that Paris had been burnt to the ground. Many even claimed hearing of an allied invasion, with British and American forces already heading to the French capital. It turned out none of it was true.

Aunt Martha barely managed to refrain Winter from leaving for Paris before they had had some concrete information, and, although she did not dread any news of Fred being hurt less than Winter, she had remained admirably collected and supportive of her nephew's wife. Winter, on the other hand, retreated into her incurable grief, able to do little else than silently cry, for deep inside she was convinced that should Fred come to any harm, she and only she would be to blame, her unforgivable sins receiving their rightful punishment. She left at noon the next day, her heart aching to leave Aunt Martha alone with her own doubts and fears, but she was in no position to offer the poor woman consolation. All she wanted was to go back and see Fred, squeeze tight onto him to feel he was alive. Then, whatever would be, would be.

Dusk fell a little later as the train was travelling westwards. The scenery was always soothing, but Winter could only think how easily this natural beauty could be destroyed by people's greed for power and control, which, in order to gain, they did not hesitate to pull out the eye of their neighbour, who, in turn, had every right to pull out their eye in retaliation. She looked at the officer travelling in the compartment with her: he had a black patch covering his one eye and a wooden hand had replaced his natural extremity. The insignia on his uniform designated he was a colonel, the medals on his tunic that he was a war hero. Had he the opportunity to exchange his medals with his mutilated body parts, which of the two would he have kept? Winter could hardly be certain of the obvious answer.

Early in the afternoon of the third day of the year, they arrived in *Troyes*, the terminal station in the *Champagne* capital. Another train would leave for Paris in two hours, and Winter was disappointed that she would have to delay her reunion with Fred even longer. Luckily, the one-eyed colonel had discerned her eagerness to return, and he soon came to inform her that a sergeant was leaving for Paris in his military jeep in ten minutes, gladly offering to take her along, if she wished to continue her journey by road. She considered it a good omen.

The vehicle was driving fast, leaving the miles behind quickly, and the sergeant was pleasant and talkative, making the distance seem even shorter. He talked about his military life, the place where he was born and his family in Germany, whom he had not seen for over two years. He took a weathered photograph out of his shirt pocket and showed it to her.

"My little Alberta was just an infant when I left her. Look at her now, a full-grown little girl!" he boasted and his fingers caressed the image of a sweet little girl with puffy cheeks and clever, bright eyes.

"I wish you can go back to your family soon, Oskar!" she told him and touched his shoulder with sincere compassion.

The man smiled mournfully at her gesture; he confessed that he did not remember when he was last touched with compassion by a human being, when he last touched someone with such a sentiment. Sometimes he thought his feelings for his fellow man had completely frozen; as if he had seen so much ice, it had literally numbed his ability to empathise with others.

"I couldn't possibly believe something like that for a man who speaks as kindly as you!" Winter objected with an emphatic urge to comfort him and, hopefully, compensate for past inefficacies to do so.

But the sergeant insisted; in his mind, it was ice that was going to destroy this world,–the deadly ability of ice equal and even superior to its incandescent counterpart, land and soul, regardless. He recalled he had never felt so helpless, never before bombs, mortars, or gun shells, but he had felt helpless there, in that endless Russian winter field, where frost was reaching deep, far deeper than a man's skin. It had been months since they had been stranded in that freezing hell. Their retreat having been forbidden, aeroplanes would fly to the fatherland only with the severely injured. He had suffered a liver gunshot a sniper had generously gifted him with and he had been waiting for his turn to board, happy to be able to leave, despite his heavy bleeding, which did not ensure him in the least that he was actually returning home. Shortly before boarding, a stretcher was brought carrying a soldier who had shot himself, so that he, too, could go along with the wounded. But when the doctor saw his wound was self-inflicted, he ordered him sent away, and he was thrown onto a pile of other inglorious sly dogs, some of whom were already dead. Many in his unit had attempted to desert, but there was nowhere to go in that vast chill-hardened plain. Some of those would-be deserters came back, others would rather die out there in the snowy wilderness. He had no idea what had become of the ones who eventually surrendered.

The wiper of the jeep was set in motion to clean off the sleet falling on the windscreen, and the sergeant's sudden silence surprised

Winter. She turned towards him with an enquiring look and saw that he was crying.

They were now driving down Opera Avenue, nothing but a few hundred metres separating them from their final destination. The *Hôtel du Louvre* was sparsely lit, an eerie aspect, very much like a Jack-o'-lantern aimed to chase away some primordial evil. A bad feeling clasped onto Winter's heart, Fred's bright thought suddenly turning into the flickering flame of a small candle in the vast frightful darkness of the world.

Fred was standing at the entrance of the *Hôtel du Louvre*, when the service jeep made the turn from Opera Avenue onto *Rue Saint-Honoré*. The tires squealed, the vehicle halted, the engine stopped. The sergeant came out to formally announce their arrival, and Fred thanked him with all due praise. Then, he opened his wide black umbrella and came down the steps. At the co-driver's seat of the jeep, he opened the door for her and helped her out, giving her his hand, dressed in a black leather glove.

"Welcome home!" he said with his so familiar voice.

"It's good to be back!" she responded emotionally and prepared for the long tight embrace she eagerly desired, the two of them together under the umbrella in the snow, a scene almost romantic.

"How was your trip?" he asked, letting go of her hand to slightly push her towards the black limousine, where the driver had already transferred Winter's luggage from one boot to the other and taken his place, the engine up and running.

"Fine, I guess!" she replied, her wings clipped by Fred's cold reception. She cordially farewelled the sergeant, sincerely wishing him all the best and, watching him depart, she breathed in deeply, as if she were readying herself for a very long dive.

"Heinz will take you home!" Fred stated without a shred of intimacy, and Winter stood for a while, her gaze into his, imploring and protesting at the same time.

"And you?"

"I have to be at a meeting!" he told her, and Winter merely nodded.

She entered the car silently–parcel delivered, mission accomplished; and her lips found nothing to say, not even 'goodbye'.

At the *Auteuil* villa, the housekeeper seemed like a vision from the underworld, the way the oil lamp was shining upon her face. Her greeting was typical, and stolid indifference frosted her interest in carrying the luggage up to the bedroom.

"Don't bother!" Winter rebuffed in the driest tone and immediately decided to go to bed, hoping that sleep could rid her of both thoughts and feelings.

Entering the bedroom was painful. On the nightstand, a lantern was waiting to be lit, but she felt darkness was more becoming at the moment. She took off her clothes, put on a light nightgown and a warm robe. It still felt cold and, instinctively, she looked towards the window, unable to tell if it was open. She did not care anyway, because she was feeling colder than an iceberg. She breathed hard and leaned against the wardrobe completely exhausted.

"Ne sois pas triste, petite soeur!"[90]

She flinched as if lightning had struck her. The figure was indiscernible, but the voice, she would know and distinguish it even if it so much as whispered in a clamour of voices.

"René!"

And there, from inside the shadows near the window, he slipped into the dim light like a ghost, haunting her with his unique ability to always appear at the times when she was most vulnerable. She glared at him and could not articulate a word, gripped by a sensation of mortal danger and a fatal attraction, just as a moth is drawn to a candle flame before it gets burnt.

"You are always more beautiful with your clothes off; beautiful and genuine like I want you!" He made a few steps towards her. "Aren't you glad to see me? ... Say you're glad to see me!" She did not speak and René kept closing in, capturing her in the magnetic field of his disarming presence. "Come to me! Stop deceiving yourself that you can deny me!"

"Stop there, please!" Winter uttered trembling, and she trembled even more seeing his smile.

"Don't be afraid! I am, too, the same man you wanted from the very first moment, the man you so passionately fell in love with!" he professed, unstoppably keeping up his irresistible advance.

"Stay away!" Winter exclaimed short of breath and her instinct instructed her to back off towards the door. "If you take another step, I'll... I'll..."

"You will... what?" he made fun of her, and Winter felt so hopelessly defenseless.

"You're insane! Have you no concern for yourself? Have you thought what will happen if someone's seen you, if Fred comes back and finds you here?" she cried in the lowest voice and listened closely in case anyone was outside the bedroom door.

"...Fred? ..." René noticed scornfully and laughed. "Yes, your adorable husband has properly cared for your safety. It's almost impossible to get inside. But 'almost' is just enough for me. You should know that by now!"

"I know that you enjoy torturing me; that's what I know!" she retaliated, swiftly attempting to escape his reach, but he caught up with her using his other hand and, with his sturdy build, he forced her to withdraw towards the wardrobe.

"No, *mon cœur*!" René objected with a fiery whisper. "It is you torturing me; when you push me away, when you deprive me of having you. I wonder if you've ever felt what that's like!" His gaze was beaming with sparking passion. His mouth so near, the air he was breathing onto her face was intoxicating. "In Zurich, you were so close I could reach out and touch you. Imagine that for a torment..." And with those words, he devoutly stroked her hair, her cheeks, her neck, her bosom. His hands were ice cold, his hair was soaking wet, his clothes were drenched. What was he doing there, on such a night, with all likely dangers? His hands gave way to his lips, and they brushed their rosy velvet against her skin, crushing every bit of her already unarmed resistance. What was he doing here? Why did he have to come back, on this night, at such a moment, with such a vehement touch and a breath as heady as a bold red wine! And the irrational want vociferating from every inch of her body compelled her to utterly relinquish her senses to this feeling, the feeling of his desire.

Suddenly, he came up for her mouth and she came to her senses and found the strength to overcome her inner turmoil and push him away.

"Stop! Stop it!" she cried. "Why are you doing this?"

Instead of an answer, he grunted with his primitive lust and stormed at her lips, hungry as a wolf.

"No!" she rejected him and she jerked away to escape to a safe distance. "What on earth gave you the impression that you can come here and put me through the mill like this? Leaving me stupid letters anyone can find, forcing me to live in a constant nightmare, to lie and deceive the only man who's ever been..." His sarcastic laughter cut off her fervent outburst. She saw René crossing his arms over his chest, while his teeth gleamed bright white in the murkiness which seemed to surround them.

"Well, von Stielen is more capable than I thought, after all!" he interjected with the sting of a scorpion in the tone of his remark. "He managed to make himself necessary to you. He dazzled you with luxuries, fed you some flattery, and you completely surrendered!"

"I will not listen to you and the spew you are gushing!" she stormed, but he was too unassailable to be inhibited by her desperate reaction: "Well, I'm not finished!" he spouted and Winter cringed into a corner, his spitfire nature making her flesh crawl. "You're stupid!" he hammered. "You don't see how he left you out to dry in Zurich, that you returned and he got rid of you, surely with a funny excuse, and, soon, you will see if he comes back to throw you out like rubbish. You think it's because of me? It's because he had his fun with you and, now, he no longer needs your services. You are nothing to him, I've told you before! You are nothing!"

His words felt like snake bite. She was not at all surprised that René knew of Fred's moves or her most horrible fears. She was only confused and angry, angry with herself, because a part of her, the faithless part, was eager to concur with him. She shook her head: she should not be listening to him, it was petty and unworthy and he knew it and he counted on her to make that mistake: "You don't know what you're saying!" she opposed breathlessly and did not convince him any more than she convinced herself.

"Oh, but you do?" he counterattacked, showing no intent to spare her: "Did you really believe your beloved spouse would remain idle here the whole time you were away? Did you think he was going to faithfully wait for your return? Do you even know why he came back without you?" His smirk could not have been more malicious, his eyes nastier and mean. "And you thought he loved you! How naive! As if he were ever capable of loving anyone. Let alone a woman like you!"

Winter was torn. René insulted her, but, more than anything, he was calling her confidence into question. Such pronounced allegations were too inflammatory to be a lie, even for his brazen impertinence. After all, had she herself not, countless times in Zurich, thought with jealousy of Marie or the exalted Elsa Walther? Hell, it could very well have been that young woman at Fred's office the other day, why else would she be sitting there so comfortably, if not because she knew she was going to be kindly received? And if it were none of them, there were so many other women, better than her or at least with better references. In fact, Fred did not even need to find a replacement for her to discard her; he only needed a flash of reason and a not-so-difficult decision. She saw René approach again. She felt defenseless and let him stuff his hands inside her clothes and take her robe off with a skillful caress.

"I'm sorry!" he whispered and placed a fiery kiss on her bare shoulder. "I didn't mean to hurt you; I just wanted you to see things for what they are!" He closed her in his arms and rubbed his cheek against her forehead. "If only you believed in yourself as I do, if only you saw how much alike we are. We were not born in silk, we weren't taught how to behave in high society and people don't bow before us as we pass, but we don't care about things like that. Not being afraid, that's what we care about. Being loved for who we are, not being judged for it, that's what we care about." He took her face in his hands, his gaze needfully running up and down into her eyes, onto her lips. "I know you! I know where you came from. I know all your secrets, all your fears, all your hopes. And I'm here, exposed to the deadliest danger because I know what we can be, you and I, Winter; together...!" He tried to kiss her, but Winter kept her lips away. She took a deep breath, tried to break loose from his embrace, and, surprisingly, he let her go. "But I can't wait for you forever! And I won't beg for your love!" he warned her, arousing all kinds of guilt in her.

"I didn't ask you to!" she murmured lifelessly.

"Oh, but you did, and you are!" he contradicted, her expression of dispute seeming too faint to refute his claim: "I am still here, am I not? Why don't you shout? Why don't you call the guards out there for help? I'm sure your master would reward you well for my head on a platter. He might even forgive you for what you've done so far!"

Winter culpably remained silent, and René felt encouraged to come and wrap his arms around her waist, burying his face into her hair. In Winter's mind, his words, the latest events, her doubts, absolute anarchy.

"So, what is it that you want from me?" she asked in all her confusion. "Abandon everything and go with you?"

"I once asked you and you refused!" he bitterly replied, and Winter choked on the knot of an intractable conflict in her throat.

"What are you asking, then?"

He turned her around to look at him, his gaze easily penetrating the cracked shield of her eyes. "You. I'm asking for you; all of you!"

"I don't even know what that means!" Winter uttered in anguish, quite conscious that the right answer could have the effect of an earthquake inside her.

"It means..." He found her hands, took them in his, ardently kissed them again and again. "... Fight them with me, Winter! Then we can be one!"

"Fight them...?"

This time, Winter's wonder originated from a completely different sentiment, and she had a kind of epiphany, making her feel foolish and illuminated at the same time. What sort of game was he playing? What was he asking her to do?

"*Oui, mon cœur*!" he heaved with his overwhelming passion. He pressed her hands onto his chest, made her feel the pounding of his heart, loud like a jungle drum. "When you face the truth, you will see that I'm not the cause of your misery, I'm your salvation. You've taken the wrong path, Winter! I can help you get back on the right one, make the difference that matters. ... Together, we can be the end of them. Imagine what we could achieve, what no one else can!"

"You on the outside and me on the inside!" she deduced, and René beamed with satisfaction, as if he had gained her most decisive consent.

Winter felt as though her entire inner self was a piece of glass which just broke into pieces, each keen-edged piece cutting open and bleeding her heart. The dark of the room grew darker, the cold colder, that tear spilling out of her eye eagerly jumped off her jaw bone and into a vast sinister chasm. Emotions turned to dust; some hopes and dreams she had not realised were there devastatingly went up in smoke. Indeed, she was feeling stupid; naive like René had told her. But she could see now; finally, she could see through him. René had laid all his cards on the table and, admittedly, he had made the perfect bluff.

"What you have in mind is never going to happen." she asserted, swirling in his arms and, slowly but decisively, backing away. "You think you're any different from those you accuse? You don't care about me, you care about what I can give you. You were never 'blind with jealousy'. My marriage to 'that German' was not something you had to forgive, it was something you wanted,–perhaps it was even part of your big plan. You played me like a puppet, and I was a fool enough to let you. Well, I won't be your puppet anymore! I don't believe a word you say and I'll be damned before I give you what you want!"

Hearing this, René's astounded frown changed to fury and, in an instant, he jumped at her and grabbed her by the throat. Winter gasped and gripped his wrist, trying to remove his hand which was strangling her. The contour between his thumb and index was pressing against her larynx, his fingers thrusting into her carotid arteries, and she could hardly breathe, her eyes were losing their vision, her head was dizzy.

"René!"

He darted off, wheezing as if some evil spirit had possessed him. His face faded into darkness, and Winter felt enveloped in an aura of death. René's figure emitted an unnatural, yet attractive, light. Small dark bubbles popped about his hair and, all around him, the volumes of the furniture melted and the room lost its substance and became a void, in which they both stood against the laws of nature.

"Who are you?" she whispered in horror, and the sound of her voice seemed to drag him up from an abyssal depth. He stood up straight, little by little taking on a more human form.

"I pity you, Winter!" he uttered with a hoarseness which made the room quake. "I'm sorry for what you've become. But you can hide behind your finger all you want; sooner or later, you'll see I'm right! I only wish it won't be too late!" He read the ambivalence in her body language, made the step that separated him from her. "Look at me!" he commanded, and something in his voice obliged her to look. "Tell me this is what you really want and you'll never see me again. But first, you will say I mean nothing to you; you will say it's him that you want, him and all that he stands for, because, if it is not so, then, when you are called upon to account for yourself, no one will believe you weren't one of them!" He took her by the arms, eliminated the last speck of distance between them. "I will not let you drown in this pit of dirt, do you hear me? I care too much to let you!" he grunted, the searing rub of his face in her hair infusing her with a torturous desire. Then he brought his burning palm to her cheek, compelled her to look into his blazing eyes: "Kiss me!" he demanded with a whisper weighty as an ultimatum, and his sizzling breath on her lips seemed like enough of a spur to give in.

She closed her eyes and breathed the desert wind his mouth was blowing, a wind with the incense of ruin. A sweet cup of poison she could just drink and be done with. But suddenly, she felt the taste of another kiss, balsam and nectar with the fragrance of a spring valley and the warmth of a Maytime sun. And she remembered how she quaked when he held her in his arms, when he touched her, a call for life, not death...

René's gaze was inviting her to surrender, but she knew now she had nothing to surrender to him. And she was sad to realise how cold her feelings towards him had grown, how much ice could be born out of that kind of fire.

"Please!" she finally found the strength to utter. "You must leave. He could be back any minute now. He must not find you here!"

René hesitated. His body was burning to be with her, his heart ached for her consensus. His eyes caught hers in their net and he saw Winter was on the verge of collapse. He did not insist.

"I know your heart will tell you what the right thing to do is!" he avowed with the certitude of a self-evident proposition and concluded with the same touch of threat always contained in his promises: "This is not goodbye for us, Winter!"

31

Generous, destructive

The house was completely quiet by the time Fred returned, well past midnight. He hung his cap and coat on the hallstand, put his pistol belt into the chest of drawers next to it, and stood a little undecided before the bottom step of the staircase leading to the upper floor. The lantern, considerately left for him at the door, was illuminating his way upstairs but his heart was veiled by thick darkness. In the bedroom, Winter slumbered on the bed, over the covers. The room was cold, and the curtain was moving in front of the window. As he headed towards it, he stumbled upon Winter's robe, stranded on the carpet. With a puzzled expression, he picked it up, closed the window, and returned inside to cover Winter with a blanket. There was a painful sadness on her face, almost as grievous as his own dejection. Breathing heavily, he took off his tunic, neatly left it on the chair in front of the dressing table, and loosened his shirt collar. An unpleasant feeling made him take a careful look around.

He went back downstairs, walked along the corridor at the side of the staircase, and stopped facing the door opposite the library. The key he took out of his trouser pocket opened his office door. He sat at the old desk, where he had often spent countless hours studying and searching for solutions to unsolvable problems, leaned back, and closed his eyes. The overwhelming weariness in him was draining. He had allowed himself a few more steps into the abyss of doubt, and now the light was already beginning to fade. A shadow of insignificance was falling upon the items on his desk: a map, some letters, typed orders, and handwritten notes. A pamphlet in a prominent position read 'GENERAL MOBILISATION'. And it continued in a text full of pompous words which could be interpreted in more ways than one. The common sentiment at the time was ambivalence; *Oberstleutnant* von H., having just returned from his long trip home, only confirmed it. With the Eastern campaign almost completely failed, it made no sense to insist, but no one dared express their objections to the *Führer*. A small conclave of fanatics, totally unrelated to war strategy, who had taken it upon themselves to advise him, were laying on his mind that they still had the strength to counterattack, when they should already be planning their home defense and considering how better to negotiate the termination of the war today, when they still had something to negotiate with. In the south, losing Corsica and going to war with former allied Italy left them with another open wound. But it was not just the military operations backfiring one after the other. It was not the objective difficulty of keeping a vast expanse under their thrall, with millions of dissidents looking for the first opportunity to rid of them, either. The most ominous fact was that the German people were getting tired; that German common people, who used to fervently cheer the idea of a Reich lasting for a thousand years and were now realising the unbearable cost of this false idea. The army had been infiltrated by corrupt elements, carefully placed in key positions to spy on officers and soldiers and secretly inform the Police on them. In case any opposition was voiced by even the lowest-ranking soldier, he was being persecuted, his family and practically anyone remotely related to him having to suffer the terrorism of the 'Protection Squadron', which offered anything but. Entire battalions of those deemed unwanted were sent away to get killed without benefit or purpose. 'No, my friends, this is in all respects unacceptable!' the *Oberstleutnant* had decisively declared at the closed-door meeting of the two of them with the Military Commander. And they could not but bitterly agree.

He enclosed his head in his hands, trying to exhale the burden of his frustration. Their fight had taken a turn for the worse and the consequences would not only be collective but also individual, because knowing held one responsible for their own actions. From his first steps in the army, Fred had learnt to be dedicated and dutiful; but the concept of duty presupposed the existence of faith. What cause could a soldier serve when it was stripped of ideals and what sacrifices should a believer make to an idol made of sand?

In the middle drawer of the desk, a large envelope marked 'Top Secret' screamed of this greatly disturbing contradiction. It contained a series of photographs, which he looked at, one by one, for the thousandth time. The officer of the Reich in him had an explicit duty as to what should be done with this highly incriminating evidence. But it had been long since he felt strongly bound by his soldier's oath. His feelings for Winter had dangerously extended a pre-existing crack in his loyalty, and developments were now coming to break up the last of its fragments.

Fred admitted that his dilemma had nothing to do with the proper requirements of his duty. His doubts plagued him as a man and concerned a woman, so simply and so inappropriately for an officer of the Reich, as one of his most devoted enemies would obscenely observe. And if he had not managed to diligently overturn the plans of this insidious schemer, there would have been no escape from his pursuit, neither for Winter nor for himself. He squeezed his fists and lips. All he wanted was to know the story behind this long-running sequel of diabolical coincidences or the well-crafted plot played out against him for months.

"Come on in!" he said calmly, raising an impenetrable gaze towards the door, where Winter was standing.

She did as he told her, briefly looking around the room, which she had only seen once, in the form of a tour around the house, when she came to settle in for the first time.

"Fred!" she whispered, and her voice revealed a deep need. "Fred!" Her hands clasped over her chest in an anxious expectation, her eyes on his face extended an eloquent plea. "I was waiting for you...You didn't come..."

"I couldn't!" Fred answered ambiguously, but Winter found the courage to take a few more steps closer to him.

"Why? What has changed since the last time we were together? What could possibly have happened for you to be so alien and distant?" She came to him next to the heavy furniture, kneeled at his feet and impassionedly touched his hand, which lay still on the arm of his seat. "I missed you! I missed you so much!" she uttered with words drenched in sweet nostalgia and leaned over to rest her cheekbone on the soft fabric of his sleeve. The touch of his palm on her hair gave her a deep sigh.

He got up, gently pulling her along. They were only standing at a breath's distance and yet none of them facilitated that much-desired embrace.

"Something did happen!" Fred told her, reluctant to prolong this unpleasant tension, and Winter was swamped with apprehension, like a criminal caught in the act. Terrified that she would face an unbearable horror, she saw Fred reach for the photographs on his writing-desk and purposefully leave them in her hands.

She looked silently, those photos of René at various locations, a loud and clear warning and provocation. There was something in his eyes, in the way he seemed utterly unaware, that demanded a closer look, and there he was, completely in character, with the perfect pose for the picture, like a model of motion photography. It was so becoming of him, that brazen self-assurance, the insolent boldness which often gave the impression he looked down his nose at the entire world. She was tempted, but she was also afraid, so she shook her head negatively, expressing ignorance and wonder.

"They were taken in Bern and Zurich!" Fred explained with a valid implication in his voice.

"What's your point, Fred?"

He did not answer. Instead, he nodded at her to keep looking and she obeyed and quickly felt that she was expecting this too. But it was remarkable, seeing her worst fears come to life and, yet, having not in the least been prepared to confront them; she felt completely unfortified, instead, naked and just as vulnerable as not having had the faintest idea.

"Oh, Fred! You had me followed?" she exclaimed crushed, not by the obvious evidence that Fred did not trust her, but by the feeling that he did not deserve to demean himself this way only to prove her guilty.

Fred shook his head negatively, but she did not see. She kept looking at the photographs as if the faces had been completely unknown. There was a still of her with Aunt Martha outside, the snowy greenery in the background; Winter was staring right into the camera and what her gaze was speaking of was not kind. Three shots were from the bench where she had been sitting. In one of them, she was talking to the heavily dressed stranger. In the next, there was a note in her hands, a note she was reading. She felt it was desperately tragic, how the simplest truth, had she the courage to reveal it, would seem like an outrageous lie, and her mind flew to an old fairytale, about a boy shepherd who falsely cried 'Wolf!' only to make fun of the villagers rushing to his aid, but when the wolf actually appeared, no one believed him and no one came to help.

"A man had to lose his life in order to keep them away from the wrong hands!" Fred confessed in the gravest tone. "Such things happen in war. People lose their lives for the wrong reasons. But this is not about the war, Winter. This is about you and me!"

Guilt weighed heavily on Winter's shoulders. For her sake, someone had been killed–another criminal act in her indictment. She inwardly agreed that none of this had to do with the war, convinced that even if there had not been war, she would still have committed the same crimes.

"For days now, I've been trying to convince myself that you have nothing to do with this; that you did not know; that it's been all his doing: René Martin's. If I'm wrong, you have to tell me! In God's name, Winter, tell me the truth!"

She closed her eyes bitterly and left the photos on the desk, exposed for anyone to see. She could easily tell him he was not wrong, but again, she would not be telling the truth. She looked at him. He was so tired... She felt sorry for him, but not in any contemptuous way; it was rather like a mother feels sorry for her child returning wounded from an unnecessary battle. She wished she could tell him he had no reason to question her loyalty, to reassure him that she was his, she was always his, even at the times when she was struggling with her own self and its shadows, even when René awakened in her the thoughts and feelings she so intensely resented, she was his. And she would continue being his, even if he condemned her to die, even if he chose to execute the sentence himself. *Oh, Fred!* So many days and nights harrowed by his doubts, judge and be judged, as a soldier and as a man, if he had done the right thing or if he would now have to pay the price for trusting the girl from the dump, who was proven as dirty in her heart as she had been in her body. She was ashamed to look at him. She was ashamed that he still hoped she could speak of any kind of truth. That he was magnanimous enough to ask for it when he should be condemning her and deciding on the most heinous punishment.

He wanted the truth. What truth, really? The truth which René was trying to convince her of a few hours ago? The truth she had invented to be able to tolerate herself? The truth he suspected? What she wanted the truth to be? She could indeed tell him that she had no idea. That would be true, from one point of view. Or she could tell him everything, let Fred find his own truth.

"I don't know what to say! ... Whatever I say I cannot prove..." she murmured and so far, at least, she could be honest. "I had returned from the Walther reception, resolved to make the best of my time in Zurich like I'd promise you, but I had this strange feeling and a bad dream... The next morning, Aunt Martha and I went out together; we talked long, but it didn't help. I needed to be alone. I wanted to go back to the places we had walked together, hoping I could fill the void of your absence. It didn't work!" She looked at him, fully conscious of the bizarre combination of truth and lie in her words, and it seemed to her that this hybrid was the only truth they could both accept at the lowest cost. "I saw someone sitting on the bench. How could I possibly imagine what you're implying?"

"And when you speak to him?"

"I only told him 'Merry Christmas' and that it was very cold!" she replied with no hesitation and let out a chuckle of greatly derisive self-scorn. "When he left, there was a note on the bench where he sat! I took it, opened it, thinking it might have a name or an address where it could be returned... There was nothing. It was a completely blank piece of paper. It was odd, but I had my own concerns to worry about!"

"The note; what did you do with it?"

"I don't know! Threw it away, I guess! It was a piece of paper with nothing on it!" she proclaimed and broke out laughing, a nervous laughter which made Fred look at her with the bewilderment of a man who had to confront a power completely beyond the human capability. When her laughter turned to tears, her deeply afflicted image was a stab to his heart. Because he had sworn to love her and that was an oath he had never stopped wanting to uphold. And while he had promised to protect her, he was pushing her to the brink of despair and, perhaps, not unlikely, madness.

The sorrowful expression on him abruptly stopped her crying, she felt twice as guilty and, for a moment, she prayed for some kind of deus ex machina to put this completely hopeless situation back in order, make it right, because she felt it, that her heart had truly taken the right path and her heart did tell her what the right thing to do was. Then, Fred collected the photographs in one hand, grabbed her with the other, and she had to follow him out of the office, through the corridor into the hallway, and then into the sitting room, paralyzed like a convict on death row, being dragged to the scaffold for a summary execution.

They sat in front of the fireplace, some flames still ascending from the smoky logs.

"Fred!"

Their eyes met; hers sank in the depths of uncertainty, determined and decisive were his. His gaze was promising of something she could not quite comprehend. She did not have the courage to ask but remained in a state of intense anticipation. She watched him place the photographs into her hands once more, looked at him with a glaring enquiry, mystified as to what he was asking her to do.

"And now, throw them away! Throw them onto the fire!"

He took both her hands to stretch them out towards the flames and she released the photographs into the hungry burning tongues: the edges curled up, the faces were blazed into obscurity. And as her sins fueled up the fire, she felt purged of every sentiment of wrong, of doubt and fear; it was a moment of revelation, a sudden perception of an illuminating truth, the strongest of truths and the only truth that mattered.

Oh, Fred!

She stormed into his generous, forgiving arms, a tempest of need and want, a cataclysm and renewal. Inside the fountains of the deep, she was gestated a novel, altered self. And out of the watery chaos she could, perhaps, finally, become someone she would be able to live with.

Hidden behind a wall, Marie bore witness to the secret agreement of this mutual reverence and worship and she perceived the cosmogony of this testament against any foreign dictate. Her eyes silently withdrew to their crypt, quietly submerged into their fathomless darkness; and, at the hour of the beast, a token of true conversion, they swore not to withhold a shred of this despicable and blasphemous conspiracy.

32

Like twilight, like dawn

The new day of an infant life dawned that morning for Winter, who woke up with unprecedented vigour. She got up to open the shutters wide; the coolness of the air was refreshing. She shook the water drops, which had settled on the balcony plants from the previous night's wet snow, and caressed the colourful petals of their flowers. A small geranium lying with its soil strewn on the marble slabs reminded her of René's attempt to breach her heart and mind, an almost successful attempt. She looked up at the life-giving sun, feeling its warmth infuse her with strength and optimism. She picked up the plant as carefully as though taking in her arms a wounded soldier. She would put it in a new pot with fresh soil and place it back where it belonged so that it could live and bloom again.

She went downstairs murmuring a tune full of sweetness and was pleased to see Marie's morose expression as she entered the dining room for breakfast with the song on her lips.

"Don't you ever sing, Marie?" she asked only to spite her and raised her luminous shield against the dark arrows hurled from the housekeeper's eyes.

Leaving early, with almost no sleep, Fred had said he would be free for a few hours at noon, suggesting that they had lunch or went for a walk together, and Winter awaited their meeting with the heartbeat of a first-time-in-love schoolgirl. With the same sprightliness, she strolled her way to the underground, the quiet suburb of *Auteuil* actually feeling like home, this little corner of the world where she and Fred had shared experiences and many, many memories.

Getting off at the city centre, she could sense a rare wistfulness to revisit its familiar streets, recognising the strange relationship of love and hate that bound her to it. A substantial part of who she was she owed to this City of Light, which sometimes shone like twilight and sometimes like dawn in her life.

On the steps of the *Opéra Garnier*, a military band was playing music. She stayed on to listen, briefly observing those who were listening along: German soldiers and officers of different ranks and ages; a man in a suit and Homburg hat with incredible resemblance to the leading character in a film she had seen with the ladies of the 'frio', while they were still in their bonding period; three young women in bobby socks and knitted coats were exchanging secrets, now and then giggling and casting shy glimpses at the musicians. Their reaction gave Winter reason to notice the attractive-looking mostly young men of the band and legitimately assume that love was potent enough a power to unite this divided world. Love and music, she might add–the full, well-blended sound of the musical instruments delivering an effectively associative sensation. With this euphoric emotion, she turned her gaze at the two elderly ladies, a few steps away from her, who had been listening intently; but then the ladies set off to leave, and one of them said to the fully agreed other: '*Boches!*'[91] Winter frowned and a gray cloud overshadowed her bright spirits. It would obviously take countless loves and endless music to eradicate the hostility between this people and its conquerors. And a highly discouraging thought crossed her mind that a war was no ailment which could be cured overnight, suddenly getting the depressing feeling that this observation applied to more personal matters than war itself.

She quickly turned around and galloped off her gloomy thoughts.

In the light of day, the *Hôtel du Louvre* looked much friendlier than the previous night, and the thought of Fred being there revived her mood.

"*Guten Tag*[92], I would like to see *Sturmbannführer* von Stielen, please. I am his wife!" she said in excellent German, and, since her identity card confirmed her allegation, the guard immediately made way for her to pass. She walked through with a sting of sadness, this already typical and completely unhindered procedure always bringing into her mind that sweet and gentle man, Klaus Molnich, who was another of those needless victims of war for whom she felt deeply responsible.

Fortunately, on the fourth floor, she was warmly greeted by Fred's secretary and she was relieved to see the youthful face of this boy with the trimmed hair and light blue eyes, who had probably been saved from the jaws of death, when Fred kept him in his service, before their Waffen SS unit was called back to the East.

"I wish you great joy and happiness for this year, Peter!" she told him and dearly shook his hand, feeling animated by a strong current of life.

After the wishes, Peter informed her that Fred was not in, but he would not be long, and she should have a seat, if she wished to wait for him. Winter smiled and, looking at the waiting seats, she saw someone else was there. At a first glance, there was nothing impressive about his scrawny, miserly figure, but that face, reflecting an overdeveloped ego and marked by a pair of cold and empty eyes, was impossible to forget. He was smoking a cigarette, which he held between two of his abnormally long fingers, and he was rudely dropping the ashes on the floor, staring at her with a smirk, despite not making the slightest attempt to greet her, not even out of politeness. Winter pretended not to recognise him.

"No, thank you, Peter. Please inform my husband that I will be right across the street, at the corner café!" she replied to the secretary and bid him goodbye, putting on her most cheerful and airy temper.

The café was glutted with German officers, drinking and smoking over loud debating, and Winter sat down at an indoor table near the bar and asked for a cup of coffee. The presence of *Kriminalrat* Blut at

Fred's office had irreparably injured her mood. She wondered what this dangerous man was doing there and felt quite confident that the reason was not foreign to her or the photographs from Zurich. Perhaps, it had been Blut who had had René and her watched–his would definitely be the wrong hands for the photographs to fall into, and it would make perfect sense if young Ditron's remarks were also to be taken into account. This man was a vicious fiend and she and Fred were on top of his attack list. It was a thought that made any faith with which Winter had armed herself in the morning flicker like a light bulb in a voltage drop.

"Heavens! Whatever may have come over you all of a sudden!" a voice with heavy German accent uttered over her head, and, flinching in surprise, Winter raised her eyes to face *Kriminalrat* Blut, the leather black coat over his uniform making him look like a devil in fancy wrapping paper. "Back at the office, you were emitting an almost angelic radiance and now you look like a beaten dog!" he continued, presumptuously sitting at her table, without waiting to be invited.

Despite her fluttering heart, Winter straightened her posture, and her instinct prepared her for battle. With this kind of people, fear had the same result as blood with a shark. And she did not mean to abandon herself to his teeth, not without a fight anyway.

"Good day to you, too, *Kriminalrat*!" she responded with clear reluctance, and the Gestapo major sneered.

"So, you do recognise me!" he scorned with a complete lack of courtesy. "A moment ago, you acted like you didn't even know me!"

"A moment ago, you hadn't spoken. There is something about the way you speak that makes people remember you!" she retaliated and Blut seemed to enjoy the innuendo. He smiled sideways, lit a cigarette with a match he threw on the floor, and blew out the smoke into her face in the most purposefully ill-mannered way.

"I heard you were on holiday in Switzerland. Do you have relatives there?" he asked with false interest.

"I have my husband's aunt!" she replied with courageous arrogance.

The *Kriminalrat* motioned to the waiter, who was circulating between the tables offering shots of brandy, to approach; he took a glass and swallowed the drink with a single sip.

"I've never really cared for relatives-in-law!" he remarked, sending the waiter away with a gesture, as if meaning to repel an annoying bug. "Or relatives in general, to be honest! They're constant trouble, wouldn't you agree?" he added and stared at her in the face like he was trying to force her consent.

"I suppose you have no family, *Kriminalrat*?" Winter reciprocated. "A family of your own, parents, siblings?"

"My paternal family remained very much immersed in their prejudice!" Blut claimed with evident disapproval. "As far as I'm concerned, my family is the Reich!"

Winter did not feel obliged to refrain her chuckle: "Such a big family! You must never feel lonely!" she mocked him with a stare just as brass and rude as his. The Gestapo major's features stiffened, and Winter was certain that, if he could, he would just love to slap her.

"It is not wise to make fun of me, *mein Frau*!" he warned her. "You would rather have me as a friend than an enemy!"

"Well, I'm afraid I usually make friends with people that I like!" she stated boldly, making the German suck his cheeks and throw at her a dour look.

"It's easy to talk like that when you are so securely under your husband's wing!" he bluntly darted at her. "But I know your game and I can assure you, you won't be feeling a winner at it for much longer!"

Winter cast a contemptuous gaze at him, recalling how nasty he had been with her in that Gestapo cell. 'I really want to see you beg' he had enjoyed telling her and, by God, if he could help it, her fate would have been no different from that of Pierre, Alain and Guillaume, Louis and Georgette, and the hundreds of others he must have ruthlessly tortured.

"I'm not sure what game it is you are talking about, *Kriminalrat*!" she asserted in a tone that deliberately showed the exact opposite. "But if you are such a game-lover, as you claim, perhaps you should take better care of your pawns!"

Blut sprang up from his seat, the thin line of his lips depicting his bitter anger: "Do me a favour, *Frau von Stielen...*" he bent over to tell her with a hiss creepier than that of a snake. "...Tell me this again, when you have lost the one and only pawn with which you know how to play so arrogantly!"

Inflamed by the blow at the German's ego, Winter could not adequately assess his clear threat against Fred, and she put a scornful face up against the sharp blades of his eyes.

It was then that Fred appeared, Winter's flushed cheeks and Blut's umbrage turning his expression dark and hard like granite: "What is going on here?" he uttered, grabbing Blut's arm with a resolute gesture, and he sounded absolutely categorical and forewarning as he whispered to him: "I will not see you anywhere near her again! Is that understood?"

Blut pulled away his arm coldly, and, instead of an answer, he silently speared at them both with his poisonous eyes. He walked away and out of the café. His car was parked nearby, on *Rue de Rivoli*. It was not a long drive, only a smoke away. He came through the entrance of an old high-rise hotel, and, completely ignoring the concierge, he climbed up the stairs.

"I'll tear him to pieces! He'll be laughing on the other side of his face soon enough!" he growled and threw his cap and gloves into a corner, looking up as if he demanded a response.

Hazy light was coming in from the window. The morning sunshine had been chased away by angry clouds. A woman's eyes were apathetically fixed upon the colourless view. She was dressed conservatively, in a long dark skirt and the same dark cardigan over a white shirt, a woman in her thirties, with rich brown hair neatly tied in a thick chignon.

"I do not want to hear about the *Sturmbannführer* today!" she objected with a flat voice and turned an ominous look at him.

Quickly overcoming his own discord, Blut crossed his arms over his chest and assumed his most sarcastic demeanour. "What's with the sour face? Bothered are we that the mistress of the house has returned?"

"Please, don't!" the woman dictated, and Blut disapprovingly shook his head.

"Marie! Marie!" he sneered.

She gruellingly pulled away from her position to approach. She reached for the buttons of his leather coat, undid them with curt moves; she slid her hands over his arms, threw the coat on the carpet. Blut plunged his fingers in her hair, his unaffectionate caress pulling it out of the chignon and loose around her shoulders. Her clothes fell to the floor, quickly and with the precision of a surgeon on the operating table. She turned her back, bent over, her fingertips touched her toes.

A roaring thunder made the room creak. Darkness fell as if it were already dusk. The wind screeched through the shutters and the window glass was whipped by heavy, impatient rain.

33

New life in the ruins

A different kind of rain fell on Parisian streets that morning, white sheets of paper pouring from the sky, covering roofs and balconies, streets, parks, even the river surface. And the city took on a festive look, as though a great power above had thrown confetti for a celebration only it was aware of.

Winter was just coming out of the Prefecture's medical services when the last of these strange paper flakes floated before her. She picked one of them up: 'Rome is falling. Berlin is coming next.' A bunch of boys and girls passed her by, excitedly waving these flyers–teenagers with their books in their hands, bright eyes, noisy faces. Only when a *Milice* squad appeared around the corner did they hold back for a minute, but when the soldiers were gone, they continued with greater intensity, making mocking faces at their compatriots.

She let the piece of paper fall from her hand. The war was ending. The tables had turned. And she wanted it, the end of the war, but the closer they were coming to it, the more she realised it would find them on the losers' side. René had warned her about this, but she did not regret her choice; she would never regret choosing Fred, for he was the only side she knew and the only side she cared about. Still, she was afraid for him; the winners would not take kindly to officers of the

Reich and Fred's position as Head of Intelligence hardly secured him the new rulers' favour.

Even so, Winter could see that Fred's evident worry and disappointment did not originate in fear for his future. In mid-February, the trial of the 'twenty-three terrorists' eventually began. They were called a vicious special sabotage unit, but they were nothing but children, fervent to revolt, as all young people should. A girl was among them, a student of philosophy, disciplined in the nature of knowledge, reality and existence, not in the nature of war, crime and the rhetoric of hate and mutual extermination. During the legal proceedings, Fred, who was one of the main prosecution witnesses, felt compelled to send a written complaint to *Polizeiführer* O. in order to designate the misconducts taking place in the trial and explicitly warn of the dangerous consequences an exemplary execution of the defendants would provoke, further fueling the already exalted resistance sentiment in the citizens. 'The enemies of the Reich cannot be allowed to continue living!' was the reply of the SS Highest Commander, who, among other statements, clearly expressed his displeasure at several of Fred's opinions, manifesting of affect inappropriately displacing his sense of duty. Twenty-two of the twenty-three prisoners were executed in the following days– their pictures were posted in central places all over the city–, while the philosophy student was to be beheaded at a concentration-camp in Germany a little later, perhaps for symbolic reasons.

As a result, Winter had kept to herself the fact that she had been feeling rather unwell for the past few weeks–gravest issues were at hand, and her beloved was struggling with forces far beyond his power. *Oh, Fred!* But now she would have to tell him the news and it was not without fear that she prepared herself for her announcement, because, in this dark time of terror and feeble expectations, she could not help but wonder if the arrival of a child was indeed good news or an unwelcome responsibility at times of no guarantee for tomorrow, of no guarantee even for today. And yet, sweetness and excitement vibrated inside her; the seed of a new generation was growing in her womb and tomorrow could not be without hope. Like the spring starting to make its presence felt, bravely blooming its new sprouts, however stubbornly the winter refused to leave.

But Fred was at meetings the entire morning that day and his shift on guard started early in the afternoon, making it impossible for Winter to even meet with him. Day after day, the same tight schedule for Fred made Winter more and more hesitant to talk to him, more and more doubtful of the blessing this was supposed to be. Then, there was a terrifying air-raid, a night of shrieking horror that lasted almost two and a half hours, spreading dread and panic. The atmosphere choked in smoke, the glow of fire in the night sky seemed to reach as far as *Montparnasse*. Dawn found the bombed area still burning. Most of the eighteenth *arrondissement*[93], near the *Périphérique*, had been completely demolished. Buildings collapsed, *Rue Championnet* was opened up like a disemboweled mattress, the metro station of *Porte de la Chapelle* had turned into a crater of debris, the flea market of *Saint Ouen* would operate no more. The victims were hundreds, countless were the injured.

Auteuil was far away and largely unaffected by the vibrations of the bombing, but the echo of the attack kept the quiet suburb awake, sharing the same ending feeling as the rest of the city. In this light, Winter promised herself to make the announcement as soon as Fred came home, but then the mourning was too heavy, there was so much pain and bitterness, that she felt it utterly disrespectful to talk about anything joyful at a time like this. Gloom remained the dominant emotion for a long time. And, even after that, Winter could not find any moment suitable enough for her to share with Fred the news of her pregnancy.

Several weeks after the bombing, and despite the poor morale and the serious supply shortages, the Desk of Propaganda insisted on holding a celebration on the occasion of the *Führer*'s birthday–in fact, it seemed that they were determined to organise an event even if it did not coincide with the happy anniversary. So, they found themselves in a fine hall, purposefully decorated with plenty of flags and pictures of the *Führer*'s triumphant rallies, remnants of a past gloriously departed. Of course, there was enough food and more than enough drink for everyone to wish a happy birthday to their leader and saviour, who evidently now lacked the capacity to do any more than drag them into the bottomless abyss of total destruction.

The party was also attended by Fred and Winter's neighbours, who, strangely, never lacked in liveliness and humour. It had been a long time since the 'frio' had met, and Winter was now feeling self-conscious about repeatedly refusing the ladies' invitations to meet. But the wives of Fred's former colleagues were considerate enough not to hold a grudge. They were a pair of overall light-hearted characters but had obviously experienced some loss of their own to know it always took plenty of time and lots of solitude to deal with the facts of death. Quickly, the ladies made certain to change the topic away from anything troublesome and disturbing; what they mostly favoured was the kind of talk they euphemistically called 'social commentary'.

"... I'm sure he is eventually going to marry her, perhaps he's just waiting for the war to be over. They do sleep in separate bedrooms though!" Gretschen Ludwig stated with firm conviction.

"Where I come from, separate bedrooms are really quite common among blue bloods, but no sexual relations at all? That's hard to believe!" Winter exclaimed in an attempt to contribute to the conversation and assure the ladies of her loyalty to their friendship.

"Well, the *Führer* has been known to abstain from all kinds of ... meat!" Uma Stobe remarked and Gretschen burst into loud laughter, immediately hiding her mouth with her palm and blushing.

"My dear, I say this with absolute certainty. The bed sheets never lie!" she was able to utter, after finally being able to exercise some self-restraint, and dreamily added, that there was a time when her own bed required new sheets almost every day.

Winter let the two women exchange memories from their erotic youth and raised her head in search of Fred. She spotted him at the other end of the hall, in the company of *Obestleutnant* von H., seriously discussing in a cloud of smoke. She sighed, feeling so sweet and mellow. When Fred touched her, there was no end to her desire, and they often did not separate from one another long after they had reached the climax–those moments when breaths were calming down again, kisses were becoming more tender and eyes were looking deep into each other's soul, those were the apotheosis of love, a rare treasure which she had found with Fred. Oh, if anyone deserved this happiness, he did, to know that he was going to be a father–and what a wonderful father he would make! Right then, Fred looked up and scanned the room for her. Their eyes met, and they both smiled.

"Ah, *l' amour*!" the ladies teased Winter, and she chortled, shrugging to admit that she was truly in love.

"Isn't it strange? That love at first sight might not mean anything after all, while the love that grows in you slowly might just mean the world?" Winter proclaimed with her peculiar mixture of German and English, emitting a warm and radiant light.

Gretschen and Uma stated almost in unison that the only men they had fallen in love with were their husbands and it was probably love at first sight, although, in Gretschen's case, the families had previously indulged in a rather long, completely unromantic arrangement, which fortunately, however, worked out for the best. Winter felt embarrassed at the thought that she might have prompted the ladies to think she had fallen in love with another man, and, indeed, at first sight. She thought of René. Yes, she painlessly admitted, she had probably fallen in love with him from the first moment she saw his face and felt his arms around her, questioning herself about him, as his shadow was falling thin and tall on the humid sewer walls. And yet, nothing remained of the one and only night that they slept together, as if she had only dreamt of it, in a dream that was forgotten the minute she woke up in the morning. As for their subsequent meetings, well, she preferred not to remember them...

Looking up for Fred again, she was unpleasantly surprised to see the appalling figure of *Kriminalrat* Blut standing in between them. With a burning cigarette in his one hand, he was looking at her; he was looking at her intently, he was looking only at her, waiting for the moment to catch her eye and trap her like a butterfly in a net. She turned her gaze away, hoping he would also go away with it, but his voice soon interrupted their company.

"Good evening, ladies!" he greeted with his distinct German accent and eagerly awaited the ladies' response, so that he could address none other but Winter. "*Frau von Stielen*, please allow me to express my special thanks for your presence with us here tonight! Although our *Führer* is not generally very fond of foreigners, I bet he, too, would appreciate the attendance of his birthday party by someone like you."

Gretschen and Uma were dumbfounded by the *Kriminalrat*'s inelegant remark and exchanged glances before turning to Winter to see her reaction.

"I thank you for your kind words, *Kriminalrat!*" she pretentiously replied. "It is always my pleasure to follow my husband to any of his social engagements!"

The Gestapo major bowed respectfully, smoked his cigarette to the butt, and then threw it on the floor.

"Would it be too presumptuous on my part to ask that you join me for a little chat, just the two of us?" he asked, a second time astounding the ladies, who were unaccustomed to such direct confrontations. "Your friends, I'm sure, can do without you for a while!" he added, basically blackmailing the ladies for their concession.

Winter followed him with a cry for help on her face, but the women themselves were so terrified, they could hardly perceive any distress other than their own. Immediately, she turned towards Fred, but even he had his back slightly turned now so it was completely impossible to see her. She took a deep breath and prepared to meet the challenge with full strength.

They walked outside onto a spacious veranda surrounded by pergolas with climbing bushes,–a scenery too idyllic for such an unpleasant encounter.

"I think your girlfriends' chatter has given you a headache!" *Kriminalrat* Blut observed with a scornful eye and corresponding tone.

"And what gives you that idea?" she reacted.

"Oh, but you are very silent!"

She threw him a sarcastic look and felt keen to tell him that she was silent because she disliked him. "I'm sorry if I bore you!" she replied instead, hoping to displease him enough to let her go.

"Bore me? On the contrary!" he declared with a very alarming chuckle.

Winter glared at him and wondered why she did not just turn around and leave. "Why don't you tell me a bit about you, *Kriminalrat*?" she suggested, obviously not out of interest.

"I'm afraid talking about myself is not my favourite topic of conversation!" he replied, to her astonishment. "Don't tell me you are surprised?"

Winter sighed, suddenly feeling extremely tired, and she found a ledge to lean against. "I must confess that I am!" she reluctantly admitted.

"Please, you must not misjudge me!" Blut continued, causing her new surprise and even greater fatigue.

"Well, if I do, you've had a great part in it yourself!" she retaliated, and he sneered.

"Do not judge Erhard Blut only as a Gestapo officer, *mein Frau*! The appearance can be very deceiving!" he stated conceitedly and ran his palm over his undercut hair.

For the first time, Winter secretly agreed with him. She had often thought the same thing of Fred, and yet, she had long since stopped seeing any other aspect of him than that of his gray-blue eyes smiling at her and his tender lips calling her name.

"I see you agree!" Blut remarked, violently dissolving the sweetness of her thoughts.

"What do you want from me, *Kriminalrat*?" she felt compelled to ask.

"Oh, *mein Frau*!" he uttered with unprecedented affection, completely bemusing Winter. "I just wanted you to know that under the right circumstances, I, like most people, enjoy life, beauty, ... love!" Winter did not like his insinuation and was not afraid to show him, but, regardless, he leaned towards her, resolved to carry on his completely inappropriate dalliance: "Under this uniform you are looking at, *mein Frau*, I'm just as human as your husband and, for your information, ... just as man!"

Winter sprang up with a strong desire to smack him but restrained herself for a reason she could not define: "I'm feeling rather cold!" she said with pure pretense. "With your permission, I will go back inside!" And she made a couple of steps away towards the French door, a little less than ten metres away, which seemed like the only refuge from him at the moment. Unexpectedly, Blut extended his hand to her arm and held her back.

"Stay, please!" he asserted, and squeezed her arm so hard that it hurt. His eyes narrowed with an evil glare and, bringing his face close to hers, Winter was given the feeling that, immediately after, a long forked tongue was about to poke out from between his pencil-thin lips. "Allow me to tell you how much I admire you!" he whispered to her. "You have something rarely possessed by a woman, and it's exactly what makes you so attractive, so damn enchanting, a quality that surpasses even this natural beauty of yours!"

"I will not listen! Let go of me or I'll scream!" Winter warned him and attempted to free herself from his grip, despite his blood-chilling laugh.

"Go on, scream, if you think you can handle the disgrace!" he thundered at her. "Besides, don't be offended! I'm rather flattering you, don't you think?"

Winter was furious, a feeling which gave her the strength to shake his hand off her arm.

"You are even more sordid than I thought!" she spurted out and decisively turned her back to him.

"And if I told you I desire you?" he impudently professed.

"How dare you!" she exclaimed, standing upright proudly and blazing into him with her eyes.

The Gestapo major jumped on her like an enraged beast, pushing her into a shady and secluded corner. Winter wanted to shout, but she was suddenly feeling too weak, unable to handle the disgrace, powerless to explain any of this even to Fred or suffer the humiliation he would be subjected to because of her.

"How dare I? What a silly question!" Blut growled and grabbed her by the cheeks. "And how unadvised that you, of all people, should make it!" In all her terror, Winter tried to pull his hand away, but his fingers were like clasped claws on her face. "Did Pierre Morné's customers ask for it any better?" he continued with vindictive malice. "I wonder: were you even paid for it? Or did they just fuck you?" And, at the end of his sentence, he kissed her with a wide open mouth, violently sucking her lips and disgustingly licking them with his rough, sticky tongue.

A loud protest breaking out from within her, she put all her courage in her teeth and bit him.

"Bitch!" he cried out and, raising his hand, he slapped her so harshly her head almost spun. His gaze was full of burning hatred. He took out a handkerchief, wiped the blood off his lips. "You will pay for this!" he viciously threatened and, straightening his hair and clothes, he walked across the veranda and entered the reception hall, calm as if nothing had happened.

Panting for breath, Winter remained where he had left her. Impulsively, she brought her fingers to her lips, touched them with her tongue, and saw her saliva mixed with his blood. Nausea upset her stomach and leaning against the veranda railing, she spat repeatedly on the greenery and, in the end, she vomited. She was feeling raped, a rape that was worse than that of her drunken customers at 'The Golden Doe'. And she wanted to go away and disappear, but the reception hall was the only way out. She staggered inside; the sight of the people there disgusted her: those orgiastic figures, eating and laughing with revoltingly open mouths, foaming and spewing blood and bile; skeletal bodies with fancy clothes, their wrinkled hands with crooked fingers and vulture claws, pointing at her, screaming: 'Whore!' She could not look at them, she could not face them. She could not...

When she regained consciousness, she was in a quiet room with soothing dim light, lying on a sofa; Fred was kneeling next to her, gently rubbing her wrists.

"F..."

"Sssh. It's okay now! You're alright!" he whispered and caressed her forehead and her hair. "You should have told me you weren't feeling well. We would have left immediately!"

It felt so painful to hear his calm voice, as though he was the only good thing left out there, a good thing that was, alas, incapable of fighting all the world's evil. She started to cry, and he took her in his arms,–an experienced, tender and strong embrace.

"What is it, my love...? What scared you...?"

Her heart pounded at how well he knew her and she squeezed onto him tightly, wishing the world would end right there and then, with her in his arms, the perfect death. He pulled her back softly, carefully examined her face.

"Your friends told me that Blut came along and took you away almost by force! Does he have anything to do with this?"

Oh, Fred! If only she could tell him everything without risking him doing anything foolish to defend her honour. Her honour! If there were a dictionary with people's faces for explanation, hers would be forever banned from a place underneath this listing. And it was not even her past at 'The Golden Doe' which would be the cause of that,–there were so many other faults for which she was hardly deserving of redemption.

"It's not Blut!" she assured him to subdue his suspicion. "I'm sorry, I didn't want to tell you like this... I wanted..." She was appalled by the idea of giving him the news as an alibi for something so vile, but she preferred to tell him a truth instead of another lie: "I'm pregnant!" she announced, shallow and unemotional, the blissful words she had been preparing for this moment having deliberately been hidden somewhere out of reach.

Fred was surprised, but his astonishment soon gave way to a smile that could light up the room: "Is it true?" he asked, but not in disbelief.

She nodded, and he was delighted, and he laughed, genuinely and wholeheartedly he laughed. Winter wept; Fred's joy sorrowed and comforted her. His gratitude was more than she deserved but she needfully made it her shield against bitterness–the world's bitterness as well as her own. Perhaps, when she had made him so happy, she was not completely unworthy. And if God had blessed her to bring a child into the world, He might not see her as corrupt and sinful as people did.

34

Hell is a place on earth

The news of Winter's pregnancy spread a positive sentiment on those close to them. The Ludwig and the Stobe couples, Karl Freier and Peter, offered their congratulations in heartfelt sincerity, and even *Oberstleutnant* von H. looked somewhat excited about the good tidings, although Winter did detect a bittersweet shadow over his eyes when he was congratulating Fred. Aunt Martha was truly overjoyed, her voice on the telephone almost tearful, and she promised to come to Paris once the due time was approaching, ecstatic that she would ultimately become a grandmother, despite never having given birth to a child herself. A family united was Winter's most eager expectation, and she was finally feeling a little more hopeful of that long-anticipated happy ending.

One of the first people to hear about the pregnancy was, of course, the housekeeper: Marie, who wept at the news, and Winter found it unexpected, unusual, and unbelievable. This woman envied her, but that was not all. Sometimes, looking at her, Winter could not help but think of the Gestapo major, both of them having something very much in common: they hated and despised her impassionedly.

Fortunately, it was early summer, and the clear and warm weather was quite permitting of the long walks Winter so much desired to escape from Marie's spiteful company. The doctor had actually recommended regular exercise, so Fred's expressed objections regarding her safety were eventually overcome.

The city always had an enormously soothing effect on Winter's psyche; it had the ability to change her perspective, and open up the picture when she felt inescapably trapped in the maze of her own microcosm. At the *pâtisserie* near the *Église-d'Auteuil*, a mother was feeding her little girl whipped cream from the lemon tart she had just bought and hardly tried herself. Further on, two extremely spry tots were running, one of them rolling a bicycle wheel with a rod, the other one chasing after in screams, obviously claiming his share of the toy. Suddenly, the chaser fell down and began to cry, abandoning the toy and his friend to run home for comfort. Winter recalled her childhood and the hundreds of times she had fallen and run to Mother to be consoled; Mother, who would magically make the pain go away, giving her back the strength to return to her games, run and roll and fight with the boys and be the little girl that she was: a girl with true grit. *Oh, Mum, Mummy!* At the underground station, a woman was having difficulty descending the stairs with her baby in its pushchair, and Winter felt obliged to offer her help. The woman expressed her thanks, but it was really Winter who felt most thankful.

Would she be a good parent? The twins had been more like children to her than brothers and they loved her, so she must have been doing something right. Her fears were too strong to ignore, though. Would she finally find in herself what it took? Once another life started to depend on her, she would have to stand strong against all the unpleasant surprises that life had in store for people. A mother could not be a cowardly and helpless creature, she had to develop will and courage, faith and wisdom. Just like Mother had been, sweet, brave Mother, whom she was only just beginning to bring back to memory, with wistfulness rather than guilt, recalling the joyful moments, not the shameful, painful ones. If only Fred could have seen her with Mother when life was kind to them, if only he could have seen her with Father...

Standing, yet again, at the square of the *Palais Royal* and gazing at the *Hôtel du Louvre*, high at the windows of the fourth floor and somewhere above the "du" of the sign, she could not help feeling that she had sensed it from the start, since the very first time she had stood there hesitant, measuring her strength to face *Sturmbannführer* von Stielen, that this man was no coincidence; he was destiny. What was her life like before him? It had been no more than two days that he was away on duty, and she already felt his absence like a missing part of her own self. She used to be forsaken and helpless before him. Now, she had a family that was flourishing and bearing fruit. Of course, she had had nothing to lose before. Now, she had everything.

She walked through the galleries of the Louvre and into the *Tuileries* garden, where she stood to admire the Luxor obelisk at the *Place de la Concorde* aligning with the *Arc de Triomphe* in the background. This area always filled her with a sense of vastness which was utterly liberating, even at the times of 'The Golden Doe', when it was so easy to be devoured by belittlement and depravity. Then, Fred came along and the two of them would stand together, right at this spot on *Pont Alexandre III*, gazing at the Tower and the boats which travelled up and down the river. He had been a conqueror, a benefactor, a companion, then a lover. Still waters ran even deeper than she had initially thought where Fred was concerned, and he was almost impossible not to fall for–Georgette had been proven right, and it must have been some providence which had kept her from saying 'yes' to the wrong question.

The feeling of a presence next to her made her turn and look. It was a little boy, ten years of age or less, his big eyes and a shy smile shining directly into her heart.

"What's your name, sweetie?" she enquired in French.

"Rémy!" he replied.

"Rémy!" Winter repeated and felt a tender tingle inside. "Are you hungry, Rémy? Do you want some money?" she asked affectionately and was fully prepared to be very generous.

"No!" the little one surprised her. "*Monsieur* gave me some earlier!" he said and Winter believed she did not quite understand the sentence.

Before she could ask the boy what he meant, he took her by the hand and pulled her along on his way. Winter was puzzled, but followed anyway, smiling curiously.

"Hey, stop!" she laughed. "Won't you tell me where we're going?"

The boy motioned her to be quiet and continued to pull her towards the edge of the bridge, down the steps to the dock, and again a little further, where smaller and larger boats quietly rocked to sleep. Winter walked after Rémy, sweetened and excited, thinking her own child could be a boy like him, one she would gladly follow into any game, however odd or absurd, looking dazzled and impressed, because children needed their parents' respect and admiration, and they needed the security of their approval. Father and Mother had been like that with her–if only time had been more benignant with them...

She stopped when he stopped, and she was still smiling when the boy dropped her hand and hurried off, after pointing with his finger to an old rust-eaten barge retired at the pier.

"Hey!" she called at him, but the boy was already far away.

Baffled, with her smile fading unpleasantly, Winter saw the boat's cabin door open wide, revealing a dark, inhospitable interior. An eerie shiver ran through her and the voice in her stomach urged her to turn away and run. Instead, she stepped onto the boat as though magnetised, walked through the iron door, which immediately screeched closed behind her, and allowed the deadly dark inside to encompass her. Absolute silence; only her breath resounded her agony. Then a match was struck and the tiny flame lit an ancient storm lamp, making the volumes around obscure and threatening.

"René!" she asserted and his figure slipped out from the shadows, which always seemed like his most natural habitat.

"It's me. Don't be afraid!"

She quivered as he started approaching her, and when his fingers touched her face, she felt as if they were the fingers of an infernal creature. Only when he brought his face to hers and tried to kiss her, was she empowered enough to back away and escape him. She turned her back on him, brought her hand to her forehead to put her thoughts and feelings in order.

"What do you want, René?" she exclaimed without attempting to hide her displeasure or distress.

René crossed his arms over his chest and leaned against a solid wooden bench.

"Now that's not very nice!" he uttered, staring at her with sheer meanness. "Is that how you people of the high society greet?"

"I don't remember inviting you!" she countered him boldly, something which obviously disturbed him.

"Well, I didn't force you in, either, did I?"

Winter smiled. Indeed, he had never forced her into anything, and yet she had never felt more abused by anyone, neither had her feelings been more hurtful and destructive than when she had them for him. What did he want this time? Why would he not just say what he wanted? Why continue this cat-and-mouse game which led to nowhere other than misery for them both?

"Let's not pretend to be ignorant anymore!" she challenged him. "I haven't changed my mind and, I guess, neither have you!"

René's face softened into such a warm expression that Winter was astonished, and impulsively recalled the first time they had met, the intimate feeling he created the way he looked at her...

"If only you knew how much I wanted it: us to be together in this fight!" he claimed and came nearer, spreading his hands to her arms and sliding them down and up again in a fully passionate caress. She let her head drop wearily and its top touched his chest. She shook her head, but he did not seem to notice. On the contrary, he leaned over and left a fervent kiss on her hair. "But I know I asked a lot of you! I can see that now!" he whispered and touched her face with flaming fingers, his eyes igniting every speck of skin on it that they touched.

"Can you?" she arduously reacted and managed to break away from his high-power field. "Do you mean to tell me this is not another one of your tricks to get round me? That there is nothing you are going to ask of me at the end of this sweet talk? Please! You've been stringing me along for quite some time, I give you that, but you can't fool me anymore."

"There's no fooling when I say I'm crazy about you, Winter!" he avowed with a rare clarity to which Winter felt extremely vulnerable. "If I believed in God, I'd swear to you how much I need you. If you would only let me show you what you mean to me..." And finishing this sentence, he walked up to her, her face entrapped in his needful hands and he kissed her with all his burning desire, with all his imperious demand.

"No!"

She pushed him away, and he was trembling with longing and denial, his seething breath, his fuming eyes like an angry volcano.

"You are still hiding behind your finger!" he feverishly accused her. "I had hoped you would have come to your senses, that you would have realised where it is that you belong."

"I have long ago chosen where I belong, René! It is you hiding behind your finger!" she lashed out at him with all her resolution, feeling for the first time the courage to openly admit to a third person her feelings for Fred: "I love this man, he's good to me and I'm happy!" She saw him frown, she saw him sneer and then he started laughing, that sarcastic, almost vile laughter she was not unfamiliar with. She shuddered but felt furious that he was mocking her feelings this way. "Yes, I am happy..." she cried out stubbornly "...as much as I can be happy and as much as I may have the right to be. No one can make me happier, René, and certainly not you!"

Her words cut his laughter, replacing it with a furious twist on the lips.

"If you repeat it enough, you might actually convince yourself!" he derisively stated.

"You don't want to understand!" she sighed, trying to dispel the sentiment of futility which insidiously clipped her strength to confront him.

"Understand what?" he surprised her with a roar and she quailed before his disdainful ire. "That you've been sold out to them body and soul? That you've bowed down, allowing them to think they can buy or scare anyone to obedience? Is that what you want me to understand?" His eyes sparked and his lips became a thin white line. He reached out to her and, for a moment, Winter was afraid he might hit her, but he just grabbed her by the waist and squeezed her onto him, the sight of her lips, just a breath away from his, a lascivious provocation. "Say you don't want me! Say it!" he dared her and, for a completely incomprehensible reason, she remained speechless. He laid a kiss on her forehead and when she did not resist, he came down to her temple, to her burning cheek, to the tip of her mouth. "We are bound together, Winter; our fate... You cannot drive me out of your life and I will not leave you...!"

And all too easily, too skillfully and effectively, he had once again struck her completely dumb. So many blatant denials in her, and yet no argument seemed enough to refute him. For a few seconds, she even felt sorry for him.

"How wrong you are, René!" she managed to tell him, swamped with emotion. "What you have imagined, for me, for us, it cannot be. I'm not the one you want! I never was the one you wanted! It has always been someone else. She... She was the one for you: Simone. And I can never be her!"

Hearing the name, René suddenly stepped back. His face turned dark, his eyes cracked, and Winter recognised this pain, a pain fully capable of feeding such stubbornness, a pain impossible to be cured with logic or even emotion. Yes, she was very familiar with a pain like that; and she felt for him, but she could not be his redemption.

"I'm so sorry, René! I truly am!" she announced with the definition of bare factuality and she determinedly headed for the exit, walking by him without a second look. Much to her astonishment, René ran after her, blocking her way.

"You seriously think you can leave like that?" he wheezed and blasted a stony glare at her.

"You're not listening to me! Why won't you listen?" she cried out, her fists against her forehead designating her despair. "You want me to say it? I don't want you, René, and I never want to see you again! Can you get it through your head now? I belong to someone else. You can't have me!" And with her look like a fiery blade on his face, she decisively turned around to leave.

René remained frozen for a moment. And then, as if scalded by hot iron, he flinched, eyes boiling their beastly rejection and a face that could bluster against all assertion and reason. Before she could open the door, he forcibly pulled her back.

"Oh, but I can!"

He grabbed her by the wrists, just like the slayer holds the defenseless animal before sticking his knife into its throat. He dragged her onto him, roughly pulling off her coat. Entrapping her between his body and the wall, he grasped her shirt with both hands and tore it to the waist, an unkind hand reaching for her breast inside the petticoat and brassiere. Winter resisted, begging him to stop, but none of her adjurations were able to palliate his embittered ego. His mouth kissed her savagely, his teeth bit her, his hand ripped off her underwear with a single move.

"René...! No!... Let go of me! Let go...!" Winter screamed, trying tooth and nail to push him off. She cried, kicked, shouted, begged. To no avail! With a primitive groan, he shoved himself into her and it was doubtful he himself felt anything other than pain and despair. Clenching his teeth, he pushed deeper and deeper, a moment of utter assimilation and a unique instance of belonging, belonging to him.

"No!" she could only howl.

He shut her mouth with a vicious palm, mistakenly leaving Winter with a loose hand, which, driven by instinct, climbed onto his face and thrusted its fingernails into his cheek. René grunted and receded wildly. He touched the spot where she had hurt him, saw the blood on his fingertips.

"Damn you...!"

He grasped a handful of her hair and threw her over to the other side. Winter bumped into the wooden bench with her belly and writhed on the floor.

"My baby!... My baby!" she panted, holding onto her abdomen and genitalia, as if trying to prevent a fatal abruption.

"What did you say?"

Winter was horrified by the hateful disgust René's eyes were storming at her: "Please, please!" she begged feeling absolutely helpless.

He stepped back, wiping his mouth clean, and he spat on the floor: "You, filthy cunt! Like it wasn't enough humiliation to be his whore!" He came to kneel beside her, grabbed her by the face. "I should rid you of your misery right here and now. But you don't deserve it..." he muttered dripping venom. As he got up, his breath rasped in his throat and he withdrew in the dark kicking at anything there was in his way. Then, he suddenly calmed down, the silence of him more terrifying than his roaring anger. He stepped back into the storm lamp light and a sinister shine in his eyes scared the living soul out of her. "I have a feeling that, from now on, you will never say no to me again!" he wheezed and the crooked smile sitting on his mouth swallowed up every trace of humanity from his face.

Winter secretly glanced at him and she could not believe how much hatred there was in his heart, which he swore needed her only moments ago. Every time she thought she had seen his true colours, he managed to show her an even darker shade. But this time he had gone far enough; he had done his worst. And there were no other means by which to hurt her.

"You haven't seen anything yet!" he threatened the moment their eyes met, and he read her mind. Winter thought she saw flames burning around him and dozens of goat-headed creatures with arrow tails dancing ecstatically at his feet. "I'll put you through hell a thousand times... And you'll be begging me to kill you!" he promised in a voice that seemed to emerge from the bowels of the earth.

He stood in front of her, ordered her up and she had to obey. He talked, and she listened. He defined and determined; she had to submit. Her blind obedience and willing sacrifice: that was what he demanded. But it was doubtful, even so, if she would ever be able to temper the cold steel in him and mellow his merciless soul.

35

If only

Her bleeding conscience was giving the dusk a crimson hue. The time had come for the abyss to look back at her, for she had been staring at it for too long, unwillingly perhaps, but she had. And she had received fair warning, but she pretended not to have heard. Fear would deafen people, deafen and blind them, so that they would never change, no matter how they suffered, because change called for the breaking down of superhuman, high-rise, thick, stone walls and, to do that, it took tons of courage and fortitude, an act of free will. It had been long since Winter felt acquainted with any of those heroic sentiments. And here it was, the gigantic demolition ready to begin, if only she had the heart to hammer the first bricks down.

Her grim task would begin as soon as Fred returned home. It would be a relieving deferment if Fred did not return that night–if he did not return for a long time, long enough for all to be forgotten, for all to be diminished into triviality... Of course, she could always leave as Aunt Martha had, disappear somewhere neither Fred nor René could find her. But she did not have the stomach Aunt Martha had, and, contrary to Aunt Martha, her enemy was still very much alive; alive and full of hatred.

Her gaze through the window was now following Fred's footsteps:

from the gate, through the garden, and up the steps to the main entrance; wide, hurried strides; the sober attire of the Reich; a large yellow envelope underneath his armpit. She closed her eyes. Her chest and stomach revolted. *Oh, Fred!*

Fred had just returned to the hallway from the library corridor when he realised that Winter was standing motionless and apathetic at the top of the staircase.

"Winter!"

The sound of his voice startled her and an insufferable pain ran through her as she brought her eyes to him. He hurriedly untied his pistol belt, left it on the chest of drawers, and rushed to hold her in his arms.

"I missed you!" he breathed like the sweetest summer breeze and his mouth had the power of an almost healing remedy.

Right then, Marie walked in, making certain to hide the green-eyed monster behind her tray of goodies; she had also been eager for Fred's return and would do all in her power to offer him the perfect dinner, the perfect nightcap, the perfect everything.

"It's nice to have you back, *Monsieur*! I'll set the table for you immediately!"

It was most fortunate that Marie felt so obliging to her master, her ambition to please him having sent her out shopping until well past noon, and then into the kitchen most of the afternoon, filling the house with the smell of freshly cooked food, a sign of home and homely welcome. Luckily, Winter did not have to cross paths with her for hours–it would have been impossible to find a convincing explanation for the look of sheer terror on her face or her torn clothes, which she immediately vanished, burying them in a secluded spot in the garden. If she were ever gone from Fred's life, Marie would be the first in line to take her place and this thought made Winter so envious because Marie and Fred had no secrets and even she would be so much better for him for that reason alone. And yet, for a while, she had believed she had actually become another, a new and better self, the self she always wanted to be. Could she have put a stop to the downfall somewhere? Which was that crucial moment, the one that would have changed the course of things, if she had done otherwise if she had made a different choice?

Oh, but what was the point in such absurd enquiries! The past was behind and nothing could change the present, despite her 'ifs' and 'perhaps' and 'might'. The only way out might be if she and Fred could leave together–yes! that would be the only correct solution, the only one she really wished for, and she would gladly go anywhere with him, live happily with him in the farthest corner of the world, even on a tiny piece of rock in the middle of the ocean...

"... If only we could leave ...!" her lips whispered, and she did not immediately realise she had spoken.

"What was that, my love?"

She turned to Fred, who was quietly having his dinner at the table next to her, and she ached at the thought that there might still be some hope.

"Yes, Fred! Let's leave! The two of us, far away, tonight!" she uttered clasping her hands in an impassioned appeal.

He laughed, because he thought she was joking, but then her restlessness, the tremble on her lips, the cloud in her eyes overmastered his initial surprise.

"But we can't just go away!" he answered in the mildest tone as if trying to reassure a frightened child.

"Yes, we can! Of course, we can! Think of it as something you'll do for me. For me, Fred, please!"

Fred sat and looked serious, the alarm in his chest warning him that the forthcoming distress he had always sensed was impending was here and about to bang on their door, demanding to take its toll on their very souls.

"What is it, Winter? I can't help you if you don't tell me..."

"Oh, but I don't want you to help me!" she ardently protested and almost jumped up from the table, taking a few uncertain steps towards the window and, looking outside at the dark greenery, she felt devoured by despair. "I'm asking you to go away with me. That's what I'm asking, don't you see?"

She cast an anguished gaze at him, and he was looking at her in his sharp perception, which always made her feel stripped naked before his eyes.

"Why don't I call Aunt Martha! You can stay with her all you want, and perhaps the two of you can return later, or...!"

But Winter was shaking her head, swamped in her frustration, and the Lord Justice inside her head was awakened and laughed at how naive she was to think she could so easily escape the final judgment. This was the hell René was referring to, and she was sentenced to live in it for all eternity.

"It's useless if you're not there..." she muttered, sensing it was straws she was grasping at, and the noose of complete hopelessness became tighter and asphyxiating around her neck.

Fred got up from the table and walked to her, deeply immersed in troubled thoughts of his own: "This is the worst of times for me to leave Paris!"

"It is, isn't it?" she said in an utterly resigned murmur. "I understand! I do! Duty must always come first!"

"Winter!" Fred's painful protest obliged her to look, and she saw his face torn, his eyes overwhelmed with a conflict she could not understand. "Please..." he begged with sore words "...please, don't do this! I can't choose between you and who I am!"

He took her by the arms, the squeeze of his hands permeating all his desperate needfulness into her, and the eyes he was looking at her with were the most human eyes she had ever, ever seen. She embraced his face with her palms, warm and sweaty, the deep yearning in their hold swamping both their gazes with loving, sorrowful tears. But Fred did not weep, she had never seen him weep, although she knew he must have wept hundreds of times inside, and most of them owing to her.

Over the nightly hours, an unnatural silence had spread its mute veil on everything. Even the clock on the nightstand had gone dumb. Only the wind wheezed through the shutters every so often, and it had not been windy for days. Twenty past three. The atmosphere was dense and suffocating. Insomnia and frustration were exhausting. She had drawn away from Fred's arms for a while now and she lay completely still on her side of the bed, pressing her lips tightly together, so that they would not scream her agony... This was how people lost their minds,–if only she, too, would go crazy, because it was madness what she was asked to do, and one could not go to war with a madman, unless perhaps just as mad... She was running out of time. Whatever was to be done had to be done now. But her limbs refused to move, in a last act of resistance. And, in her stomach, emotions were fighting against her most dreadful fears.

Finally, she managed to get up. If she lay down a little longer, she would certainly go mad, but she would not escape René's ire, not even so: he would definitely find a way to get back at her, he was so good at finding ways to hurt her. She peeped at Fred, asleep on his back, his favourite sleeping position, which always allowed her to cozily nestle next to him at night and dream the dreams his fragrance inspired. If she could just get back into bed with him, close her eyes and sleep forever! She did not want to do this; she did not. And yet, she clenched her teeth, her neck muscles contracted: enough!

She prowled to the dressing table at the other end of the room, found his clothes resting neatly on the chair. Her hand crept into his trouser pocket; then into the other. When she touched what she was supposed to find, her blood froze for a second. It was decided then! She got up determinedly and swiftly sneaked out of the room.

The wind protested for her indecency, it made the window creak and Fred opened his eyes. He had always been well prepared for the unexpected–but was this really unexpected?–and coming out of the bedroom, he did not really expect to see any light in the bathroom or, downstairs, in the kitchen and the sitting-room, but he checked, anyway, for the benefit of the doubt. Past the staircase and into the corridor, he noticed the key of his office door in the lock; a thin line of light gushing out from the inside coiled his heart like barbed wire. He opened the door, saw her sitting in the armchair in front of the desk, the yellow envelope, her petrified face.

"What's the meaning of this?"

"Please... Come in and close the door, Fred!"

"I demand an explanation!"

"And you will have it!"

As he came to sit in the armchair opposite her, instead of his own seat behind the desk, Winter felt somewhat encouraged. Her anguish had dried up every trace of saliva in her mouth, she was frightened to death, but it was too late to change her mind.

"I want you... I need you to listen... to hear me out before you make up your mind about anything, Fred. This is the moment we have both been dreading, the moment of truth. But you must believe, no matter what you hear, no matter how it sounds, that I remained faithful to you. And if I dare speak to you tonight, it's because I had to remain faithful ... faithful to you!"

She raised an imploring look at him, her heart banging almost out of her chest, but the cold in Fred's eyes, the smirk on his lips hurt her like a knife.

"Don't waste your breath on worthless introductions! You have my fullest attention!" he provoked her, sitting back in the armchair and crossing his arms over his chest.

Winter looked away with a bitter smile. The outcome of her dare would most probably be dire. But this Gordian knot around her neck could not be undone in a way that was easy or risk-free. It had taken her long to realise she would have to either cut it or be strangled by it.

She hid nothing this time. She spoke of the night when she left home, the den of *Rue Goubet* haunting her dreams until she returned, only to haunt her ever more after. Her lungs had almost exploded from running and grief. She could not tell when she collapsed or how she had been carried for safety into the damp chambers of the sewers. She only knew that when she saw him, a bizarre familiarity mixed with her fear and suspicion of him. His name was René, he was from Lille, his hazel eyes dived into her and engraved their fatal legacy. She could not help feeling guilty for leaving his shelter; why did she leave? She did not know, only that she had to. Then, in the darkest hour, a British girl before an SS German, terror and despair overflowed. She devised a lie, and Pierre

Morné played along. 'You know what it is that girls do around here,' he had told her, and she had not really believed it would come to that, but it did. 'The Golden Doe' became another much despised home for her, but she slowly grew to love its people, some more than others. And she would dream of René, a girlish dream stung by envy for that Simone, who had stolen his heart before her, a figure so powerful, he would still look at her in her eyes and desire her in the way he touched her. Oh, she was well aware of what René was. He had not tried to hide it, he wanted her to know everything about him, and love him for it. 'And you?' she had asked him a pale morning in the catacombs, after a frantic dance, his burning hands over her arms, those hungry eyes inside the mirror. He wanted to change her, he wanted to make her the same as him: free and militant, brave and fearless. It would have been beautiful if she could have become like that then, if she could detect in herself even a grain of that valour, the self-denial necessary to sacrifice oneself for a greater cause. But she was not like him; she wanted to live...

It was right about that time, when his figure emerged, distinct and important: *Sturmbannführer* von Stielen, the major, Fred. She owed him everything, and she was grateful, but he did not want her gratitude and, in the end, it was not gratitude that she wanted to give him. When he entered her life, René's image inexplicably began to flicker. But he was like a reflection on the surface of water, which dissolved into irregular shapes when a stone was thrown into it, but was easily restored when the water again calmed. She never felt to have had any control over him. There was a mysterious bond between them, and it was not the romance that had entrapped them, once and never again, in the same sheets. As if he gave flesh to all her fears, all her guilt and her denials, to every insecurity and dissatisfaction, to every pain she was carrying in her soul. And he was attractive and repulsive at the same time, merging with her very self, impossible to be rid of, no matter how persistently she refused him.

She brought her eyes to Fred's expression, effortlessly breaking through its haggard surface. He was a blessing and a curse for her, salvation and condemnation; because he was such a man that she could not help but love with all her heart; because he had accepted her the way she was, and only a fertile ground did he lay for her to change as much as she wanted and was able to. How she had accused him of this incomprehensible behaviour in the beginning! Like the hordes of the Great Inquisitor's believers who needed manipulation to get through their lives. And yet, there had always been something very familiar about him, too–in another way familiar to the way she had felt for René. It was a sweet, empowering emotion. She had never had this feeling before, not since she was a child.

But once Fred had become precious to her, René gained another arrow in his quiver. He knew how to bring to life her worst nightmares, but it must never have occurred to him that, when one was pushed to the edge of the cliff, they might just make the impossible choice to jump. And so, she was here now, resolute not to give her executioner another weapon to hurt her with, except perhaps the satisfaction of seeing her lose what she had been struggling to keep for so long; because, if Fred did not forgive her, René Martin would, in a way, have won. But, at least, it would have been her decision how to have 'nothing to hide and nothing to fear' anymore.

The next morning, he would be waiting for her at the *Montmartre* cemetery to exchange his lenience with a small step into hell, through which he would get her a thousand times. The countdown had begun. This time it was an envelope–her adorable husband had been away for two days, he would bring it with him. She did not ask him how he knew this; it did not impress her: René always knew...

Fred's expression had something of a cast iron furnace fueled up to a melting point. For a moment, a morose smile settled on his lips, revealing a painful state of mind.

"Open up this envelope!" he told her and his reaction astounded Winter and she pulled back, shaking her head. "Open this envelope!" he repeated in a commanding tone, and Winter felt she simply had to comply. She took the envelope, opened it carefully, and spread its contents on her lap. It was a bunch of reports and official documents, some scattered notes on them written in Fred's handwriting, pointing to certain references by lines and arrows. René's name was affluently mentioned. She shook her head, sincerely admitting that she did not understand. "His real name is Lebrun! I have been looking for him as Martin, but his name is René Lebrun!" he informed her with a strict censure in his voice. Winter was surprised, but she gestured she did not consider it strange for René to have changed his name. Fred also agreed with a nod, but that was not his point: "Look at the photos!" he urged her, and Winter felt more reluctant to do so than before. He persisted with his gaze.

And Winter looked, a relentless fear stirring up the acidic fluids in her stomach.

René in khaki uniform, he had one of those Adrian helmets on, exactly the same as the toy helmets Stepfather had brought the twins for their fifth birthday, a rare gesture, perhaps it was out of enthusiasm that he had money in his hands again, Mother's money. A family picture; René's family. Oh, the sun was shining so bright over the fields, over the faces, and in their smiles, the smiles born out of familial happiness and love. Then there was the ultimate murk. Hay and grain, old tools and wood around, a body suspending from the ceiling. The sun was shining on this young girl no more, the dried blood on her lips, her crudely cut hair explaining her sadness. A sign hanging from her neck called her a whore, and her dress was torn open to prove it. There was a wooden stool; it had fallen to the floor, only an inch below her toes. Her greenish colour was horrifying; no one ever deserved a colour like this, much less a girl so young and pretty. She had a fair complexion, sun-kissed brown hair, and two earthen dollops for eyes in another photo, a portrait from before. And Winter felt she recognised her, a face from the past, a past she had never lived except in another universe.

"Now, turn it over and read the name!"

She did not feel she needed to, but she turned the picture anyway, tears rolling unstoppably from her eyes. The name, the place, the date, it all felt like ancient knowledge: René had a sister. And her name was Simone...

36

The light in darkness

The dawn was beautiful; painfully beautiful; those layers of purple, orange and yellow, the vast light blue–how they compared to the gloom inside her! She could hear the howling of wild dogs from afar. An atmosphere of death surrounded her. The image of the hanged girl was harrowing; she could almost feel the swinging of her toes, hear the bump the stool made as it tumbled under her feet. Would she be calling out his name? Was he there, looking at her? Simone! All this time she had been envious of her, and René had had the nerve to do so many other unimaginable things, but never to tell her the truth about who Simone was. Could this be the death she felt was due to end the drama? Or had there to be another: her own most appropriately? At this thought, something flinched in her abdomen, and Winter remembered she was no longer alone, not even to think.

"My life!" she whispered and caressed her belly, suddenly flooded by a warm, healing wave.

Now the purple veil came to enwrap and appease her, infuse her with a positive power: trust. She trusted Fred not to allow his ego to get the better of him. Fred had always been strong; his love had been stronger than the circumstances. She was glad that her love for him had finally found its strength, too. And he would see that; he just had to.

But she knew how much she had hurt him. And Fred was only human. She smiled bitterly. She had finally broken down the walls; the dust cloud from the demolition was suffocating, like it must have been at that bombing in Spain, where Fred had suffered an almost mortal wound. How many times had they almost died? Almost! A near miss, which was enough to keep them alive! Perhaps that was, after all, what was really necessary. A flimsy crack of light where darkness prevailed, and her love for Fred had already grown to be an open window. But the war was still raging. A battle lost, a battle won... screams... screams...

Wait a minute, what was that? That was not in her head, that was real: the screams, they were real, and they were coming from downstairs. A vague premonition pushed her out of the bedroom and to the top of the stairs. For a moment, she doubted the sight before her very eyes. She had never seen Fred so close to insanity, so crude and ferociously brutal to anyone.

Until only a while ago, Fred was left alone in the office, the time following a harsh truth urgently calling for silence, retreat and contemplation. It did require a lot of courage from her to do what she did; or a lot of despair, for that matter! He could grant her this ultimate act of bravery, but what about the entire volume of lies the charade played behind his back this whole time was made up of? For a strange reason, he believed her confession, and when she claimed she had been faithful, he knew, faithful she had been. But she had systematically been deceiving him, keeping those guilty secrets hidden from him. For every time he had implored her for the truth, for every time she swore of her innocence, and every single time he trusted in her, while she had kept quiet, playing along with René Martin's game–yes; he was certain she had never taken part in any of his illegal activities.

He revisited her every word. Once again, he realised he believed her when she said she was afraid to tell him the truth: he himself had ascertained as much, and he knew her so little then–such meaningful truths were revealed that day in the celestial surroundings of *Chantilly*. And he also believed she had misjudged René Martin's intentions, feeling entrapped when the time had passed for a forthright admittance to her mistake. Fred had spent little personal time with René, but he had studied him carefully. Winter's descriptions matched his exact idea of him: demonic. But that hardly relieved her of the choice she had made, the choice not to trust him with the truth. Jealousy stung him, his ego raged; those petty sentiments he had so often encountered in others, exploited even to serve his purposes. He had always considered himself better than that; he was not. He reflected on all the instances she must have pretended to him in order to rebut his suspicions, on the times she might have been thinking of Martin while they were together, sharing moments of warm companionship and love. He was feeling robbed of something of his, something dear. And he was the perpetrator, Martin, who had been so brazen as to rub it in his face that he would always live in his shadow. Because Martin knew the truth, while he was in complete, ridiculous ignorance.

Those conflicting emotions were excruciating. He used to be clear-minded, firm and decisive, and, now, he did not have the faintest idea whether he wanted to punish or forgive her; if she deserved his contempt or his compassion; if he hated or passionately loved her. Damn that vile serpent! He should have unearthed him from whatever hollow he had been lurking in and crushed him. This was not only Winter's fault, it was his own, as well. She might have been weak, but he? He had promised to protect her and he had failed pitifully.

He turned towards the lamp spilling its pale light over the desk. He grabbed and flung it to the other end of the room. It was finally dark. He could not stand any more light in this plain of the apocalypse.

It was then when an uncanny feeling whirled in him, as though a sinister presence had visited him, and his hearing became extraordinarily sharpened, his senses on full alert. He took a few steps towards the half-open door of the office, a kind of murmuring in the background and a mordant instinct had the effect of a magnet: to the end of the corridor and to the side of the stairs.

"Please, try again! I must speak with him now! ... No, I can't call back later, it's very important!" the voice said in secrecy, and in an instant, Fred realised it could not be Winter's voice–Winter did not speak French so well.

Coming out into the hallway, he saw Marie with the telephone receiver in her hand. The woman froze. She did not even think of putting the telephone down before Fred reached her and grabbed the receiver. He brought it close to his ear as if he were afraid that, any moment now, some rabid beast would burst out of it.

"I'm sorry, Madam, the *Kriminalrat* is not answering! Would you like to leave a message?" the voice on the other end of the line replied. "Hello? Hello?"

Fred hung up the telephone and his eyes glazed dangerously: "Blut? You were calling Blut?"

Stillness. Great devastation often had this effect even on the strictest, most suspicious vigilance. And on her part, it was a now or never situation, one of those moments when circumstance comes before decision and sets things on their course.

"Well, someone had to do something to get this hussy out of here!" Marie reacted unexpectedly, shocking and scandalising Fred.

"What did you say?" he uttered, his face deformed by astonishment and mad rage.

"I said someone had to do something! After all you've heard, you are still thinking about it?" Marie lashed out at his completely destroyed face.

"Shut up!"

"How do you live with yourself? To be humiliated by this slut; and I had to stand by and watch, watch you stoop lower and lower for her!" she attacked him, completely forsaking the obligation to keep up appearances.

"Shut up!" Fred wheezed and grabbed her by the wrist with no awareness of the force he was applying. The pain made Marie scream; her envy and denial exacerbated her.

"What I have done for you all these years! And you still chose this strumpet! If you don't get rid of her here and now, I swear I will!"

"I said, shut your damn mouth!" Fred growled and beat her with a furious fist, causing her to fall to the floor. He brought his hand to his forehead, desperate for a reason to keep his right mind. It was inconceivable what was happening, what he was hearing... He turned his back; he could not stand to look at this betrayal.

"Blut was right!" Marie spurted out, wiping the blood from her mouth, raising a resentful, vindictive gaze. "You're nothing but a charlatan pretending to be great. You're wrapped around the whore's finger and, perhaps, that is all you deserve!"

Shaking her words out of his head, his eyes fell on his pistol belt on the chest of drawers, unusually and carelessly left there, he might say, were he in a position to think straight, but now its presence seemed like an almost divine intervention and the only way out of this insane infuriation. He took the pistol out and pointed it at her, his eyes manifesting he was just a moment away from surrendering to his fury and planting every one of its bullets into her.

"Go ahead, then!" Marie howled in a frantic delirium. "You had better kill me! Because when I open my mouth, there will be no saving you or your slut!"

He felt the trigger recede under the pressure of his finger and longed for the gunshot to bang away the madness that trampled over him.

"Fred! Fred... please!"

Winter's scream, like a signal from another world, shocked him to the core. He turned to where her voice had echoed, confused that she was there, standing in the middle of the staircase, her hands clasped to her face, a face crushed, drowned in tears, and eyes almost exploding with anguish and supplication. In a tenth of a second, his mind was stormed by images of her, rooted deep inside him, unruly images, invincible, persuasive even... He stood there looking at her and he seemed to slowly ascend back from a murky chasm, gradually releasing the pressure on the pistol trigger, regaining self-control, becoming himself again. The final pieces started to fall into place: the people he had believed in, both traitors of his trust. And yet, they had nothing in common. Strangely, perhaps, but they had absolutely nothing...

He let the pistol hang loosely in his hand, shed another regretful look at the housekeeper. Then a crooked smile appeared, making his face resemble a poorly painted caricature, a sign of a fleeting thought in his mind transforming into a scheme.

"No!" he murmured. "You deserve something better!"

And, despite her resistance, he grabbed Marie by the arm and dragged her to the cellar, where he locked her up and took away the key. Marie was punching at the door, cursing and swearing vengeance, but Fred had sealed himself to her threats. With steel coldness, he glanced at the large floor clock standing against the opposite wall. It was ten past seven. Immediately, he picked up the telephone and dialed a number. Winter approached, anxiously observing his abnormally controlled moves, his perfectly composed expression.

"Karl!" he said, and Winter understood he was calling Karl Freier. "Get the plan of the *Montmartre* cemetery and meet me there in two hours. And, Karl. keep it quiet... I can't. I'll explain later!" He hung up, breathed deeply, turned and calmly looked at her.

"What are you going to do?" she asked, beforehand terrified at the answer.

"What I should have done a long time ago," he stated in a flat tone like some kind of sound steamroller had passed over his voice.

Winter felt a sharp pain in the middle of her chest.

"Fred!" she implored him and anchored on him with the forceful instinct of survival and the urge to protect him. "Please, don't go! Send a squad or something and don't go, I beg of you!" Fred did not reply, and Winter saw it in his determination that the closing act of this drama he was going to take up all by himself. Out of hurt ego, perhaps, or... out of excessive love. "Fred!" she muttered sadly, impressing the look of him into her mind: the masculine outline of his chest underneath the white vest; his neckline, where the veins protruded like subcutaneous ropes; on the skin of his face, newly grown thorny hair; his lips a little drier; his wrinkles a little more visible; the grey in his eyes bleary and saturate... "Fred, if anything happens to you, I will die!" she exclaimed, blinding tears flooding out onto her cheeks.

He gazed deep into her blazing eyes, softly wiped the tears with his fingers. His hands on her arms, he tightly held onto them for a moment. Then, he pulled her away with a kind, but decisive move.

"No, Winter, you will not die!"

And his words were gentle, filled with that sentiment, which always gave Winter confidence and hope; they were heartening and benign, warm and affectionate like his love; but they were also absolute and definite, undeniable, as factual statements usually are; and they had something of a desire, a wish and a command, for which reason they were utterly, regrettably, and so frightfully compelling.

37

By the demon within

Like a ghost before dawn, René Martin jumped the fence in the west wing of the *Montmartre* cemetery and found himself the only living soul among the sepulchres. He was not afraid of the deathly silence, neither of the shadows playing hide and seek around the tombs before lying down to rest out another day of eternity. The dead did not frighten him–it was the living he always had to beware of. He proceeded on the paved path with precaution, however secure by the conviction that the conquerors would not eagerly step into a cemetery, as they would not set foot in the catacombs, the sewers and anything underground, probable to remind them how feeble their arrogant sense of power really was. He stood in front of a marble monument, not far from the fence; 'Mort Escalier', it read, and it was an austere square building with a dome, set on a concrete platform with two grassy steps. A rusty latch locked the iron door, impressed with representations of ancient funeral rites. He lifted the latch and opened it up, entered and pulled the door shut.

Early daylight entering from the skylights in the dome was lovingly falling on the tomb. René was drowsing off with his back against its base, his newly acquired Schmeisser submachine gun near, in case it was needed. But it would not be! He recalled his last encounter with

Winter: she was all warm inside, despite the repugnance, and he wished there had been another way, that she had left him with a different option. There was a time, promising time, when he wanted to win her over, offer her the precious gift of freedom. But she proved undeserving of such a gift. She had sold herself out to the conqueror, every molecule of her miserable existence, and she was impenitent.

Many had succumbed to this temptation! Many who could have been saved had they received proper, timely guidance; if they had not relinquished their beliefs, giving in to the unforgivable defect of the human nature to desire its survival above all else. They would even forsake their own blood,–they should know blood could not tolerate being forsaken.

He waited for her: helpless, betrayed and traitorous, her self-destruction would soon be complete. Her guilt and the wrath of the deceived husband would diligently fulfill the task, and all he wanted was to be somewhere nearby, to triumph as she would drown in her own filth. *How could I bear to look at you like that?* And yet, he could.

Next, it would be von Stilen's turn. There was someone who would delight in the information he had to offer on the much-overrated Commander of the Intelligence Service and his honourable wife. When he was done with them, there would be nothing left but their dust under his shoes–he who laughs last, laughs longest, would he not agree? The *Sturmbannführer*. He was but a lieutenant at the time. Did he really think he could ever forget his face?

The sun was moving a little higher in a perfectly cloudless sky; morning, and people would start with another busy day, much like a swarm of bees around the hive. Mistresses would get about their household; workers would set off to work, children to school. The market would open, the shop keepers would step out to observe the day's traffic, anything to add to the overall disposition towards normality.

The *Montmartre* cemetery remained largely untouched by the bustle of the city and life. In the sepulchre where Mort Escalier now resided, the atmosphere slowly began to warm up. René started feeling the heat a bunch of sunbeams spread upon his eyelids. He breathed deeply and stretched out his neck and shoulders. Then, he heard footsteps from outside. His eyes cracked open, and he reached for his machine gun, quickly glancing at the watch on his left wrist. It was twenty to ten.

The heavy door opened a few centimetres at first, wider and wider a moment later, evidence of reasonable hesitation. A woman's figure appeared inside the bright white, dazzling light, her slim legs and slender waist as attractive as ever, but her shoulders were hunched by the burden of guilt and a headscarf attempted to hide the shame of the most sinful act: betrayal. He could not see her hands though; where were her hands? But the thought flickered and passed, not lingering long enough to warn him.

"You're early!" he exclaimed and lowered the gunpoint away from the doorway. "It's good to see you've taken matters seriously after all!" He left his firearm on his thighs and put his fingers into his trench-coat pocket looking for a cigarette. He pulled one out and put his fingers back in the pocket, this time looking for a match. "Well, get inside, will you? I take it you did make sure no one followed you!" he slurred somewhat irritated.

As soon as he saw the woman moving inwards, he bent over the little flame to light his cigarette, but before he could take the first puff, a strange moan violently distracted him. The woman had taken three or four clumsy steps towards him and, in the short distance that separated them, he could see it was not Winter's familiar face, but another, which he did not have the time to identify. His attention was now drawn to another figure making its appearance, a male figure in Nazi uniform.

Within moments, and while the male figure was already firing at him, he grabbed his machine gun and began to shoot blindly in the direction of the invaders. While the figure used the woman as a shield, some of René's bullets hit her low in the chest and abdomen, and injured her, fatally no doubt. René himself had a burning sensation all over the upper part of his right arm and he glanced at the blood drenching his trench coat sleeve cursing, because it was the side of his shooting hand. Reflexively, he reached for his firearm with the left but the German, who had never stopped holding onto his human shield, shot at him again, this time brushing past his left ear, warning him against any movement. He felt a fleeting, but very annoying surprise. He was caught in a trap like a rat; how was that even possible?

"Von Stielen!" he affirmed, once the male figure had come near enough to discard the bloodied woman's body close to him and relieve him of his weapon.

"We meet again!" Fred uttered, satisfied to see the frustration in René's eyes, but, more than that, to see René's face, his scarred cheek, confirmation of struggle against a repulsive foe. He then followed René's gaze to Marie, now lying down like a useless object with her hands tied behind her back, her eyes shut, a thick piece of cloth shoved inside her mouth. "Your accomplice, don't you recognise her?" he mocked René, who was only just beginning to remember who she was. Fred pulled the gag out of Marie's mouth, cut the ropes off her wrists with a small Swiss army knife, and threw them away, behind the tomb, where they would not be visible. Then he stepped back to a safe distance,–he had underestimated his opponent once too many times, he would not make the same mistake again.

René was able to tame his confusion quickly. He smiled sideways and let a scornful giggle escape his lips: "You got me there, for a moment, von Stielen! I thought you had brought your beloved to die by her lover's fire. But that would be too forward a concept for you!" he provoked him and laughed at the end of his sentence.

"If I were you, I'd worry more about myself!" Fred sufficed to say, pulling the yellow envelope out from his tunic and throwing it in René's face.

The contents of the envelope slipping out, Simone's photographs first and foremost, shattered René's sarcasm and a blend of regret and resentment clouded his expression.

"So, the little tart decided to talk to you!" he concluded, once again feeling the sting of an unpredicted shock. "I confess I did not expect she could actually go through with it, but, after all, she did hang around me for quite a while!" he boasted and immediately smiled with contempt: "But you? What's your excuse cleaning up her mess? I would expect more from someone with your credentials!"

Fred was offended but did not fall into the trap. "Keep your opinions to yourself, Martin, for they interest me not! I am here for one reason and you know damn well what that is!"

René nodded. "You have every right to hate me!" he agreed with pretended understanding. "Nothing will ever be the same between you and her!" He made a step forward, smiled nastily. "You just want to beat the hell out of me, don't you?" he challenged him. "I lured her, that's true, but she enjoyed every bit of it, I assure you!"

He observed Fred's stern face with an unwelcome feeling of dismay. He, who had the unique gift of reading behind even the most inaccessible look, could hardly discern whether his tactics now had the desired effect. To be honest, he did not count the *Sturmbannführer* for a proper man, capable of proper manly feelings. But, if he had a chance to get out of this predicament, then, he would not only have to believe his enemy was capable of them, but also that they were of an explosive enough substance to lead him astray.

"Well, I'm right here!" he arrogantly dared him. "Although wounded, I'm willing to take you on! Come on! Let's settle our scores like men!" He brought his right fist close to his cheekbone, the left one slightly forward as a first line of defense. His eyes became two glowering cracks firing small thunderbolts, and his mouth wore the perfect sneer to show he was not only unafraid, but already certain of victory.

Silent and controlled, armoured with his discipline, and unmoved by the challenge, Fred looked at him calmly. "Don't be a fool, Martin!" he spurned with a voice which had the ballistic effect of a catapult. "I have nothing to prove to you! I have you exactly where I want you!"

René broodingly stared. Bitterness deformed his mouth and an ancient hatred steamed from his face: "You should be thanking me, von Stielen; you should be down on your knees grateful that I was not then what I am now!" he told him emphatically, and Fred reciprocated with a contemptuous smile, but the smile quickly froze on his lips. "Remember a bombed-out landscape?" René spurted out with words deadly like a poisoned arrow. "You were wounded. You were asking for help. A moment before, you had blown a man's head off. It belonged to my brother..." Fred's features turned dark. Unconsciously, he brought the fingers of his left hand under his right shoulder. René cried out an eerie laugh. "Yes, it's a small, small world; and chance is a fucking bitch!"

He stood upright, fearless and proud, his impertinent eyes plunged into Fred's broken gaze. The most powerful weapon of man against man was memory, and, more efficiently, the memory of horror.

They looked at each other. So close to one another, they seemed like two sides of the same coin. War strangely divided and united people. It united them with similar feelings, common instincts, the same purpose. Then Fred pulled the trigger. Once, twice, three times. René fell onto his back, with three bullets stuck in his chest. Eyes wide open, an insolent smile on his mouth hardly extinguished. Fred did not feel the slightest satisfaction, not even relief...

"It's time to go, Friedrich!" Karl Freier came through the sepulchre door and stood uncertain, looking at Fred's head hanging down, his back hunched over, the pistol fallen from his resigned hand. A couple of paces away, the two bodies lying in a pond of blood screamed of tragedy. He touched Fred on the shoulder and he flinched: moisture in his eyes, a suffering face, despair. "Friedrich..."

Fred glimpsed at his friend, his closest and most trusted friend. In his concerned countenance, he read that he was looking up to him to be masterful of himself and full of his renowned courageous determination. And he sent a smile, a tender, pacifying smile at him, brother in joys and sorrows, brother in arms in battles past and new ones to come: "I'll be right there!" he sighed and Karl Freier was reassured and gave his consent with a little pat on Fred's arm, before stepping out to inspect the outside perimetre.

Fred reset René's weapon to firing position and left it next to him for an alibi. He took a deep breath, closed his eyes, and turned his back to the scene. When one moved a stone for ages rooted deep in the ground, they had to be ready to face whatever was lying underneath;

and it was not the first time he had to look at this monster in the eye. The world was small, René Martin was right; and they were even smaller, insignificant people.

A burst of gunfire in the vaulted tomb shook Fred's body and violently interrupted his thoughts. The excruciating burn in his lower back and stomach informed him that he was injured. He put his hand on the wound and looked; it was profusely bleeding. The sight made the pain perceptible, but more overwhelming was his awe and wonder. His logic was categorical: it could not have been Martin. He turned in amazement: Marie! It was Marie... A second burst shot across his chest, shortly before Karl Freier barged in like crazy to return the fire. The woman's body convulsed several times and her last breath came out with a groan.

Fred lay down, looking at his blood flowing in small streams along the grooves of the eroded cobblestone; a simple breath seemed like a huge struggle. This was most unexpected and unfortunate! He would have to be there to make certain their story was made credible, to erase any suspicion against their allegations regarding the events of this day; to stand up against one particular foe, whose simmering hatred would hugely motivate him to prove every single argument of theirs false. On her own, Winter would be easy prey for him; and he had been dying to get his claws into her.

This thought impelled him to muster every bit of strength remaining in him and turn to Karl Freier, grab him by the lapel of his tunic and pull him near: "Take Winter to Zurich..."

The blood gushing from his mouth swallowed his words, the muscle in his limbs abandoned him. Karl Freier's agonising voice, calling to him that he should hold on, faded. But he was feeling calm, without fear, even the pain was gone. Two cold, but gentle arms embraced him; he welcomed them. They took his senses and scattered them in the atmosphere; it was liberating. And it was peaceful, like snowfall at night. A snow falling upwards and back into the white cloud from which it was born.

38

Let the snow fall

It's snowing. I'm looking at the falling snowflakes. Look, if you can. But you can't. You can't anymore. I'm looking instead of you. Snow is falling. A thick white blanket has already covered everything out there. The snow! The first snow of this winter, the first snow of a new life: it always snowed inside of me as it snowed all around, but this is a different kind of snow. Or there's a different eye looking at it.

I am Winter Pale. Outside it's snowing and I'm staring at the image in the glass. I see you and you see me. The time has come. The time you may have anticipated or the one you may have suddenly realised was inevitable, and, facing up to this shocking revelation, you felt utterly helpless and unprepared. Perhaps you wanted another ending for this story, I know I did. I'm looking at my reflection in the window and I stand alone, separate from it. My thoughts, my feelings. I choose, I make mistakes; they teach me how to be. And if there's one thing I've learnt from this life you've put me, like Destiny, in this world to live, is that no one need speak for me anymore–not even you.

I'm looking at your smile, bittersweet like your feelings, as befits a loving farewell. Because you wanted it to step out of the narrator's role and live the adventure of your own life. You needed it to set yourself free of our minds and souls, and you desired it to give up the divine power granted to you by the muse, which no human should hold on to for too long. We are like a mirror of each other, you and I. Who defined whom? We'll always wonder. You gave me life; I gave you wisdom, a deeper knowledge of yourself, walking hand in hand together for so many years, on a parallel course, where we both had to struggle with the mysterious wonder of living. You can rest assured now and let go. I'm going to treasure you deep in the veils of the existence you have given me; I'll remember you with affection, and you, every time you go through these pages, you will recall everything we lived together, every moment of joy, of pain, of love and hate, of fear and predicament. You will visit me every now and then. I will welcome you, and we'll look back, gratified and wistful. But now, my spiritual creator, I am ready to part from you. Henceforth, I'm the sole creator of my story and I'm its only narrator.

The story begins with my childhood, my wish to return to its bliss. The tragedy of man begins the moment he is separated from his mother's womb and adulthood is a snowstorm, for which I wonder if anyone is ever prepared enough. I used to think of life as a fairytale with a happy ending, but I know now it is not. This tale is not governed by the rules of fiction, it pertains to no certainties, and no matter how many pages you skip, there's no telling when the happily ever after will be, if ever. You stumble and fall. If you're strong, you get up again. The struggle is endless; only, if you look closely, eventually you see that, with every fall and rise, you ascend to a different level. There will be sunshine, there will be clouds, there will be rain and even snow; you have to keep on climbing.

"Come, look at the snow! It's so beautiful!"

Next to me lies my little one, an angel in his crib: his gray-blue eyes, his honey hair, two tiny hands reach out. I hold him and he feels me; he's happy and I smile. I gave him his name, he gave him his strength and the premature baby survived against the odds.

"Are you looking at the snow?"

Grief has withered Aunt Martha like her many decades of age never could. She did not wear black, but her spirit lies in darkness and she suffers. She had a son who was not hers, now she has a daughter she might as well have cast away and despised. But she didn't.

"... The heart was weeping and crying so small
Are you hurt my child, are you hurt at all?"[94]

Holding the baby, she regains that old vigour I remember her with, first seeing her at the *Auteuil* villa. She had come for a wedding and she beamed of cheerful youth and enthusiasm, because her child was happy and her heart rejoiced. Truly Fred was happy then and so was I, more than I thought, more than I could ever believe. He believed for the both of us. He had so much faith. His faith taught me to believe.

"Why don't you go and rest? I'll put Freddy to sleep!"

She knows I like to sit by the fire on a cold winter evening. We would spend hours in front of the fireplace, Fred in the armchair, and I would sit on the soft carpet at his feet, my head against his knee, his fingers in my hair. Oh Fred! He made me feel so alive, with senses I never knew existed, and I miss him.

Now, I have to live my life without him and, guiltlessly, I admit I can. 'You will not die, Winter!' meaning to tell me that life goes on and never backwards, grateful even for the pain–the pain which is fortunately there to amplify every other emotion.

In an armchair that looks very much like his, in front of a fireplace that reminds me of him, I come and sit every night. I read from Fred's favourite books; I read from Father's poetry scrapbook. Two photographs now hide in its pages; two voices give the verses life. They'd pause and break as they read, not ashamed to expose their souls, for they were beautiful. It is much like a poem, life: each one reads it in a different way, each making their own interpretations. It's just that, sometimes, you need someone to start you off, to give you a direction, so that you won't pointlessly wander around in the labyrinth of meanings. You don't seek an understanding of poetry; you don't seek an understanding of life. You feel life and poetry, and hopefully understand yourself.

I have come to understand a lot of what he used to tell me, as well as what he decided not to explain, to which I failed to find the meaning at the time. Fred's mind travelled at light-speed. He was ahead of many who would like to see him crumble, and he was certainly much ahead of me. God knows what would have happened, if he hadn't asked Karl Freier to take me away, and if, at that time, when all I wanted was to give in to my grief, with no foresight of the consequences, his words hadn't been there to remind me of my obligation to carry on, for the sake of myself, for the sake of our child, for the sake of living.

He was the devil in absolutely no disguise, *Kriminalrat* Blut, he'd never believe our story. And he must have known Marie better than we all thought, because he was never convinced she had anything to do with René. With Fred out of the picture, the wife and Karl Freier missing, he had every opportunity to make of the facts whatever would serve him best. It was a treacherous act no doubt, and every single person in Fred's closest circle was strictly interrogated: Peter Schwarz, the Ludwigs and the Stobes, even *Oberstleutnant* von H. would not escape the inquisitive interest of the Gestapo. To retaliate for the absence of hard evidence, Blut persuaded the SS- and *Polizeiführer* to deprive Fred of a proper military burial. He was cremated like a common criminal and his ashes were thrown in the rubbish. As for Karl Freier, I haven't seen him since he left Zurich.

Shortly after, a rumour spread that the *Führer* had been assassinated. Coup instigators took over in Berlin, and, in Paris, the General Military Commander sided with them, ordering the arrest of all the SS, including Blut and his party. *Oberstleutnant* von H. had his own part in this putsch. Too much intrigue and the balances to keep so delicate... He managed to hide away for a while after the coup failed. But, when they caught him, they tortured him brutally and executed him as a traitor.

It was Peter who wrote us the news, after he had surrendered, like many others, to the American side. The war was lost and he was nothing but eager to return home, an only child now in a family which used to be of six. His mother would hold him tightly and finally smile again-a single joy, yet so powerful even against four bitter sorrows. It's the strangest feeling, happiness! The most conflicting of all. You feel it when sunshine follows an overcast day; when pain goes away, intensifying the feeling of relief; and it's there when you finally realise that what you really are decides for you before you even know it. And so it was for Fred, who could not choose between me and who he was, yet he died that morning at the *Montmartre* cemetery a man and not a major; not as a soldier, but as a simple man for a human passion.

Young is the night. The snow is falling. In the dim light, souls reveal themselves and they converse better. I'll sit here and read. Perhaps I'll fall asleep a little later. The fire will continue to burn for as long as I sleep, and the snow... let the snow fall; even after I've woken up.

THE END

Afterword

Thank you for reading *Winter Pale*.
I hope she moved and inspired you as much as me.
Would you like to stay updated with news about my books?

- Join my mailing list at: **http://eepurl.com/h8q2Ln/**

Kindly take a minute to rate and review *Winter Pale* at the retailer where you purchased it. Other readers will be grateful to know what you enjoyed about this book.

- Don't forget to navigate through my website, where you will find *Winter Pale* extras, previous newsletters, bio trivia, and a comprehensive portfolio of mine. The place to look is: **https://www.marinakoulouri.com/**

I hope to meet with you again through the pages of another book. Until then, keep reading!

Endnotes

1. *^German for "Attention!"*
2. *^"L' Adieu" by Guillaume Apollinaire. Collection "Alcools" (1913). Translated into English for the purposes of this book by Marina Koulouri.*
3. *^German for "Thank you, sir".*
4. *^Special Operations Executive (SEO). An organisation formed in WW2 to conduct sabotage in Nazi occupied countries and to assist local Resistance.*
5. *^Guy Fawkes Day.*
6. *^Excerpt from the sonnet "Whoso list to hunt" by Sir Thomas Wyatt (1503-1542).*
7. *^French for: "Good evening, miss!"*
8. *^SS rank equivalent to Major.*
9. *^French equivalent to "Good heavens!"*
10. *^A German equivalent for "Right away!"*
11. *^German for "Excuse me!"*
12. *^Translated: "Don't be sad, Miss; we are going to have so much fun together!"*
13. *^French for "That's how things are!" or "That's life!"*
14. *^Sir Thomas Wyatt op. cit.*
15. *^Illegal French newspaper of the time.*
16. *^French for: "Ladies and gentlemen!"*
17. *^French for: "My darling! My angel! My precious!"*
18. *^"My jewel!"in French.*
19. *^Short for "Sicherheitspolizei", meaning Security Police.*
20. *^In German, 'du' is the second person singular, while 'Sie' is the polite way of address, indicating formality and respect.*
21. *^Refers to Hercules in Greek Mythology.*
22. *^"Good evening, sir!"*
23. *^"The madam's coat?"*
24. *^William Butler Yeats, "Aedh Wishes for the Cloths of Heaven" (1899) from "The Wind Among the Reeds".*
25. *^After the war, the square was renamed to Place André Malraux.*
26. *^"Stop! Entrance is forbidden!"*
27. *^"Please, please!"*

28. ^*Translated: "One people, one realm, one leader!"*
29. ^*SS rank, close equivalent to British army Second Private.*
30. ^*"Come in!"*
31. ^*'Liberty, equality, fraternity'. The national motto of France, which first appeared in the French Revolution.*
32. ^*SS rank equivalent to the British rank of Colonel.*
33. ^*Police force rank equivalent to Major.*
34. ^*The armed forces of Nazi Germany, including army, navy and air force.*
35. ^*Stalingrad is located on the western bank of the Volga river.*
36. ^*Red berries warm pudding with cold cream, traditional German dessert.*
37. ^*An expression of anger in French; close equivalent to "Bloody hell!"*
38. ^*"Yes!" in German.*
39. ^*Borrowed from French to mean the "elite" in this context.*
40. ^*"Out! Quick!"*
41. ^*Refers to the Höhere SS und Polizeiführer, a Nazi party official who commanded the SS, Gestapo and all uniformed Police.*
42. ^*Berlin borough where training school for the Security Police officers was established.*
43. ^*French expression of endearment meaning: "My heart!"*
44. ^*Open-air market for selling secondhand, antique, and other printed works, found along the Seine in Paris.*
45. ^*"A little princess", Frances Hodgson Burnett, illustrated by Ethel Franklin Betts, 1905.*
46. ^*"Peter Pan in Kensington Gardens" by J.M. Barrie, illustrated by Arthur Rakham, 1906.*
47. ^*Written and illustrated by Beatrix Potter, 1903.*
48. ^*By Edith Nesbit, illustrated by C.E. Brock, 1906.*
49. ^*Refers to A.L.O.E.'s "Bible Picture Book. Stories from the Life of Our Lord in Verse", published by T. Nelson and Sons, London and Edinburgh, 1871.*
50. ^*French for appetizers.*
51. ^*Member of the Milice troops.*
52. ^*Refers to the statue of Boadicea and her daughters on a chariot, which can be seen at the crossing to the north edge of Westminster Bridge in London.*
53. ^*Refers to the famous passage in the Place de la Madeleine area, better known today as Village Royal.*
54. ^*French for tearoom.*
55. ^*Meaning "master of the house", the job of a maître d'hôtel in a hotel or restaurant is to make certain everything related to dining and serving is to the customers' satisfaction.*
56. ^*French term loaned to many languages to indicate good manners and familiarity with the customs of good society.*
57. ^*Excerpt from "Pietà" in "Das Marienleben" (1912) by Reiner Maria Rilke. Here in free translation by Marina Koulouri.*

58. *^German for: "Good day, miss!"*
59. *^Excerpt from "Der Hochzeit zu Kana" ("The Wedding at Cana"). Reiner Maria Rilke (op.cit.).*
60. *^Stands for "Rasse und Siedlungshauptamt", the SS Race and Settlement Main Office, which was responsible for the safe-guarding of the "racial purity" of the SS. This also meant overseeing and approving of the marital decisions of unmarried SS officers.*
61. *^Wehrmacht military rank, equivalent to the British Lieutenant-colonel.*
62. *^Frédéric Chopin, Waltz in A minor, B. 150, Op. Posth.*
63. *^French term which refers to the business of making high-quality trend-setting fashion clothes.*
64. *^Johann Pachelbel, Canon in D minor.*
65. *^Organisation Todt (O.T.). A civil and military engineering organisation in Nazi Germany.*
66. *^German for "Augsburg taste".*
67. *^Excerpt from "An Mignon" (To Mignon) D.161 (1815), a song by Franz Schubert, inspired by J.W. von Goethe's eight-volume novel "Wilhelm Meister's Lehrjahren" (Wilhelm Meister's Apprenticeship).*
68. *^German expression of endearment, similar to: "My darling!"*
69. *^"Le Soulier de satin" (The Satin Slipper) (1929) written by the French poet Paul Claudel. The information in this chapter is drawn from the Greek edition "The Satin Slipper" (translator: Pandelis Prevelakis), French Institute Athens Publications, Athens, 1968.*
70. *^Mutterkreuz (the Cross of Honour for the German Mother) was ordained in 1938 as a sign of gratitude to German mothers for bearing many children.*
71. *^Three classes of the Mutterkreuz: i) Gold Cross, for eight or more children, ii) Silver Cross, for six or seven children, iii) Bronze Cross, for four or five children.*
72. *^Paul Claudel (op.cit.), Day Two, Scene XI, The Moon. Here in free translation from Greek by Marina Koulouri.*
73. *^SOE members arrested in Paris in 1943.*
74. *^From "Stehn zwei Stern am hohen Himmel" ("Two stars are standing up in the sky"), a German traditional song first recorded in the late 19th century.*
75. *^French for "my sweet".*
76. *^French for "shoemaker".*
77. *^A bicycle rickshaw used as a taxi.*
78. *^Refers to Ivan Fyodorovich Karamazov from "The Brothers Karamazov" (1880), the last of Fyodor Dostoevsky's novel, vol. I, chapter VI.*
79. *^Reiner Maria Rilke "Das Stunden-Buch" (The Book of Hours) (1899-1903), third book, "Von der Armut und vom Tode" (From the Poverty and Death) (1903), page 86, verse 23-24.*
80. *^Refers to Edgar Alan Poe's poem "The Raven" (1845).*
81. *^"Never give all the heart" (1904) by William Butler Yeats.*
82. *^Literally meaning "swimming lights".*

83. *^A kind of alcoholic beverage made from fruit juice.*
84. *^Autumn is game and mushroom season in Zurich.*
85. *^German for "Merry Christmas!"*
86. *^It is undetermined whether this tradition existed in WW2 years, however, here it is used in terms of poetic license.*
87. *^German for "Please, wait!"*
88. *^Refers to Fyodor Dostoevsky's "The Brothers Karamazov" (1880).*
89. *^Well-known Swiss bank established in 1856.*
90. *^French for "Don't be sad, little sister!"*
91. *^A disparaging and offensive term of the French language, referring to German soldiers in World War 1 and 2.*
92. *^"Good day!" in German.*
93. *^An administrative district in Paris.*
94. *^"A mother's heart" (1881). The poem first appeared in the French novel "La Glu" (The Slime) (1881) by Jean Richepin. Translated into English by the Irish poet Frederic Herbert Trench, and included in his book "New Poems" (1907) with the title Jean Richepin's song.*

MEET THE AUTHOR

MARINA KOULOURI comes from Greece and she started writing stories as a teenager. She loves languages and history, and she is interested in social matters, philosophy, and religion, all of which can be traced back to her writing.

She writes Historical Fiction because she likes to explore non-contemporary times, discovering the differences and similarities of people's ways and thinking. War stories move her for the intensity of emotions they arouse, as people are called upon to face situations far exceeding their individual capacity. This condition puts many human attributes sleeping within each and everyone in times of peace to a strenuous test with results no one can be absolutely sure about. World War 2 fascinates her, not only as a complex historical event, open to multiple interpretations, but also as an experience that affected the lives and psyche of millions of people, being the most massively destructive war in the history of the modern world.

Her stories are distinguished for their cinematic feel because she simply adores cinema. She enjoys a good Hollywood action thriller, but mostly she is into the European film aesthetics, while she finds extreme interest and pleasure in many Asian–Iranian, Chinese, Korean and, of course, Japanese–directors who like to dig into people's souls as they struggle to overcome the obstacles put in their way by social circumstance.

She is a published author of a novel (2011) and a short stories collection (2021) in her native language, and she has been a LGFF winner (2021) and nominee (2012) for her short fiction screenplays. A stage play she wrote in 2009 was successfully staged at the *Théâtre du Soleil* in Plaka, Athens, and she has translated several fiction screenplays from and to English and Greek.

She has had plenty of desk jobs in her time, but what she really loves to do, apart from writing, is teach English.

Marina values her readers' opinions and welcomes constructive criticism, so feel free to rate and review this book. You can interact with Marina leaving a message in her website inbox or by joining up with her on the social media, following the links on the next page.

WEBSITE
https://www.marinakoulouri.com/
FACEBOOK PAGE
https://www.facebook.com/marinakoulourigoespublic/
INSTAGRAM
https://www.instagram.com/marinakoulouris/
TWITTER
https://twitter.com/marina_koulouri/
YOUTUBE
https://bit.ly/3IJBKNP/

Acknowledgments

Noone had read my manuscript as a whole body before but, when he did, he embraced it with care and enthusiasm. My first and most sincere thank you has to go to my editor, **David Flack**, an Englishman from far away, but never too far from home.

Better wed over the mixen than over the moor, they say, and it could not have proved to be more accurate than in the case of my graphic designer. I'd been searching literally all over the world, but he was right next door to me, and absolutely wonderful! **Ilias Karampinis**: a true magician of design.

And suddenly it was pointed out to me that the reference to songs, poetry, and music in the book could result in some serious copyright issues. Careful research was essential, the necessary attributions in the text and licenses to be obtained, all had to be absolutely clear and problem-free. From far away India, a learned, thorough and most kind copyright lawyer, **Kanwar Lal**, gave me all the advice I needed for which I can't thank him enough.

I was close to writing another novel with the attempts I made writing the blurb for this book. A condensed, but still illuminating and intriguing text for the back cover is often the nightmare of a novelist who is so much into the story that it is almost impossible to decide what to leave out. **Nicola Cassidy**, a writer and screenwriter herself, made it possible with her inspiration and her amiable, enthusiastic personality.

I couldn't neglect to thank all the creators, administrators, fellow writers and book lovers in that extremely supportive Facebook group, called **Aspiring Writers United**, to whom I often turned for questions and opinions, to discover a treasure of knowledge and ideas, while, seeing there were other writers with the same difficulties and concerns about writing and publishing as me, was indeed a powerful morale booster.

My special thanks to the authors of the highly informative, greatly inspiring books I came across in my research over historical facts and era. To name but a few, I would have to mention **Gerard Walter** *Paris under the Occupation* (1960), **Julian Jackson** *France. The dark years 1940-1944* (2001) and *The Fall of France. The Nazi invasion of 1940* (2003), **David Pryce-Jones** *Paris in the Third Reich. A History of the German Occupation, 1940-1944* (1981), **André Zucca** *Les Parisiens sous l' Occupation. Photographies en couleurs* (2008), **Johann Voss** *Black Edelweiss: A Memoir of Combat and Conscience by a Soldier of the Waffen-SS* (2002), **Pierre Assouline** *Lutetia* (2005), and many others, together with military magazines, travel guides and websites, which took me to the time and place and made everything so real.

Many warm thanks to **my brother** for accompanying me to that beautiful journey to Zurich in the summer of 2007, where we tasted our very first *Pinot Noir* on the top of the *Uetliberg* mountain.

Last, but not least, I'd like to thank **Paris**, this magnificent city that stole my heart, conquered my hopes and dreams, and occupied the sweetest of my memories and my most exciting inspirations.

MORE FROM THIS AUTHOR

COMING SOON!

The outbreak of war, Blitz Krieg, Occupation.

Resistance, persecution - the ingredient to make heros.

Eventually, life just has to go on.

And it does!

Join Marina's Newsletter and be the first to know.
Sign up at: http://eepurl.com/h8q2Ln/

Passion:

1. a strong, uncontrollable emotion.

2. suffering and death (esp. of Jesus).

Condemned to die by the hand of whom impassionedly loved her, Simone accounts for their forbidden relationship, shedding light into the darkest corners of René's character.

A story within the story of Winter Pale.

A story in its own right nevertheless.

Curious about Marina's next work?
Join her Newsletter at: http://eepurl.com/h8q2Ln/

CPSIA information can be obtained
at www.ICGtesting.com
Printed in the USA
LVHW110748071222
734732LV00027BA/551